ᴠ

Twilla's Story

RACHEL GRIPP

To Sherri

An avid reader

Best Wishes

Rachel Gripp

Twilla's Story
Copyright © 2018 Rachel Gripp

ISBN: 978-0-9859396-7-0

DEDICATION

This novel is dedicated to my brother, Orlando DelleDonne and my sister, Lina DelleDonne Davies, in remembrance of our childhood years and how memorable they were.

TABLE OF CONTENTS

STORY BACKGROUND

Cyrus Stockton was known as a man of vision. Although he came from generations of enormous wealth and had vast real estate holdings, including huge tracts of land, his real interest was not on the family's lucrative banking business. The man was more concerned with educating the young.

In that endeavor, he directed the fortune he amassed and inherited to the opening of Stockton, a private college, along the eastern border of Pennsylvania, between the municipalities of Easton and Stroudsburg.

It started narrow in scope but one hundred fifty-two years later, it had become a thriving college with a municipality of its own, one with elected officials and law enforcement. Although Stockton remained a private college, it needed continued growth and recognition. And to that end, two of Stockton's finest fulfilled that need.

The mayor of the town, Ed Maines, and his brother-in-law, police chief, Sam Wilkerson, a former detective with Philadelphia's police department, were always busy with their separate obligations. While Ed continually met with corporate and political bigwigs to bring business to the area, Sam renewed his friendships in law enforcement at conferences, conventions and funerals.

As more new businesses came to Stockton in 2017 and enrollment reached an all-time high, the flavor of success was felt everywhere.

Then the unthinkable happened. A shooting occurred.

PROLOGUE

She rushed to the safety of her apartment, shaken by seeing him and terrified of having been found. How could that have happened after years of anonymity?

The recognition was apparent on both sides, their hatred for each other undeniable. How long had he been watching her, following her, thinking she was the one? In the effort to be certain, did he study her daily routine and then search her apartment, checking the bedroom closet first? *Was that how he found her? She would never know. He was much too clever.*

Sinking into an upholstered chair, her anxiety intensified as she recalled their accidental meeting. Recognizing him with his false portrayal had fueled an immediate reaction. It was then that she realized the full extent of his plan and her impending danger. He could not risk his position or allow her to jeopardize his standing. His primary objective now became survival. The real one would come later. She had to be prepared for any course of action and it had to be now.

A plan began to take shape as she rose slowly from her chair and walked to a desk where a large book lay idly facing her. A look of deep satisfaction crossed her face as she reached for a pen.

ONE

THE SHOOTING

Amy Gregson sat in her car tapping the steering wheel nervously, watching the tiny droplets of rain splatter the windshield. Fortunately, she had parked her little Rio near Temple Twin, the connected engineering buildings whose breezeway led to the campus quadrangle at Stockton College.

Having no umbrella, she would try to cross campus before the downpour started. Was 'getting wet' a deliberate move on her part? The clouds looked ominous even then, when she left her apartment at Ravencrest much earlier for a restaurant breakfast. The umbrella would have been an extra thing to leave behind and she could not afford loose ends.

Today had to look like the normal routine of an 'absent minded professor' crossing campus in the rain for a scheduled lecture. Of course, the meeting to cover a colleague's classes the following week validated her early arrival and was, in fact, a blessing in disguise. All the essentials needed for an escape were with her. Now it was time to set the plan in motion.

After exiting the breezeway, she raced across the quadrangle to Hawley Hall, the Home Economics Building, ignoring the rain and sudden pain piercing the upper back of her body. Throwing open the heavy metal and glass door with all her strength, the

1

young woman fell into the arms of Twilla Hale who waited at the entryway for her friend and colleague.

"Help me!" Amy begged, blood flooding her clothes as she opened her hand to expose a gold ring. "Find Mark," she gasped before lapsing into a comatose state.

"Call 911!" Twilla screamed at the passing students on their way to class. "I think Miss Gregson's been shot!"

No sooner had she spoken when a crowd began to circle the crouched instructor whose arms held the bloodied body of a familiar faculty member.

From the corner of her eye, Twilla glimpsed a man's shadow, an elongated apparition that suddenly appeared on the entry wall, and an uneasiness began to mount deep within her. She assumed by his dress that he was neither student nor faculty. But within seconds, the specter of the man in a long coat had suddenly disappeared, causing her to slip the gold band inside her jacket pocket.

"Coming through," An emergency medic yelled, followed by a group of men that included the campus police and two detectives. Within minutes of a cursory examination, the medical team removed Amy's body while the police cordoned the hall and emptied the building.

"You stay here," barked a man who introduced himself as Detective Clisten Barr. "We need to talk. What is your name and what were her last words to you?" His piercing eyes narrowed at the disheveled woman's appearance; his mind questioning where this homeless-looking waif fit in.

"Twilla Hale. I teach here," she stammered, still in shock by the bloodied body of her colleague. "Are you saying Amy's dead? Was it really a shooting?"

"What makes you think she was shot?" The fact that she would ask such a question led him to believe the woman knew more of her colleague's personal issues and could be useful during his investigation.

"I saw the blood when she fell in my arms and I didn't hear a backfire noise or anything like that. But then I was inside the building. There was no knife, so Amy must have been shot crossing the quad." She saw little point in bringing up her father's gun collection or his hunting days many years earlier.

"Everyone's a detective." The detective muttered to himself as he jotted down a few notes during their conversation. "And what were her last words to you?" He repeated his former question.

Twilla steeled herself, knowing a multitude of questions would be forthcoming. Something told her to be defensive in commenting to the authorities, regardless of her friend's condition. The ring and Amy's plea to 'find Mark' meant that she had to decipher the meaning of those things on her own. Yet everything seemed so surreal: the shooting that involved her personally, and even more important, where it took place. None of it made sense. Stockton was just a small private college nestled in the mountains of Pennsylvania, halfway between Easton and Stroudsburg.

"Amy just said, 'Help me.' She collapsed after that and I yelled at the students passing by to call you. No. I said, 'Call 911.'"

"Why were you meeting her?" He ignored the clarification. Politeness had no place with the detective.

"Since Amy was set to cover my classes next week, we were going over my course material. My father's having surgery," she explained with a painful sigh. "I gave her my lecture notes a few days ago and thought if she had any last-minute questions, I'd still be here to answer them. I plan on leaving tomorrow."

"Subject."

"Excuse me."

"What subject do you teach?"

"Home Art," Twilla answered, then catching his derisive laughter, thought the tall, dark-eyed man's arrogance was too insufferable for more conversation and began to walk away. She didn't care how important the handsome man was, Twilla wanted nothing more to do with him. She did not like Detective Barr. Not only did she find his laughter belittling, the detective never gave her the opportunity to mention her full teaching schedule; he was too busy satisfying his own ego. She had met too many people like that, so full of themselves.

"We are not finished here." He followed her.

"Then arrest me," she bristled. "I've got Amy's blood all over me and I need to shower and change."

"You can do that later. Right now, I need your clothes."

"Fine!" Twilla dripped with anger as she edged the yellow-taped area to her lab, knowing full well he was behind her.

Inside the room, carved wooden trays, small lamp bases sculpted of driftwood and an array of wooden accent pieces sat on rows of long work tables waiting to be finished. Running vertically to them, along a bank of windows sat several other long tables. They displayed an abundance of tools: very sharp ones used for carving, others for sanding, and bundled grades of polishing cloths. In one corner, somewhat apart from the others, sat containers of chemicals, paints, varnishes and shellacs. The overall combination gave the room a studio effect rather than a classroom laboratory.

"This won't take long," her voice trailed off. Then ignoring him after the directive, Twilla grabbed a long lab coat from one of the room hooks and entered a large storage closet. Before undressing, she placed the ring inside her shoe and pulled one of the gray laboratory bags from a shelf. "Here." Twilla gave him the bag of clothes. "I think we're done now." She wanted to go home and shower. The lab coat felt like it was sticking to her underwear and by every count was uncomfortable.

"No. We are not," he corrected, towering over the thin woman whose height barely brushed his chest. "I need to know your relationship with Amy Gregson, along with several other questions. Where is your father's surgery taking place? What city? Is that your home? How can I contact you if I need more information?" It was obvious from her shocked expression that he caught her totally unprepared for an inquiry.

"What is your problem?" She stiffened, provoked by his rapid line of questions.

"Are you always this hostile?" he interrupted her.

"You should be searching for the shooter instead of asking me useless questions." She crossed in front of him to a filing cabinet and pulled her handbag from the top drawer. After closing it with a slam, she turned to leave before a further argument ensued.

"That's my intention, after I get your statement or has that thought not occurred to you?" He followed her out of the lab, frustrated by her lack of cooperation.

"Then you're wasting time questioning me. I don't have anything else to tell you."

"Nevertheless, I still need to know where you're going tomorrow and a phone number for contact purposes." Although his request was standard protocol, she was the only current lead he had to the shooting, and the detective wondered why the young woman was so snarky with her responses. Her terse answers were less than satisfying and her dark eyes refused to make-contact with his. The woman was hiding something…something connected to the shooting…something she did not want him to know.

"Right," she bristled again. After jotting-down the information on a blank grocery pad she carried in her purse, Twilla tore-off the top sheet and gave it to him.

"This must come in handy," the detective offered dryly, referring to the grocery sheet he waved back and forth in his hand.

"You can always add bread and eggs to it." Her sarcasm deepened as she began to walk away.

"Just a minute, Miss Hale." The harshness of his resonant voice made her turn quickly to face him. "If you can think of something that would help find your friend's shooter, please let the department know." He gave her his card.

"Right!" Twilla answered cynically, turned and walked away. She would have to be drowning in deep shit to call him for anything. Although his looks could wilt any woman's petunias, the detective was arrogant, humorless and without feelings. But more than that, he made Twilla feel her Home Art class was a joke and that did not sit well with her.

But little did she know his thoughts.

Twilla's testy response caused him to wonder even more about this teacher as he watched her exit the building. He needed to investigate this small-statured woman who consistently objected to his questions. And although she used sarcasm as a defense mechanism, little escaped him. His years of experience made him a proficient in body language, and Twilla Hale knew more than she was telling. He would question her later. Right now, the detective had to notify her boss about the shooting.

When Twilla fled the building, it was no longer raining. She decided not to cross the quadrangle, and instead, traversed the sidewalks fronting the other campus buildings that bordered it. One, however, caused her to pause momentarily as she made her way to the breezeway of Temple Twin.

After four years at Stockton, she now realized why Jordan Hall, the building used for music study, sat farther back from the others. It must have been planned that way to showcase the music program the college offered. Twilla remembered seeing groups of students gather on the large lawn fronting it for the annual spring festival, an event that filled the air with song, but she never thought much about it until now.

Then, for some reason, her thoughts took a different direction and Twilla became frightened again but didn't know why. Was she thinking about the man in the long coat, the one who watched her hold Amy's body and then suddenly disappear? Was that the reason she wouldn't walk across the quadrangle? Was Twilla afraid of being openly exposed the way Amy was? Was she afraid of being shot too? Why would anyone shoot Twilla? She never harmed anyone.

Then again, why would anyone want to shoot Amy? Was it an accident or did someone shoot her deliberately? That sudden thought triggered something she had not previously considered. Was her colleague in trouble? If so, it had to be something very serious and life threatening, considering what just happened. And although Amy was a very private person, Twilla felt justified in asking that question when her colleague recovered. Giving Twilla a ring and asking her to find Mark implied an element of great trust, and although flattered by the thought, Twilla was more concerned about the current situation, and the shooting scenario played out in her mind once again.

Amy already had the ring in her hand when they met. That meant she planned to pass it to Twilla should something untoward happen to her. *It also meant that Amy knew her life could be in danger and she was taking precautions. But for what? Finding Mark?* Was there a time factor involved?

Was Twilla to find Mark while Amy was recovering? How was that possible? A series of unanswered questions inundated her thoughts.

Why had Amy given her a ring in the first place and what was the significance of it? How was it connected to the shooting? Who was Mark? What was the relationship? Could Amy possibly have a child, a son perhaps? How was Twilla supposed to find him? Why was it so important? Why? Why? Why? Why was this happening to her?

After exiting campus from the breezeway of Temple Twin, Twilla walked quickly to her little black Chevy but stopped suddenly. Parked one car away from hers was Amy's innocuous silver Rio. Upon impulse, she tried the door and found it unlocked. There on the front seat lay her folder of lecture notes. She grasped them quickly, closed the car door and, sliding into her own car, drove away.

Now another question churned her mind as she left the campus area. Why did Amy leave the notes in her car instead of taking them to their meeting? There was only one reasonable explanation. She didn't want the folder to get wet. Although that explanation did not satisfy Twilla, she had another concern, one that worried her.

What was she thinking? Had she done something illegal by retaking her own lecture notes from Amy's car? How could that be? They belonged to her. If the police say she acted illegally, Twilla had a very plausible excuse. She had to find another teacher who could sub in her absence and needed her lecture notes for that purpose. Finding a sub at this late date was going to be difficult, if not impossible. Those thoughts continued to cross her mind as she pulled into the driveway of her condominium at Stoneledge. It was only after a quick shower and change of clothes that an unexpected phone call came in.

"Yes. It was a shock. No. I haven't heard anything more about Amy's condition," she said, referring to the shooting. "I think the detectives will notify you again if something is needed." Then Twilla became silent when the real purpose of the call became clear. "I really appreciate that, Dr. Shelden."

Twilla was overcome by Felicia Shelden's generous offer to cover her classes the following week but had no idea what to suggest. Her department head was brilliant in her own right. Would she really want Twilla's lecture notes? "Oh," she responded to Dr. Shelden's request. "I can drop-off the outlines today for all three courses," she offered, but hearing another alternative, said, "Then I'll leave them in the desk drawer at the lab. Thank you so much." Twilla heard the click on the other end.

"That was a shock," she said aloud. "Who would have thought?" Twilla began to laugh at the idea of Dr. Shelden teaching her classes. Although her department head would do well teaching the course in Family Economics and the one in Home and Family Living, Twilla could not picture the woman wearing a lab coat or soiling her hands for Home Art.

Twilla crossed the living room to her desk and grabbed a folder with clean copies of her outlines and work notes from the top middle drawer. Directly below the folder sat a snapshot of Amy and Twilla with a leashed Lily at nearby Tavis Park. "Oh, my God!" Twilla screamed, her thoughts churning.

She raced to the kitchen, grabbed a set of keys off the counter and fled to her car. She needed to get to Ravencrest Apartments ASAP.

When Twilla arrived at Amy's apartment building, she went directly to Mrs. Benson's flat, knowing the next-door neighbor had a key to her colleague's apartment. "I need to get in," she explained. "Amy was shot crossing the quad this morning and this place will be crawling with police before too long."

"Oh, no! What happened? Why?" the elderly woman questioned, visibly shaken by the news.

"No idea. An accident or a disgruntled student, maybe."

When Mrs. Benson opened the door to Amy's apartment, she began screaming immediately. The unit was in shambles: furniture overturned, smashed decorative items and papers strewn everywhere. Torn stuffing from upholstered furniture lay scattered about the room. A wooden leg pulled away from a three-legged table seemed incongruous in the room's setting as it sat tilted against a bookcase bereft of books now lying on the floor.

"Lily! Lily!" Twilla yelled, totally ignoring the woman whose screams were silenced by the whimpering of an apricot Peekapoo bounding toward Twilla's open arms.

"You're ok now." She petted the small, frightened dog whose cold, black nose nestled in her armpit for protection. Twilla's soothing voice seemed to have a calming effect as she crossed into the kitchen looking for dog food and treats. "I need a shopping bag to put these in." She told Lily whose head surfaced suddenly, her black-button eyes approving the idea before returning to the safety of her armpit. The dog seemed to feel safe now, knowing Twilla would take care of her until Amy came home.

As she placed cans of dog food and treats into the found bag, her eyes fell on a three-ringed notebook that was thrown on the floor in a corner of the room. It was not just an ordinary notebook. It was Twilla's cookbook, the one with her mother's recipes. Amy had wanted to experiment and perhaps adapt one or two of them for her cooking classes. However, a tab projecting from the binder's upper-right corner told Twilla a folder inside was something Amy wanted her to read. Twilla wondered if it was an article on foods or related to the gold ring. No. The latter couldn't be possible. Amy had no idea she would be shot crossing the quadrangle, so why would she write instructions connected to the gold ring? That idea was too preposterous to pursue and Twilla gave it little thought.

"Could you slip my cookbook into the shopping bag for me?" she asked Mrs. Benson when another thought occurred to her. "Do you know where Amy keeps Lily's leash and food bowl? I'll return them when she's better."

"What are you doing here?" a booming voice demanded. "I thought you were leaving."

Even before turning around, Twilla knew it was the bark of Clisten Barr. "I'm helping my friend." She faced him in defiance.

"How? By turning this place upside down?" Although his tone was derisive, Twilla knew the question was just his ridiculous way of gleaning information.

"We found it this way when I unlocked the apartment," Mrs. Benson interrupted. "Why would someone do this? Amy is such a sweet girl."

"Was. She died twenty minutes ago."

"Oh, no!" Twilla uttered in disbelief, questioning his credulity. "It can't be true! I don't understand any of this." Her eyes swept the room before resting on his. "I thought it was an accidental shooting and now this." Without being aware of it, Twilla's eyes began to glisten, her thoughts racing. *Amy was dead, her apartment ransacked, and Lily was now an orphan. Twilla would never again see her colleague walking Lily in Tavis Park. Although they were not the closest of friends that thought saddened her greatly.*

"It might have been," he interrupted her thoughts, "but from the looks of this place, someone did an exhaustive search. Whatever it was for, it had to be important. No. I think we're looking at murder. So, tell me, Miss Hale, just what, exactly, are you doing here?"

"I came for Lily." In conveying the reason for her presence, Twilla's words were distinctively garbled. Her thoughts were still on Amy's death and the nine-pound orphan in her arms. "That is until Amy recovered. Now, I'll just care for her…"

"What's in the bag?"

"Dog food and my cookbook. Amy teaches, taught," she stammered, correcting herself, "foods and nutrition. She wanted a few of my mother's recipes." Twilla placed the shopping bag on the kitchen counter knowing he would check it as she stood by watching him, her thoughts racing. *Were all handsome men this annoying? Unfortunately, the ones she knew were neither handsome nor interesting. But then a Christmas gathering at the Dean's house last year hardly qualified.*

"You're taking her home with you?" he asked as the Peekapoo turned her head to face him. "She's small but very cute." He scratched the top of the Lily's head lightly.

"I may not have made it clear earlier. My dad's having heart surgery. I thought having her around might give him a lift. My parents lost their dog last year. Tom was eleven...a pure mongrel," she added, placing the leash on Lily.

"What do you know about Amy Gregson?" he asked after moving the checked shopping bag toward her.

"Other than she's thirty-five and taught here for six years, not much...was thirty-five." She corrected herself again, still in disbelief.

"Family?"

"I don't think so. Sometimes she'd spend the holidays here or go skiing."

"Where? Poconos?"

"Different places...out west...north east...different ski resorts, I think. But I'm not sure. She was a very private person."

"Where did she spend her summers?"

"Travel, workshops. I don't know. Different places."

"For being a friend, you don't seem to know much about her."

"We only became close last spring. That's when my lab was moved next door to hers. We also shared the same class rooms for our lectures. Being thrown together so often, we'd eat lunch at the cafeteria or grab a cup of coffee, but I never went to a restaurant breakfast with her. That was her daily routine; a good breakfast and then a drive to Starbucks. Amy must have spent ninety minutes every morning to break the fast. Breakfast was her bag, not mine."

Twilla paused for a moment, knowing the detective expected her narrative to continue.

"When Dad's surgery came up Amy offered to cover my classes. That's what colleagues do. They cover for each other when situations arise. That's about it!" Twilla gave no further explanation. "I was not interested in questioning her personal life." Twilla grabbed the shopping bag and guided Lily out of the apartment as several police officers entered. Engaging in further conversation could be dangerous. *To whom, her thoughts questioned? You don't know anything. You have a ring with no real significance and a dead woman's directive to find Mark. Until this makes any kind of sense, you are whistling in the dark, feeling your way up a blind alley.*

Clisten watched her exit the apartment in silence. His mind, however, was ticking rapidly with one thought. The woman not only knew more than she was telling, she had the face of a guilty party. But what exactly was she hiding?

TWO

DISCOVERY

When Twilla took the outline and work notes to her lab as prearranged with Dr. Shelden, she ran into Delsin Peck and became brightened by his presence.

"Hey!" She greeted the man who as head of operations and maintenance took care of her lab needs at Stockton. "Think there's still life left?" She referred to the carving tools he held in his hands.

"Shelden ordered new ones but has little hope with the current budget. I'll see what I can do about sharpening these," he said before changing the subject. "What are you doing here? I thought you were going home."

"I'm leaving these work notes for Dr. Shelden. She's taking over my classes," Twilla said, sliding the papers inside her desk drawer.

"I thought Amy," he began.

"She was shot crossing the quad," Twilla interrupted.

"What? How? Why?" It was apparent by his shocked questions that he had not heard the news.

"I don't know. She was to meet me for a final briefing but collapsed in my arms."

"Where is she?"

"Emergency took her to the hospital. The police are all over her apartment. I had to leave." At that point, Twilla determined not to mention the update of Amy's death.

"I don't understand." His head swayed from side to side.

"The dog. I had to find Lily after it happened. I thought I'd watch her until Amy got better."

"Then that explains Shelden's presence. You two must think alike." His mind took a different turn. "She's next door."

"In Amy's lab?"

"Maybe she's covering her classes too."

"Thanks, Delsin," she answered appreciatively before going next door.

"Hello, "Twilla greeted the woman sitting at a desk strewn with assorted files.

"Just more paperwork," Dr. Shelden explained. "Anything new on Miss Gregson?"

"The police were at Amy's apartment when I went for her dog,"Twilla said, purposely making no mention of her colleague's demise. It was Detective Barr's responsibility to make that official notification, and she did not want to be involved. Nor did she want to answer more of Dr. Shelden's questions. The woman was notorious for asking them.

"I didn't know you were close." Dr. Shelden expressed surprise.

"I'm not...we're not." Twilla continued to speak in the present tense. "I see her walking the dog when I go jogging at Travis Park. When this happened, I thought someone should take care of Lily. Did I do the wrong thing?" A worried look crossed her face, again on purpose.

"No. That was a very humane gesture," Dr. Shelden quelled her fears. "Are you're taking the dog home with you?"

"I thought Lily might be a cheerful pet to have around with my father's coming surgery. She's very small compared to the mongrel we had, but the dog seems very gentle and might be

good for him emotionally right now," Twilla replied before allud-
ing to the reason for her presence. "I left the outline and notes in
my desk drawer as requested. I had no idea you'd be here."

"I gave Miss Gregson the wrong folder several days ago and
came by to retrieve it. Just suggestions for a course of study. You
know how regulations constantly change." Her eyes fixed on
Twilla's.

"I certainly do." Twilla agreed. She began to feel uneasy by
the woman's steady stare and was impatient to join Lily who sat
waiting in the car. "Thank you for filling in for me. I should be back
sometime next week. I'll phone with an update on my father's
condition."

As the woman watched Twilla leave, she had a few thoughts
of her own. Although the young instructor was very clever with
her evasive answers, Dr. Shelden had determined many weeks
earlier that a connection between the two colleagues existed. But
had the young woman become Amy Gregson's confidant? Did
these two women share secrets? She would learn soon enough.

Pulling a cell phone from her pocket, she immediately tapped
a contact number. "Now talk to me. I'm completely alone. Exactly
how far along are you with our plans?"

"Did you miss me?" Twilla addressed Lily as she entered her
car. "I think we'll go to the park for a few minutes. You need to get
out and stretch." She studied her little bundle for a moment then
headed toward the benched and grassy area fronting Tavis Lake.

Within minutes after leashing the little Peekapoo, the end of
it slipped out of Twilla's hand and Lily dashed away, bounding
toward a huge black and white sheepdog lying at the feet of an
elderly man sitting on a bench. The man picked-up the leash while

talking to the little Peekapoo who seemed far more interested in the sleeping sheepdog than anything he had to say.

"I can tell you are new at this." He referred to the leash escapade, as he watched Twilla bundle the dog on her lap when she sat down beside him.

"Yeah, I kinda am, but I'll get the hang of it, I guess."

"You just get her?" The white-haired man asked quietly.

"More inherited, I think. My colleague got hurt this morning, so I'm keeping Lily for a while."

"Colleague? You teach at the college?" He caught her nod. "So, you're keeping Lily until your colleague recovers. That's nice of you to take-on the responsibility of a dog. Sam, here, eats everything in sight and snores like a trumpet." At the mention of his name, Sam rose on all fours and began sniffing Lily's nose. "Don't worry, he's very gentle."

"He's beautiful."

"Pet Shoppe just finished with him. I can't groom this long-haired hound. That's my grandson's job. Sam's his dog, but I'm the designated walker. That's my role. Isn't that right, Sam?" His question got no hint of response, for Sam seemed to be taken with Lily's little black nose.

"Maybe you can give me some pointers."

"Peter, but everybody calls me, Pete."

"Twilla." She shook his hand.

"So. Twilla. How long will it take your friend to recuperate? If it's only a few days, you won't need much help, other than dog food."

"No. Lily will be with me for a while. I just got word she died in the hospital." She lied about the timeline, feeling it made her dog inexperience more credible, but gave no further information about the shooting.

"Then you're a real novice at this."

"No. We had a family dog, a mutt, really, but Tom died last year. Since my dad's having surgery Tuesday, I'm taking Lily with me. I thought she would be good to have around."

"I recognize you now." The old man studied her. "You jog along the lake sometimes."

"Sometimes," she agreed. "So, what should I do about taking care of Lily?"

"Papers?"

"No. No! She's trained." Twilla shook her head causing him to laugh.

"I meant her pedigree."

"Oh. No clue."

"Shots?"

"Amy never talked about that to me."

"Basics then. You have Lily's brand of dog food?" He caught her nod. "When you get back, see if your friend kept records of Lily's pedigree and health problems. They must be somewhere in her possession. If you come up empty, call the vets in the area. Someone had to treat her for shots if nothing else. But you should try to get the dog's history before starting from scratch. Maybe, by that time, you won't have a problem."

"What does that mean?"

"The family may want the dog."

"To my knowledge, Amy had no family."

"I find that strange. Everyone has family. Some people won't admit it, but there's always someone hiding in the family cracks."

"Are you here every day?" She changed the subject after checking her watch, "Around two?"

"Come by. Sam and Lily seem to like each other, and I'll help in any way I can," he said, watching her bundle Lily and the leash in her arms.

"Thank you." She waved goodbye.

"Take care." His parting message rang in her ears.

He should only know. The thought drummed her brain.

Within the hour Twilla had a change of plans and was heading toward her valley home at Mount Penn, a suburb of Reading, Pennsylvania.

She eyed Lily who lay curled on the cookbook she retrieved from Amy's apartment. "Who would have thought we'd be leaving this early?" Twilla asked aloud, blowing a kiss up to her third-floor unit at Stoneledge Condominums, one she dearly loved.

As she drove along the highway, Twilla had mixed emotions about going home. Although she loved her family, sometimes it was tough being together. Their thoughts and interests were no longer ones she shared with them. Not true, she corrected herself. Twilla and her father seemed to be on the same page most of the time. Her mother, however, was a different story. The woman's harangue would start within the hour of her arrival. That never seemed to change. Twilla had a little over an hour to think about it. Too bad Stockton wasn't further away. Maybe she should start looking for teaching jobs on the west coast.

THREE

QUESTIONS

It did not take Clisten Barr and his team long to search Amy Gregson's apartment. Although they checked the strewn shambles for possible clues, tying the shooting to someone with a motive was their main priority.

"Other than a confirmation at Sugarloaf over Christmas, there were no pictures or correspondence of any consequence. I found a folder of paid bills, but that's not what we're looking for." Tony Mistretta, the detective's new partner, was the first to respond.

"Sugar Loaf. That ski resort is at least 500 hundred miles away, Carrabassett Valley, Maine," Clisten mused. "That's about an eight-hour drive from here. What about other reservations?"

"You mean ski resorts?"

"Those and other places she may have traveled on a regular basis."

"You're trying to establish a pattern," Tony said, thinking he understood Clisten's approach.

"No. We're trying to learn what Amy Gregson was hiding. From the looks of this place, she was hiding something. Whatever it was, it had to be important and we don't know if the intruder found it. But if we can make a connection with her past-history, we might find the motive for her shooting and the person who killed her." Just as he was making this explanation, his cell phone began the beat of a strange rhythm.

20

"What?" The detective couldn't believe the caller's narrative. "I'll be there in an hour." Then turning to his assistant, Clisten said, "Tape the place when you're done. I don't want anyone in here."

"Who was that on the phone?"

"Thistle," he said, referring to Bill Thistle, the county coroner.

"He found something, didn't he?" Tony pressed.

"More than I suspected. You cover this. I need to see the next-door neighbor."

"You think she knows something?"

"I'm hoping she can give us some information on the dead woman, but I have my doubts. Nobody shares anything these days."

Tony watched him leave the apartment without saying anything further.

Clisten Barr was careful in his approach with Mrs. Benson. She had been very upset with the condition of her neighbor's apartment and could not understand why someone would want to steal from the teacher. She had nothing of value that would warrant theft. Of course, the woman never equated the neighbor's death with murder. In her mind, someone capitalized on Amy's tragic accident with a home invasion of her apartment.

"Hello." Clisten presented his shield. "Remember me. I came with the police next door."

"I remember." Mrs. Benson studied him behind her thick bifocals. "You have more questions." She ushered him into her apartment and directed him to the living room sofa. "I really don't know much."

"How long did Amy Gregson live in the apartment?"

"About six years. When she got the job at the college, I think."

"Where did she live before that?"

"Come to think about it, we never talked about that. Never came up."

"Where did she go on vacation? Did she ever say?"

"Up north, out west. She was always going somewhere different. Ski resorts, you know. Amy tried them all."

"Do you know which ones? Did she mention any one in particular?"

"No. Amy would look for good deals. At least, that's what she said before deciding on a particular one."

"How about summer? Where did she go on vacation?"

"Tours. She took a lot of tours around the country and in Europe. She'd look for good deals there too."

"But you don't know where she went?"

"She went to a play in New York City. I know that. She told me she loved it."

"When was this?"

"This past summer, I think. Maybe it was spring break," her voice trailed off, her memory fading.

"And who took care of her dog while she was away?"

"You mean Lily?" She caught his nod. "Amy got the dog just this past spring, I think. Lily was just a little thing when Amy brought her home. Now that we're going into September, she's gotta be somewhere around six months."

Realizing the woman was mixed-up with her timeline on Amy's travels and the current month of October, Clisten had little hope the woman could be of any help. "Do you know where she bought the dog?"

"Why? Did you want a Peekapoo too?"

"I thought she may have bought it from a friend."

"I don't understand your logic at all. You should be looking for the person who broke into her apartment. A friend wouldn't do that."

"You are absolutely right. Thank you for your help." Clisten hurried away as quickly as he could.

The woman had to be bordering senility with the kind of answers she gave. But he had to credit her. The woman did have a key. What more could she offer in her mental state? He would have to think about that.

Within the hour, Clisten Barr listened to Bill Thistle explain the results of his autopsy through a series of x-rays and photographs.

"So, what do you have in addition to her being shot?" He watched the man grab a clip board nearby before speaking.

"The female victim had brown eyes, brown hair, weighed 130 pounds and was 64 inches tall."

"So, statistically, Amy Gregson was a small-statured woman."

"That's true, statistically speaking, but there is much more here than meets the eye. Aside from the fact that her left leg is slightly shorter than the right one and a heel cushion was glued inside her shoe, this woman had extensive work done to her body. Her face had been reshaped, her breasts augmented, and she had extensive hip surgery. With operations of that magnitude, you're looking at months if not a year between surgeries and total recovery."

As Clisten snapped a picture of the displayed photograph, Thistle directed the detective's attention away from the dead woman's face to another facet of the examination. "If you examine the x-rays, you'll notice healed broken ribs and scar tissue from bone fractures in the arms, legs, hands and hips. The latter may account for the difference in leg length."

"Meaning she had been abused."

"Multiple times. You can see the scar tissue." He pointed to an x-ray. "But then, at some juncture, she underwent extensive surgery to conceal her identity. Although you can readily under-stand why she would want to get away, that's not the whole of it."

"I'm not following you. The abuser would be our prime sus-pect in Amy Gregson's murder. It fits."

"That's just it!" He insisted loudly. "There is no Amy Gregson. She doesn't exist. I had our team go through different data bases. We came up with nothing. Not even a fingerprint match."

"You are not helping me," Clisten complained loudly as he exited the morgue.

"Then bring me someone with an identity!" Thistle shouted back.

Shortly before four o'clock that afternoon, Clisten Barr drove to the college on the off-chance he would find Felicia Shelden in her office. Catching the department head unannounced and without an appointment meant her answers to his questions would be unrehearsed. The detective also knew the murder of a faculty member would bring notoriety to her department and a cloud on the whole college. Although scarring Stockton's repu-tation was to be avoided at all costs, he wondered if mayor Ed Maines could put a partial lid on it; his own boss, Sam Wilkerson did not have the clout necessary for that kind of thing.

But Detective Barr was not really interested in the publicity surrounding a dead teacher. What he wanted was the truth… both good and bad. Dropping by unexpectedly seemed the best way of getting it. He had gleaned very little information when notifying her by phone of the shooting and then later, Amy Gregson's demise. Maybe his sudden appearance would jog her memory for more details about the dead woman.

When he entered Dr. Shelden's office, he found the depart-ment head sorting a stack of papers cluttering her desk.

"Excuse me," he apologized. "I happen to be in the area where the shooting occurred and wondered if you could give me a few minutes of your time." He continued talking hurriedly to draw her in. "How long was Miss Gregson employed here as a teacher?"

"Associate professor," she corrected. "Six years."

"And was she well-liked by the students?"

"Very much indeed. That's why I believe her death was the result of a random shooting."

"We are following that line as a possibility," he lied. "But right now, we are having trouble locating her family. I was hoping you could provide some information for us."

"Amy had no family. Her parents died years ago, and she had no brothers or sisters. I checked her employment record when I was told about the shooting. Everyone on campus is nervous. You can understand that." She pulled a folder from a large file cabinet and scanned it. "There's no family listed."

"But there must be references. Employers always ask for them."

"We have two." Her finger traced a line with information."

Clisten took a pen and pad from his pocket to write the names and addresses of Thaddeus J. Stevens, an attorney at law in New York City and Dr. Rebecca M. Givens at High Coventry, an elite girl's college ninety miles away.

"You still have their letters of recommendation?"

"Oh, yes. 'They're in the file here." She displayed the letters.

"I would like to borrow them, if I may. They could help me find some distant relative or someone who knew Amy Gregson. I will return them next week." Then changing the subject, Clisten said, "I would like to look at her office while I'm here. We are extremely anxious to put this case to rest."

"It's just down the hall." She rose from her desk to walk with him. "I knew you would need to check her office."

"Thank you. I won't be long."

"I would appreciate your keeping me informed. Amy Gregson will be missed by the members of our faculty."

After searching the victim's office, Clisten left the building without any additional information. He had no need to search further. They had already established the trajectory route of the fired bullet. The shooter had crouched on the rooftop of Temple Twin, the building facing Hawley Hall across the quadrangle, to accomplish the woman's premeditated murder.

He checked his watch and tapped a number on his cell phone. "Find anything?"

"Nothing of real interest. Not even spent clutter. It's just so bizarre. Everyone has clutter."

"I want you to check two names for me," Clisten said, ignoring his partner's commentary. "I'm going to inspect the quad again before coming back to the station."

"You get something from the neighbor?"

"Department head."

"Ok. Shoot. I'm ready when you are." Clisten heard the rustle of papers, then offered the two references from Dr. Shelden.

Standing outside Hawley Hall, Clisten felt at odds with himself. Something didn't feel right. There was something he had overlooked. As he crossed the quadrangle to Temple Twin, it suddenly hit him. Where was her car? Where had Amy parked on her way to class? What kind of car was she driving? He tapped-in a number and began taking notes. Within the hour, he spotted a silver Rio at the exit area of the quadrangle. A one-word parking tag hung from the inside mirror…Faculty.

Clisten took a handkerchief from the pocket of his trousers and after testing the unlocked door, began a cursory examination of the stark interior to a glove compartment which yielded nothing but insurance papers. "How can that be?" he questioned aloud. "Not even a flashlight." Clisten sat still for a moment deep in thought when his eyes fell on the mirror tabs. He pulled them down hoping for something to fall, and in his disappointment, uttered, "I don't know what you're hiding, Amy Gregson or whoever you are, but you did one helleva job erasing your life."

Clisten took out his cell phone again and tapped-in a number. It was important to have the car taken to the pound and scrubbed for clues. Although he had real doubts about finding something to advance the case, he wondered if the trunk was as empty as the car.

When Clisten returned to the station that afternoon, he knew from his partner's expression that the inquiry did not go well.

"Thaddeus J. Stevens died several years ago, and his office has no record on Amy Gregson. They never heard of her."

"And the other, Rebecca Givens?"

"Long retired. No address forwarded. Apparently, the staff is filled with young administrators. The people I talked with never met the woman. So where do we go from here?"

Clisten shook his head. "Too many dead ends here. I need a fresh look at the case."

"Where are you going?" Tony watched his partner walk toward the building exit.

"I just need some air." He needed to be alone with his thoughts. Something still wasn't right. That thought kept nagging him.

FOUR

AT HOME

As Twilla pulled into the long driveway of her family home, her mother rushed out of the house to greet her. "I'm so glad you're here." The small-statured woman hugged her tightly. "Let me look at you."

"Mom, it's only been a month since I left. I couldn't have changed that much."

"You will be civil," Agatha instructed, holding her daughter at arm's length. The strong words were more of a directive than a statement. She referred, of course, to the stormy relationship between Twilla and her sister. "Julie will be arriving tonight, and I want the weekend to be as pleasant as possible. Dad's scheduled tests are on Monday. Surgery's Tuesday."

"I'm aware of the schedule, but is he...?"

"He's fine, but I don't want him upset."

"Then tell that to Julie," Twilla snapped unexpectedly. "Is she coming alone or bringing another stray with her...again?"

"Why can't you just get over it?" Agatha scolded. "It was a long time ago." Her mother did not want a rehash surfacing, particularly now, when her husband was facing serious surgery. All she wanted was a little family peace.

"Why should I?" Twilla objected. "The family just sluffed it off as some crazy mistake. Like her date didn't know he was crawling into my bed instead of Julie's," she complained. "Then

28

he abandoned her a month later. It's the same old, same old…a collection of losers."

"Don't go there," Agatha cautioned as she watched her daughter remove a suitcase from the car trunk and roll it near the porch steps. Her curiosity peaked as Twilla crossed to the passenger side of the car and retrieved a small bundle sitting on the front seat and began leashing her.

"Oh, how cute. She's such a light apricot," her mother cooed while the Peekapoo stepped to a nearby bush to relieve herself.

"Lily." The mere mention of her name set the dog's black button eyes peering at the lady talking to Twilla. "I had to take her."

Twilla gave her mother a quick capsule of Amy's death, making it appear as a random shooting.

"You never talked about her. Were you close friends?" she asked, then catching Twilla's negative response, said, "How old was she?"

"She had me by nine years, but Amy was only four years older than Julie." Then realizing her mother's confused look, she clarified her statement. "My colleague was thirty-five years old.

"Oh, dear." Agatha's mind took a different direction. "But that shouldn't be a problem."

"Now what? Just tell me." Her mother was always going from one crisis to another.

"We took one of the neighbor's new puppies."

"From the Haskell's next door? A retriever?" She caught her mother's worried expression. "Don't worry. It won't be a problem. Lily is very shy. She'll be glued to my armpit while we're here."

"We better go in. Matthew will be wondering why we're taking so long. Remember what I said. No fighting with your sister!"

"Are you giving her the same mandate?" Twilla challenged. "It works both ways."

"Twilla. Please." Her mother sighed. "Just be civil…and watch your mouth."

"Why don't you just say what you mean for a change? You don't want me to swear like a drunken sailor or lace my conversation with profanities if Julie brings someone with her tonight. Isn't that what this is all about?"

"You're just like your father!"

Twilla thought about her comment for a split second and realized her mother knew nothing about synomatic speech, her made-up term for profanity synonyms. *'Oh, shit.'* had a multitude of meanings other than *excrement*. It could mean a forgotten paper, a ripped shirt or a missed meeting. No explanation was necessary; it was covered...just like the English *'bloody hell.'*

Her mother always made it sound like every other word Twilla uttered was blasphemous. Not so. That her vocabulary was extensive with expletives, she credited her father first; and then later, her college peers. But giving credit where it was rightfully deserved, the latter group did enrich her vocabulary with profanity in other languages as well. It was part of her 'enrichment' program.

Her mother's exhortation was an old story; if Twilla could refrain from swearing during class instruction, why not tonight? Or tomorrow? Or forever? They had gone down that road before, many times in fact. Twilla was cautioned every time Julie brought someone home to meet the family. Yet, during all those shared dinners, she couldn't remember ever swearing in front of a guest. It may have happened later, when only the family gathered and Twilla thought the man was an asshole.

It is what it is, Twilla told herself. Forget about it. There would be a new crisis to contend with tomorrow. There always was with Agatha.

Twilla watched her mother sigh in resignation, before rolling the suitcase into the house. She started to follow her but stopped suddenly. Holding Lily firmly on the leash, Twilla tapped her key ring to unlock the car door and, after adjusting Amy's folder inside the three-ringed cookbook, grabbed the hard-covered binder from the front seat and locked the car again. "Ok, Lily. We're on go."

⁓

After unloading the luggage, cookbook and leash in her bedroom, Twilla raced to the family room with Lily in her arms.

"Hi, Dad," Twilla greeted the thin man sitting on a recliner. Bending down to kiss his cheek, she noticed how sickly he looked and tried to hide her concern. "I see you have a friend." She acknowledged the golden retriever lying nearby, her voice, cheerier than usual.

"It seems we both do." His face broke into a grin.

"Lily." She repositioned the dog from her armpit to face the altered man. "Her owner met with a fatal accident so I'm taking care of her," Twilla explained, repeating the same story she gave her mother.

"She's really cute, but what about family? They may want her."

"I'll know about that when I get back," Twilla lied. "Since Amy was a colleague of mine, the department head will keep me informed." That, too, was also a lie. Dr. Shelden lived in her own little world. The only knowledge she'd have on Amy's family would be at their initiation. The department head would simply check Amy's application records, learn of the deceased family and end her research. Case closed. It was that nosy detective that would dig further.

To her knowledge, Amy had no family. Nor did her friend ever mention relatives. In fact, Twilla knew nothing of her colleague's personal life. It was only lately that they had become close. But they were never close enough for personal exchanges. Amy never volunteered anything of consequence. She was vague about everything connected to her past and family.

Of course, Amy knew Twilla's father was having surgery. She had to know; the woman was covering her classes during the week's absence. Twilla may have mentioned her sister's expected arrival, but she couldn't remember telling her.

"So, we ended up calling him, Luke," her father continued, unaware his daughter's thoughts had strayed from their initial conversation momentarily. "He's almost five months old... smaller now, bigger later."

"Aside from being pretty, Luke seems very gentle."

"Yeah, I guess he is."

"He doesn't wander too far from you, does he?"

"You noticed already?" He seemed surprised. "What gave it away?"

"He hasn't even tried to sniff Lily."

"Put her down and he will."

"Ain't gonna happen." She stared at the larger dog and began to walk away.

"You going to the kitchen?"

"What do you need?"

"Water."

After serving her father, Twilla raced upstairs to the bathroom where she immediately set Lily down on the hall floor, adjacent the bathroom entrance, and cautioned her to 'stay put.'

Of course, the little elitist ignored Twilla's command, and taking a few steps inside the bathroom, sat on her haunches and stared at the sitting woman.

"Ok, if that's the way you want to play it." She told the black button eyes staring up at her.

Of course, Lily had no idea what Twilla meant by that statement, but thinking she had the woman's approval, the Peekapoo sprawled out on the floor and waited. Eventually, a treat would come her way, if she was patient.

"What can I do to help?" Twilla asked her mother who stood peeling potatoes at the kitchen sink.

The question seemed rather ridiculous since she held the small leashed bundle in her arms, fearful that Luke would be bounding into the kitchen to sniff Lily before they made it outside. She looked away momentarily as if listening for something.

"I turned on the TV. He's watching football."

"Some things never change," she sighed. "What are you making?"

Although the question concerned food, Twilla studied her mother quietly, her eyes encapsulating the woman's whole demeanor. She looked tired and worn…altered like Twilla's father… both prematurely gray and growing old. But how could that be? They were not yet sixty. A few years from it, in fact. Had they looked like this before she left for Stockton or was it the absence that caused her to take a fresher look at her parents?

"These are going in a pan of water right now." Agatha brought her thoughts back to their conversation, referring to the potatoes. "Later, I'll put them in the oven with chicken. Everything's done."

"The menus for dad's diet, isn't it?"

"He'll eat the chicken and noodles I made for him. We'll have the chicken, carrots and potatoes."

"It'll be just the four of us, right?" She watched her mother turn away to wipe her hands on a dish towel. "Well?" Twilla waited.

"Julie's bringing a friend," she sighed once again but at a louder pitch. "Now, don't start. I can't take this bickering between you two. He's leaving right after dinner."

"Which one is this and what does he do for a living…that is, if he really does work?"

"Julie just met him recently. Yes, at a bar." She answered Twilla's question before it was asked. "He lives and works in New

York City, like Julie. He's a consultant for some big company and travels a lot."

"Right," Twilla barked. "Her last guy traveled so far across the country, he was never heard from again."

"Now you're being crass," her mother snarled. "Julie can't help being so beautiful. If she's searching for Mr. Right, what's the harm in dating different people? I don't see you bringing anyone home," she continued the harangue.

Twilla slammed the kitchen door in anger and took Lily outside for sanctuary, knowing deep in her heart the momentary peace she felt would not last. Julie would be arriving within the hour and all hell would break loose. All attention would be slanted in her direction.

Suddenly, Twilla wished she had an excuse for not being there. '*That's not true*,' Twilla chastised herself. Her dad meant the world to her.

She may not have been the family favorite, but her father appreciated her accomplishments much more than those of her sister's. He verbalized that once…very privately to her. With her achievements, the goal was to make a good independent life for herself.

Julie's, on the other hand was to make a good marriage and be independently wealthy.

Independence meant different things for the two sisters. Although her plainness was never mentioned, it was always understood that she had to work harder to achieve it. Twilla had to face the prospect of going through life alone. Alone and financially independent.

Now, at twenty-six, was she supposed to reconcile and accept the thought of spinsterhood? Not Twilla. Being single was not a synonym for spinsterhood. Besides, weren't spinsters supposed to have cats? She certainly did not fit that category. Lily would attest to that.

FIVE

JULIE

"Hey!" Julie rushed into the living room excitedly, hugging each parent on cue. "I couldn't wait to get home." Then, she turned to the tall dark-haired man who stood idly by watching her, waiting to be introduced. "Come." Julie took his arm. "This is Russell Weatherly."

"Hello." The man shook hands with Matthew Hale and turned to acknowledge Agatha, when Twilla entered the room with Lily in her arms.

"Twilla, I want you to meet Russell." Julie's excitement could not be contained.

"Hello." A wide smile crossed Russell's face, his dark eyes meeting Twilla's, as he petted Lily's forehead.

"Hi," she responded, their eyes fixed on each other. In that brief instant Twilla felt an intense chemistry mounting between them and became very disconcerted that this gorgeous man belonging to her sister would have this effect on her. "This is Lily."

At the mention of her name, Lily peered-up at Russell momentarily, then snuggled closer to Twilla.

"She feels very safe with you." Russell smiled. "Sometimes animals read people better than humans do. They seem to know who is worthwhile," he added, a message his eyes translated to Twilla's.

"She's really not her dog," Agatha said, urging them to sit down. "Her owner was shot and later died. Some random shooting, isn't that right?" She directed the question to Twilla.

"That's the current thinking, but I'm not privy to what the police may have uncovered."

"You sound like you don't think it was random," Russell offered.

"The woman collapsed in her arms," Agatha interrupted. "She told me all about it."

"Mother!" Twilla chastised. "I don't want to discuss it."

"I'm sorry. Your colleague was obviously close to you," he said, his words stinging in her ears.

"How did he know Amy was her colleague? Was he involved somehow or just conclude that she was? She could not chance a slip of the tongue, regardless of his effect on her.

"No. She was not close to me. Our labs were next to each other in the Hawley Hall. She was to cover my classes when the shooting occurred."

"But you have her dog," Russell insisted. "That alone would make someone think you were close."

"I'd see her walking the dog when I jogged in Tavis Park."

"So, you took the dog."

"Only until family comes."

"You told me she had no family," her mother volunteered.

"None that I know of, but the university would have that information. In the interim, I thought I'd take care of Lily. It's me or the dog pound and I certainly didn't want that."

"Well, you're taking Lily makes sense to me. And I do think it sounds like a random shooting." Julie's concluded.

"I feel the same way," Twilla agreed.

"Well, now that's settled, let's have dinner before Russell has to leave us." Agatha began directing everyone into the dining room, making certain her seating chart was followed.

"Where are you going?" The question popped out of Twilla's mouth unexpectedly as she walked into the dining room.

"He has an appointment in Reading tomorrow morning," Julie quipped before Russell could explain. "He drove so I'll need a rental." She sank into her usual seat at the dining room table.

A frown crossed Twilla's face. "I don't understand."

"I drove my car." Russell explained, taking the seat next to Julie's.

"I'm flying back to New York after dad's surgery." Julie glared at Twilla who sat across the table from her. How could her sister be so dense? "I just wanted Russell to meet the family. Coming here wasn't really out of his way, but he needs to leave right after dinner." While Julie spoke of her travel agenda, all eyes were watching Agatha heap plates of food on the table.

"Now that you've given us Russell's itinerary, I think we should eat before he has to leave us." Agatha's words were more of a hint to move on to another subject.

"The table looks beautiful, Mrs. Hale. I heard you were a wonderful cook." From the wide smile crossing the woman's face, Russell knew his compliment hit home.

"She is." That was all Mr. Hale could add.

It was shortly after dinner when Russell followed Twilla and Lily to the walled alcove behind the family home. He lit a cigarette, took a few puffs then crushed it with his foot, placing the dead butt into his pocket for a later disposal.

"Nothing is more satisfying than a Parliament after a wonderful dinner." He approached the woman who was scarcely visible against the brick wall.

"Parliament?" From the tone of her response, it was obvious the woman's knowledge of cigarette brands was very limited.

"They're popular in Europe." He brushed away the small talk. "I was hoping for a chance to be alone with you."

"I don't understand." She looked-up to face the tall, handsome man who inched closer and closer to her, the chemistry between them increasing in the pale darkness of the night.

"I think you do." He kissed her eagerly, edging her lips open with his tongue, his woody scent engulfing her, awakening deep within her a feeling of want as he pressed her yielding body with his against the wall. Within seconds, his hands cupped the cheeks of her lower back, positioning her to him. "I know you do."

"Then you are mistaken." She pushed him away from her, and grabbing Lily in her arms, raced back to the house.

Russell watched the small figure disappear, knowing in his heart he would be seeing her again. He had read the signals loud and clear. The raw chemistry between them was there.

After Russell left the Hale home, the family gathered in the family room and began to talk about their dinner guest.

"He seems like a nice young man," Julie's father began the conversation. "When will he get in?"

"Within the hour, I think. He'll probably meet with his co-workers in the hospitality suite. I think that was the plan. He'll text me at some point."

"I gather it's serious." Her father pressed harder.

"I don't know," she faltered.

"What do you mean?" Her mother questioned. "You must feel something."

"It's just too soon, I guess. We've only been dating a short time."

"From what I saw, there was more than an inkling of interest," her mother challenged. "You should have some idea if a relationship is developing." Agatha stopped speaking and waited for a reply.

"Russell's not one to rush into anything," Julie insisted, "and I don't want to scare him off."

"Then you are serious." Her father found the latter part of her comment amusing.

"Unrequited love is not something that interests me."

"Then it is serious," he repeated in earnest. "If the relationship fails to blossom, don't waste your time trying to encourage it. It must evolve normally between two people. I know it hurts, but that's the way of life and love." It was the only advice he could offer his beautiful daughter.

"What do you think, Twilla?" He asked his younger daughter. "You've been very quiet." All eyes suddenly focused on the small woman sitting in the corner holding Lily in her arms.

"I'd drop the whole matter."

The strangeness of her response made Julie demand a further explanation. "What is that supposed to mean?"

"He's too good-looking."

"With your experience, what would you know about the likes of handsome men?" she snapped back, shaken by the comment.

"Attractive men don't want to be tied down, particularly when there are so many butterflies swirling their net." Twilla knew she could not offer more of an explanation and decided that leaving the room was her best option.

"What is her problem?" Julie demanded angrily, when Twilla had gone.

"She's just going through a hard time, what with the shooting and dad's surgery on her mind. Just ignore her. She doesn't have your beauty," her mother cautioned, "and she's not outgoing enough to really understand the way of relationships."

"You can't possibly fault her for being introspective," Matthew interrupted, disturbed by Agatha's comment. "That's been her nature…a book in hand, a stray dog at her side. That's our Twilla."

"Our Twilla's going to be an old maid." Agatha faulted his logic. "She's plain. Everyone can see that…her straight hair, the pale skin and no make-up…this picture only emphasizes her plainness. She won't even try to mask it with cosmetics. That is the full composite of our Twilla. In all honesty, what man would want her for a mate?"

"I think you are being exceptionally cruel about our younger daughter." He rose to exit the room, fearing his temper would get the best of him.

"Of course, you would think that. She's your favorite!" his wife shrieked, but her stinging comment brought forth a piercing reply she had not expected.

"There's only one in this family who plays favorites and it sure as hell isn't me!" Matthew shouted back loudly. "You have been doing this for years and it stops now, unless you want to live in New York City permanently with Julie. I mean it!"

The two women watched an angered Matthew Hale quit the room as they sat in silence.

"You shouldn't have said that," Julie reprimanded her mother. "You made him angry and that's not good, particularly with his condition."

"I know I was wrong, but Twilla sets me off with her crazy comments. I never know what she's really thinking. She was the same way as a child."

"Mom," Julie pleaded. "Keep those thoughts to yourself. You know we've always been very close. I know you love me and have the best intentions, but Twilla's here now and should be included. Dad must remain calm before surgery."

"You're right. I'll take care of it."

She watched her beautiful daughter rise gracefully from the couch and then dutifully kiss her forehead before leaving the room.

Agatha sat in silence, her thoughts spinning. Although she loved Twilla, she was right about her daughter. Twilla was plain but Agatha never said she was ugly. However, the facts were clear.

Both daughters were dark-haired, dark-eyed, small and slim in stature; however, the similarity ended there. Where a glamorous beauty whose dark eyes shone with a luminous brilliance, her counterpart's plainness had more of a dull effect. Then, Agatha thought about their differences in comportment.

Whether gorgeous clothes draping Julie's beautiful figure and porcelain skin, were part of her work ethic as a buyer for Morgan's Department store, or part of a genetic make-up that defined her, it had little effect on her younger sister who constantly lived in casual apparel. If manufacturers were to make it possible, her younger daughter would probably sleep in denim pajamas. The thought of denim pajamas and Twilla's affinity for garments of that fabric, brought a smile to Agatha's face, as she slowly left the family room for an apologetic conversation with the man she loved.

While the conversation was taking place downstairs, Twilla was upstairs, her thoughts running the gamut of castigation to castration as she lay across her bed.

What a dumb ass! How could I allow it to happen? How could I be so stupid not to see it coming? Approaching me like that…I must be losing it. She continued the reprimand when another thought entered her mind. *What about Julie? Should she tell her? What could Twilla say? "Your boyfriend's a jerk. If he's not loyal now, why would you pursue marriage?"*

Twilla thought long and hard about Russell's betrayal, the man's physical manipulation of her, and the knowledge that this information could ruin or damage a relationship between the two sisters.

What's the point of saying anything? Twilla would never see Russell again unless a marriage took place and she doubted that would happen. The man did not impress her as wanting a singular woman. No. He was far too interested in releasing his sperm in more than one vaginal bank. He proved that rationale tonight. In her mind, it was best to let the relationship play out. Julie was smart enough not to be played. Although somewhat fragile, she could take care of herself.

However, it was not long before Twilla's thoughts were interrupted.

"Twilla." Julie tapped her sister's bedroom door. "Can we talk?" She heard Lily whimper and Twilla's soft response before the door opened.

"I thought you'd be here a little earlier." Twilla crossed the room and patted the side of the bed, encouraging her sister to sit.

"Twill," she used the pet name from their younger days. "It is serious."

"I figured. But on whose side?"

"You have to ask?"

"I don't want to see you hurt."

"It's too late. I'm already in love with him. It's so stupid since we only met recently. I have feelings that I've never experienced before. No other man has affected me like this. I know he feels something for me. I'm sure of it." Twilla began to feel the pain of Julie's insistence. Her love was pure: his actions proved otherwise.

"And you brought him home, thinking he would say something after meeting Mom and Dad." Twilla caught her nod. *What could she say about this undeserving cad without divulging their exchange earlier that evening?* "What does he do? I mean that he could swing by on his way to a meeting?"

"That wasn't a problem. He's an executive with Simex." It was obvious from Twilla's expression that she was clueless about the company. "From what I understand, it's a large corporation with central offices in New York. Russell travels throughout the country attending conferences and big trade shows. Apparently, he brings in a lot of business. But, truthfully, Twill, I don't know what his job description is. We don't talk about work when we're together."

"Have you met any of his friends?"

"Only a very charming Brian Mills."

"They work together?"

"No. Brian's an architect. I think they were roommates or fraternity brothers at Penn. Why are you asking these questions?"

"I just wondered if you had met his circle of friends. I'm sure he's met yours."

"No. You're wrong. I was at a local bar with two of my co-workers when we met. When they left with their husbands, he came to my table and bought me a drink. I met Brian later that night when he dropped in for a nightcap."

"Really?" Twilla forced a laugh. "What's this watering hole called, 'The Whiskey Greet?' Sounds like a colorful place."

"I wish. McCaffery's. It's around the corner from the department store. Some of us eat lunch there."

"Regularly?"

"No. I can't get away on-a-daily basis. Why? Why are you asking me these questions?"

Twilla began to laugh again. "Don't get in a twist. I was hoping you'd take me there when I visit you. It sounds like my kind of place…a busy bar with good food."

"Actually, the bar food is good."

"So, do I get a promise?"

"Of course. But, what do I do about Russell?"

"I'd give him a month. If he doesn't come around, go elsewhere. You're too smart and much too beautiful to waste your time on a one-way street."

"But I hurt, Twill." A tear streamed down her cheek causing Twilla to take the end of her pajama top and wipe it away.

"Listen." She embraced her sister. "If the SOB doesn't come around, I'll shoot him and then we can drink to his memory at McCaffery's." Her words immediately impacted laughter as she blew over the top of her index finger and cocked thumb of an imaginary gun.

"You are so funny!" Julie tried to control herself.

"Feel better?" Twilla became serious.

"As a matter of fact, I do. If he doesn't come around, maybe I'll shoot him myself," she said, exiting the room.

"Now that's a good call!" Twilla crowed as she watched her sister close the bedroom door.

Twilla waited a few minutes after Julie left her bedroom before taking any action. She feared her sister's return for another recap on Russell and unstated love. Then feeling it was safe, Twilla took one of her ruled tablets from the nightstand and began writing down every scrap of information Julie uttered about meeting

Russell, his employment and the tavern, McCaffery's. Trying his charm on her that night only underscored his pretended interest in her sister. It was time to conduct a full search on Russell Weatherly before he broke Julie's heart completely. Twilla knew he was a player but could she prove it?

Suddenly, her thoughts took another turn. Was he just a plain ordinary rogue or did he have an agenda of his own? Was it at all possible that Russell Weatherly was connected in some way to Amy Gregson and the ring? *He said colleague. How did he know she was Twilla's colleague?* Was he using Julie for information, knowing Twilla was the last person to see Amy alive? Could that explain his advances that evening in the yard? Would he think this plain unadorned woman, so engulfed and mesmerized with emotion, would give him the information he wanted? Was this his plan? Sway her now; question later. Twilla rationalized the sense of it. Was this narrative too farfetched? Maybe she was losing it. Twilla cast the thought aside and pulled the hidden folder from the three-ringed cookbook under Lily's pillowed head.

"Come on, darlin." She tried moving the dog back on the pillow. "Let's see why this folder's inside my cookbook. Amy must have clipped some new articles on foods and nutrition." But those meaningful words mattered little to Lily, who, by then, positioned herself for a quick belly rub, before turning away to sleep.

"You little traitor," Twilla said complying with her request. "When do I get one of those?" But she stopped speaking suddenly after opening the folder. Her eyes fell on what appeared to be an inventory page of Dr. Shelden's. Having it in Amy's possession immediately stirred her mind with questions.

Why would Amy keep an inventory of lab equipment that spanned decades? Twilla's finger followed the listings, order numbers, and shipment dates of several refrigerators, ranges, microwave ovens and the larger more expensive cooking equipment used in Amy's classes. On another page, along with a scribbled notation, was an equipment inventory of two home management houses. Along with refrigerators and stoves, the list included washers and dryers.

"What the hell is this all about?" Twilla asked herself as she read Shelden's memo that said, "See DR on this." And once again, she questioned Amy's reason for having the file.

As she sat in bed trying to decipher the note, Twilla began to wonder if the file and Amy's death were connected. She thought about it for a moment.

Only her department head would have had access to inventory records. Then, how did Amy get possession of this file and what did it mean? Was this the same folder Dr. Shelden was searching for in Amy's lab, the one given her by mistake? If so, why didn't Amy return it? She must have kept it for a reason. But what? What made Amy hide it in Twilla's cookbook? Why was the file so important? Twilla had to think about this logically.

The file belonged to Dr. Shelden. That was a fact. But according to the notation, she had to see DR about it. "Who the hell is DR? Were these someone's initials or was DR a medical doctor?" she said aloud. "Did Amy know this person?"

Why would Shelden have a file that spanned a twenty-year history of expensive equipment from her department? One separate from departmental records. There had to be a reason for it. But what? For what purpose? None of it made sense. Then again, why would Amy keep it? What was she doing with it? Was she busy checking serial numbers and dates? Why would she do that?

Intuitively, Twilla went back to the first page of the file and jotted down the current numbers and shipping dates adjacent two refrigerator brands listed. If the inventory proved real, she would find those two pieces of equipment in Amy's lab.

Twilla began to lose focus after studying the file so long. As she slid the folder back inside the cookbook binder, a recipe with several notations in Amy's handwriting caught her attention. Twilla skipped a few pages and found a few more notations.

"I can't stand this," Twilla whispered to herself as she climbed into bed. "What did Amy get me into?"

Her eyes fell on Lily quietly sleeping on the pillow. What would become of her? Was there someone in Amy's life who would care for her, or even want her? Taking care of an animal was a huge responsibility. Twilla had come to learn that. But Lily was so small, so helpless and so sweet. Who could possibly resist her?

Deep down in her heart, Twilla hoped no one would come forward for Lily. She had grown attached to the little Peekapoo in their short time together. In a way, it was like having Amy back with her. Twilla's eyes began to glisten with that thought, a tightness growing in her chest.

Although they were never close friends, a relationship between them did exist. They did enjoy having meals together, their conversation never lagging. Each encounter seemed to bring them closer together. In time, a real friendship could have existed. Twilla felt certain of that. The fact that Amy offered to substitute when she went home for her father's surgery indicated some form of closeness between them. They were bonding. Of that, she was certain.

A tear inched down Twilla's face. Now she would no longer see Amy standing by her classroom door watching the students enter. Nor would she eat the fruits of her cooking classes or see her friend walking Lily in Tavis Park. That would never occur again. Amy was dead. When all was said and done, Twilla lost her one real friend and Lily was left an orphan. Twilla sat-up in bed, a flood of tears washing her face.

SIX
COOKBOOK STUDY

The next morning a sleepy Twilla heard her mother's voice over a rhythmic tapping at her bedroom door. Agatha listened for a response amid Lily's barking. "Did you hear me? Do you want sausage or bacon?"

Within minutes, Twilla stood facing her mother, with Lily close behind sniffing her bare feet. "No, I'll just have toast and coffee. I brought some work home I'd like to finish this morning."

"I just thought it would be nice to have a family breakfast since we're all together. Couldn't you finish your work when Julie and I run errands this morning?"

"You're going into town?"

"The bank and supermarket. Next week will be hectic with dad's surgery. You can come with us, if you want."

Shopping with her mother and sister was not something Twilla would relish. Been there, done that, hated every minute of it. However, she found the thought of being left alone at home very appealing. Her father would be glued to the television set watching football, golf or whatever sport suited his fancy, while she examined the cookbook for a meaning of Amy's intermittent scrawl.

"Okay. Bacon. I'll have two slices," Twilla acquiesced.

"Eggs?"

"She'll have one, over medium, and a slice of toast." Julie walked down the hall, answering her mother's question. "That's how Twilla likes her eggs. See, I remembered," she addressed her sister standing in the open doorway.

Twilla eyed both women with disdain: one was casually dressed; the other, smart and very chic. She, of course, fell into neither category. "Give me five minutes to slip into my jeans." Closing the door slowly, Twilla heard their footsteps fade away and wished she were back in her unit at Stockton.

Later that afternoon, Twilla sat on her bed thumbing through the mixed pages of a three-ringed cookbook and wondered why Amy left it in such disorder. The pages were not numbered sequentially, and the recipe chapters followed no logical order. Soups, fish and meats were all mixed together while appetizers, desserts, breads were lumped in the canning section.

"What was Amy up to?" she asked the Lilliputian sidekick asleep on her pillow. "I don't get it." Twilla fingered every recipe until she found one with a notation in Amy's distinctive curly-cue scrawl. Although the recipe title had been altered, the ingredients and measurements remained the same. Was this notation one of Amy's cooking fantasies or something deliberate? A something for Twilla to follow? It was time to check.

In a cookies and bars section, Amy's fancy writing finally caught her attention. Her colleague labeled a simple brownie recipe as Baby Ruth's Brownies.

Twilla grabbed the tablet from her nightstand, found a blank page and wrote the word, *Ruth*. Within minutes she found a Graham Cracker Pie Crust recipe that was starred with a fanciful flourish. Once again, she jotted down the word, *Graham*. In the workings of Twilla's mind, the heading that included *Cracker* took second place to *Graham*. Nevertheless, she wrote *Cracker* along the page margin, just in case the word had meaning.

As she continued reading and writing, Twilla realized a code was in the making. Were these messages meant for her as a means of finding Mark? Paging through the cookbook recipes, she soon added the following words to her list: *Brindle Street* Biscuits, *A 1* Prime Rib and *High* Garlic Tomato Sauce. With Chicken Mushroom Crepes, Amy added: An Authentic *Coventry* Recipe.

Now she realized why the cookbook pages were not categorized. It was done purposely. Twilla had to follow the page disorder and list Amy's specific notations to decipher her code. She wondered why Amy needed a code in the first place.

Did something scare Amy into making these recipe notations? When did she do it? Was this puzzle really meant for her or someone else? She and Amy were never really close as confidants exchanging secrets. They were friendly enough for coffee or lunch after meeting in the park; however, they were not friends in the social sense. Yet, Twilla recalled Amy's mention of something important but could not remember what it was. Her thoughts then shifted back to the coded notations.

Not only did Amy create a code, she made it appear innocuous for some strange reason. Who could possibly be suspicious of scrawled notations on recipes? It was done all the time. But the reasoning behind these notations was totally different.

"Amy knew something was in the wind," Twilla told herself. "She created a code for protection. But from whom? Why was it needed? Was she afraid of someone or something in her past catching up with her? She never talked about her personal life. What was Amy hiding?" That thought kept rolling over in her mind, when something else occurred to her.

Whatever Amy was hiding, it concerned Mark. Twilla had a gut feeling about that. Amy was smart, scared smart with a hidden secret to protect.

She remembered Twilla's spirited thirst for adventure during their conversations. Amy also knew if anything happened to her,

Twilla would retrieve the cookbook, examine it for her mother's recipes and pursue the scrawled clues. If that was her intention, the recipe notations and gold ring were keys to finding Mark.

Was that it? Was that the purpose of dismantling her cookbook? Twilla would have to read it a second time before reformatting the sections in proper order. That had to be done as a precaution, as well as assimilating the content to make it look like a standard cookbook. Then someone reading it would think nothing of the notations listed. In fact, she would add a few of her own.

Then, she wondered about the inventory list. Was that a separate issue or were the two related? What about the ransacked apartment? How did that fit in? Was the person who searched Amy's apartment also responsible for her death? The thought made Twilla shudder. She had the cookbook, the inventory list and the gold ring. The intruder had nothing.

Twilla remembered seeing the shadow of a man in a long coat when she held Amy in her arms at Hawley Hall. That mere glimpse triggered a sinister foreboding, one that stirred deep within her at the time. Did he have something to do with Amy's murder? Would he remember Twilla holding her and think Amy gave her the very thing he wanted?

"If so, I'm running out of time," she said loudly, "so get your arse in gear."

Twilla rolled her body out of bed and began talking to no one in particular. "I feel like I'm back in the fifth grade reading a juvenile mystery...the kind where every scrawl is supposed to mean something." She glanced briefly at Lily. "Like you really care." Twilla scolded the little Peekapoo whose black button eyes looked-up at her from the pillow. "As long as I feed you and rub your belly, you don't have a care in the world."

Having gotten the attention she wanted, Lily rolled on her back and offered her belly again.

"Traitor, when do I get mine? I keep asking that question and you never do anything." Twilla rubbed Lily gently for a few minutes, and before realizing the dog's intentions, found Lily licking her nose.

"I love you too." She bundled Lily in her arms, only to be taken back by someone calling her name.

"Twilla."

As soon as she heard her mother's voice, Twilla set Lily back on the bed and, after stashing everything into one of her dresser drawers, slowly opened the bedroom door and pretended to be groggy.

"Have you been here all this time?" Agatha studied her. Staying in her room for hours was strange behavior, even for Twilla. "Are you alright?"

"I must have dozed off," Twilla yawned.

"Then it was a good thing you rested. You must have needed the sleep." Agatha accepted her daughter's plausible explanation. "I want you to see what Julie bought me."

Twilla already knew what the item was. In all the years of her sister's gift giving, only the blouse color changed. "Come Lily." Twilla embraced her. "Let's go see Nana's surprise."

Saturday evening passed quickly in the Hale household. A thrilled Julie received a phone call from Russell who suggested they have dinner upon her return to New York. Agatha displayed her new blue blouse saying she would wear it to church the following morning. Matthew sat glued to his chair watching a football game, while Twilla, feigning tiredness, escaped their company to further study her cookbook before reformatting it. But in her attempt to reorganize the cookbook, she found two index pages glued together with a photograph tucked in between.

Twilla studied the photograph of the two women and a dog. She recognized Amy and Lily immediately but had no knowledge of the second woman's identity. She was older. Although that was evident by her graying hair, her face was not wrinkled by age, nor her body stooped in stature. Wherever the picture had been taken, the woman's broad smiling face seemed to glow as she hugged Amy. No. The photograph said more than a woman hugging another one holding a dog. A genuine feeling came through. Much more than a friend. An aunt, perhaps. The woman was too old to be Amy's sister. A cousin? A close loving relationship between the two existed. That was definite. That the photograph was hidden and not to be found by anyone other than Twilla was also definite.

Was that part of Amy's plan too? Of course, it was. In reorganizing the cookbook Amy knew Twilla would tear the glued pages apart. The picture was another clue, an important one that had to be kept safe and well hidden. But Why? Did it have something to do with finding Mark?

Twilla tiptoed to the dresser for her purse. She slipped the small photograph inside her wallet among the other snapshots. In her mind, it was the safest place. The wallet was always in her possession, and anyone seeing the pictures would not ask questions, unless it was that nosy detective, the arrogant beast she tried to avoid.

There was a quiet round of activity the following morning when the family bustled about, getting properly dressed for the Sunday service. Matthew and Agatha were the first ones' downstairs, waiting for their daughters to appear.

"I'm surprised Twilla's not down yet," Matthew started the conversation. 'She's always been very prompt."

"Julie's the one who takes time to dress; Twilla never cared much for fashion."

"I think you're wrong, Agatha." Her husband looked approvingly at Twilla who now stood before him in a rose-colored jacket dress and a matching Derby hat whose turned-up brim was held in place by a cluster of gold beads. Aside from the matching shoes and purse completing the outfit, Twilla chose a gold necklace that lay flat on her bosom, a gold bangle bracelet and swirled gold earrings to add an even more chic element to her very expensive wardrobe, the one that broke the bank of her last paycheck.

"Twilla, you are absolutely breathtaking," her father sighed appreciatively. "I've never seen you look more beautiful."

"How about me?" Julie entered the room. "Do I pass muster?"

"You always look gorgeous," her mother prevailed. "But that's who you are."

Agatha's hurtful comment did not go unnoticed, however. For at that very moment a cursory eye-exchange took place between a father and his younger daughter…the ugly duckling who had suddenly turned into a swan.

"Shall we go," Matthew led the way to the family car. "I'd like to get a front pew if we can."

Later that day, Twilla did something very useful. She bought a dog crate for Lily. There was only one problem. Lily did not seem to like it. The little elitist preferred freedom by day and Twilla's pillow at night. A traveling enclosure be damned. She had the passenger seat of Twilla's Chevy.

It proved to be a long arduous week for Twilla who was forced to listen to her mother's complaints and her sister's dreams of love, when their priority and continued concern should have been Matthew's condition after surgery. Although the doctor had been positive on Matthew Hale's recovery, Twilla worried about his care upon discharge and verbalized her concern.

"I'm sure he'll be fine in your mother's hands," the surgeon reassured her.

"True, but I'm considering the help of a private nurse…at least for the first few weeks. Julie and I work in different cities and I think we'd feel better if a private nurse took care of him. It would be less of a strain on my mother during the day."

"I can check the registry, if that's the direction you want to take."

Twilla's eyed her mother and sister before unloading an idea she had been considering. "I was thinking of hiring our neighbor, Mrs. Haskell. I know she takes private cases." Although Twilla knew it would be a perfect fit, she noted her mother's disdain.

"She's only a practical nurse," Agatha interrupted, not enthused with her suggestion.

"That doesn't matter, mom. She's still a professional and lives right next door."

"This would give you time for a needed rest," Julie offered. "You've been looking after dad for so long, you could use the help. Let Twilla approach her."

Her sister's last remark played havoc with Twilla's brain. Why was she elected for the job? Why couldn't the three of them approach Millie Haskell? God knows they knew the family for years. Millie and her father were in the same class in high school, even graduated together. Some even speculated a blossoming romance between them but that rumor never had legs. Could that explain the dirty look from her mother? How stupid. She was a widow now. The woman needed money and took as many private cases as she could, without jeopardizing family time with her crippled son and granddaughter.

Ned's tragic accident suddenly came to mind…the car spinning out of control, killing his wife, Leslie, and leaving six-year-old

Tessie unharmed. That was years ago, and computer repair became the handicapped man's livelihood. And it was not unusual to see the father and daughter play computer games from her bedroom window.

"What do you think?" Julie said, bringing Twilla up to present time.

"I think it's a good idea. The three of us should approach Millie."

"Sometimes, I think you are in your own little world. I already made that suggestion and mother agreed."

"Then we'll see Millie tonight and get everything resolved before dad comes home," Twilla said, somewhat confused by the change.

From their facial expressions, it was clear that they agreed. The only one who had not voted was Matthew, but that didn't matter. He would have been overruled.

When the hospital discharged Matthew Hale the following Saturday, Agatha thought his release was much too soon as she waited for the papers to be signed. She did, however grudgingly, feel better about hiring professional help, but secretly wished it could be someone other than Millie Haskell. She, too, had heard those rumors of the budding romance with her husband, but while Millie's husband, Scott, was alive, Agatha had pegged it to idle gossip long dead. The families had been close friends for years. In fact, spending Super Bowl Sunday together had been a tradition with the two families until Scott died. Still, with a widowed Millie in her house, Agatha certainly did not want a repeat of past speculation.

Was she being foolish? For the past three years, Millie's status as a widow never bothered her. Why should it now? Was she no longer sure of her husband's feelings? Was their marriage that much in jeopardy? Agatha thought long and hard about it. No. Matthew never gave her cause to believe a troubled relationship existed between them. If anything, he was still as loving as ever. Any problem arising would be of her own making. She would keep those thoughts to herself. She would think of her widowed neighbor as a trained nurse who could help with her husband's recovery. And although Agatha accepted that premise, it did not mean she would be less observant.

"Mrs. Haskell will be at the house when we arrive." Twilla told her mother after ending a call on her cell phone. "She needs a list of Dad's medications and his discharge instructions."

"You handle that while Julie and I take care of your father." Agatha quickly divided their duties. "We'll put Dad in bed and go over everything with Millie when we get home. I want all of his medication in the house before you leave." Her eyes fell on Julie.

"Before who leaves?" Twilla questioned.

"I am. Tomorrow." Julie offered. "I talked it over with Mom. You'll be here and so will Mrs. Haskell. You don't need four people taking care of Dad, and it's not like he's in any danger."

"That's not the point!" Twilla fumed. "It's the caring, the support system he needs right now that's important."

"Dad already knows how I feel, so I don't have any regrets about leaving."

Twilla knew it was a losing argument. If Julie did not understand the importance of "being there" for her father, the innate concern that comes naturally with loving someone so important in your life, then there was nothing Twilla could do or say. This feeling had to come from within. Obviously, Julie did not possess that quality.

"How did you know I would be staying on?"

"Mom told me you called your department head for an extension." Julie ignored her sister's continued frown. "So, I felt it was okay for me to leave." Her voice trailed off as she walked toward the nurses' station.

Although her remark was intended to reaffirm the logistics of her leaving, this did not sit well with Twilla. It merely confirmed her sister's selfish streak. How into herself, she really was. She did not care about anyone, other than herself. It was obvious that her own personal life was more important than an illness in her own family.

"Twilla!" Her mother pointed to a doctor approaching them. "Get the instructions. Julie went for your father."

As Twilla spoke with the doctor, she noticed Julie wheeling her father toward them. He looked so small. Had he lost weight or was the wheelchair too large? One thought crossed her mind. She was glad for the extension.

SEVEN

BREAK-IN

As Twilla drove along the highway on her return to Stockton one week later, her thoughts were not on Lily, who lay fast asleep on the front seat, nor on her father's speedy recovery. She concentrated on two discoveries: the folder holding Amy's hidden inventory, and the notations on the cookbook recipes. How was she to proceed with that knowledge? Twilla was no code-breaker spy. She was a fish out of water who needed a school of help. Although that thought made her smile, she suddenly felt stupid.

Was Twilla being dumb doing what she did? They did it in spy movies and on television crime series. So, what would it hurt? No one would know she unstitched the tiny seam of her outer jacket and sewed the ring inside before re-stitching it. Between the fabric and the lining, the ring could not even be felt. As long as she continued wearing the outer jacket, the ring would be safe. With the coming cold weather, it seemed like a perfect James Bond move. Maybe she wasn't watching closely enough. Spies were never into sewing anything but mischief. That was the kind of thing they sowed.

As her thoughts continued in that direction, she heard Lily's soft whimper. "You awake now? We'll be home soon." She pulled a bagged treat that sat inside the car's beverage holder. "Here you go, Sweetie." Lily eagerly took the treat and once again settled down to rest. "I've got your dinner," she said, thinking of the dog food she left at home, "but it looks like I'll have scrambled eggs. I'm not stopping for groceries."

Within thirty minutes, Twilla pulled into the parking space of her unit at Stoneledge and, after leashing Lily, stood by patiently to watch her water a nearby shrub before entering the building.

Minutes later, Twilla's body slid down the open doorway of her unit, her loud screams shattering the silence of the hall, a shaken Lily in her arms. Neighbors in the units nearby rushed to help the fallen woman. "Call the police. Ask for Detective Barr," she pleaded as they brought a shaken Twilla to her feet. "I've been robbed. I've been robbed." She kept repeating the phrase.

"What happened? When did you get back?" Clisten Barr questioned a now composed Twilla as Lily's head burrowed deep into her armpit at the sound of his strident voice.

"How long did it take you to get here?"

"Answer my question."

"I thought I just did," she snapped angrily. At that point, Lily emerged from her shelter to reaffirm Twilla's response, her black button eyes rapt with attention.

"Ten minutes." He watched his partner and an investigative team enter the unit.

"Try twenty-five."

"And you know this how?"

"My watch keeps great time."

"You could have gone inside."

"And have you scream at me for entering? No thanks." Twilla bristled with sarcasm. She felt Lily squirming for release, and setting her on the hall floor, watched her race inside the open doorway and disappear.

"You must not have a very good opinion of me."

"Can we go inside?" Twilla ignored his comment as she entered the ransacked unit. "Why would someone do this? Why rob me? I have nothing of value." Her eyes encompassed the extreme disarray as she went from one room to another. Furniture was overturned, clothing and papers strewn everywhere. Every drawer in the unit had been emptied on the floor except the silverware drawer which remained intact. She turned suddenly and realized another detective had been following her, notebook in hand.

"I'm Tony Mistretta, Detective Barr's partner." He introduced himself. "Is anything missing? I mean that you can see right now."

"I have no idea," Twilla shot back. She was angry...angry that something like this could happen to her and frustrated by the whole damn situation. "It will take me weeks to get this place back to normal, let alone learn what's missing."

"What's missing?" Clisten asked upon entering the kitchen at the tail-end of the conversation.

"That's what he just asked. How would I know? I just got home to find my place ransacked and my question is why. Who would want to rob me? I have nothing worth stealing." Her eyes remained fixed on his as she spoke.

"I don't think this is a robbery. Whoever ransacked your place was looking for something."

"Why would someone do that? What could I possibly have to warrant searching my unit? That makes no sense."

"Yes, it does. The timing's too close."

"I'm not following you." She shook her head.

"You're a colleague of Miss Gregson's. Maybe there's a connection."

"To a random shooting? That's ridiculous. Anyhow, Amy and I weren't that close."

"But you worked together," Tony interrupted.

"That's true, but I didn't know anything about her, really. I never questioned where she spent her vacations. In fact, other than having Lily, I don't know anything about her personally. We were never together that much." She lied deliberately, knowing the connection, if there was one, had to do with the inventory or the ring so neatly stitched inside the corner of her jacket.

"Are you alright?" Clisten asked, realizing she was visually shaken. "Maybe you should consider sleeping somewhere else tonight."

"Why? Do you think whoever did this, might come back?" Her eyes riveted his, demanding, yet afraid of the answer.

"I doubt it, but you might be uncomfortable sleeping here tonight."

"I don't have much choice. I'm not close to any of my colleagues, this place is a wreck and I have classes tomorrow. I've got to start somewhere, but this really pisses me off." His eyes followed her pointed finger. "My grandmother's vase." She crossed the room and was ready to pick-up the two porcelain pieces when Clisten's rushed to stop her.

"Wait! There may be prints on those."

"Oh, please," she stiffened. "It was probably knocked down when the furniture was overturned."

"You don't know that. Find me a plastic bag," he demanded.

Twilla ambled carefully around the ransacked living room to get one of the plastic bags she stored under the kitchen sink. To her surprise, the cleaning supplies and bags were intact. As she rose, Twilla found Tony hovering for one of them and, following the man into the living room, watched him carefully bag the broken vase.

"That should do it for now. I want you to call, if you're missing something, regardless how small it is," Clisten demanded. "It doesn't have to be valuable," he said as the team began to leave the unit. "Perhaps you should put me on speed dial for now."

He scrawled something on a card and gave it to her. "My private number. Call me if you find anything. I want to close this case as soon as possible."

Twilla watched everyone leave, and then began calling Lily. After a frantic search she found the Peekapoo hiding under her bed. When Lily refused to come to her, Twilla became confused. Was her refusal connected to Amy? Was Lily beginning to miss her? She had heard stories of dogs pining for their masters, but never knew of an actual case. Was this happening now? How could she handle it? Amy was never coming back.

Twilla sat on the rumpled bed quietly, waiting patiently for Lily to appear when her eyes fell on the card in her hand. Without thinking she pulled the cell phone from her pocket and involuntarily entered Clisten Barr's name and number in her list of contacts. Shortly after completing the entry, her thoughts returned to Lily and she was on her hands and knees, amid the strewn clothing, jewelry and dresser knick-knacks crowding the floor, peering under the bed.

"Come on, Sweetie. Come to Twilla," she cooed and begged ever so gently, when the shattering clang of the doorbell interrupted her pleas. "Oh, crap! What does he want now?" she railed, her tone suddenly changing.

"I forgot something." Clisten ignored her as he strode toward the kitchen, leaving Twilla to close the door and follow him.

As she watched him take a pair of latex gloves off the counter, the doorbell rang again.

"You are expecting someone?" They chorused simultaneously.

"No." Her eyes met his. "But don't leave," she demanded, withdrawing from the kitchen to answer the door.

"Russell." Twilla stood in shock. "What are you doing here? How did you know my address?"

"What happened?" He stood in the open doorway, gazing at the ransacked living room, intentionally ignoring her questions. "What's going on?"

"I've been robbed, so you can't come in." She turned away quickly and raced back to the kitchen. "Please don't leave me. I'm begging you," she whispered, motioning him to follow her, totally unaware Clisten had heard her conversation and slipped on the gloves to give his presence credence.

"Russell, this is Detective Barr who is following the robbery. Why are you here? Where's Julie?"

"I'm on my way to another conference and thought I'd stop by to say hello." He glanced from her to the detective.

"What is it that you do?" The question was one the detective was accustomed to asking.

"Regional director for Simex. I'm headquartered in New York City."

"I'm not familiar with the company. Is your conference about a product or a service you sell?"

"A little of both, really. We service everything we sell. Think of it as an umbrella with an array of products and services."

"The company sounds very diverse," Clisten said, dialing a number. "Yes, you can bring them in now," he spoke into the phone before addressing Twilla. "I think we'll know more in the next hour when the team comes to scrub for evidence." That, of course, was a lie. They had already been there.

"I'd better be going then." Russell turned to leave the open doorway.

"My love to Julie." Twilla watched him saunter toward the elevator before returning to the kitchen where an inquisition waited. Detective Barr would, no doubt, question the visit. That Russell was linked to her sister, and not Amy, didn't matter.

"Now, young lady, what was that all about? Why was my presence here so important?" He volleyed a continuous line of questions while petting a contented Lily, resting comfortably in his arms.

"How did you do that?" Twilla stared at Lily in shock, ignoring his questions. "How did you get her to come to you? She was hiding under the bed and wouldn't come to me."

"When Lily heard my voice, she just ran into the kitchen and wanted held. She was shaking." He continued stroking her.

"But why? Was it because someone broke into my unit?"

"I don't know the reason, but she wanted to be held. Now answer my question. Why did you want me to stay?"

"Maybe I should tell you," Twilla rolled her eyes, "but you'll think I'm crazy. I met Russell when I went home for my dad's surgery. He came to our house with my sister, Julie, who by the way, is crazy about him."

"Then why did he stop by? Did you encourage him in any way?"

"You can't be serious!" Her strident voice echoed the room. "I don't trust the SOB. He tried hitting on me in the back yard when Lily was watering the grass. That did it for me."

"Meaning?"

"My sister is gorgeous, intelligent and has a terrific job in New York. She's a high-fashion buyer for a big department store, dresses to the nines and has a beautiful apartment. She is so smart and should have her pick of any man the way I see it. And although I love her to death, her choice in men sucks."

Somewhere along the line, the detective seemed confused by her never-ending narrative. "And your point is?"

"We may not see eye-to-eye on a lot of things," her finger poked his chest, "but neither of us is blind. I look like an unmade bed most of the time and live a very casual lifestyle. There is no comparison. So, what does this handsome man, someone who has his pick of the litter, want with me? No. He's after something and it's not just a roll in the hay. I'll show you what I mean." Knowing he would follow her, Twilla walked into the bedroom where her purse lay on the dresser. "I made these." She showed him her written notes on Julie's first meeting with Russell, their growing relationship and her deep feelings for him.

"You really don't trust him." The detective was impressed as he scanned her detailed notations.

"No. I don't. I plan to learn everything I can about Russell Weatherly. There's something about him that doesn't ring true and I don't mean his hitting on me. There was a reason for that, and by damn, I'm going to find out what it is."

"I'd like your notes."

"Why? Don't you trust him either?"

"Your condo has just been ransacked. I don't trust anyone," he said, his words now penetrating her brain.

"I'll make a copy." She marched into the living room where a toppled desk, computer and small printer lay on the floor near a gashed printer stand. She stood staring at the mess momentarily, then said, "You make me a copy." She exchanged the tablet sheets for an unwilling Lily. "Why is she so mesmerized by you?"

"She knows how charming I can be." Twilla watched him stuff the papers and latex gloves into his pants pocket.

"Right!" Her edgy one word reeked with disdain as she walked him to the door. "By the way, I need a favor. I want Lily's history and thought there might be some record at Amy's apartment. Since I'm assuming it's still sealed, can we arrange to meet there tomorrow afternoon, around one?"

"That's fine but you're wrong, you know." He returned to their initial conversation. "I'm sure someone out there might find you attractive." He closed the door quietly behind him. *'If only, she'd do a make-over.'* But he kept that thought to himself.

Twilla leaned against the opposite side of the door unques-
tionably pissed. *"Was his left-handed compliment supposed to
comfort her? Was it supposed to mean that someday, a Mr. Right
and Ugly would find her attractive?"*

The nerve of him: him with the clean-shaven face, the bright
dark eyes and resonant voice." Her thoughts about Clisten Barr
continued to roll when Twilla suddenly realized Lily had neither
eaten nor peed.

"I left an extra bag of dog food here when we visited dad,"
she told Lily. "I'm almost afraid to put you on the floor. You're not
going to hide from me, are you?" she cooed, setting her down
gently.

Lily followed Twilla around the kitchen in a normal fashion,
and after eating her meal, strolled outside to water the grassy
area. She knew that at the end of her leash was someone who
really loved her.

A short time later, Lily lay circled in Twilla's arms on a rumpled
bed, in a room strewn with human clutter.

Several hours later, a jangling phone awakened her. "Hello,"
she yawned.

"Twilla."

"Mom, what's wrong? Has something happened to dad?"

"We were worried. You didn't call when you got home."

"I was so tired. I must have dozed-off," she lied. "I'm sorry.
What time is it?"

"Eleven o'clock. We're glad you're ok. Maybe it's a good thing
I called. Get ready for bed, dear. We'll talk tomorrow."

Twilla listened for the click of her mother's landline. "Why
can't people leave us alone?" she asked Lily who responded to

the question by licking her face. "I knew you'd understand." She wiped her cheek with a tip of the bedsheet.

Within minutes, the woman and her Peekapoo were fast asleep.

EIGHT

TONY

Tony Mistretta was waiting for clarification when Clisten entered his office the next morning. "Why are you wasting time on this?" He pointed to the broken vase that belonged to Twilla Hale's grandmother. "You knew there wouldn't be any fingerprints on it. The team would have told us if there were."

"I thought you handled cases like this before," Clisten said, somewhat puzzled by the question. He studied the deep-furrowed frown crossing his partner's face and wondered what the dark-eyed man was thinking.

"I have," he offered, "but taking the vase makes no sense, unless you have some plan in mind." Tony studied the man in silence, almost demanding an answer, and soon realized his thoughts had been correct. "You do have something in mind."

"Maybe it would be better if I clarified my actions. We are working as a team," he said, his words slow in coming. Explanations were so unnecessary with Leggin, but that part of his life was over. His former partner was dead, and Tony, his replacement.

"Sometimes the action I take doesn't seem to make sense. But I do it for a reason. It will all come together at some point."

"I figured as much but why the vase?"

"It gives me the opportunity to see the Hale woman again. I'll have the vase glued, and when I return it, I'll have the chance to question her further."

"You could have her come to the station."

"Wrong setting. It has to be inside the ransacked unit."

"Meaning she might remember more if questioned in her own surroundings."

"That's not it exactly. The Hale woman knows something. She's just not aware of it. It could be some miniscule detail about Amy Gregson that seems meaningless. And it's tracking the minutia that could lead us to the person who shot her."

"How can you be sure?"

"I'm not. I don't know if her rummaged unit is even connected to the Gregson's murder. But with my years of experience, my gut tells me to pursue this avenue."

"That's why you get the big bucks." Tony drummed Clisten's desk before turning toward the door.

Clisten watched his partner leave and wondered about the man's actual experience in detective work. Would Clisten be forced to explain his every action on the Gregson's homicide? He just detailed the most elementary one concerning the heirloom vase and the psychology behind it.

Making a victim think you were sympathetic to the situation, whatever it was, and really cared about the outcome, long before asking questions, was paramount in any investigation. So, giving the mended vase to Twilla Hale, before a casual grilling in the comfort of her home, was an elementary tool some detectives used. Was Tony that dense?

He thought about his dark-eyed partner who was so well-groomed. Other than being a replacement who transferred from Philadelphia to fill a vacancy, Clisten knew very little about the detective who became his partner. That he might be somewhat dense caused him to think further about the man.

They were not that close in age. He guessed a difference of seven to ten years. With Clisten at thirty-four, Tony looked older; early to mid-forties, he thought. Although Clisten was taller, Tony was much thinner, almost rail-like. Then too, the man's thick head of hair was much darker, his ruddy complexion a direct contrast to Clisten's ivory skin. However, descriptions, in this case, mattered little since neither was being sought by the police.

Approaches to cases and resolutions were the chief issues between them. His partner did not think deep enough for motive, or even attempt to link Amy Gregson's shooting and the ransacking of her apartment to Twilla Hale's vandalized unit, even though a quasi-relationship, however distant, did exist.

The timeline in both cases could not be overlooked. The facts were there. Both units had been pillaged. Although the timeline for Amy's was uncertain, Twilla Hale's condo must have been rummaged shortly after the shooting, when the woman left town. Who would have known about that? *'All her students and Dr. Shelden's department,'* his unconscious mind answered question.

Then again, why was Amy Gregson's apartment overturned in the first place? Was it pillaged by the same person who shot her? Did he ransack her apartment and then vandalize Twilla Hale's condo? What was the shooter looking for? What hadn't he found at Amy Gregson's apartment that made him check Twilla Hale's?

The same question kept coming back to him, over and over. What was Twilla Hale hiding? Those questions brought his thoughts back to his partner.

Maybe he had been too hard on his new partner. The man had been with him for only a few weeks and hadn't fully grasped his routine. But Clisten knew deep in his mind he was not ready for a replacement. The bond with Leggin had been too strong. Even now, to this day, he was not convinced his former partner died at the hands of a mugger. That the perpetrator was caught did not ease Clisten's pain. And although the evidence against the man was staggering, it meant nothing. What had it really accomplished in the end? The money for drugs brought death to a detective's family and a jail sentence for the addict. What was the point?

That thought continued to sadden him as he reflected their time together. Although memories of Leggin Floyd would stay with him forever, they were just too painful. The two detectives were always on the same page.

Was he being too hard on his new partner? Perhaps, he expected too much all at once. The man needed time to adjust. Clisten could, after all, be a hard ass. Leggin told him that all the time. The word *time* jarred his thoughts. He had an appointment later that day and things to do before that meeting would take place.

Inside his pocket were tablet notes on Russell Weatherly. Once copied, he would return the originals to Twilla Hale that afternoon at the Gregson apartment. Of course, he would pretend interest in the man relative to her vandalized unit. However, he planned to question the woman on her relationship with Amy Gregson while they casually checked the apartment for Lily's history. He intended to use a subtler approach, giving the stubborn instructor no idea that she was being interrogated.

Yes. Clisten had a lot to do before meeting Miss Hale, but first, he needed a haircut.

"I hope I haven't kept you waiting," Twilla yelled, racing down the apartment hall, breathing heavily. Her appearance caused the speechless detective to stare unabashedly at the disheveled woman whose high-arced ponytail swayed wildly from side-to-side as she ran to meet him. The picture of the galloping woman reminded him of Bosco, the frisky donkey he rode in Grand Canyon one summer. His swinging tail never stopped swirling either. "I just got out of my lab and rushed right over." Twilla caught him ogling her work clothes as he led her into Amy's ransacked apartment, where she stood frozen in shock. "It's still a mess."

'*You should talk,*' he thought, eyeing her ripped jeans and stained shirt. "We're still trying to find her family or some living relative."

"What happens if you don't?"

"That's not probable. Someone, somewhere, is related to Amy Gregson. The trick is to find that person."

"And what if you fail?"

"That will not happen, Miss Hale."

"What makes you so sure?"

"Why do you doubt me? Do you know something about the woman's personal life? Something you can share with me?"

"You really are a piece of work," she answered slyly. "If I'm clueless about Lily, how the hell would I know anything about Amy? She was a very private person. Now where should we look for Lily's history in this ransacked mess?"

"Among papers. We'll check all the drawers first, then the living room floor."

"Why are you being so helpful?"

"Finding Lily's history could provide leads to Miss Gregson's family. Why do you ask?"

"I keep wondering how your mind works. I was right. You had an ulterior motive for coming. You weren't just being a Good Samaritan." He caught the cynicism of her words with a sharp rebuke of his own.

"And you aren't thinking straight!" he barked, totally annoyed with her. "Whether or not she was a close friend, we both want the same thing: the person who killed her. Or have you forgotten that? You're searching for Lily's history, and I'm doing the same thing for Lily's owner. Now, let's get on with it."

"Ruff! Ruff!" Twilla barked back loudly, her arms akimbo in defiance of his bossy attitude. However, her loud barking soon faded as she turned and headed toward Amy's bedroom.

As Clisten watched her leave, the smile across his face widened. The unkempt woman did have a sense of humor after all.

Too bad she kept it so well hidden. It was only minutes later that he heard shouts of success.

"It's here." She pointed to an open box in Amy's dresser. "She kept a record on Lily. There's the name of the breeder who sold her, along with the date and cost, and the vet who is currently treating her. I'm so excited." However, her enthusiasm was short-lived as she watched the detective remove the box from the drawer. "What are you doing?"

"I want to look through these papers before releasing them to you," he said, sitting on the bed.

"Oh, hell." She sat down beside him. Twilla knew he didn't want her checking the contents with him, but she didn't care. "Is he good?" She pointed to the name of the vet listed.

"One of the best."

"How do you know that?"

"I'm a detective, remember?" Although Clisten thought his remark funny, her scowl told him she did not share his amusement. "No. Jay Harris has a good reputation in town." Clisten gave her the box as he rose from the bed.

"That makes me feel a lot better. Now, I can make an appointment for Lily," she said, following him to the front door of the apartment and out of the building. "I want to thank you for helping me find her history."

"Glad to help." He started to walk away.

"Detective Barr," Twilla yelled. "I don't know what you're wearing but it smells nice."

A quizzical look crossed Clisten's face at her outburst. "The barber's aftershave." He shouted back and took a few steps toward the untidy woman who had a mild fragrance of her own: turpentine. "Are you hitting on me?"

"Why? Because I said, 'You smell nice?' I just wanted to say something pleasant to show my appreciation and couldn't think of anything else. I'm sorry if I offended you." As Twilla turned to walk away she couldn't resist a further comment. "You do smell a lot better than your partner. He reeks of musk. The smell almost knocked me over when I gave him the kitchen bag for my grandmother's vase."

"Miss Hale," he called her back. "I forgot to give you these." He removed the tablet notes from his pocket. "You gave me these on Russell Weatherly. With Lily in mind, I completely forgot about him. Good luck with your investigation."

"Are you going to check on him?"

"Our paths are different."

"How so?"

"Yours is personal. Mine has a criminal bent."

"That's where you're wrong, Mr. Barr. He crossed that line the night we met. You don't switch women in the blink of an eye without some ulterior motive, and I don't mean sack hopping."

"A true cynic."

"My counterpart should talk…," Twilla objected, leaving him abruptly. Different paths indeed! A friendly exchange between the two of them was impossible.

"One more thing, detective," Twilla yelled turning around to face him again. "There is no way in hell I'd ever hit on you," she announced boldly, but with an added declaration. "If we ever dated, which we won't, I would always wonder if you were interested in me or the information you could extract. It would be like an inquisition without the robes. You never quit. That's what drives you."

Clisten watched the woman walk to her black Chevy and drive away. The disheveled woman certainly spared no words on how she felt about him. The thought made him smile. She was a snippy little thing, smelly as hell, but passionate with her opinions. The woman was right. The case was on his mind, front and center.

He stood for a few moments after the car disappeared and taking a pen and pad from his jacket pocket, wrote the words,

Herman Banks and puppies. Talking to the breeder was an avenue to pursue. Hopefully, the man would remember something during a conversation with Amy Gregson, some fact that would advance his investigation. He doubted Twilla Hale would give the breeder any thought. She was more concerned with the veterinarian. Of course, he knew Jay well. The man was part of his golf foursome. Clisten needed to talk with him first, before his appointment with Miss Hale. Then he would talk to Herman Banks. The man was the only lead Clisten had.

According to Tony, the two references from Dr. Shelden never panned out. That they both fizzled still nagged his psyche. One dead and the other essentially missing made no sense. The Givens woman had to be somewhere. But where? What could he go on? His only bet now was with the breeder.

Clisten would keep this lead to himself. No sense in creating more disappointment in the department. There were no other avenues to explore. The detective would check with the Hale woman again when he returned her grandmother's vase. Maybe in the comfort of her home she would remember something about Amy Gregson. However, his hopes were diminishing rapidly. Although Twilla Hale expressed no real relationship with the dead woman, she was hiding something. Clisten truly believed that. He also believed the woman cared little about appearances. She did look like an unmade bed, one with a ripped sheet and torn comforter.

That she wasn't hitting on him certainly cleared the air and made it so much easier to question her. Yet, Clisten wondered why he thought she might be interested in him. Was it the mention of the aftershave? It made no difference now. They were on the same page. Nothing between them was personal.

NINE

A COLLAR

Upon entering her condo that same afternoon, Twilla greeted Lily as the dog rushed to her side. Bundling the Peekapoo in her arms, she kissed Lily's nose while taking the leash off a nearby hook. "We're going out to water the grass," she said, gazing into Lily's black eyes.

A short time later, Twilla sat browsing her computer for more information on Dr. Jay Harris, the veterinarian Amy used for Lily, and feeling satisfied with the results, made an appointment for the following day.

"You're such a good girl." Twilla took Lily into her arms again and was ready to give her a doggie treat when the doorbell rang.

"Miss Hale." Twilla immediately recognized Detective Barr's distinctive voice before opening the door.

"Did I miss something at Amy's?" She peered up at him through the open doorway.

"May I come in or do you always leave your callers hanging in the hall?" This, of course, was a reference to Russell Weatherly's unexpected visit. As his usual custom, Clisten baited her deliberately, hoping the still disheveled woman would give a more telling response.

"Oh, please!" she smarted, deflating his plan for information, and ushered him in. It was only when he cleared the doorway by inches that his height became obvious to her. Up to now, she never thought the detective was anything but a pain in the ass.

"Hi Lily," Clisten greeted the dog pawing his leg. "Come here." Gathering her in his arms, Clisten walked into the kitchen and placed the dog on the island counter. "Now, let's see what you're about."

After loosening Lily's collar and placing it flat on the counter beside her, he pulled a switch blade from his pants pocket and began to prick the single file of holes.

"What are you doing?" Twilla demanded, trying to remain calm by the size of the knife and the skillful way he used it.

"I needed to check." He caught her staring at the blade and immediately answered her unspoken question. "The knife belonged to my partner and I usually keep it in my glove compartment. But it does come in handy."

"Are you looking for a microchip or something that would plug one of the collar holes?"

"Nothing that sinister. Dirt, maybe. Just to learn where the dog might have been, or the collar laid. A very long shot…to start with."

"To start with?"

"Something's been nagging at me since the break-in. The person who ransacked this place must think you have something he needs, something important."

"He? I have something important. Here…? Like what?" Her staccato-like questions caught him by surprise.

"Don't get in a twist." Although he spoke softly to Lily, Clisten was really addressing Twilla, trying to calm her. "I thought about this after we parted and wanted to follow a hunch. It may be nothing." He padded the dog collar end-to-end with his hands and examined both sides.

"You think Lily…?"

By his expression, Twilla knew questioning him was futile. She watched his fingers trace the inside part of the collar for something unusual. Then he repeated the process on the reverse side before placing the collar gently back on Lily.

"I don't understand," she said, watching him pet and scratch Lily's head.

"Think about it. When you returned yesterday, your unit had been vandalized; however, the date it took place is uncertain. Correct?" She nodded in agreement. "When I came back for my gloves, you told me Lily had been hiding under the bed and wouldn't come to you." Once again, Twilla agreed. "When she came to me, Lily was shaking."

"She might have been scared by the burglary."

"But what if something else frightened her?"

"Like what?"

"I don't know." She caught his frown. "Lily hid under the bed just as soon as she came home? Right? You couldn't get her to come out."

"So, what are you telling me?"

"What if it was a repeat? What if Lily had been hiding under the bed when Amy's apartment was being ransacked? You went to get her right after the shooting. Remember?"

"You're right. So, when the same thing occurred in my unit, Lily got scared and hid under the bed."

"Maybe, but I was thinking along different lines. You have something in your possession that belonged to Amy Gregson: Lily. I thought she could be the common link for ransacking both units, but there is nothing in or on the collar."

"Could Lily have a chip?"

"She probably does, but that's in case she gets lost or stolen."

"Couldn't she have another chip somewhere else?"

Her question caused him to laugh. "You've been watching too much television."

"I can ask, can't I?"

"What do you mean?"

"I have an appointment tomorrow with Dr. Harris. He's going over Lily's history with me. I could ask him then."

"You should have him examine Lily thoroughly while you're there. He's a very good veterinarian."

Lily sat on the counter listening to their voices, her head moving from one to the other. Finally, when the words no longer flowed they stood facing each other in silence.

"I'd better go," he said, and after placing Lily on the floor, walked toward the door with Twilla following him. "Sorry for the bother. I had to follow-up."

"I understand." She closed the door slowly and leaned against it in thought. Could she have been wrong about the tall, barking detective with the piercing brown eyes? He had been so gentle and soft spoken with Lily. Maybe he loved dogs and hated people. Some people were like that. Of course, none of it really mattered now. She had what she wanted: Lily's history.

But then she remembered the detective's words. He was trying to link Lily to the ransacked units and perhaps Amy's murder. Twilla had more than one possession of Amy's, other than Lily. She had four: the inventory, the recipe notations in her cookbook, the ring and a picture of Amy with an older woman who could possibly lead her to Mark. Was the intruder looking for these things? How were they related to finding Mark? A shiver ran through her body as her thoughts unfolded. What had she gotten herself into? Twilla became frightened. Could she be the next victim? Was there someone she could talk to? Someone other than Clisten Barr? Twilla couldn't talk with him. He would be angry because she withheld information from him, information that could move his case forward but hinder finding Mark.

Twilla didn't know where to turn or whom to trust.

While Twilla was musing about the detective and his theory, he was on his cell phone right after their meeting ended.

"Hi, Jay," Clisten greeted the vet. "I'm calling about an appointment you have tomorrow with Lily, Twilla Hale's dog. I need you to do something for me. Yes, an ongoing investigation."

As Clisten drove to the station, his thoughts centered on the possible danger that faced Lily and Twilla Hale, a threat the woman was not even aware of. The detective had remained silent on the other possible link between the two ransacked units: if Lily were hiding during the ransacking of Amy's apartment, she might be able to recognize the person…either by sight or smell.

Yet, Lily had been with Twilla Hale, miles away from Stockton, when her home invasion took place. So, why was Lily shaking when she ran to him? Was it the recall of a bad memory or for protection? If the latter, from whom?

None of it made sense. Yet, one thing was certain. The intruder was looking for something the Hale woman possessed. Had the murdered woman told Twilla Hale something, or perhaps, given her some precious item before she collapsed? From the moment they met, Clisten felt Twilla Hale was hiding something from him. The woman knew more about Amy Gregson than she cared to admit. He had to question her more thoroughly when he returned the vase.

Still, the thought that Lily might be able to recognize the person who ransacked Amy's apartment really bothered him. She was such a cuddly little thing. Maybe he was just taken with her black button eyes peering-up at him through her furry face.

As he pulled into the parking lot, Clisten knew his partner would question his prolonged absence. He would probably make another snide remark about the broken vase, his insinuation clear. Why was he so interested in the detective's personal life when Clisten never questioned his? As partners, their chief concern was solving the case, nothing more. There would never be a closeness between them.

In his mind, no one could take Leggin's place. They were so much alike…in thought, ideas and approach to cases. Lengthy conversations were often unnecessary. Of course, a murder in town or at the college was rare. Rare indeed. He had dealt with suicides at the school, but this was his first murder. Most calls concerned some sort of robbery. However, the mugging of Leggin did not sit well with him. His gut told him something was not right about it, but he was overruled by the evidence, the police chief and even the mayor. As much as he respected Sam Wilkerson and Ed Maines, Clisten did not agree with their decision. He felt the drug addict had been framed but could not prove it.

Clisten walked into the building prepared for an inquisition. The haircut would never account for his lengthy absence.

"Where have you been?" Tony began firing his line of questions.

"You mean aside from the haircut?"

"The barbershop must have been busy. You've been gone for hours."

"Obviously, nothing happened, or you would have contacted me."

"True, but I was hoping you picked up some new information, or," he emphasized, "you got a haircut for another reason." A grin crossed his smooth-shaven face.

"You're right on the last assumption. I got tired of the hair edging my neck." Clisten started to laugh. "The damn stuff's itchy." When Tony began laughing with him, Clisten knew his remark hit a home run. However, the cajolery was short lived. A call from Bill Thistle summoned them to the morgue.

The coroner led them to a small table when the two men arrived. "I did a small 'mock-up' of the victim's face," he said, referring to Amy Gregson. "I mean without the plastic surgery. It's not perfect, but I thought it would give you a clearer picture of what she could have looked like before the cosmetic work. I emphasize the word, 'could.' This is not my area of expertise, but I thought it might be helpful."

"Look at the shape of her face, her cheekbones…she looks different," Clisten said, completely surprised.

"Wow. She does look different. I would never have guessed it was the same woman," Tony agreed.

"Don't go 'gaga' on me," Thistle interrupted. "Remember, I said, 'Could.' I'm not saying she did look like this before plastic surgery. It's not a real 'before and after' scenario; it's merely a possible guide."

"Maybe so." Clisten snapped a picture of the woman's face from his cell phone. "In this day and age, you never know what might come in handy. Appreciate your doing this." He started for the exit with Tony following him."

As Bill Thistle watched the men leave, his thoughts verbalized. "They really don't know what they're into. Did I do the right thing, giving them two faces to follow?"

What's your problem? His thoughts answered the question. *They should be thankful. What else do they have to go on?*

TEN

TAVIS PARK

On Tuesday afternoon, long after her appointment with the veterinarian, Twilla took Lily to Tavis Park and walked around the lake for a long walk. After finding an empty bench facing the water, she sat down, nestled Lily on her lap and unsnapped the dog's leash. She needed time to think and the quiet serenity of Tavis Lake made it a perfect place.

In only a matter of weeks, her life had changed. It wasn't just taking possession of Lily. She was the brightest aspect of it. But it was at the expense of her colleague's death, regardless how distant the relationship. Still, Amy must have trusted her; otherwise, she would not have given her the ring or altered the cookbook recipes. Although separate, they were connected somehow. They had to be clues to finding Mark. That was the only thing that made sense. And deep within her being, Twilla knew she was right. Still, something had to be done.

A plan began to take shape in her mind. First, Twilla would arrange the recipe notations in some order. Second, once she solved the puzzle, she would follow every avenue to find Mark. If she had to give up her weekends, so be it. Third, she would place the cookbook on the shelf with her other cooking tomes. Carrying it with her continually could draw unnecessary suspicion.

Unfortunately, her time to initiate any plan had been limited. Between straightening her ransacked unit and getting Lily's history, Twilla had been too busy to concentrate on other areas that needed her attention. Yet, the inventory folder weighed heavily on her mind. Something told her to hide it inside a new cotton pillow protector as a precaution. Since the pillowcases had been checked already, it seemed like the sensible thing to do…sensible and safe.

Now Twilla had to make another decision. Tomorrow, she would go into Amy's lab and complain about needing new appliances since the intruder invading her condo scratched and dented hers. She would take the number listed on a refrigerator then match it to one of those on the inventory sheet.

Twilla was deep in thought when she was suddenly jarred by a man's friendly greeting. As soon as Pete addressed Twilla, an upstart Lily leaped from her lap to sniff Sam's furry leg.

Within seconds of getting the message, the sheepdog stretched his furry body flat on the ground and allowed Lily to step inside his two front paws and lick his nose.

"Well, it looks like they're settled and you're not."

"What do you mean?"

"When a pretty lady like you is lost in thought, something's bothering her. Something important."

"No. I'm really happy, thanks to you." Twilla smiled at the elderly man who sat down beside her.

"You found Lily's vet." He seemed pleased.

"I didn't think you'd remember us." Twilla could have bitten her tongue after the statement left her mouth. Fearful he would equate her statement with his age, she tried to clarify it. "I mean you and Sam must meet so many people here…in the park."

"I may be old, Twilla, but I'm not senile. The marbles are still fluid."

"I was hoping you could give me more pointers."

"On Lily or something else?"

"What do you mean?" She studied his wrinkled face and became aware of something that had never occurred to her when they first met. The white and black patches of his hair matched the coloring of his sheepdog. They really were a matched set.

"I hate to keep repeating myself, but something's on your mind. You were so lost in thought, you never saw me wave to you." Pete caught her deep sigh as he spoke.

"I told you when we met, my colleague was shot and then later died in the hospital."

"So, they found her relatives and you're losing Lily."

"I don't think Amy had family."

"We had this discussion before. Everyone has family, regardless how distant."

Twilla shook her head. "I don't think so. She never mentioned anyone to me. I mean never. I talked about mine. She never did."

"That's strange. I agree. But that's not what's bothering you."

"How do you know?"

"I'm good at reading people." He took Twilla's hand. "How was it at home?"

"Dad's surgery went well. From all reports, he's recovering nicely. We hired a nurse to take care of him."

Inwardly, she was shocked that he remembered so much of their conversation. Did he write it down after she left him or was he that lonely? Now, she was being ridiculous. Of course, he would remember their first meeting. Nine-pound Lily was taken with Sam immediately on sight. She spun-away from Twilla, rushing to meet the huge, furry sheepdog, her leash whirling in the wind…

The man would have to remember that scene, particularly when he caught the leash. Then too, how many sheepdogs would put-up with some little runt constantly licking his nose?

"You've got that sorted out, so what is troubling you?" Pete jarred her thoughts again.

"I don't know," she blurted suddenly. "My sister's boyfriend hit on me at home and someone ransacked my condo while I was away."

A bewildered Twilla stared at the man who broke into gales of laughter. "Don't mind me." Pete continued to laugh. "Your two problems are the extreme poles of each other."

"That may be, but they're real." Twilla went on to explain Russell Weatherly's overtures, his later visit and the home invasion that was being investigated by a gruff Detective Barr.

"Is Julie gorgeous and shallow?"

"Why would you even ask that?"

"I'm talking shallow in terms of academic or realistic thought, not shallow as being superficial."

"I don't understand."

"Of course, you do. You're a smart woman. Little gets by you."

"Then don't misunderstand me. I love her to death but there are times she makes me so mad. Julie is very intelligent, extremely beautiful and has all the credentials of an educated woman; but her taste in men is another story. Russell's just one in a long line of losers and it's too bad because Julie has everything going for her. She's got a great job in New York along with a fabulous apartment. My sister makes far more money than I do. So, who's the smart one?"

"You're equating brains with money. Beauty and success. That could be the wrong approach. Maybe it's the sum-total of you that attracted this man initially. Although looks and brains may be great attractions, it's the chemistry that always wins in the long run."

"I'd love you to death, if that were true. Although I found him physically attractive, I also felt he was using his animal prowess for a purpose. Did he want to alienate me from my sister by trying to seduce me or was it for another reason?"

"Are you thinking he might have ransacked your apartment and came by later to check on you?" Pete became quiet for a moment. "That doesn't make sense, unless you have something he wants. What could it be?"

"I have no idea." She ignored the possibility of another seduction attempt since her disgust was so blatantly obvious that night. "I found the condo door open and the unit vandalized. The neighbors called the police, but that dumb detective has no clue who did it."

"Clisten Barr?"

"He's heading the case."

"Be careful what you tell him. He's a very sneaky detective. His brain's like a computer. It stores everything connected to an investigation, putting the data in perspective. Before you know it, the case is solved."

"He and his partner must work well together," she said, remembering their shared responsibilities after her home invasion. Each seemed to inspect different areas before coming together with their thoughts.

"That was true of his old partner, Leggin Floyd. They were a pair. More action than conversation. He died of a mugging that went bad. But that's today's crime: mugging for drug money."

"Then Detective Mistretta is his new partner."

"I'm sure both were called to investigate your home invasion. Was there a problem?"

"No. I just like to know who the players are." She said, sorting them out. "So where do you fit into this scheme?"

"I don't. My wife died years ago and I'm just a retired detective who walks my grandson's dog. That's how I pass time. When you're my age, people think you have less to offer. It's sad, really. Just because I can't run fast, that doesn't mean my brain is slow."

"Then why don't you determine who trashed my condo?"

"I don't think I can do that?"

"Why not? You have time on your hands."

"Because you don't trust me."

"Yes, I do."

"Then tell me what you're really hiding. Someone broke into your place for a reason and you're scared of something being found, if it hasn't been already."

"How do you know?"

"I told you before. I'm good at reading people. Of course, I was also an investigator in my younger days. But that no longer counts." After checking his watch, he rose to leave. "C'mon Sam, tell Lily goodbye," he told his sheepdog before turning to Twilla. "You take care of yourself, young lady."

Twilla watched them disappear, knowing full well the message Pete left behind. His offer was conditional. She had to tell him everything. Yet, there was nothing she could divulge without putting Mark in harm's way. At least, that was her current thinking. The ring and recipes were connected; the inventory list, a separate animal. She felt certain of that. Still two questions remained unanswered. Was her condo ransacked for information on Mark or to retrieve the inventory file? She had yet to sort that out.

"Come Lily," Twilla said after leashing her. "We'll walk a little before you water the grass. I have to think long and hard about seeing Pete and Sam again."

Before thinking about that, she had a lot of research to do, one that included an exhaustive search on her computer. Still, first things first. It was dinnertime for Lily.

Miles away from Stockton College, a conversation was taking place.

"What's going on? I haven't heard from you?"

"I'm working on a new plan."

"Your last one wasn't so hot."

"Your carelessness wasn't either." What followed was the slamming of a phone by a very angry man.

ELEVEN

CORKY

One whole day had passed and Clisten's frustration level rose even higher that Tuesday morning when he thought about Bill Thistle's art work: Amy Gregson's altered face. The whole case was enigmatic. There were no loose ends; no real avenues to pursue, and it bothered him. The two names given by Dr. Shelden never panned out. His partner had checked those possibilities. Attorney Thaddeus J. Stevens was dead, and Tony found no trace or forwarding address of Dr. Rebecca Givens from High Coventry.

That there was no trace of Dr. Givens or the real identity of the shooting victim, portrayed as Amy Gregson, exasperated him. Where could he go for answers?

He thought about the three people: one long deceased, another lost and the dead victim, an alias. At least that was the official thinking since the identity of Amy Gregson began with her teaching stint at Stockton, some six years earlier.

However, his thoughts shifted as he drove into the parking lot of the police station. He remembered asking Jay to check Lily's chip when Twilla Hale brought her in that afternoon. From the coded chip, Jay would contact dog registries for owner information. Although this was a way of returning a lost dog, in this instance Clisten wanted to check any irregularity that might appear on Lily's registration papers. No matter what it took to get that information, he told Jay it was critical to his case. He also assured his friend of confidentiality. Nothing would be written in the case log. The secret would remain between the two of them.

Entering his office, Clisten sat at his desk poised to make a phone call when Tony tapped his open door.

"You must have been lost in thought. I passed you ten minutes ago."

"I need to have my tires checked. Something's not right."

"Maybe your pressure's down," he answered quickly, before changing the subject. "So, what did you think of Thistle's creation yesterday? Amy Gregson's altered face gives us something new to work with, doesn't it?"

"In what way?" Clisten said as a way of testing the man who replaced his former partner.

"Missing Persons. I can start there. Maybe I'll find a match." Tony turned to leave when another thought crossed his mind. "Did you return the vase?"

"What?"

"The woman's vase."

"It's being glued."

"Oh." He shook his head in acknowledgement and left Clisten's office.

Within minutes of Tony's departure, Clisten closed his office door quietly and was ready to call Jay about Lily when something else caught his attention. Through his office window he watched his partner circle Clisten's parked car for a visual tire check. Did Tony not believe him or was the man being a good partner wanting to offer help? Either way, he found the man's actions strange. Certain he had not been seen, Clisten determined to archive the incident and resumed the business of contacting the veterinarian, when a series of interruptions occupied his entire morning. One of which was Amy Gregson's car. After a thorough examination, they found nothing inside to determine a hint of her identity. The trunk held an untouched spare tire.

It was late that afternoon when Clisten remembered to phone the veterinarian.

"I found something rather strange in my records." Jay began. "When Miss Hale left the dog leash in her car and went to get it, I scanned Lily's chip. After they left the office, I checked the scanned number with Lily's registry base, the one used for lost dogs."

"And?" Clisten asked, growing impatient with the long winded-narrative. "Nothing matched."

"Not quite. The dog is registered to Amy Gregson. She is the legal owner. But the phone number listed on the registry is different from the one in my patient file."

"Then give me everything," Clisten said, jotting down the information on a small pad he carried for private use at home. He studied the area code of the registry phone number. "It's long distance."

"Just remember the facts, Clisten." Jay's voice held an edge. "I did not insert the chip in Lily, so Amy Gregson had the services of another vet. What's strange is the two different phone numbers. Registry services caution pet owners to update their address and phone number with each change of residence. It's their means of contact for a found pet, reported lost. For some reason, maybe an oversight, Amy updated her current address on the registry but left an old phone number. There must be a certificate with that same information. She'd need it to transfer ownership, although I doubt she'd ever sell Lily."

"Did you mention any of this to Miss Hale?"

"There was no point in stirring up trouble. If Amy has relatives, they might want the dog. I've witnessed that before."

"I owe you." Clisten thanked his friend before ending the call.

A smile of satisfaction inched across his face as he slipped the pad into the pocket of his trousers. In the recesses of his mind, he quietly thanked Twilla Hale for giving him the idea to have Jay check Lily's chip.

∾

Clisten sat back in his chair thinking how to handle the new information. It had to be done privately. He couldn't search the office data base without someone asking questions. But then he often worked late hours and could return when the office was deserted, but only if it became necessary.

To get started, he would begin a search on his home computer to identify the person whose phone number was listed on Lily's registry. Clisten would create a private file, keeping it permanent and away from the prying eyes of the office. It was a way of keeping his word to Jay. The matter would be entirely confidential.

When Clisten got-up to stretch, he turned toward the window and was somewhat surprised. Tony's tan Toyota was no longer in the parking lot. Where had his partner gone? Clisten thought he was checking the office data base for missing persons. Had he gone for a quick bite without telling him? Why would he do something like that? Regardless of the man's reasons, Clisten wanted to go home and begin a search of his own. As he walked down the hall toward the exit door of the station, the ringing of Tony's phone jarred his thoughts into answering it.

"Hello, Cueball! I shouldn't even be calling your ass. I haven't heard from you since you left." A raspy voice exploded with indignation.

"Who is this?" Clisten demanded.

"Frank," the voice stammered, realizing a stranger had answered his colleague's phone. "Detective Frank Corky from Philly Central. Where's Tony Cueball, my former partner?"

"He's not here right now but I can take a message." Clisten pulled a sheet from the note pad on Tony's desk.

"Nah. Just tell him Corky called."

"Before hanging-up, what's the private joke between you?"

"What do you mean?"

"Why do you call him Cueball?"

"Either you're blind or dumber than shit. The man's bald."

"Can you text me a picture of Tony Mistretta?" A bewildered Clisten asked in a quiet whisper.

"Yeah, but what's twisting your shorts?"

"Our Tony Mistretta is one hairy gorilla. I don't want a fax of his picture coming through the office." Clisten's hushed voice continued. "Send it on my cell phone."

"Give me your number and take mine."

After exchanging information, Clisten gave the man further instructions. "I'm on my way home. We need to talk after I get the photograph."

"That's just the beginning. I want to know what happened to my partner." The man's concern had now turned to anger.

After ending their conversation, Clisten deleted the man's phone number from Tony's bank of incoming calls. Then he turned from his partner's office to the main desk where Sergeant Qurlan usually sat monitoring the day's business. Finding the area deserted, Clisten took the opportunity to browse the transfer file of his new partner but ignored the service page, knowing it was not applicable. Within seconds, Clisten snapped a picture of Tony on his cell phone and exited the building.

Clisten sat at the desk in his home, studying the picture Corky sent before tapping his phone.

"What took you so long?" bellowed Corky's raspy voice.

"Are all the people from Philly in a rush? I just got home."

"You don't get things done, moving slow," he grumbled.

"Then move on this: your picture of Tony doesn't match ours." Clisten caught the man's pause. "I snapped a picture of the one we have on my cell phone. It's from our files. It may not be a great photograph, but it's clear enough for identification purposes."

"Send it and I'll call you back."

Once the call ended, Clisten followed through with the man's request and waited for the return call.

"Who the hell is he?" The hoarse voice roared.

"One of yours, supposedly. His papers are in order. I checked his file before taking this picture. So, you tell me how the switch happened."

"How the hell should I know? Nobody tells me nuthin."

"Don't play with me, Corky. You can't unglue what's between partners. You knew he was leaving."

"A temporary assignment. A favor between Healy and Wilkerson." He emphasized the last two words. "Something they worked out."

"Healy?"

"One of the heads here. Real good guy though. It was kind of an exchange, a quid pro quo. You're short a detective and Tony's taking early retirement."

"I don't buy it. The man looks too young for retirement."

"You got the wrong guy. My partner had years of service. Tony was caught drunk and disorderly too many times. Anyhow the retirement thing was not on the transfer papers. It was an understanding he had with Healy. The temporary assignment was a way of saving his pension, but Tony had to transfer sooner than originally scheduled. So, what happened?"

"He died."

"Was he sick?"

"What makes you ask?"

"Then you don't really know, do you?" Corky smarted, his frustration mounting as reality set in. "He asked for a three-month fill-in."

"He was killed by a mugger," Clisten interrupted before the detective could say anything further. This was not the time for detailing Leggin's personal life or the mention of a sick grandchild hundreds of miles away and the crisis it entailed.

"Well, his request had to materialize first," Corky explained, thinking back to the way it was processed. "If it worked, Healy could save Tony's boozing ass before retirement, while helping Wilkerson with a temporary replacement. Later, things would go back to normal. At least, that's what I understood."

"Then how did phony Tony show-up with legal documentation? Although our department is not the CIA, it would take an alias with brass balls to pull this off. Even with the right papers, how was the exchange made and where is your partner?" But as soon as Clisten spoke, he realized the unspeakable truth. "Corky, I'm sorry."

"I don't want sorry!" He exploded. "My partner's missing, presumed dead, and I want the bastard who killed him!"

"Hold on, Corky!" Clisten interrupted the detective's harangue. "You can arrest the man for impersonating an officer, but where's the evidence of murder?" He tried calming him. "Where's the body?"

"What's your full name?"

"Detective Clisten Barr. Why?"

"Because I'm going to beat you to death after 'offing' your fake partner."

"Hey!" Clisten shouted him down. "I'm on your side, remember? Don't take the switch out on me."

"Then don't tell me I need evidence to beat the shit out of this perp." He screamed back to the calm voice on the other end.

"Listen, I know you can prove false identity, but you better be damn careful. Make sure your paperwork's in order before you come for him."

"Why are you being so cooperative?"

"Because I don't want him in our department and I know how you feel. The one killed in the mugging was my partner. Personally, I think Leggin was murdered but I can't prove it."

"And you think 'this' Tony might have killed him."

"I never thought about it until now. But if he could pull this off, setting-up some crazed addict for Leggin's mugging would be a piece of cake. Still, it makes me wonder why he came here… why this assignment? Something brought him to the area. I feel it in my gut." Clisten paused, his thoughts racing.

Did the fake detective create the sudden vacancy in his department? Was there's a link between Leggin's death and the Gregson case? If so, Clisten never made the connection. But he sure as hell would now.

"And you think whatever it is, it's on your turf."

"That's the only thing that makes sense. Why here? There must be a reason. I don't know if you read about the murder of Amy Gregson, an associate professor here at the college. That seems to be the current menu of conversation. The media vultures were here swooping dirt."

"That's always the way it is with them. They're known to follow every crumb of news and won't let us alone. We call them the Hansel and Gretel Group. They go around scraping-up every piece of tragic shit to make the daily news." Corky could hear Clisten laughing at his remark. "That may sound funny to you but it's true. Some are nice, but most will play 'kiss-ass' for a scoop, particularly if it's sorted."

"So where are we going with this?"

"I'll call you after I get the authorization and paperwork. I owe you, Barr." He ended the call.

Clisten continued to sit at his desk, and in a trance-like state, tried to picture Frank Corky in his mind. During their conversation, two descriptive things were paramount: a raspy voice and Corky's need to throttle him. So, in his unique way of solving puzzles, he combined these known facts into a quasi- portrait of the detective.

Frank Corky had to be a big man, big enough to thrash him, and perhaps middle-aged, with a raspy voice and Roman nose. He added the large nose in deference to the raspy voice and colorful language used by the detective from Philadelphia. Not quite satisfied with his portrayal of Frank Corky, Clisten's curious nature got the best of him. After a search of Philadelphia's finest, an image of Frank Corsi appeared on the screen, surprising Clisten on one hand and satisfying him on the other. Although the name was different, he was right on target with Corky's description!

Then for some reason his thoughts moved from Corky in Philadelphia to Stockton and Tony Mistretta, the imposter.

Exactly why had the man chosen Stockton? Was it accidental or deliberate? Choosing a place like Stockton was illogical, unless he wanted to come here. His reason had to be dangerously important particularly when the real Tony Mistretta was obviously missing, probably dead. But how did the imposter know Corky's partner would be coming to Stockton on a temporary assignment? How did he get that information? Corky would certainly check on that. After all, who would know Tony's habits better than his partner?

It was the thought 'of knowing' that brought him up short. Who knew Leggin Floyd better than Clisten? There was no way his partner would have been drawn-in by a drug-crazed mugger. And as these thoughts began to materialize in his mind, Clisten wanted to arrange the facts he hypothesized in some logical order. He took a sheet of paper from his desk and began writing.

The imposter came to Stockton for a specific reason. He had probably visited the town before, staying in places where identification was unnecessary.

During that time Tony must have seen Leggin around town, perhaps even followed him. Since Tony was set to replace him, why murder the detective? Did Tony advance the timeline because Leggin discovered something that would have jeopardized his plan?

Leggin Floyd was a smart man with very good instincts. Since he knew a detective from Philadelphia was to be his temporary replacement, had they made contact? Would Corky have that information? Leggin never mentioned it to Clisten. In fact, every conversation they had regarding the temporary leave concerned the family situation, a hopeful resolution and his determination to return to Stockton and resume a normal life again.

That Leggin became suspicious of phony Tony was the only thing that made sense. His partner would follow the scent of wrong doing wherever it took him, and what he discovered must have been the motive for his mugging death. Imposter Tony could not allow Leggin to live. He had come too far for his plan to fail.

Leggin may have been older and smaller in stature, but he was a smart investigator. Following a hunch about Tony was probably his downfall. Although saddened by the thought, Clisten never believed a drug-crazed addict murdered his partner; however, he was told the case was officially closed and ordered to leave it alone.

Brushed aside by those in charge, Clisten knew he would clear Leggin's death in the end, as would Corky with his real partner. That was the other side of the coin.

The imposter must have watched the real Tony, perhaps made friends with him to glean information. When the time was right, he murdered the real detective and switched places. How did that happen? How did he obtain the needed transfer papers? Where did they meet for something like that to occur?

These questions continued to play in his mind and Clisten felt there was only one thing to do. He tapped a number on his cell phone.

"You better have something new," the raspy voice snarled. "His whole apartment's dusty. The man who sublet it never moved in."

Realizing Frank Corky's anxiety, Clisten thought it best to talk with him at some later time. This was the man's moment of truth: his partner's death was now more fact than probability. "I just had a few thoughts. I'll call you later."

"If you got something, spit it out."

"You might want to write this down."

"Why? Do you think you're talking to some moron?"

"No…it's just…"

"That I find my partner's place empty and know he's lying dead somewhere, I should be sad." Corky finished what Clisten was trying to express. "Well to my way of thinking, sad comes after pissed. I'm going to nail this sick son of a bitch and you're going to help me. So, spit-out what you got."

After Clisten finished his narrative, he wasn't sure if Corky agreed with his theory on Leggin's death or the surveillance of his partner during the planning stage. Corky just grunted and abruptly ended the call. His sullen behavior was expected; he was still in the pissed stage. But the call did give Clisten further insight. If contact was made between the real Tony and Leggin, Corky didn't know about it either. Words often explode in the pissed state and there was no volatile exchange to indicate his knowledge of the two men making contact.

102 | RACHEL GRIPP

A short time later, when Clisten remembered to call about the number that appeared on Lily's registration papers, the operator told him it was not a working number. Why would Amy Gregson make-up a phony number? Did she do it deliberately to hide any trace of her through Lily? He would alert Jay of that fact, although the information would be meaningless to him.

On a hunch, Clisten phoned his partner and listened to the ringing telephone. Was the man out and about or had he skipped town? The latter part of that question worried him.

TWELVE

GUNTHER PRATT

Twilla woke-up feeling very tired Wednesday morning. She went to bed late, her fault, of course. Trying to understand Amy's inventory file was trying, even for her. Nothing made sense.

She continued to remain silent about it because Amy had kept the file hidden and out of Dr. Shelden's hands. So, to her colleague, the file had meaning. However, its real significance was now lost forever; Amy was dead and Twilla had no way of learning its importance. Of course, if the inventory were damning to the department, Shelden would want it back. She had to cover her ass.

But facts were facts. In descending order, the inventory sheet listed a number for a new refrigerator supposedly housed in Amy's lab. Since it was not there, Twilla had made it her business to check the numbers on all three lab refrigerators. It came as no surprise when those numbers matched the ones listed third, fourth and fifth on the sheet; however, the refrigerator whose listing number ranked second was also missing. So, where were these two refrigerators?

Something was very wrong. Did Amy think a scam was going on...a pretended delivery of new equipment going elsewhere for sale? Amy must have thought Dr. Shelden was involved in a scheme to recycle new and old equipment for money. If so, the woman could not have acted alone. She would have needed help with removal and delivery. Although the list included the two home management houses, Twilla wondered if an inventory file also existed on her lab equipment. How far reaching was this money scam and who else was involved? How could this be happening?

Twilla was in over her head and knew it. There was no way she could sort this out. She had neither time, nor resources for investigative work. Still, she had to look at both sides of the issue.

What if the inventory file were meaningless and misplaced? Dr. Shelden, the department head who enjoyed such a long history at Stockton, would want it filed accordingly. In that case, a list of old equipment and numbers would not match those in her lab.

Still, Twilla could not overlook Amy's desire to keep the inventory file or the fact that two refrigerators assigned to the lab were not there. Maybe her colleague had witnessed something illegal or overheard an untoward conversation.

Then too, if the file were meaningless why would Dr. Shelden continue searching for it so feverishly? Wouldn't the inventory be an open record and filed in the accounting department or some department of record? All of this made Twilla suspicious. Amy must have felt that way or she would have returned it.

No. Amy knew something was wrong. In searching for a place to hide the file, she must have thought of Twilla's cookbook. Who would think of searching there? Suddenly, that question led to another.

Was the person who ransacked Amy's apartment looking for the missing file or information on Mark? That thought brought it even closer. Did the person who ransacked Amy's apartment also vandalize hers? She thought again of the man in the long coat the day Amy lay comatose in her arms. Recalling that glimpse rekindled the growing fear deep within her.

If only there was someone she could talk to...a person she trusted. She thought of her father but dismissed the idea. He had enough on his plate just trying to recover. The man would probably do better if her mother would just leave him alone.

Thinking of her father brought a new-found friend to mind. Would Pete be able to help her? The man had already sensed something was troubling her during their conversation in the park. He was not affiliated with the college and had been some sort of detective before retirement. At least, that's what she thought. Twilla wouldn't ask him to investigate the file contents, she just wanted to know what they meant.

But right now, she had to feed Lily before class. Maybe she would take Lily for a walk by the lake later that afternoon.

In another part of town, a different conversation was taking place.

"We're on our way. Is he in?" Clisten listened to Corky's raspy voice so filled with anticipation.

"Not yet. But I was told he stopped by the station last night."

"When last night? What was he doing?" He fired a continuous line of questions.

"That's what I heard when I came in this morning. He was probably checking our data base for a missing woman. I told you about our current case."

"So, he doesn't suspect anything."

"I don't think so, but then nothing's certain in life."

"This is just what I need right now, some smart-ass philosopher spewing the precepts of life. Let me know if he comes in." He rang off without adding anything further.

Corky's abrupt rudeness caused Clisten to smile. The man was typical city: a harsh attitude on life and a mouth that wouldn't quit. Still, he was anxious to meet the big man with the raspy voice. As Clisten pictured him standing there, Sergeant Qurlan brought him out of his daydream.

"This was just brought in." He placed the glued vase belonging to Miss Hale on his desk.

"Is PB still here?"

"No. He was in a hurry."

"I'll catch him later. Thanks." Clisten watched the burly man leave, his thoughts racing as he stared at the vase. "With everything coming down today, this is the last thing I needed," he grumbled aloud. He sat staring at the vase, before realizing it could no longer sit on his desk. Holding it gingerly, he placed it on the floor in a non-traffic corner of the room and began to smile. The vase sat in a perfect spot for a spittoon!

An hour later, Clisten walked down the hall to the main office and confronted Qurlan, who sat at his desk busily involved with paperwork.

"Have we heard from Tony this morning? He should have been in by now," Clisten said casually.

"Oh." Sergeant Qurlan remembered. "Tony called this morning to remind me about the note on his desk."

"What note?" he asked turning toward Tony's office. Inwardly, Clisten was irritated but couldn't show it. "Did he say?" Qurlan shook his head and went back to his paperwork as Clisten entered his partner's office.

It was only after reading Tony's note that Clisten realized its full intent, causing him to slowly tap a contact number.

"Don't bother making the trip. He skipped." Clisten knew the information would infuriate Corky but he tried to remain calm after relating the news.

"What the hell are you telling me?" Corky's voice boomed through the phone.

"Tony left a note on his desk. He's following a clue and won't be in."

"That doesn't sound suspicious to me. That's what we do to solve cases. He could be telling the truth." His acceptance of a normally followed routine did not sit well with Clisten. He wasn't buying it.

"No!" Clisten spat emphatically. "A note for my benefit would have been left on my desk, not his. And following a clue is a great excuse for not coming in. Although Tony wants me to think he's working the case, it has the opposite effect and just reinforces my original thought. He's buying time."

"I'm still coming," Corky interrupted. "He murdered my partner and may have killed yours. We know this perp came to Stockton for a reason. He won't leave until he finds what he's looking for. Got any ideas?" The detective paused, waiting for a response.

"No. There isn't anything to follow on my end."

"What about the case you're working on?"

"Maybe, but it seems remote." Clisten hesitated. There were now several avenues that had to be pursued; dead ends according to Tony, ones that could lead to the real identity of Amy Gregson. "What about your end? Have you found anything?"

"I'm working a lead, but I thought it would be easier if your partner talked to me. A private conversation of sorts." Clisten caught his meaning immediately and wanted no part of it.

"I think it would be better if you worked your lead instead of coming here. Your presence would send the station into an uproar and we certainly don't want that right now. Let's keep his arrest between us for a day or two while I quietly look around town."

"I hear you." Clisten heard the man's coarse growl before ending the call.

Clisten sat at his desk, thumbing through the notebook scrawl for two names worth checking. They had already been investigated by his partner supposedly; however, Clisten now questioned the results Tony gave him. Did the man uncover something that could lead to the real identity of Amy Gregson and keep that information for his own purposes? If so, why? What was the common link between them? As these thoughts progressed, his eyes fell on the names he sought: Thaddeus J. Stevens in New York and Rebecca Givens at High Coventry, some ninety miles north of Stockton.

Within minutes, Clisten was speaking to a woman who answered the phone number listed beside a man's name.

"This is Detective Barr from Stockton." He introduced himself. "I'm trying to contact Thaddeus J. Stevens for information on a current case."

"I wish you people would start sharing information and stop bothering me," she said, annoyed by the inquiry.

"Excuse me." He remained calm. "I don't understand."

"I told the other detective from Stockton that Thaddeus died five years ago. His sons run the firm now. Don't you people share information?"

"I am so sorry, and I do apologize," Clisten sweetened his tone. "My partner is on vacation and I'm trying to make sense of his scrawl. I can't read his handwriting. The name of the client is on one line, but somehow, Thaddeus' name is on another. Since there is no further notation, it left me wondering about his status.

I am so sorry for disturbing you." He echoed those sentiments again. "I know you are very busy." Clisten could not have been more understanding or charming.

"We do try to cooperate with the police." Her attitude softened.

"If you could possibly check your files for the name of Amy Gregson, I'd really appreciate it." He continued oozing charm.

"Sorry to disappoint you but that name is not in our files. I checked thoroughly before returning the other man's call."

"Trying to read his notes is very difficult. I really appreciate your helping me." Clisten's voice dripped with sincerity.

"Bessie." She identified herself. "Bessie Long. I was with Thaddeus when he opened his first office. I've been with the family for years."

"Does the name of Rebecca Givens mean anything to you?"

"Something tells me she had Thaddeus do a document for her years ago, but I don't remember what it was."

"Bessie," he said, his resonant voice soft and yet melodic. "Would you call me if you remember anything about the document?"

"Don't count on it but give me your cell number."

After Clisten gave her his phone number, he said, "You are a wonderful lady, Bessie. Call me, Clisten. When I come to New York, we have a date for lunch."

"Most people forget old ladies. That's why so many of us wither on the vine."

"I've got a very good memory and the only vine we'll enjoy comes from a grape." He heard laughter as she ended the call.

Clisten sat at his desk thinking about the conversation he just had with Bessie Long. What was the nature of the document Thaddeus J. Stevens prepared for Rebecca Givens? Was it connected to Amy Gregson in some way? If so, what was the relationship between the two women? There had to be a connection somewhere: Amy Gregson gave her as a reference on the employment application. Thaddeus did too. He eyed another phone number and tapped it on his cell.

Within seconds a sweet voice answered, "High Coventry."

"This is Detective Barr from Stockton, I need to speak with someone about faculty information."

"You want general services. Just a moment while I transfer your call."

Clisten waited, hating the bureaucratic red tape that followed every school expansion; this was what the ideologues called economic success.

"General services," the woman began, "how may I help you?"

Clisten repeated his earlier routine of identifying himself and went straight to the business of Rebecca Givens. However, he expressed no surprise when the woman transferred his call to HC records.

"HC Records," a man's dry voice answered. "How can I help you?"

Clisten listened to the same identical greeting he received from the other departments that transferred his call. *They must get these people in a room and have them rehearse the same script over and over.* The thought ran through his mind as he sat drumming the desk.

After identifying himself for the third time, Clisten took more of a provocative tone. "I certainly hope so. I've been transferred so many times, I'm beginning to lose patience."

"That's the price of progress. At least that's what they tell me. I liked it better when we were small."

"You been there a long time."

"Too long. I'm retiring at the end of term."

"Then you must have known all the faculty before the expansion.

"It was much easier to know them on a personal basis."

"What about Rebecca Givens?"

"What about her?"

"I'm trying to locate her or her family."

"She was always a quiet woman…a good administrator, but Dr. Givens always kept to herself. She went to faculty functions, but I don't know too much about her; things like where she went on holidays or after term. She was never gone long though, just a few weeks in summer."

"How do you know so much about her routine?"

"She was a good-looking woman. Just because I shuffle papers, that never stopped me from wanting to get inside her file cabinet."

Clisten laughed inwardly at the older man's remark. He had never heard sex phrased that way before. This was his *learning something new every day.'*

"Do you happen know where she is? I need to contact her, a simple routine for my current case," he said knowing most of his statement was a stretch of the truth.

"Good luck with that. After she retired no one heard from her. Some say Rebecca moved to Europe; others think she died."

"What do you think?" Clisten tried cajoling him. "You were interested in the woman."

"Gunther Pratt always takes rejection seriously. You have to with the quiet ones; otherwise, they sneak-up on you and cut-off your balls."

Now, Clisten was really enjoying the conversation. It was informative, personal and very amusing. "What exactly did she do to you?"

"I walked her home from the campus one night and tried French kissing her when we got to the front door of her place."

"And?"

"She was very agreeable at first."

"But then Gunther screwed up." Clisten interjected, as the old man's romantic encounter unfolded.

"Big time. Wrong message. Slid my hand up her skirt too soon."

"What's the matter with you? You were too anxious…much too soon."

"I just wanted her. For years, I dreamed of taking her to bed, spending a life together, pruning her roses. What I got instead was being kneed in the balls. She never talked to me after that."

"So, you don't know where she is." That the man could offer no more information was obvious. "Then can you fax me a copy of her file with her picture?" he asked offering the number.

"The file includes her picture," he assured Clisten. "I already sent it to the other detective in your department."

"It must be misplaced. He's away on vacation so I'm stuck checking reference information before closing the case. Does the name Amy Gregson mean anything to you?"

"No. I don't think so." As he spoke, Gunther began the task of faxing the information to Clisten.

Clisten began browsing his cell phone for a picture of Amy Gregson's faculty face, the one recognized by the students. "Can you give me your cell number? I'd like to send you a picture of someone who might have known Rebecca. I want to know if you remember seeing her."

Clisten took Gunther's number and immediately sent Amy's picture to him. He waited few minutes before Gunther broke the silence with a return call.

"She may have been the woman who went away with Rebecca at the end of term. But that was a long, long time ago."

"Did she come often?"

"I might have seen her twice, but I'm not sure. I always felt there was some reason Rebecca retired early. Some people thought she was ill and had to retire. Of course, they also thought she died."

Gunther, how do you know so much? Were you stalking Rebecca?" he asked boldly.

"Although it wasn't mutual, I wasn't blind to her 'comings and goings.' We lived in the same complex on Cyrus. I just never wanted her to think I was some pervert. My passion was real; my intentions, honorable. I wanted to marry her. I think I still would, if she'd have me. That is, if I knew where she was or was still alive."

Listening to Gunther's plight, a feeling of sorrow began to engulf him. Clisten heard so much regret in the man's voice. It expressed a loss that could never be recovered. But this was so much more than unrequited love: this was years of loving a woman who disdained his very existence. How could he not have understood that?

"If I learn what happened to Rebecca, you will be the first to know." Clisten felt obligated to give him that information.

"Is that a promise? You have my cell."

"And you have mine," the detective said, repeating his number again. "I need to know one more thing. When you spoke to my partner, did you have a conversation with him about Rebecca, the kind of personal information you shared with me?"

"No. It was all very impersonal. He just wanted employment information. When I told him, there was no current address listed, he requested her file. I sent it to the address he gave me."

"Do you remember what it was?"

"That struck me funny. The address was not a police station."

"Does this sound about right?" Clisten asked, offering Tony's home address.

"That sounds about right."

"We're trying to keep our information private and away from the press. We had a shooting at the college. You may have read about it."

"What's Rebecca's involvement in that?"

"Strictly peripheral. She was listed as a reference. I either follow it or get accused of sloppy detective work. I'm required to check everyone. You know how that is."

"Amen to that," Gunther agreed. "Clisten," he said slowly, "I'm holding you to your promise."

"You will have the facts: good or bad. That I promise."

"Thank you."

As Gunther ended the call, Clisten detected a tremor in his voice. Was the man thinking of what could have been, so many years earlier? What kind of damn fool was he? In his frenzied hunt for sex, he ignored the cardinal rule every red-blooded male followed: start slow with a little romance before hopping to the next stage. What was the matter with him? Even after the blunder, a groveling apology followed by a 'hands off' date would have gone a long way in reaching Gunther's objective, which of course, was to bed the woman. Poor Gunther, he had to release the passion he carried in his pants much too quickly.

How would he react in such a situation? It wouldn't happen. He wouldn't slide his hand up some woman's skirt. That was for damn sure. If Clisten really wanted the woman he'd probably rip-off her clothes and take her on the spot. Of course, she would want him to do that. Otherwise, the exchange would be meaningless emotionally, or in legal terms, rape. That scenario was too farfetched anyhow. There was no one that gave rise to a bulge in his pants.

Clisten continued sitting at his desk deep in thought. A link existed among three people: Thaddeus prepared a document for Rebecca and Amy vacationed with her. The central figure linking Thaddeus J. and Amy Gregson was Rebecca Givens. So, it was imperative that Clisten find her. Gunther mentioned the complex on Cyrus. Certainly, someone there would remember her. Maybe he would make a trip to High Coventry. It could prove to be very worthwhile.

He wrote their names in his tablet and added Herman Banks, Lily's breeder, to the list. Although unworkable, he also scribbled the old phone number still on Lily's registration. The breeder was an avenue left unchecked and Clisten expected to change that very soon.

Loaded with questions, Clisten would visit the man tomorrow for information on Lily and her owner, Amy Gregson. He had to get back to solving the case; yet questions about the imposter, Tony Mistretta, kept popping into his head.

As these thoughts continued, his eyes fell on the repaired vase sitting in the isolated corner of the room. A visitor would think nothing of it. The vase was merely a decorative feature that brought color and warmth to the Spartan-like office.

Still, he had to get rid of it. Clisten couldn't chance having the vase broken again by some clumsy move. Since he wanted to interrogate Twilla Hale in her own setting, maybe he would visit her that evening…pop in unannounced and catch her by surprise. The woman was deliberately hiding something. That thought continued drumming in his mind. She withheld far more about Amy Gregson than she admitted. He had to uncover those secrets.

Visiting later that evening would be ideal…perhaps some-where around eight. She would be totally relaxed when he dropped by casually to return her grandmother's vase. What could be a more perfect time to question her? An interrogation would never be expected, and he could soften the whole inquiry. Clisten began to revel in the daydream of his strategic visit when his thoughts turned elsewhere. He had to find Tony Mistretta.

But first Clisten had to check on something of great impor-
tance. He had to be there when Gunther's fax came in. Rebecca
Givens was the key: she could unravel the motive for Amy
Gregson's murder. Of this, Clisten was certain.

THIRTEEN

A LOVE PRETENSE

Before taking Lily for a walk Wednesday afternoon, Twilla thought of calling home to check her father's condition. It almost seemed like a daily ritual since returning to Stockton.

It had been a long morning. After coming home from class, she finished her three-day project of turning the unit back to its natural state and now realized there was nothing more she could do. Twilla could try to repair the gashed printer stand or buy a new one; however, she would decide that later, when she was flush with money. At that moment, she wanted to get out in the fresh air while it was still sunny. That, of course, was impossible; she had to call home first and listen to the forming of a crisis.

"Mom." Twilla heard a taint of anxiety in Agatha's voice. "Is something wrong? Has something happened to Dad?" She feared the worst. "I don't understand what you're saying." Then after a quick response, said, "Oh, you had me worried." Twilla became silent, neither responding nor interrupting when her mother began a furious two-level harangue.

"What do you want me to say?" Twilla answered trying to remain calm.

She was aware of her mother's conflicted feelings about Millie Haskell, the nurse they hired to care for their father. That the woman dated him before each of them married was an issue her mother refused to let go, particularly now that Millie was a widow. Her living next door only exacerbated the worsening

117

relationship. However, the immediate problem dealt with none of these issues. Plain and simple. Millie insisted her father walk; Agatha thought Matthew should rest.

"I'd say stay out of it." Twilla continued her thread of conversation. "Millie's a trained nurse; you're not. She knows what's best for a quick recovery. If Dad's making progress, leave it alone. When her visits end, you'll be there for him. In the meantime, get your hair done and do all the things you need to do before becoming temporarily housebound."

Twilla had no sooner finished her directive when Agatha ambushed her with another problem.

"For God sake, she's a grown woman!" Twilla screamed in anger. "You have enough on your plate with Dad. Let Julie solve her own problems." She was half-way through her response when Agatha interrupted. "I don't care!" Twilla shouted down her mother's intrusion. "The world is filled with unhappy people. She makes it sound like everyone has a life of champagne bubbles except her."

"Why are you being so mean?" Agatha smarted. "Julie would comfort you if you were unhappy. She was crying when I phoned last night. Something's wrong. I know it. But she wouldn't tell me."

"And you want me to call her."

"She'll talk to you. Even with your differences you were always close."

"I understand."

"You'll call."

"Of course."

"You won't mention my telling you…"

"How many times have we had this conversation?"

"You're right. I just thought…"

"How's Dad," Twilla interrupted her. She did not want the rehash of a repeated past. Julie was always going from one romantic crisis to another, while Twilla stayed steady as her shock absorber, deflecting all those nasty problems in her hour of need. If nothing else, she was a good listener. She also loved Julie to death, although sometimes Twilla wanted to choke her sister over her choice of men.

"He's on the mend actually."

"Tell him I called." She tapped the end button on her phone before her mother could think of sharing some other problem.

"Come Lily." Twilla grabbed the leash from a kitchen hook. She stepped back a minute and stared into space, an idea taking hold in her mind. "What if," she said aloud but never completed the thought verbally. Instead, she walked into the bedroom with Lily following her. After placing the leash on the bed, she removed the inventory file from pillowcase and took it to the living room to be copied.

Twilla examined the big gash on the table leg while the printer spewed her needed copies. After returning the original file back to its hiding place, Twilla placed the papers inside her purse and, after leashing Lily, left the condo.

As Twilla drove toward Tavis Lake, she wondered if giving Pete the file was the right thing to do. However, after arriving at their regular spot, those thoughts were suddenly interrupted as Lily pulled the leash from Twilla's hand and raced toward a bench where Pete sat with a sleeping Sam at his feet.

"Lily seems to find us wherever we go." He addressed the woman flying after her dog, who at that very moment was licking Sam awake. "She's taken with him. There's no doubt about it."

"I don't see him fighting her off," she said, removing Lily's leash.

"He wouldn't. She's a pretty lady like you," he said, as they watched Lily's body resting between Sam's two front paws, her small tongue licking his nose. "You see how she's positioned him, don't you?"

"I don't understand."

"It's the only way they can communicate. Sam's a huge sheepdog. She likes him and it's mutual. Look at the way her tail is wagging."

"Pete...," Twilla dawdled with a possible implication. "She's young and he's..."

"Her boy toy for the moment," he interrupted. "That'll change but you have to get her fixed."

"When?" Twilla's eyes were the shape of two saucers. "How?"

"Same as with all females. Your vet will help you out."

Twilla felt embarrassed for being so stupid. "I just didn't think that far ahead."

"No one ever does and then one day it just happens. Now you won't be alarmed when it does."

"I'm learning a lot from you."

"That's a surprise." Pete was unconvinced. "Aside from your father's condition and your sister's boyfriend, you never mentioned the real problem bugging you."

"As of today, there's more to my sister's story."

"Twilla, we can go on and on about Julie, if that's what you want."

"You remembered her name!" Twilla remarked, shocked with his recollection. She mentioned Julie and Russell only once at their last meeting. Pete had to be writing this down on some tablet.

"Because I'm old, you must think my brain cells died." He brought her out of her reverie. "I take an interest because Sam likes Lily and he's a good judge of character." His comment brought a broad smile to Twilla's face. It was so different from the reason he gave when they first met. Bringing in Sam's judgment of character was amusing and very clever. "Now, if I were to guess, I'd say your sister has another crisis on her hands and needs your help, but I'm not interested. I want to know what's really bothering you."

"If I could give you a definitive answer, I would. Right now, I'm scared and confused."

"Because of the break-in?"

"I don't understand why me? Why my place?"

"We went over this before. There has to be a reason, Twilla."

"Meaning?" Her eyes met his. "What are you saying?"

"There are only two reasons for theft, or in your case, a break-in: loot or hidden information. Now, don't take this the wrong way, but you don't look like a person dripping with money. So?"

"You think I'm hiding something."

"Are you?"

"Damn it, Pete. I really don't know. I'm totally confused."

"Trust me, Twilla." He urged her. "I'll try to help you in any way I can."

Twilla sighed, her eyes still fixed on his, "After Amy died, I found an inventory file in the cookbook she borrowed from me. I checked the equipment in her lab and the refrigerator numbers don't match." She went on to explain the discrepancies. "I checked every refrigerator but only one stove unfortunately. I ran out of time." Twilla paused and waited for his response.

"And you think your condo was ransacked for the file."

"I don't know. I have so many questions running through my mind. What makes the file so important? Why didn't Amy return it to Dr. Shelden? Since it was given by mistake, why keep it?"

"Is there any way I could see this inventory file?"

"Why? What would you do with it?"

"I'd study it first. Then I'd try to determine its meaning."

"I already tried that."

"Not from my perspective. Remember, I spent my life investigating cases."

"I'd want a promise of confidentiality."

"I can't promise that." Pete shook his head. "If I find something criminal going on, I'd want to report it."

"That's why I can't trust you."

"Twilla, you would not be involved, but if the college is being ripped off, someone should be arrested.

"What if the list is meaningless?"

"It stays between us."

"Promise?"

"Twilla!"

"I brought copies with me." She grabbed the folded papers in her purse and said, "The originals are in my unit."

"Put them somewhere safe."

"You think my condo could be ransacked again."

"That's a distinct possibility," Pete agreed, scanning them. "Give me the number of your cell and take mine. I might have some questions after I study this."

"I don't know how much help I can give you. None of it makes sense. I only kept the file because Amy did."

"If you have a safety deposit box, put the papers there. If something criminal is going on, the prosecutor will need the original file."

"Prosecutor?"

"We are a long way from any of that. Don't worry about it. This whole thing could amount to nothing. I just want you to take precautions."

His reassuring words seemed to calm her almost immediately. "I spoke with my mother before coming here. She wants me to call Julie. I guess my sister's going through a bad time with Russell."

"And, of course, you will." He laughed. "I'll tell you what. You talk with Julie and I'll work on these." He held up the file papers. "C'mon Sam. It's time to go home." Before turning away, he said. "I meant what I said about you being pretty. I know you don't care much about that sort of thing and that's too bad. You should let people see how beautiful you really are inside and out."

Filled with mixed emotions about his left-handed remark, Twilla watched the image of the man and his dog get smaller and smaller, totally unaware of Lily's soft whimpers. He had given her a compliment with a caveat. In other words, she could be beautiful if she really cared about her looks. So much for subtext. Why didn't he just come out and say she was a mess that needed fixing?"

Did her peer group, the other academics in her circle, feel that way about her…that she needed a makeover? How would Twilla know? She could not remember anyone talking fashion or cosmetics to her when they gathered at faculty meetings, before, after, or in the ladies' room.

Twilla couldn't think about that right now. She had too much on her plate. Between Amy's dying request and Julie's romantic problems, her life had become more complicated than ever. No. That kind of thing would have to wait. Yet, Pete's words continued to linger in her mind.

Within an hour of coming home and after a quick shower, Twilla changed into her favorite pair of threadbare jeans, tied her hair into a pony tail, and then, accidentally spilled spaghetti sauce on her sloppy sweatshirt as she prepared dinner. Once the meal was over, Lily sat on the couch with Twilla and watched her tap a few numbers on her cell phone.

"Hey, I wanted to check in. We haven't talked for a while."

"Not since you returned to Stockton," Julie agreed. "Did Mom tell you to check-up on me?"

"Why? Is something wrong? She didn't mention anything when I called about Dad this afternoon." Twilla wasn't lying; she was just evading the truth.

"You don't normally call during the week."

"That's true." Twilla laughed. "I'll hang-up and call this weekend."

"No. Please don't."

"Don't call or don't hang up?"

"Something's wrong. I feel it. Russell's going to be traveling more. Trips overseas, I think. He gave me that impression but I'm not sure. I'm not sure of anything anymore."

"I don't understand."

"When I got back in town, we went out to dinner and then afterward we came back here…to my apartment."

Certain she did not want to hear about their detailed encounter, Twilla interrupted her. "What did he tell you?"

"After making love to me, Russell said his company was sending him London. Then Russell kissed me goodbye and told me he would be in touch."

"How long has it been?"

"Three days."

"Now you are being ridiculous," Twilla said in disgust. "It takes a day to fly overseas. Give the man time to settle in. You're worrying over nothing."

"Think so?"

"Absolutely. Do you know where he's staying?"

"He couldn't remember. West End somewhere."

"I wouldn't worry. Russell will call this weekend and you can tell me all about it."

"I'm glad we talked."

"Me too." She pressed the end button.

"Can you believe this crap?" Twilla's arm circled Lily. "She gets so hyper over every little thing. I'd have dumped that creep a long time ago. But then, Julie doesn't know about the yard episode. Better we keep it that way."

Lily, of course, had no idea what Twilla was talking about. She only heard a soft voice speaking to her and hoped somewhere in the conversation a treat was in store. However, those thoughts were interrupted by the doorbell and she raced behind Twilla to see who was ringing it.

"Russell!" Twilla stood staring at him. She could not have been more surprised as the conversation with Julie lingered in her thoughts.

"I was in the area and wanted to see how you were getting along."

"You mean after the break-in?" Although she shrugged it off carelessly, Twilla knew the real reason for coming was not his legitimate concern for her; it was one she would have to handle quickly and permanently. "Hanging in there, I guess. Want some coffee?"

Following her to the kitchen, he watched her place two mugs on the island counter and moved swiftly to embrace her.

"There's no point fighting what's between us." He brushed her lips. "I want you, Twilla. I know you feel the same way about me." However, before he could say anything further, his words were interrupted by a persistent ringing of the doorbell.

Pushing him away, Twilla raced to the door, and seeing Clisten Barr holding her grandmother's heirloom, set the vase on the floor quickly and threw her arms around him. "Listen to me," she whispered, running her lips along the side of his clean-shaven face, "Whatever happens, don't leave me." Her lips then moved to meet his.

Although taken by surprise, Clisten felt an arousal surging through his body as he pressed her to him and kissed her long and hard. The moment their eyes re-met briefly, their lips merged again. And before any verbal exchange could take place, Twilla reluctantly broke the embrace.

"I'm glad you were able to make it, but Lily and I ate already," she said knowing he would take the hint. "Oh. Russell came by," she added of the man who emerged from the kitchen and stood watching them.

"You're dating Twilla's sister, I recall." Clisten seemed un-moved. From the tone of his voice, it was obvious that he disap-proved of the man's visit. "Did she ask you to deliver something?" Russell's dropping by twice within four days of Twilla's home invasion made the detective increasingly suspicious.

"No. I was just in the area again and wanted to check on Twilla after…Sunday."

"I'm fine, thanks to Clisten watching over me." She smiled sweetly, then glancing up at him, asked, "How's Julie?"

"Wonderful as ever. In fact, she made a wonderful dinner last night."

"Give her my love." Twilla ushered him to the door.

As soon as Russell left the condo Twilla stood behind the closed door and began her usual tirade. "I told you. I was right. To begin with, Julie doesn't cook; she makes reservations. Secondly,

I just talked with her tonight. She hasn't seen him in three days. He told her he'd be traveling overseas. No. His coming here again tells me he's after something and it's not a roll in the hay. The sex is just an excuse."

"Did he hit on you again?"

"In the kitchen," she motioned with her hand. "I offered him coffee, but he was after something else. That's when he grabbed me." She caught him staring at her. "What's the matter?"

Twilla followed him into the kitchen and saw him wet the end of a paper towel before drawing her to him.

"I wasn't sure when we kissed, but you do have a little sauce stuck on the corner of your mouth." He rubbed the area gently. "That's better," he said, his eyes fixed on hers.

She was drawn by the closeness of him, and a wanting deep within her began to swell as she lifted her face to meet his lips again. "I had spaghetti." She paused, clearing her throat.

"I know. You've got sauce all over your sweatshirt."

"I didn't know it was on my face. I'm surprised Lily didn't lick it off."

"You fed her spaghetti?"

"Only a few strands with her dog chow."

"That's not good for Lily, Miss Hale."

"After our performance tonight, don't you think we should be on a first name basis? I mean neither of us kisses indiscriminately." Then Twilla was taken back for a moment when a sudden thought occurred to her. "Oh, God. I'm so sorry. You could be in a relationship or even married for all I know."

Clisten ignored her comments and knew she was following behind him as he retraced his steps to the front door. This was not the time for an interrogation. The detective would have to wait until things cooled between them. He turned to face her directly. "My friends call me Clis. I am not married, and you look like hell. But I do like the way you kiss."

Without any further discussion, he gathered her in his arms, placed his hand on the small of her back and brought her to him. Wetting her lips with his tongue, he penetrated the hollow of her mouth while pressing the lower portion of her body directly against his. An immediate surge of raw passion flooded their locked bodies as his increasing readiness became apparent. He heard the heaviness of her breathing and felt her body yielding to his.

"How far do you want to go?" He ached with hunger, his whispered voice hoarse with longing.

"The next room." Twilla surrendered, her body limp with expectation.

She felt the buoyancy of her body being carried and caressed as she lay cradled in his arms, a heightened passion coursing wildly between them, knowing their melding bodies would soon reach the climatic end she yearned for.

Lily stood watch in the darkness of the bedroom. She barked at first, being too small to jump on the bouncing bed, and then began to whimper. Getting attention from no one, she went to her little bed in the corner of the room and sulked. After a while, Lily finally fell asleep.

FOURTEEN
REGRETS

When Twilla opened her one eye Thursday morning, she was lying flat on her stomach, her one arm dangling over the edge of the bed while Lily licked her hand.

"What?" She asked stupidly. "I don't want to get up." Her eye went to the clock on the nightstand. "Ah, shit. I got class in an hour."

Twilla threw off the twisted covers to take a quick shower but sat on the bed completely puzzled.

"How did that happen?" A naked Twilla asked her dog as she looked down at the socks on her feet. "He must think I'm a twit. Why didn't you tell me?" She questioned Lily again, her tone somewhat harsh.

Lily raised her head abruptly, her black eyes staring at the scolding woman, thoughts of her own racing angrily. *"What's her problem? I'm not her keeper. The dumb ass should have kicked him out of bed and let me sleep on my pillow. She wasn't looking out for me, so why should I care about her socks?"*

Within the hour Twilla showered, fed Lily and was deep in thought as she drove toward the college.

"I doubt he'll be thinking of me this morning?" Twilla said aloud. "He's probably laughing his ass off." With that thought in mind a scowl deepened across her face. "Who but an absent-minded academic would wear socks when making love?"

After chastising herself thoroughly her thoughts took another turn. He had been so gentle, so thoughtful, a far cry from the arrogant man she had met weeks earlier. If he knew, he didn't mention it. A man of his experience would know he was dealing with a novice. And the memory of their night together inundated her thoughts as she began to relive them.

She lay in his arms and felt the serenity of being fulfilled. Words were so unnecessary. A prolonged kiss readily explained the raw need for each other a second time, and Twilla wished she could relive that moment again. Now, she wondered about the purpose of his visit. Was it just to return the vase? It probably was.

Clisten kissed her upon leaving, but he never mentioned seeing her again. In some ways, that was a blessing. A relationship with him would be disastrous. She would never know if he were interested in her personally or questioning her for his investigation. Nevertheless, she had no regrets of their night together.

Her thoughts began to fade as she turned onto the main road leading to the college.

Across town, and somewhat earlier, a ringing phone jarred Clisten Barr awake.

"Where the hell have you been?" The raspy voice questioned. "I tried to get you ten times last night. I even called the station. They thought you went home, but I knew better."

"I was working a case." Clisten sat-up against the headboard of his bed. "I must have turned-off my cell."

"Nah. I'm not buying it. If you were working a case, the phone would have been on. You were following what we call 'a dormant lead.' She had to be hot."

"Ok, Corky," Clisten sighed in resignation. "When you finish busting my chops, can you tell me why you called?"

"They fished my partner out of the Schuylkill last night or what was left of him. The ropes weighing him down got loose somehow and a boat propeller hit the river's floating debris."

"Jesus."

"That's all you gotta say? If I wanted a priest, I'd have called Father John." He scolded the detective. "I had to identify Tony or what was left of him."

"I'm sorry, Corky, but I lost Leggin too."

"I told you before; I don't want sorry."

"I haven't found him, if that's why you called. I spent a concerted five hours checking the town haunts. This was after I broke into his apartment. His clothes, or a lot of them, are still there. The apartment looks like it's lived in, but I think he skipped."

"What makes you say that?"

"No notes or papers anywhere. Tony was always taking notes. There was no clutter. It's always there, no matter how clean you are. No. He's gone."

"Where do you think he is?"

"I don't know where he is now, but Stockton is still the key to his coming here. He planned everything to get into our department, including murdering your partner and possibly mine. The why, now becomes clearer."

"Clearer, how?"

After the shooting, I told him to check the two names Amy Gregson gave as a reference. He lied saying they were dead ends, but I checked both. They are definite leads, ones he didn't want me to know about. Whatever brought him here is connected to Amy Gregson. That's the only thing that makes sense."

"And you think he killed her too."

"I don't have any real evidence…yet."

"That does it for me."

"What's that supposed to mean?"

"If he's not with you, he's not here either. He's tracking those references. I'll check my partner's watering holes to learn where they met and follow anything I can find."

"Smart move. Let me know if anything turns up."

"Just keep your phone on, Romeo."

"Believe what you want, big city man. You got far more blossoms to sniff than I have here in Stockton."

"Yeah. Yeah. Yeah. The wife's no shrinking violet; one hanky-panky and I become a soprano in the church choir."

Corky's response made Clisten laugh. To think the raspy-voiced rascal had a wife came as a surprise. For some reason, he pictured the man a singular loose cannon. At least he came on that way. "Listen," Clisten changed the conversation back to the case. "While you're tracking Tony's watering holes, I have a new lead of my own to follow. It'll take me out of town."

"Whatever," Corky snapped back. "Just keep your friggin phone on. You can check Cinderella's corset later."

"You're impossible." Clisten snorted but Corky had already ended the call.

Whatever was going on in the man's head had nothing to do with the case. Although Corky's assumptions were correct about the turned-off phone, why would the detective jump to that conclusion? Was that his way of ragging Clisten or had Corky dealt with this kind of thing before? Had the real Tony screwed around when they were working cases?

A thought suddenly occurred to him. Since Corky was checking his partner's haunts, he would also ask questions about the women Tony met when frequenting them. Then he would recall the man's habit with romantic conquests; the ones he talked about, the ones that panned out.

Strangers meeting at a bar wasn't unusual; nor was the routine. After a pick-up, drinks and conversation, turning-off the phone was instinctive…when a night of bonding occurred afterward.

Bonding, Clisten smiled. That was one way of putting it. So, in Corky's mind, he equated Clisten with Tony's telephone pattern. It was a *'Do Not Disturb'* sign.

Was it true? Was Corky right? Although Clisten turned-off his phone, he did it before entering Twilla's condo. His plan was to interrogate the woman in her surroundings and not be interrupted by a phone call. However, the entire night changed direction, solely because of the unexpected visit by Russell Weatherly.

If only, she had not kissed him, a pretense to discourage the man's stay, the night would have ended differently. The moment she embraced him, pressing her body to his as their lips met, he was filled with an escapable want. Was that why he continued to linger, when the unwanted suitor was gone? Also gone was his intended interrogation. Only the fragrance of her supple body remained.

Concentrating on their 'bonding' the previous night started to affect him physically, and he immediately thought of poor Gunther Pratt. Why would he suddenly think of him now? He already knew the answer. But his case was different. He didn't need to put a hand up her dress. The thought made him laugh. Twilla wore crappy jeans and a shirt splashed with spaghetti sauce; no skirt was involved. Nor was there a question of what was to follow. The more he thought about it, the more vivid the recollection.

"How far do you want to go?" Clisten remembered asking, so wrought with passion.

He had pressed her body to his, while plunging his tongue into the hollow of her mouth, a precursor to a heightened expectation. And although she went limp in his arms and was noticeably filled with emotion, her unexpected reply caused him to act immediately.

"The next room," she sighed softly.

It took only moments in the darkened room to fully possess her. Afterward, he began to explore the suppleness of her naked body; his tongue licking throat, his hand touching every curve and indentation. His adventurous foreplay resulted in repeating that special moment again. It was even better a second time for both…the signals were there. The want for each other had not diminished…and her socks were still intact. The thought that her feet were covered when the rest of her body was naked made him smile. There was no doubt about it. Twilla Hale was caught up in the moment of passion. She wanted him. Sock removal was the last thing on her mind.

That she had been with no other man before was obvious by her tightness and unsure leg placement. By repositioning and taking the woman gently, Clisten was certain he had satisfied her. Yet, for a beginner he was surprised by her skillful response in the lovemaking department. Was it instinct or his prowess that made her so flushed emotionally?

After a long-lasting kiss, he had left her comfortably in bed. It was much better that way. They would not see each other again…not privately. There would be no third bonding. However, with a town the size of Stockton, the chances of their meeting again somewhere were high. Yet, that presented no problem. A friendly greeting and his busy schedule would excuse him from any extended conversation.

Yes. Clisten was certain he could prevent a repeat of their encounter. He wanted no part of Twilla Hale. His private life was settled. That's how he liked it; no woman to meet him at home. He could come and go as he pleased. Living alone was perfect for detective work. People reported to him, not the other way around.

Clisten took a deep breath. Why was he having these thoughts about Twilla Hale? *"Because you're stupid and did a dumb thing."* He began a stern reprimand of himself. In all his years of detective work, the one directive he held dear was to steer clear of all women being questioned or investigated. He had held fast to that dictum until Twilla Hale crossed his path. How could he even attempt to question her about Amy Gregson after last night?

At every turn he found her annoying, obstinate and without a shred of deportment. She always looked a mess and usually smelled of some chemical that would demand a clothespin for his nose.

"Why did she have to smell so good last night?" he asked himself. "Why am I thinking about it? Life is full of regrets and stupid mistakes. I need to move on with the case." He would have to go elsewhere for answers. With that thought in mind, Clisten needed to see a man about a dog. But first he needed to re-check two phone pictures that were important to his inquiry.

As he drove out of town, Clisten's thoughts about Twilla Hale continued to linger. This annoyed him so much outwardly, that by the time he arrived at the farm owned by Herman Banks, Lily was almost an asterisk to his inquiry.

"Do you recognize her?" Clisten asked after identifying himself as a detective of Stockton's police department.

The small beady-eyed man studied two different cell phone pictures of Amy Gregson. "I get so busy. They all seem to come at once, you know. Busy schedules, I guess."

"I think she might have come with another woman." The detective paused momentarily, thinking the added statement would jog the man's memory.

"Buyers seldom come alone. After checking a litter, they always want help with the selection."

"I guess that makes sense."

The breeder suddenly became distracted and, turning his attention to a mournfully howling dog and a young disheveled boy holding his food bowl, yelled, "You can feed him now." Then Herman Banks returned to his previous conversation with the detective. "Sorry I couldn't help you. As you can see it gets a little hairy around here." As he spoke, the man turned his attention to a newly arrived couple. He then led them to a small litter of puppies, indicating a previous visit had taken place, dismissing the detective completely.

Clisten entered his car and drove slowly away, thinking of the hours he wasted visiting a breeder who could not remember Amy Gregson or her purchase of Lily.

Of course, that was not quite true. As soon as Clisten's car disappeared from the long driveway, Herman Banks left the couple momentarily and made a quick phone call.

"The detective showed me two pictures along with his badge. Before and after surgery. That means they'll continue to dig. Just be careful. I'm tossing this phone."

When Twilla came home from class, she began working on a thought that kept gnawing at her. Since the cookbook hid a picture and coded words, they had to be related to finding Mark. But was that right? She sat at her computer browsing a few locations, and within a few minutes, printed a map.

Taking her scrawled list from the cookbook, she copied the words on a sheet of paper before cutting them piecemeal to see if they fit with the computer street map. Now she was certain. Amy's word additions were clues to a long-held secret. And one of them was a street in High Coventry. If she followed the street would she find the name and address of the person listed in the clues? Was that also true of the photograph? Logistically, if the word clues proved to be true, she should also find the woman pictured in the snapshot with Amy and Lily. Only then did the apparent question become paramount. Would the pictured woman lead her to Mark?

It was time for a decision. Would she pursue this on her own or did she need help? For the time being, Twilla decided to visit High Coventry on her own that weekend, just to make sure she was on the right track. But for now, she felt very tired and needed a break. After shelving the formatted cookbook and its contents, Twilla tossed the word cuttings into a shredder. She wanted no trace of Amy's secret should another home invasion take place. With everything in its proper place, it was time to prepare dinner.

A short time later, Twilla pondered her map and the scrawled cookbook list again in preparation for her journey to High Coventry Saturday morning. The inventory file was nowhere in her thoughts. The matter of finding Mark was much more important. She replaced the list back into the cookbook and turned to Lily.

"What am I going to do about you?" She asked. "Since I can't take you with me, I'll need to find a sitter. Someone who knows you." With that thought she tapped the contact number on her cell phone for Mrs. Benson.

FIFTEEN

MRS. BENSON

It was after four when Clisten returned to his office after visiting Herman Banks. Although the man gave no information on Amy Gregson, his body language spoke volumes after seeing both pictures.

That the police had photos of the woman 'before and after' cosmetic surgery unnerved the man. He tried hiding his shock by turning his concentration on the howling of a dog, but Clisten knew it was just a smokescreen to divert his attention.

Still, the inescapable fact remained. The photographs of Amy Gregson had upset the man and Clisten wanted to know why. There was a connection. He was certain of that. But finding it was another matter. It went far beyond the purchase of a dog.

What, exactly, was the relationship between Amy Gregson and Herman Banks? Were they just good friends? Did the friendship include Rebecca Givens? Had the two communicated with each other after Amy's death? The man's phone records could be a lead; if not in learning the real identity of Amy Gregson, then perhaps in finding Rebecca Givens.

It was then that Clisten became aware of the folder on his desk. It was the file on Rebecca Givens from Gunther Pratt. He had ignored the fax after it came in, concentrating instead on gleaning information from Herman Banks, his live lead.

When he opened the file, a picture of an attractive dark-haired woman, older than Amy Gregson, smiled openly at him.

The picture must have been taken years earlier, when she first applied to the prestigious college, long before becoming an administrator Of course, by now, with all the passing years, the woman had aged. Would he be able to recognize her? He could have a computer image of her face updated from her registration picture. Although it would give him a current picture of her face, it would also raise questions that demanded an explanation.

No. It was better to do this on his own. By now, the woman was gray or prematurely gray, and her face somewhat wrinkled. Her body mattered little. He wasn't bedding her. He'd leave that to Gunther.

Still, there was something else to consider, something much more important. What, exactly, was the relationship between the relatively young Amy and the older woman? Was she a relative? An aunt perhaps? Clisten started salivating at the prospect of finding Rebecca Givens and a plan began to unfold in his mind.

After studying the file, he would go through Herman Banks' phone records to see what spilled out. There had to be a link. Somewhere, someone must have seen both women together. Suddenly, a smile crossed his face as an idea occurred to him. "Maybe. Just maybe," he mused, leaning back in his chair to digest Gunther Pratt's material. The man could have the answer without realizing it.

Gunther Pratt…the frustrated man who put his hand up Rebecca's dress in a hurried frenzy to make love. What a crazy misguided bastard!

"Who are you to talk?" he chastised himself. "Weren't you just as hungry? What dumb ass?" He continued castigating his actions of the emotional night, when the ringing phone jarred his thoughts.

"What?" he yelled into the receiver.

"Don't what me!" Corky roared back. "Every case hits the outhouse at some point."

"And what makes you say that?" Clisten snapped.

"It's either that or Cinderella's getting to you."

"You're right. The lead didn't pan out."

"Nothing on the murdered woman?"

"No. But now I have a file that Tony requested. Without my knowledge, of course."

"You mean of the two dead leads?"

"Uh-huh. One came through."

"And you think it'll lead us to finding phony Tony."

"Why would he send the file to his home address? He didn't want me to know the lead was real. No. The link is there. He'll try to find Rebecca Givens on his own. Although Amy Gregson used her as a reference at the college, my gut tells me there's something deeper between them. So, what do you think?" After getting no response, Clisten asked, "What's happening on your end?"

"I checked my partner's last watering hole. He was celebrating his departure with the whole joint."

"And?"

"Some of the regulars say he left with a man to go meet some babes. It was the last time they saw either of them. Since everyone knew about Tony's transfer, they figured he had already left town."

"Were they able to identify the man?"

"Only by John Landis. I showed them phony Tony's picture on my phone. The one you sent me."

"The name and picture matched."

"Exactly. But I've got nothing. Nothing on the data base either. I'm back to scrubbing my partner's place again." Clisten could hear the frustration in the man's gravelly voice.

"I'm thinking of going to High Coventry on Saturday to see a man who worked with Rebecca Givens. If I question him in person, he might remember things that could help me find her. I know Tony has to be looking for the woman too."

"You think Tony's in High Coventry? How far is it from you?"

"Ninety miles, maybe."

"And you think he's there."

"I can't be certain, but it's the only lead we share. What would you think?"

"Just keep your phone on, Romeo!"

"Then quit dropping my shorts." Clisten laughed as he ended their conversation.

Corky wasn't laughing. His thoughts were on High Coventry.

Clisten leaned back in his chair once again to read the file on Rebecca Givens, yet his thoughts couldn't erase Corky's frustration. There was nothing more he could do. Clisten had to find Tony, arrest him for impersonating an officer, and then Corky could charge him for the murder of his partner.

Clisten's thoughts shifted to his own dead partner. If only he had evidence. Nothing could change his mind. Leggin's mugging was a murder. A murder committed by phony Tony. He was sure of it but needed proof.

It was in that vein that Clisten turned to Rebecca Givens' folder. He had to find the woman. His gut told him she was the key to finding Tony and the hidden story of Amy Gregson, the woman of changed identities.

"Identities," he mused. "Maybe. Just maybe, there was someone he overlooked."

Clisten felt somewhat smug as he snapped the file picture of Rebecca Givens on his cell phone. Why had he not thought of it before?

"Because you didn't have her photograph," an inner voice answered his question.

"Well, now, I do and someone close to the Gregson woman might be able to help me," he said aloud, checking his watch. "She should be home. It's dinnertime."

Within minutes, Clisten slid the file inside the desk drawer, grabbed his jacket and sailed out of the building.

"Well, I certainly didn't expect to see you," a surprised Mrs. Benson greeted the detective from the door of her apartment.

"I don't understand." Clisten studied the gray-haired woman with interest. Granted, she had said some very strange things during their first encounter, but her mind was not completely addled with age. He was certain of that.

"The other detective." She reminded him. "You came together when Amy's apartment was ransacked. I heard a noise over there this afternoon, so I knocked on the door. He told me it was a routine inspection. What with the taped door, I guess you must be careful who goes in there. I mean, other than the police."

"We do have to be careful that way," Clisten repeated her words, knowing this information changed his primary reason for being there.

"If he already checked it, why are you here?"

"I remembered seeing some legal documents that could help our investigation," he said, making his reason sound plausible, "but I must have left the duplicate key at the station. Then I remembered Miss Hale telling me you had a spare." As Clisten spoke, he knew phony Tony did not have a key; the felon used other means.

"Just a minute," she closed the door only to return seconds later. "You will return this." She held the key tightly in her hand.

"Of course." Without her knowledge, Mrs. Benson had given the detective more information than she realized.

✍

Clisten spent a great deal of time in Amy Gregson's vandalized apartment. He went from room to room, searching for clues to Tony's treasure hunt. What was the man looking for? More important, what was left there to chance a break-in? Although his story to Mrs. Benson sounded plausible, the link was there. The object of his search was connected to Amy.

After inspecting the entire apartment and finding nothing, Clisten found himself in the woman's ransacked bedroom where his eyes fell on two heaps of shoes from an open closet. And remembering Bill Thistle's description of Amy Gregson's slight handicap, noted that every padded left shoe sat in one pile while its companion, the other. Did Tony inspect all of Amy Gregson's shoes or just the padded ones? Studying one left shoe would be enough for identification purposes, while two could prove further confirmation. But why inspect all of them? There had to be another reason. Had the woman hidden something beneath the pad in one of her shoes? That seemed to be the only logical explanation for the extensive search. Yet, Clisten would never know for certain, unless he found and questioned his false partner. His eyes moved away from the mounds of shoes to the rest of the clutter-filled room.

As his thoughts shifted, memories began to flood his mind. He remembered sitting on the bed with a gross-smelling, garment-stained Twilla Hale going through papers on Lily. Little did he know then just how vulnerable she would make him feel.

Clisten shook his head as if to dust the cobwebs from his thoughts and concentrated on searching the bedroom furniture, starting with the dresser. As he went through each of the drawers sequentially, he noticed a few of the contents had spilled on the floor.

In his attempt to right the tossed items to their respective drawers, the label of a multi-colored scarf caught Clisten's eye. It read 'The Market Shop at Coventry.' Clisten folded the scarf carefully and slipped it into his jacket pocket. Could this be a clue to finding Rebecca Givens?

"No. That would be too easy," he said aloud. Still he wondered what Tony had found and then realized several more accessories had the same label. Had Tony noticed them too? He had the Givens' file. Gunther Pratt attested to that. Perhaps the trip to High Coventry would prove fruitful in finding Tony after all. The man was nowhere to be found in town.

Clisten was certain of that. It wasn't often he searched the 'hellholes' that edged legality. However, in trying to find Tony, he walked that invisible line and sought cooperation in that endeavor. If Tony had been hiding in Stockton, he would have been unearthed by those Clisten helped in trying times.

"There's nothing here," he said, dismissing the bedroom from his thoughts. He walked toward a small desk in the living room and emptied the paper contents of a middle drawer. "When I return the key, I'll need these to 'back up' my story."

In less than two minutes, Clisten Barr stood at the door of Mrs. Benson's apartment, equipped with a bunch of Amy Gregson's class schedules.

"I take it, you found what you were looking for." Mrs. Benson took the offered key, just as the phone rang, giving Clisten the opportunity to enter her apartment.

"Yes. I can watch Lily." She listened carefully to the other end of the conversation. "I can do that."

"That was Twilla Hale," she said after ending the call. "I'm going next door and I don't want to be arrested." She challenged him abruptly. "Some of Lily's toys are still there."

"Is Lily staying with you?" He ignored her testy attitude.

"Just for an overnight. Twilla's leaving Saturday morning and asked me to babysit. God knows I love that sweet dog."

"Yes. She is very gentle," Clisten agreed before changing the subject. "Did Miss Hale say where she was going? She's supposed to check with me before leaving town." Catching the woman's quizzical look, he added, "The Gregson case is still open."

"Twilla's going to a spa. Where? I don't know. Ask her yourself, if that's the law." She shrugged her shoulders. Then being very dismissive, said, "I see you got the papers you wanted."

"Some. But not all for the estate." Clisten reached into his pocket for his cell phone and displayed a picture of Rebecca Givens. "Have you ever seen this woman with Amy Gregson?"

Mrs. Benson reached for her glasses on a lamp table to study the picture. "No. I can't say that I have. Is she dead too?"

"I have no idea."

"Did you ask Twilla? She may know her."

"That's a very good thought," he said, thanking her.

'The woman was a shrewd old bird,' Clisten mused as he walked to his car. His years of experience told him to be patient, wait and watch.

Within ten minutes, the detective was following a car to a nearby hotel. He entered the lobby from a side door to watch a woman make a call from a nearby telephone booth.

The case was getting more interesting by the minute. Was she calling Herman Banks or Rebecca Givens? Clisten would know soon enough. The phone company kept track of public numbers as a matter of record.

So, what was Twilla Hale's involvement in this? There was more to the story than the one given to Mrs. Benson. That she was going to a spa for an overnight did not fit the behavioral pattern of someone who ignored every grace of cultured appearance.

He pictured a distraught Twilla Hale in a sauce-splattered shirt and spaghetti sauce edging the corners of her mouth, as she rushed to him with an urgent kiss holding a message. Twilla wanted protection from Russell; yet in the end, she wanted him. He tried dismissing the wanton emotion surging deep within him. Somehow, some way, he had to stop thinking about her.

Where was she really going for an overnight? What spa, if her story rang true? He knew of only one within driving distance of an overnight. Would she be staying at the hotel nearby? He could check on that easily enough. At precisely that moment, Clisten's thoughts were interrupted by Mrs. Benson exiting the hotel.

Following her again proved uneventful since it led him back to her apartment at Ravencrest. Since nothing further would happen that evening, it was time he went home.

SIXTEEN

PLANS

On a freaky whim, Twilla drove to the town's beauty salon after depositing the inventory file into her safety deposit box late Friday morning. She had not planned on getting a new hairdo or a manicure, for that matter. But the night with Clisten Barr kept creeping into her thoughts, and she needed to do something about her looks, particularly after his remark about her appearance, notably, the spaghetti sauce on her face and shirt. The remark made her wonder again if other people, particularly faculty members, looked at her that way too. Was she just another academic drudge whose work was more important than her appearance? How ridiculous! She had beautiful clothes, ones Twilla wore to church. Still, they were nothing compared to her sister's stock of coordinated outfits.

However, those thoughts soon evaporated once she saw the softer look of her new hairdo. Yes. She was very pleased at the 'new Twilla.' Now, she really had to do something about her wardrobe and thought of visiting the dress shop nearby. Those thoughts, however, were interrupted by a man halting her.

"Hey, Twilla, you didn't answer my memo."

"Memo?" she questioned. "I don't remember getting a memo from you, Delsin."

"I put the reminder in your office mailbox. We're doing the floors tomorrow. We scheduled the date months ago. Don't you remember?"

"I must be losing it. I completely forgot."

"Just don't plan on working there. It'll be a mess."

"I won't be in town."

"An escape, I hope."

"Just a Saturday overnight."

"Sometimes, a one-nighter works out better than extended stays. Have fun." He patted her shoulder. "I'll see you Monday."

Twilla watched the man walk away before entering the dress shop. And as expected, the balance of her checkbook was much less when she left.

When Twilla got home, thoughts of her new clothes completely vanished once she pulled the hidden list from the cookbook. However, while she was examining the material for High Coventry, Lily started pawing her legs and whining loudly. Twilla knew then she would have to delay the undertaking and slipped the paper into her purse.

"You want some attention, don't you?" She scratched Lily's head. "Being by yourself all day gets lonely." Her voice fell soft with understanding. "Would you like to see Sam?"

That universal language triggered an immediate emotion. At the mere mention of his name, Lily's flagged tail wagged profusely as she raced toward the door.

"Just a minute, young lady!" Twilla stopped the dog in her tracks. "I can't forget this." She grabbed the leash off the hook and bundled Lily in her arms. Once Twilla opened the car door, Lily scampered inside and began to bark.

"OK." Twilla turned on the ignition. "Captain Kirk's Starship is heading to Tavis Lake. Now stop barking!"

Lily became quiet and subdued as they drove along the highway; however, once they reached Tavis Lake, she bolted from the car and raced along the scattered benches until she found a sleeping Sam and started licking his face.

"You better get used to it," Pete greeted her as she finally reached his bench, leash in hand. "Maybe it's puppy love." The thought made him laugh. "Look at the way she sits between his paws and licks his face. To let her do that Sam has to lie prone. So, we know they're enjoying each other."

"True but she's not getting any exercise."

"You're missing the point. It's so obvious. She wants his company, not exercise. He fulfills some sort of need. Lily must be left alone most of the day."

"That's true. I leave the TV on when I'm gone, but it's not the same as real companionship."

"They seem contented. We should leave it at that."

"Of course, you're right." She agreed reluctantly, before changing the subject. "Have you learned anything new?"

"I'm getting there," he reassured her. "It'll take time, but I think I understand why your friend did not return the file."

"What do you mean?"

"I may not be the shiniest nickel, but I do know theft when I see it. It's small change but that's the beauty of it. Nothing would be noticed unless someone like Amy got Shelden's file and started tracking the inventory."

"I don't understand."

"Think about it this way. Say every couple of years, your department head replaces some equipment from Amy's lab or the home management houses. And say, maybe she used this replaced equipment, like a refrigerator, in a summer home or gave it to relatives. Or suppose," Pete held up a finger to further explain, "a piece of new equipment, again a refrigerator, was listed on the inventory but never made it to Amy's lab. We're talking stoves, refrigerators, washers, dryers, dishwashers. All major appliances."

"Essentially, you're saying the file is a fabrication. Regardless of the time frame or unaccounted number, equipment was kept, given away or sold one piece at a time."

"I can't think of it any other way. What was missing from the lab or home management houses, over a span of twenty or more years, was so insignificant, there was no real oversight. But one thing is certain: she had an accomplice. Shelden couldn't have moved this stuff alone."

"Who? Why?" Twilla gasped in shock. "She has it made. Everyone respects her."

"That's the point. Who would ever suspect Shelden of altering an inventory or stealing her own equipment? Of course, we know what she's done. Now, I have to learn who else is involved."

"Amy must have known something was wrong."

"Shelden really screwed-up when she inadvertently gave Amy the file. To say the woman must be nervous is an understatement. If the college discovers her theft, she's fired."

"Are you going to report it?"

"It'll get resolved," he ignored the question. "I'm more concerned about you. Someone must think you have it."

"You're referring to the break-in?"

"Exactly. It will happen again, if it hasn't already."

"The file's not there. It's in my safety deposit box."

"Good girl." Pete glowed. "Now I want you to position any papers or files inside your desk drawers at home. Arrange them carefully, so you'll know if anything's been moved. I'm sure your office has been searched by now."

"Don't you think I'd know if someone searched my office?"

"Not with the kind of skills I'm talking about," he cautioned. "Right now, Shelden can't take chances. She'll send someone to search your condo again and it will be thorough."

"Then how would I know if my unit's been searched?"

"You wouldn't unless the person gets sloppy. That's the reason for the desk arrangement." Pete drove his point home. "Once the hammer comes down, it will all be out in the open and you won't be connected. Your boss will think Amy sent the file to someone with clout."

"You really think so?"

"Yes. I really do. That's why you're going to forget all about this, once I have the original."

His overly concern made Twilla wonder if he had withheld something more from her, and she felt the need to press him again. "Your investigation is further along than you led me to believe."

"Twilla. It's Friday!" He groaned loudly, wanting to end the discussion. For safety purposes, it was better that she knew nothing more about the investigation. If questioned by her boss, Twilla would have nothing to offer, no slip of the tongue. "Take the weekend off. Go somewhere with Lily. I don't want you worrying about this."

"As a matter of fact, I'm staying at the big hotel in High Coventry Saturday night. I'm thinking of doing their spa, but didn't make an appointment, so that may not happen."

"Sometimes change is good, like your new hairdo. You didn't think I noticed, did you?" He acknowledged her surprise. "Twilla, you are a very pretty lady. Too bad I don't know anybody young enough to appreciate you." His words trailed off, as if his thoughts were scattered elsewhere; and then, just as abruptly, he focused on her again. "Same time Monday?"

"Around two o'clock?"

"Don't forget to bring the original file," he reminded, "and remember to fix your desk."

Pete turned his attention to the sleeping dogs and said, "Come Sam. It's time to go home. You'll see Lily next week."

After leashing the dogs and a few words of farewell, they walked away in different directions: A Sheepdog happily keeping pace with his master and a whimpering Peekapoo saddened by their parting.

"Come Lily. You'll see Sam again on Monday." She encouraged the dog as they walked to the car. "Are you hungry or just getting horny? I'm getting a little worried about your carrying-on with Sam," she continued to drone. "We should definitely have a conversation about the birds and bees."

Then in an aside, added, "What do I know about the birds and bees? The birds, if there were ever any, flew away a long time ago, and the bees were never interested in my hive, so what the hell am I talking about?"

She looked down at Lily walking so gingerly beside her, and said, "Do dog owners have this kind of conversation with their pets? They must have at some point. Don't you think so?"

Twilla thought about her statement for a moment. *Of course, they do. They're aware of the signals, those signs of interest. The vet wouldn't have a clue of Sam's sex appeal. Still, maybe Pete was right. Sam was big, broad, and very protective. Maybe he was Lily's boy toy after all and she was just a shameless flirt.*

Twilla continued her stare. Who would have thought it? *Her precious Lily…turning into a brazen slut!*

Suddenly, Lily stopped abruptly, as if she had read Twilla's thoughts, and focusing her two black eyes on her, sat down and would not move.

"I'm sorry," Twilla pleaded. But she knew her thoughts were not forgiven as she watched Lily lift her leg and water her shoes.

Twilla studied her wet sneakers, a deep frown crossing her face. "OK. I'll give you that one!" She scolded, taking a few more steps forward. "Now get in the car."

A short time after dinner, Twilla began checking her purse for item confirmation. She pulled a picture from her wallet and studied the photograph of Amy with an older woman. Could the clues from the cookbook lead Twilla to this woman in High Coventry? The town was the only location given in the entire assortment of clues. It was the only thing that made sense. She had three major things to work with: a name, Ruth Graham; an address, A1 Brindle Street and the location, High Coventry. If Twilla went to this address in High Coventry, would the pictured woman be there? She had to try.

It seemed too easy, yet she had no other alternative. She had to follow the clues. That was it. There was nothing more she could do. Twilla folded the material, slid the picture back into her wallet and stashed everything into her handbag. It was time to move on to her next order of business: the desk drawer.

She began by positioning the few folders and tablets inside the center desk drawer. Of three pencils lying there, Twilla placed two side-by-side with the third topping between them pyramid fashion. She closed the drawer carefully before opening it again. The pencils had not moved. Perfect, she thought. Then Twilla inverted the upper pencil and set the pyramid right once more. Completely satisfied with the arrangement, she closed the drawer slowly.

Although she completed the task as Pete instructed, Twilla felt she needed more evidence to indicate a break-in, something a little different.

When her eyes fell on the wastebasket near the desk, an idea popped into her mind. She wedged it between the desk leg and companion chair. The arrangement looked like a haphazard move of someone in a hurry. Anyone seeing the jammed wastebasket would think nothing of it; but she had to test her theory. When she pulled the chair from the desk to get into the middle drawer, the wastebasket moved back toward the wall without making a sound on the carpet.

A look of profound satisfaction crossed her face. She could dismiss worrying about a break-in and concentrate on finding Mark.

Of course, Twilla was never aware of the car that had been following her lately or of the driver who seemed to know her daily schedule. Nor did she know that her condo had been quietly searched while she was at Tavis Lake that afternoon. But Twilla did think it strange when Lily went into hiding as soon as they got home. Had someone been there…searching her unit?

Coaxing her Peekapoo from under the bed took forever. She thought of calling Clisten Barr, but that idea soon vanished when a shaken Lily raced into her arms and caused her to wonder what triggered the reaction in the first place. Twilla had seen her bundle of joy shaken once before…but that was when her condo had been burglarized. She had no suspicions then.

But Twilla was not without suspicions now. Those included Russell's bank of lies, ones he told Julie, before visiting her with his outrageous declarations. There had to be a reason for his visits or the man was a nut. She had made it very clear: he wasn't getting any part of her.

Twilla wasn't interested in pursuing his motives for visiting her. Her concern was his pretended interest in Julie and the amount of heartache he would inflict with that fabrication. Maybe Pete could help her expose him as the collective rat he was. She had to stop thinking about this. What if it wasn't Russell at all? What if everything was connected to Amy's murder?

Twilla had to stop thinking about Russell and Pete. She had to concentrate on finding Mark. Twilla couldn't tell Pete her real reason for going to High Coventry. He would have discouraged her from the start: *It's too dangerous a trip with so little to go on.* She could hear him now. But then again, Twilla wondered if her actions were even legal.

Regardless of outcome, Twilla could not tell anyone her real reason for going to High Coventry. She thought about the man in the long coat when she held a dying Amy in her arms. Did he have a role in her murder? Was he also searching for Ruth Graham in his effort to find Mark? But even more important, would he be in High Coventry too?

Suddenly, her thoughts turned to Clisten and their night together. Russell's contrived overtures were no longer in her thoughts.

Within a short while, Twilla and Lily lay entwined asleep.

Twilla had little knowledge of the feigned lover's pretense and less of the man following her.

What was at stake for one was much different from the other. *Yet the importance for each was the same.*

SEVENTEEN

FRIDAY

Tony's search of Amy Gregson's apartment weighed heavily on Clisten's mind as he sat on his favorite lounge chair in the living room of his home.

It was fortunate that Mrs. Benson mentioned him. Otherwise, Clisten would never have known the man was still in town. So where had he been hiding? The detective had combed the whole town looking for him without success. With his connections, someone would have contacted him. Of that Clisten was certain. He had done too many favors over the years: looked the other way, in what could have been embarrassing or bordering illegal situations.

Still, what was Tony looking for? What was so important that he risked going there? Had he found the fruits of his search? What had Amy left behind to chance discovery? Was it enough to kill for? Was it a motive for murder? As these thoughts rattled his brain, a pattern began to emerge.

Somewhere, somehow, Amy Gregson and Clisten's fake partner were linked. It had to be a relationship of sorts, maybe even marriage. Whether it existed before or after the woman's cosmetic surgery was an unknown. However, since the x-rays showed multiple fractures and bruising, the link between them probably occurred before surgery. If true, then Tony would have known the history of the woman's tormented past. And perhaps, it was the battered woman syndrome that eventually caused her to run.

At that juncture the story became more definitive.

After repeated assaults, Amy Gregson devised a plan to escape her miserable existence. It had to be unique and strategically safe for the long haul, which meant forever or a long, long time. And she had to have help to accomplish a clean getaway.

Somehow, after a successful escape, the woman immediately put a second part of her plan into action. She underwent a complete change of identity, *including cosmetic surgery*, and then moved to a location she felt safe from discovery.

That part of the scenario led to several questions.

To get a new identity, her documents had to be forged. So, she needed someone who could do that kind of work. The young woman must have known people with questionable connections or had friends working that route for her. However, which group selected was of little consequence. *That she had help was of greater importance, and it became abundantly clear that Amy had a circle of people protecting her.* But why? The concern for protection led Clisten to pursue another avenue regarding the woman's identity.

Amy Gregson could not have had cosmetic surgery without someone helping her during the healing process. Discovery at that time would have exposed her entire plan and placed her life in jeopardy. The identity change, which had been kept so secret, was too important at that venture. Amy had to rely on someone she trusted implicitly, someone who would lock those secrets forever. The only name that came to mind was Rebecca Givens, the referral used on Amy Gregson's job application at Stockton. That thought turned Clisten's mind inward.

Of all the cities across the country, how was his town chosen? Were others considered, ones thought safe from discovery? Was the list of those locations also matched with available jobs?

Clisten scratched his head, leaned back in his chair again and began to review his former thoughts.

If Amy had to select a location, one considered safe and had job opportunities, how did she whittle down the list of cities to Stockton? Was the small size or remote location the major factor in selecting this town? A small private college could easily be overlooked by someone searching crowded cities for lost people.

Then Clisten recalled Amy Gregson's referral by Rebecca Givens and Stockton's proximity to High Coventry, the town where the older woman worked as an administrator in its very prestigious and elite women's college. Obviously, a connection between them existed. It was the only thing that made sense. That being the case, Dr. Givens must have arranged a teaching job for Amy Gregson as part of her escape plan. The woman may have even padded her teaching credentials. But why go to that extreme?

There could be only one answer. The two women were related and the battered one needed protection.

Clisten sat quietly in thought, trying to digest the scenarios that crossed his mind. If the planned escape had been carefully executed and in place for at least seven years, including the year of healing, how had Tony found her? Had he conducted a search by questioning every known relative and friend? If the pursuit led him to Stockton, how did he identify her? Then Clisten remembered his conversation with Bill Thistle at the morgue. After locating the woman, her slight gait could be his confirmation. Still, why was it so important to find Amy Gregson, and what went so wrong that led to her exposure and murder?

Was there something he overlooked? Was there another motive for her escape, one that demanded more protection? She had been assaulted so many times. He had seen the X-rays. But was that the only reason she ran away? Clisten began to have doubts. No. The woman was hiding something: something Tony desperately wanted, something worth killing for. That thought led him to another avenue.

After finding Amy, did he stalk the woman to ascertain her daily schedule and then comb her apartment without fear of discovery?

Of course, in his search, Tony had to be careful not to disturb anything. Unfortunately, he was totally unaware of the dog. That intrusion caused a small, frightened Lily to hide under the bed, while retaining the smell of a very bad man.

Clisten based that evidence on Lily's trembling behavior when she rushed into his arms after Twilla Hale's unit had been vandalized. His fake partner was there during the investigation, along with the smell of musk. He must have ransacked the Hale unit in search of something connected to Amy.

The Gregson's apartment entered his thoughts again. In his continued hurry to find the object of his search, did Tony pillage the place before or after the shooting? Although Clisten had no factual evidence, he theorized it occurred before her death for two reasons.

When Clisten and Tony went to the Gregson's apartment shortly after the shooting, the apartment had already been vandalized.

Clisten believed the woman knew her apartment had been quietly searched long before the obvious ransacking took place. *Not only did Amy Gregson know the perpetrator, she also knew the purpose of his search. Her life, as she knew it, was over.*

Had Amy alerted someone? Perhaps she did. However, in doing so, she would have cautioned those who helped her to close ranks. But why? The woman was dead. Why make the investigation so difficult? Why couldn't he get answers to simple questions? Since he was being stonewalled at every turn, Clisten began a question and answer review.

Why did Tony search her apartment initially? Obviously, Amy had hidden something he wanted, something so important, that on his second try, he ransacked the apartment that very morning before shooting her.

Then again, how did the murder fit into the equation? Finding the battered woman just to kill her defied common sense. Since Tony just checked the apartment again, that alone meant he hadn't found the object of his earlier searches. And if his intent was to kill her anyhow, it would have been much more logical to do it after he had the object in his possession.

"No." Something drove him to kill her before he found the object of his search. "But what," he mused. "What happened to make him alter his plan? It had to have been sudden, unexpected and threatening."

Then, it hit him. Only one reason made sense.

In disguising her identity, she discovered his. Amy must have seen him in town with Clisten and noticed his standing as part of the police force. Once Tony discovered she had seen him, he ran out of options. What could he do? Phony Tony could not allow her to reveal his identity fraud, particularly after murdering Leggin and Corky's partner. Silencing her immediately was his only option and, having followed her previously, he was well-aware of her daily ninety-minute breakfast routine. Clisten would include those facts in his report.

The morning after Amy had discovered his fraudulent identity and while eating her early restaurant breakfast, Tony ransacked her apartment and then waited until she crossed the quadrangle before shooting her.

Still the question remained. What was the secret Tony searched for and why did three people have to die in that quest? Clisten was determined to find the answer.

His thoughts turned to Amy Gregson. What was her mental state after seeing Tony? He suspected shock and fear. The man had found her after seven years of a lethal hunt. The woman had no choice. She would expose the fraudulent detective and take her chances with the law as a battered woman. That he would be sentenced could give her time to start over in a new city. Of course, she would have no knowledge of his murdering two men. Her concern would be acquiring a new identity and hiding the secret Tony wanted.

Then Clisten remembered his own visit after Tony's search that day. An array of scarves crowded one dresser drawer and he slipped one of them into his trouser pocket. All of them had The High Coventry Shop label as the boutique of purchase. Was that coincidence or a shopping habit? Nevertheless, it could be a lead. Did Tony notice the labels too?

From that observation, Clisten realized one glaring fact: everything led to High Coventry and a recap of that investigation began.

Gunther Pratt knew and loved Rebecca Givens, the retired administrator at High Coventry. As requested, he sent Clisten her file. A week or so earlier, the man sent the same school records to Tony. Of course, the man never acknowledged the file. However, Clisten did learn the woman's true status after Tony skipped, but it was of little consequence since he could not locate her.

This was the same Rebecca Givens who gave Amy Gregson a reference for her teaching position at Stockton College. Then too, she must have accompanied the young teacher to the dog breeder's farm for Lily. And despite the man's pleas of ignorance, Herman Banks, the breeder, was there somewhere in the mix. *Was he the one Mrs. Benson called from the hotel?* Once Clisten had the phone records he would know for certain. Although it would merely confirm a line of contact, the game Mrs. Benson played was not new to the seasoned detective. Herman Banks was the intermediary. After Mrs. Benson's phone call, he was to give Rebecca Givens an update of the visit to Amy's apartment by two detectives that day. *Had they found something new*? This, Clisten clearly understood. What he did not understand was the loose cannon who could muddy the waters: Twilla Hale.

Why was she going to the spa in High Coventry for an over-night? Why now? Was there something she had to do that specific weekend? Something for Amy? Did he have to follow her too?

Once again, everything pointed to High Coventry. Regardless of outcome, he was going there tomorrow.

His thoughts suddenly shifted to Corky. There was no point in alerting him since Clisten had no idea where Tony was now. Clisten had been everywhere in that endeavor. However, at this point, the detective believed two things.

If Tony's search that day proved fruitful, the man would be long gone and good luck in finding him. If not, Tony would be looking for Rebecca Givens in the event Amy Gregson gave her information or something of value. The woman's life would be in danger but neither Mrs. Benson nor Herman Banks would be aware of that. They were more concerned with what the detectives found in Amy's apartment. It all seemed to fit.

What didn't fit was Twilla Hale.

That Twilla Hale knew much more than she told the detective the day of Amy's murder weighed heavily on his mind now. He remembered telling Tony that same thing, adding he would get her to talk in the setting of her home. That was the night he took the vase to her unit. That was also the night Tony skipped town. That too was the night...

Clisten had to forget Twilla Hale and that night. He had to concentrate on the facts as he saw them. If he was so convinced she knew something, Tony would share that same thought. Had he searched her unit a second time? There was no report of it being vandalized again.

"What's the matter with me?" He smacked his forehead, chastising himself. "There would be no trace. A clandestine search would be clean, swift and without a hint of intrusion." Yet, whether it happened was of no consequence now. It brought nothing to the table.

Clisten began shaping the puzzle pieces when he remembered a shaken Lily racing into his arms. Twilla had tried coaxing her from under the bed as he recalled. Now it all added up. A logical sequence unfolded.

It began when Tony conducted a quiet yet fruitless search of Amy's apartment for something she had hidden. That caused Lily to hide under the bed the first time. *Clisten felt certain Amy was aware something was not right.*

Then Tony ransacked Amy's apartment the day of her murder. Again, to no avail. That's when Twilla Hale appeared on the scene to take custody of Lily. Then, thinking there was a relationship between the two colleagues, Tony ransacked the Hale unit. After finding nothing, he did a third search of Gregson's apartment that very day. That was the one that mattered.

Did Tony find the object of his search? Was it the motive for Amy Gregson's murder? He would soon know.

The answer pointed to High Coventry.

Clisten planned to question Guenther Pratt again with the hope of learning more about Rebecca Givens. Although the man answered all his phone questions, a face-to-face conversation usually elicited information long forgotten or thought to be of little consequence. Anything the man remembered could be helpful in locating the woman. He was not concerned about the interview. It was the other thing gnawing his brain.

He was worried that Twilla Hale was also going to High Coventry. If Tony's search for Rebecca Givens failed, Twilla Hale would be his last and only link to Amy, her contacts and the hidden object he sought. He would have to follow her.

Clisten had the strongest urge to call but decided against it. Instead, he would make a point of meeting her accidentally. Through conversation, Clisten would determine her real reason for being there while trying to protect her. He was certain the spa trip was just a cover. Why was she doing this? Why was she making him so crazy?

He pulled the cell phone from his pocket and tapped-in a number. "Yes. Detective Barr here from Stockton. I want to check a reservation."

EIGHTEEN

HIGH COVENTRY

C listen left his home early Saturday morning with two priorities: the first was to question Gunther Pratt further on Rebecca
Givens; the second was to uncover Twilla Hale's real reason for
going to High Coventry. This time he was determined to get the
information she withheld.

Upon entering the small town, he checked his map then
turned into the parking lot behind the Coventry Hotel on High
Street, a heavy traffic road running parallel to Coventry Avenue,
the main artery that crossed the bustling community with its
busy shops and restaurants.

As he drove slowly between the rows of parked cars, searching
for an empty space, Clisten caught sight of a small black Chevy
that had a Stockton decal on the back window. Bingo! The car
belonged to Twilla Hale. Coincidences like that did not happen
that often, particularly with his track record. Still, he would check
the vehicle before going into the hotel.

He continued driving slowly when a tan Toyota also caught
his attention. The vehicle which was parked five cars away from
the Chevy fronted a two-car formation and could move-out at a
moment's notice.

Instinctively, Clisten knew the car belonged to Tony. His fake
partner took that specific parking space to follow Twilla Hale in
the hope she would lead him to…what?

Granted, Clisten mentioned the woman's withholding information, but he never intimated that it would lead them to High Coventry. Why would he? His concern was getting Twilla Hale to divulge some secret information about her colleague, not some town ninety miles away.

Clisten circled the row that held Tony's car for a parking space. Finding one, Clisten sat quietly for a moment and then reached into his glove compartment for Leggin's switchblade knife as a justification for his actions. He slipped it into his pocket, locked the car and walked slowly toward the Toyota.

A few minutes later he returned to his car, slid the knife back into the glove compartment and tapped a number on his cell phone.

"Where the hell are you, you dumb SOB?" Corky growled loudly.

"Where the hell do you think I am? I told you I was going to High Coventry on a hunch."

"No. That's not right," his growl corrected. "You were going there to interview a man Tony already contacted."

"That's true. But I'm calling you because I found Tony's car. He's here… somewhere. I'm calling the local police for help."

"Where's the car?"

"In the hotel parking lot, why?"

"Because we're inside the hotel."

"We?"

"Stop with the questions. I'll wave when we get to the back door for the parking lot. You flag us to the car."

Within minutes, Clisten waved to a man that fit Corky's imaginary description. Accompanying the hefty middle-aged man was a humongous giant with a tank-like body.

"This is Lupo." Frank Corky greeted Clisten with a handshake. "He plays the ponies when he's not patrolling the streets."

As he turned to acknowledge the man, Lupo's large out-stretched hand completely engulfed Clisten's and began pumping it.

"That's quite a grip you got there," Clisten quipped, wondering if his cramped fingers would ever feel the same again.

"He's good at everything." Corky agreed, totally unaware of the detective's true feelings. "So, where's the car?"

Clisten passed several parked cars then stopped at a vehicle next to the tan Toyota. "I don't know if we're being watched, but it's that one." As his fingers pointed across and downward to Tony's lifeless car, Clisten was stopped from saying anything further.

"That's my partner's car with new plates!" Corky shouted loud enough to draw the attention of people parking nearby. "He must know lots of felons." The detective lowered his voice. "I can't wait to get my hands on the son of a bitch."

"Enough." Lupo held him in check. "You said by the book." Lupo then turned to Clisten and waited for him to finish his narrative.

"When you inspect the trunk, I think you'll find a high-powered rifle. It's the one that killed Amy Gregson. I think he planned to use it again. That's why he kept it."

"On you?" Corky expressed surprise.

"The woman I'm looking for. This time I may have help."

"He's got a flat tire." Lupo interrupted their conversation.

"Imagine that," Corky snickered as he turned to Clisten. "How do you want to handle this, you sneaky Barr Bell?"

"If Tony hasn't seen us, we should wait to arrest him. If he has, the car is of no consequence. He'll leave it."

"Since he knows you're looking for him, wouldn't it be better if you go inside and Lupo and I waited out here? We can identify him from the picture you sent, but he doesn't know us. It would be good if you could steer him to the parking lot. With a flat tire, he can't go anywhere unless on foot. My car's parked in the row behind this one if he runs. I think it's better that way."

Clisten was slow to respond. That he was not in agreement with Corky's plan was obvious. "It doesn't seem right, somehow. Neither of us has jurisdiction. I'm surprised you're here."

"Everything pointed to this place. The two of you...here at the same time. I think he's been in hiding all this time, watching and waiting for you to make a move. By coming here you'll make him bolt. It's the only thing that adds up. The man you're interviewing has to be the common denominator."

"He will think I have new information on the case."

"True. But don't underestimate him. This is the man who manipulated our files and killed my partner."

"And mine," Clisten interrupted him. "If I can't prove he murdered Leggin, he'll pay for killing the Gregson woman."

"That's what I've been saying. Go talk to your sources. We can take care of him with the locals."

Clisten checked his watch. "It's almost ten. I have to interview two people."

"Get the evidence to build your case. A stake out for us is no big deal. I'll text you with an update."

"Make sure you open the trunk before they impound the car," Clisten was emphatic. "Take pictures of everything but bag the rifle. That son of a bitch is not going to get away this time around." Although he spoke to Corky, his thoughts were on Leggin.

As they watched the detective walk toward the hotel, Lupo said, "The man's sharp. He didn't want us to be alone with Tony Baloney and you know it."

"I never said he was a jerk."

"Then why did he go?"

"He's leaving the decision up to me."

"Are you going to kill him?"

"Is his tire flat?"

Lupo always had a deep understanding of flat tires.

Upon entering Corky's car, they sat in silence waiting for the man to appear, neither truly prepared for the outcome. Would they need handcuffs or a gun?

Lupo knew the frustration and rage his friend suffered. It had been a subject many at the station whispered about when Frank Corky wasn't around. But even in their quiet moments, all of them wanted a piece of the imposter who killed their colleague and friend.

Lupo could understand Corky's wanting to kill the perp. Aside from a deep sense of satisfaction, it would be the sweetest taste of revenge, an iced cake full of bullet holes.

Maybe so, but probably not. But then, who really knew?

When Clisten entered the hotel from the back-parking lot, he faced a wide carpeted hall, hanging chandeliers and a series of doors along a corridor that opened to both meeting rooms and those reserved for more festive occasions, commonly known as ballrooms.

He turned the corner slowly, thinking Tony might be lurking somewhere nearby; however, what he faced was a large bank of elevators. Now, Clisten needed some perspective on the hotel layout.

To get to the main reception area of the hotel, away from the elevators, hotel guests had to climb a wide marble step, which stretched the entire breadth of that section. On the landing stood three marble columns, Ionic in design and only there for show, its utilitarian purpose was to create an aura of grandeur.

Clisten popped his head around one of the columns for a further peek at the reception area. From his vantage point, a low-walled dining room filled with clattering noises and chatting people seemed to fill the left side of the enormous lobby. The cocktail lounge, which stood adjacent the restaurant, had a few patrons sitting at scattered tables, while a bearded man at the very end of the curved bar seemed to be enjoying his morning paper.

Directly across from both the dining room and cocktail lounge stood a large concierge desk and a very long reception counter, behind which stood four employees. A small gift shop cornering the room was only a few feet away from one of the pillared columns.

Of course, in the middle of the lobby were countless easy chairs, couches and tables.

Clisten digested the layout slowly, and then closed his eyes to see if he could picture it in his mind. As a detective, it was important that he know the details of the lobby, particularly if he encountered Tony. The man had to be in the hotel. Otherwise, his car would not be parked in their lot.

Suddenly his thoughts took a different turn. He had been right in his thinking. Tony was following Twilla Hale to see where it would take him. *He must think she has information, something he wants.* Did Tony think she would lead him to Rebecca Givens?

Clisten had to do something but what? To help her, he had to find Tony first.

Clisten peered around the column again. He studied the patrons in the dining room before concentrating on the bar. The bearded man reading the paper began to stir an unspent interest in him. If he were clean shaven, Clisten felt certain the man sitting on the bar stool would be his fake partner. The wavy hair and facial features were discernibly obvious as was his rail-like frame.

Identifying the man was something that came naturally to a trained detective, but Clisten found Tony's calm, undisturbed attitude very disconcerting. There he sat…so cool and unafraid: a fugitive and murderer.

Clisten needed a plan. It had to be done quickly and in a very tempting way. Clisten took the cell phone from his pocket and made two calls.

NINETEEN
STAKEOUT

Twilla Hale sat on one of the easy chairs in the lobby of Hotel Coventry and selected one of the magazines on a nearby table. Becoming totally engrossed in an article on dogs, she never felt the quiet tapping on her arm by Clisten Barr who had just walked into the hotel through the front entrance. A guest watching him would assume he used valet parking.

"Hello." Twilla rose to greet him.

"Twilla, I need your help." He brushed her lips. "Smile and point to the back-parking lot."

As he watched her follow his instructions, he shook his head and, taking her arm, led her to the front entrance of the hotel. Once outside, Clisten tapped a number on his cell and mumbled a few words.

"Don't ask." He looked at her sideways as they stood huddled together for what seemed an eternity.

"Can we at least talk?"

"Later. Right now, we're waiting for my car or pretending to be."

"And you think I don't make sense."

"You look beautiful, by the way. Really beautiful."

"Really?" She looked up at him, fixing her eyes on his, inwardly happy she wore one of her new outfits. "That's the nicest thing you've ever said to me." She could see the frown deepening across his forehead and immediately regretted the remark. "I'm sorry. I guess that was rude. You have been very kind to me and Lily."

Minutes later, his words were stifled by the loud blaring sirens of police cars converging on the parking lot of the hotel. "Go to your room and wait for me," he shouted over the deafening noise. "We need to talk."

Twilla watched him race around the corner of the building and chalked-it-up to the nosy detective's interest in what had just occurred. She equated his thirst of following police sirens to that of chasing firetrucks when he was young. Of course, that was just her thinking. Maybe he never chased firetrucks, or maybe police sirens just make him nutsy.

It was probably neither one. The man was just plain nosy. He had to know what was going on every minute. Some guest probably had a heart attack going to his car. It didn't matter. Clisten Barr had to know about it. Little did he care about leaving her!

What was Twilla to do? She had come to High Coventry for a reason. Waiting for the detective's return would spoil her plans. She thought about the map marked with clues, the picture of two women with Lily and the ring Amy gave her. Twilla had worked so hard putting it all together; all with the hope of finding Mark. Now, she was in the crosshairs of a nosy detective.

If she followed the map and Clisten found her somehow, Amy's secret would be revealed. If she waited in her room, the entire day would be shot. Regardless of what just occurred, she had to protect her colleague's secret at all costs.

Twilla entered the elevator knowing she would be forced to make a reservation for another weekend. Although unhappy with the prospect of returning to High Coventry again, her thoughts shifted back to the detective.

Clisten seemed to look at her in a different way while they waited for his imaginary car to appear. Did he find her attractive or was it her new clothes and hairdo that sparked his interest?

Maybe it was the combination of both. Of course, it could be neither. Detectives were trained to notice details and he was far superior in that category, right down to her sauce-stained shirt. That was probably it. He was surprised that her clothes were unstained today. But deep in her thoughts, Twilla did not believe it.

When the elevator stopped, Twilla walked down the hall, her mind on finding Mark. It was like a clock had stopped; her thoughts were no longer on Clisten Barr.

While Twilla was in a tizzy about Clisten Barr's chasing police sirens, the detective stood listening to a quick recap as the local force positioned Tony Mistretta into a police car.

"You should have seen him." Corky did a hitchhike thumb at Lupo. "Man, was he fast! When Tony got to his car, he noticed the slashed tire and got nervous. He thought someone was watching him. He was getting ready to run when this linebacker pinned him to the hood and cuffed him. That's when I called the police."

"Wish I could have seen it." Clisten watched the two patrol cars drive away. "Did you get the rifle?"

"It was in the trunk along with two handguns. He should have ditched the rifle since it connects him to the shooting in your case. That would have been the smart thing to do."

"He couldn't. Not yet." Clisten reminded him again, his thoughts on Rebecca Givens. Once found, she would have been Tony's next target. She was, after all, the last known link to Amy Gregson and could possibly provide him of needed information. Killing her would be a matter of expediency, once Tony got what he needed.

Although he wondered about the detective's comment, Corky never asked for a further explanation. Instead, he changed the subject completely.

"Without your plan, we couldn't have caught the SOB so smoothly. How did you come up with it?"

"Let's just say I'm following a person of interest who also happens to be a colleague of the murdered woman. She came to High Coventry with some purpose in mind."

"And you came here to follow her," Corky interrupted.

"She holds the key to the murder of Amy Gregson but doesn't know it. I'm sure Tony's been following her, but I don't know where he 'holed-up,' since I couldn't find him. My phony partner thought she could lead him to someone who had the information he desperately wanted. She was in danger and didn't know that either."

"So, what are you going to do?" Lupo asked.

"I'll talk to her later." Clisten shrugged. "We need to get Tony's arrest processed without tramping his 'legal rights' bull shit. We'll go to the station for booking then I'll leave. You check on the arraignment and transfer to your jurisdiction. Your case will predispose mine. We both know that. I really have to do this interview and maybe another one," he said thinking of Gunther Pratt.

"You sure? No argument?"

"What's the point?" Clisten shook his head. "He killed a cop. That's murder one. Our combined evidence starts there."

"Wait a minute." Lupo halted the conversation by turning to Corky. "Aren't you going to tell him what we found?"

"You mean the rope?" Corky shrugged.

"In the trunk," Lupo clarified.

"Tony had rope in the trunk?" Clisten wondered why it was brought to his attention. "How is it significant?"

"It'll match." Corky went glum, causing Lupo to take Clisten aside.

"Partner was tied up, weighted down." Although his voice was hardly audible, Clisten caught the meaning immediately.

Corky would use the rope to match the one used on his dead partner, before he was weighted down and tossed into the river like so much debris.

Turning to Corky and speaking in a very calm manner, Clisten tried to assuage the man's sadness. "Finding the rope may be difficult in dredging up memories, but it will help your case. That's the best thing you can do for your friend. You owe him that."

"Is that what you're doing for Leggin?" Although his manner was subdued, Corky's question hit home.

"I'm going to use every piece of evidence I can find to convict Tony of Amy Gregson's murder. That conviction, along with yours, will satisfy me. That bastard killed Leggin. I know it but can't prove it. However, his being convicted of killing a police officer will do it for me. Now, do you understand?"

"You have a funny way of putting things, but I understand what you mean." Then with a quick nod, said, "Follow us."

As he followed Corky and Lupo to the local station, Clisten thought about the day's sorted activities and wondered how he would explain his crazy behavior to Twilla Hale.

It was somewhere around one o'clock when Clisten phoned a sleepy Twilla Hale.

"Hello," her husky voice greeted him.

"Clisten Barr, Twilla," he said then paused. Something didn't feel right. "Were you sleeping?"

"I was," she yawned.

"What's your room number?"

"Why? Are you sleepy too?"

"This is no time to be cute," he growled. "We need to talk."

"Five-sixteen."

"Make sure you're dressed."

"Oh, for Christ sake, you are a pain in the ass!" She ended the conversation abruptly, and then made the sign of the cross.

Clisten eyed his phone and smiled. He loved getting this messy, smelly, disheveled woman riled-up. Although her quips were spontaneous and clever, she was the real pain in his ass. What exactly was she hiding? He would know shortly.

As he rode up the elevator, he re-adjusted his thinking. Twilla Hale was far from disheveled when he saw her earlier. She was a strikingly beautiful woman. "She makes me crazy!" he said aloud, as he pictured her that morning. "But that mouth. It won't quit. Her wanting to know if I was sleepy too..." Those thoughts soon vanished when he reached the fifth floor.

When Twilla opened the hotel door, she had hoped Clisten would pull her to him and kiss her passionately. Instead, he sat her in an easy chair and grabbed the one facing her across the table. She couldn't remember him looking so serious or downcast. His troubled thoughts had to be connected to her presence in High Coventry. Twilla was sure of it. That was his reason for wanting her to wait for him. *So much for kisses and passion!*

"I don't have time, Twilla. I need your help again." His voice ached with desperation.

As he agonized with her, pleading urgently for her assistance, Twilla stared at him in silence. *What exactly did he mean? Was it about Mark? She had to know.* "I don't understand. How can I possibly help you?"

"You can give me the motive for Amy's murder." As soon as those words escaped his lips, Clisten noticed her shocked expression. It made him wonder if she understood the statement.

"How could I possibly know that?" she demanded hotly. "If that's the idea circling your attic, you better try another house," she continued the tirade. "That I would have pertinent informa-tion about Amy's life is ridiculous. She never mentioned her fam-ily, friends or anything of real substance to me. That's how it was with our relationship."

"Did she ever give you something personal or valuable? Twil-la, please don't lie to me," he sighed deeply. "We have someone in custody and it won't stick unless I have the motive for Amy's murder. It's very important that you tell me everything you know about her."

"Who is it? Do I know the man who killed her?"

"That's privileged information." He shook his head. And although his reply was immediate, her last question made him curious. Was Twilla still withholding information and did she unconsciously make a slip?

"What makes you think it's a man?"

"I can't think of one single woman wanting to kill Amy." But the words no sooner left her lips when she thought of Dr. Shelden and how far she might go to protect herself from arrest. "But then I can't think of any man off-hand either. Everyone liked Amy."

"Then tell me what you know about Amy Gregson. Just talk and we'll sort it out together. Please." He reached across the table for her hand. "Please, Twilla."

Twilla felt helpless. Although she wanted Amy's murderer to be prosecuted, she felt an obligation to her friend. Twilla had to find Mark. However, the rustling of something being slid from an opened envelope drew her attention to a photograph of a woman.

"Have you ever seen this woman with Amy Gregson?"

Twilla recognized her as the woman in the photograph with Amy and Lily. This was not the time to lie. "Who is she?"

"Her name is Rebecca Givens. I need to find her. I think she holds the key to the murder of your colleague." His eyes hooked on hers as he spoke. "Your expression tells me you have seen this woman."

"What makes you say that?"

"Facial expression and body language. I've been doing this kind of work for a long time. I'm good at my job. Now, I need you to level with me."

"No." Twilla sighed in resignation. "I haven't seen her. That is the truth." Her eyes searched his for belief. "I'll prove it to you."

Arising suddenly from her chair Twilla walked to the dresser and, removing several papers and a photograph from her purse, placed them on the table.

"I don't know the woman you call Rebecca Givens, but I do have a story to tell. There is also Amy's dying wish which I intend to follow, with or without you."

Clisten sat quietly, absorbing each detail Twilla uttered, from finding Amy's cookbook clues to the pasted photograph between the pages.

Finally, Twilla placed the gold ring on the table and said, "Her dying wish was that I find Mark." She removed the ring from the table and returned it to the inside zipper of her purse. "I intend to do just that."

Clisten studied Twilla's sober expression. Whatever the ring symbolized, it was of great importance to her. Perhaps finding Mark was another part of the key to his case. If so, Twilla Hale would not be searching alone.

"May I?" he asked shuffling through the papers laying on the table. "I take it you got these word changes from the cookbook." He said, waiting for some response, but for some reason she was slow to reply.

"It would be better if I gave you an example. Under the recipe for brownies, Amy added the words, Baby Ruth's, so someone would think they were something special. I knew they were clues after I went through the whole cookbook and saw Amy's scrawl.

She never formatted it according to the table of contents either. That wasn't like her. No. Amy wanted me to have this information. Although I put it all together, I don't know what it means."

Twilla watched the detective pour through her notes and map, mumbling to himself as he put the puzzle pieces together. He took a pen from his jacket pocket and began writing all over her notes. He glanced across the table at Twilla and smiled. "I think we have it. Ruth Graham at number A1 Brindle Street in High Coventry."

"That's what I came up with." He noted her agreement and slid the map toward her, thudding his fingers on the written clues.

"These directions should take us to Rebecca Givens or someone who knows her."

"What if they're wrong?"

"Then we've taken a nice fall drive. C'mon," he urged, getting up from his chair.

Clisten began stuffing Twilla's papers into the envelope that held Rebecca Givens' picture and waited for some saucy reply.

"That's it? That's all there is?" she demanded, groaning loudly, while sliding into her coat.

"No. Since I haven't eaten all day, I might buy you dinner."

"What makes you think you're alone on that score?"

"You didn't have lunch after I left?"

"What did you expect? You told me to go to my room. I guess I fell asleep."

"I am so sorry, Twilla," he began sympathetically, then with a twinkle in his eye, said, "But not sorry enough to stop somewhere."

An explosion of laughter followed his remark as they left the room. "You're going to pay for this." She continued to laugh. "I am going to order one of everything on the dinner menu."

"Great idea," he rebutted. "I hope you'll remember the limit on your credit card!"

The banter continued as they exited the hotel to a very deserted parking lot, *neither realizing a truism: laughter can bring people together.*

TWENTY

REBECCA GIVENS

After leaving the hotel parking lot, Clisten and Twilla soon realized they were heading toward the outskirts of High Coventry. As they followed the plotted map, driving eastward along the busy thoroughfare of town, it became clear that Coventry Avenue, the town's busiest artery, became Brindle Street, a long winding country lane with acres of farms dotting the landscape. Although each farm was owned independently, taken collectively, they all looked the same to Twilla. It was like being in an art gallery or museum. Every barn and silo, peppering the skyline, stood solidly detached and farther away from a two-story frame house and gravel driveway that housed a parked truck.

They continued driving through the sparsely populated area when Clisten noticed a small service road extension and turned on it abruptly.

"What are you doing?" Twilla's demanded loudly, critical of the of the directional change. He was not following the planned map.

"Call it a hunch."

He continued driving down a narrow dirt road when a bank of four posted mailboxes caught his attention. After stopping abruptly, he scanned the mailboxes quickly and smiled. The letter address for the sparsely populated area seemed rather strange, yet the location was uncommonly smart for one inhabitant.

While the addresses on Brindle Street followed the numbered order common to all houses, every mail box on the service road or Brindle extension had the letter A before the number. This, Clisten gathered, clarified mail delivery for the *added* service extension.

However, upon further inspection, Clisten found the numbering strange. The first mailbox started with A4 instead of what would normally be A1. Clisten put the gear in park and began to scan all of them more closely.

Scrawled in black paint across the A4 mailbox was the name Mortimer. The A3 scrawl named Blackburn, while the A2 lettering belonged to the Penning family. However, it was the last mailbox that drew Clisten's undivided attention. The name Graham appeared in black letters across the A1 mailbox.

"Oh, my God!" Twilla whispered. "I never thought…"

"Don't get too excited. We don't know what to expect."

Clisten switched the gear from park to drive and moved slowly down the narrow road, looking for numbers while trying to avoid a variety of potholes.

"That's Mortimer." Twilla pointed to the two-story frame house some fifty feet back from the road, a broken A4 plaque near the front door. The rusted wrecked cars and worn tires that lay scattered in the front yard were stark reminders of projects long forgotten. "What a junk yard!" she bellowed as Clisten drove on, "It's a good thing these houses are so far apart. They need display space."

"I'll watch the road; you find the numbers." He ignored her running commentary.

"There's Blackburn." She pointed to the second frame house sitting as far back from the road as Mortimer's junk palace. "Holy crap! This whole place must be Cuckoo Corners! Either Blackburn's a nut or likes pots. They're all over the yard." And for some unknown reason, the statement triggered an altered version of

I've Got a Lovely Bunch of Coconuts as she burst into song. "*I've got a love-a-lee bunch of flower pots. See them all a scattered in the yard. Big ones, small ones, some as big as your head.*"

As Twilla began to sing, Clisten started to chuckle. He had no idea the woman had that kind of crazy humor bottled inside her. "Did you see an A3 sign?"

"Yep." Twilla halted her song. "Near the front door. Right above the statue holding a pot of weeds. The flowers must have died months ago." Then Twilla cautioned him. "Go slower. You're approaching the Penning place," she said of the third two-story structure that sat as far back from the road as the other two. "Must have been part of the building code," she muttered, half aloud.

"If you mean a set-back so many feet from the road, that's a normal requirement in every building code. But there's a particular advantage here."

"Meaning?"

"This extension is probably zoned agricultural like Brindle Street, which means acres of land, deep set-backs and lots of privacy for people who do not want to be found." He knew from her expression she understood his meaning. "Where was the A2 sign? I missed it."

"There's an A2 sign posted on the front porch but nothing in the front yard and no car on the driveway. Either these people are near normal or the house is vacant."

"Or they're away," Clisten interjected, adding another reason to her list.

Within minutes, Clisten stopped in front of a sprawling Victorian style home with a wrap-around porch and a detached two car garage. To the right of the front door was a plaque with the A1 address. Although vintage in appearance, the house and grounds seemed too well manicured and incongruous within the four-home area. This, of course, would be a conundrum for anyone who did not have Clisten's listening capacity.

"How do we approach her if she is Ruth Graham, the woman in the picture?" Twilla demanded, anxious to get on with the program.

"Breaking the ice is the first step," Clisten said calmly. "You have the ring." He turned into the long driveway paralleling the side of the house and parked. "I'll chip-in when necessary."

"Cute!" she snapped at his unhelpful response, taking the envelope he gave her.

Knowing she was nervous, Clisten took her arm and said, "Just tell her Amy gave you a puzzle to solve and it brought you here."

He followed her to the front entrance and watched Twilla push the doorbell button, wondering what the hell she was really going to say when the woman answered. *"Hello. I'm selling Girl Scout Cookies, or I need to find Mark."*

Although her hair was grayer and facial lines deeper when she answered the door, Twilla recognized the small-framed woman immediately from Amy's hidden photograph.

"Miss Graham?" Twilla asked. Receiving no answer but recognizing her as the same woman pictured in the photograph, she continued her plight. "I'm sorry to bother you," she started again. "My name's Twilla Hale. I've come a long way to find you. Amy sent me." Twilla reached into her purse for the gold ring. "Amy's dying wish was for me to find Mark."

"You're the teacher she talked about, the one taking care of Lily." she mused, then realizing the awkward situation confronting her, acknowledged the young woman's companion and ushered them into the living room. "Please." She motioned to the sofa, asking them to sit. "What is this about? You mentioned Amy." As she spoke her eyes were fixed on the ring.

"We were colleagues." Twilla began. "She offered to cover my classes when I went home for my father's surgery. We scheduled a meeting to finalize my class plans, but when Amy reached Hawley Hall, she had been shot. She fell in my arms and told me to find Mark. That's when Amy gave me this ring. She was too injured to say anything more and I had no idea what she meant. It just happened so fast."

"May I see it?" She opened the palm of her hand for the ring.

Twilla and Clisten exchanged glances but remained silent when the woman took a magnifying glass from an end table drawer to examine it carefully.

"It is Amy's, isn't it?" Twilla caught the woman's nod as she returned the magnifying glass to the table drawer.

"It's her wedding ring if I'm not mistaken and you were looking for something to identify it." Clisten's keen observation caused the woman a disquieting moment. "A mark or scratch," he added.

"The two are hardly noticeable." The woman acknowledged.

"I didn't see them," Twilla said, caught by surprise.

"You weren't supposed to." Clisten ignored her. "Only Rebecca Givens could authenticate the ring or am I wrong?"

It was then that Twilla captured the full meaning of his words. *Ruth Graham was really Rebecca Givens. Was that her real name? Why was she using the name Graham? What the hell was going on?*

Clisten's statement caused the woman to rise from her chair in total dismay. For years, everything had been going according to plan, one so carefully devised and implemented. Security and safety were key. However, since Amy's death, the layers of taken precautions were beginning to unravel. How could she stop the bleeding? What measures could she take now? Was there no way out? The woman feared not for herself but for what she was protecting…what she had been protecting for years!

"Who are you and what do you want?" The woman demanded, addressing him directly.

"Tell Gunther to join us and I'll tell you."

"What you are talking about?" She tried dismissing him.

"Gunther, Gunther Pratt!" Clisten's yells echoed the house like the clamor of a bell tower. Then after identifying himself, he reminded the man of their phone conversation some weeks earlier. "I'm not here to cause trouble. I need clarification and Rebecca wants closure."

"How did you know?" A tall and very skinny, gray-haired man entered the room. "We've kept this place secret for years, although I still keep a small apartment for show."

"I'm a good listener. The neatly trimmed rose bushes gave it away. You mentioned wanting to spend a quiet life with her, gardening and pruning her roses."

"And you remembered that?" Gunther asked, shocked that a stranger, although a detective, would recall something so insignificant.

"Well no. The first thing that came to mind was sliding your hand up Rebecca's skirt."

"You told him that?" The woman scolded. "Why would you say such a thing?"

"Because he loves you," Clisten interrupted, "and to make his side of the conversation more believable. He was protecting you from being found. Sifting through an inquiry to determine your degree of safety had to be impossible. So, he conjured a believable story of his own. Obviously, I fell for it." He began to smile at the thought.

"Twilla, I heard you say Amy sent you. What did you mean?" It was now Gunther's turn to ask questions.

"The clues were in my cookbook. Amy added words like Graham Cracker pie crust instead of just plain pie crust and Baby Ruth Brownies. After putting her changes together, like Ruth Graham, I knew it was a code, but I didn't know what it meant or why it was necessary. Then I remembered her dying wish. She must have been afraid of someone or something and used the code as a precaution."

"That makes no sense," he interrupted her discourse. "How could she be sure you'd find it? It could have taken months before discovery."

"No. Amy knew me too well. She borrowed the cookbook for my mother's recipes. So, after retrieving it, I found misplaced sections that had to be rearranged. That's when I discovered her code."

Twilla opened the envelope she had been holding, pulled out the papers and gave them to Gunther who began scanning them immediately.

"I see you also have a map," he muttered half-aloud.

"Yes. I plotted the coded words on the map for High Coventry, but I wouldn't have been able to find the house without Clisten. In the back of the cookbook, I found this photograph glued between two pages." Twilla held up a picture of two women with a dog.

"So that's how you found me," the woman acquiesced, injecting herself back into the conversation. "Now that you know I'm alive, what do you really want from me?"

"To find Mark. That was Amy's dying wish."

"I'm sorry but I can't help you," she said calmly.

"Can't or won't?" Twilla disregarded the woman's negative response with contempt. "You're my last hope."

"I can be of no help to you. Perhaps it would be best if you left now."

As she addressed Twilla, Clisten sat by silently, absorbing the futile exchange between them. It was time to step in.

"Rebecca, if I may call you by your given name, I know you want full disclosure of Amy's death to further protect Mark. I think I can ease your anxiety on that score."

"How so?" Gunther piped up, curious by the detective's display of confidence.

"Do you know this man?" Clisten tapped a picture of Tony Mistretta on his cell phone. "It's very important that you tell me the truth."

"Why is that?" Gunther continued to ask questions."

"We are holding this man in connection with the murder of Amy Gregson. That's all I can tell you, but I think you know his real identity." As a detective, Clisten felt an obligation to remain silent.

The displayed picture caused the woman to slide back into her chair. "It's Jonathan!" she cried, dropping the symbolic ring Twilla quickly grasped. "So that's what happened. He found her before she could escape. Now everything's going to come out," she moaned, her eyes growing moist. "We were so careful."

"But you knew that could happen when you helped her initially," the detective interrupted. "The possibility of his finding her always existed. Once he did, Amy's life was no longer viable." Although the facts he stated were true, Clisten hated hurting the woman.

"How can you be sure it was him?" Now it was Gunther who needed confirmation.

"We have the evidence. Now thanks to you, I have the motive."

"Which is?"

"Protecting Mark." As the words rolled from his mouth, Clisten studied Rebecca Givens closely and from her reaction determined his premise was correct.

"The story goes something like this," Clisten said and began a narrative. "An abused woman flees with her young son to a family member long considered a disinterested loner living hundreds of miles away. The woman disguises herself through cosmetic surgeries, takes time to heal and then with help, gets a teaching job. The child lives elsewhere, seeing his mother only when deemed safe. Meanwhile, the abusive father hires someone to search for them or does it on his own. When he finds Amy in Stockton, his carefully made plans go awry when they meet accidentally. Finding Mark then becomes secondary to his own survival.

"Was it that obvious?"

"No." Clisten continued. "I saw the x-rays of her broken bones, along with the cosmetic scars. The medical examiner detailed the amount of abuse to me, but he also mentioned the padded heel of her left shoe, indicating the possibility of a slight limp."

"Then you know it had to be done."

"Why didn't she go to the police?"

"Her local hospital informed them of the beatings, but since she was pegged a terrible undeserving wife, the cops did nothing. Jonathan Grant was their pal. They hung out at the same bars and were buddies on weekends. My great niece had no alternative. She had to run or be killed. He did it, didn't he? No matter how far she ran, he found Amelia and killed her."

"Amelia Grant?" The detective questioned, relieved somehow knowing the woman's real identity. "How far did she run?"

"From Cleveland. She was working on her Master's in Education when they met at Ohio State. Unfortunately, they married almost immediately."

"Then it must have gone downhill after the baby was born."

"Within a year, I think. The beatings took a toll on her. Broken bones, bruises. His drunken rages. She feared for the child."

"Why you? You weren't in the loop."

"That's exactly why she contacted me. The family favored the silver-tongued fox. I should say Amelia's father and sister. Her mother died years earlier. I heard he was dead too, but her sister is very much alive. I believe Chloe Moss was hatched in a bath of amniotic vinegar. She is one mean spinster. No love lost there."

"Then how did you finally meet? Did you drive from High Coventry to Cleveland?"

"Yes." She nodded in agreement. "After developing a plan, we created the identity of Amy Gregson with forged papers and had her and Mark simply disappear."

"We, as in Herman Banks? How does he fit in?"

"My third outcast cousin on the Graham-Banks side of the family and his wife, Tula. Amelia called him from a pay phone the night before she was murdered. He went to get her the next day but was too late."

"Does he wear a long coat?" Twilla interrupted.

"Sometimes. Does it matter?"

"I saw the shadow of a man in a long coat when I held Amy in my arms."

"It's possible. He was to meet her at Hawley Hall."

"And Mrs. Benson?" Clisten disrupted their conversation, feeling it irrelevant to the information he so sorely needed.

Before Rebecca could answer, Twilla could not contain herself. "Mrs. Benson! She can't possibly be involved in this!"

"Tula's sister, Henrietta." The woman ignored Twilla's outburst. "Although we formed a perfect triangle for protection, no one knew what Jonathan looked like except me. I saw his picture before destroying everything for identification purposes."

"Then how would they be able to identify him if he came too close to be finding Amy?" Clisten cleared his throat. "Amelia?"

"They had his description in case some stranger came around asking questions. Amelia always mentioned his thick head of hair and his stick-figured body." Rebecca gave him a knowing glance. "Herman would contact me immediately if anyone started questioning him or Henrietta. He was my direct contact. When he told us of the shooting, we knew Jonathan had to be responsible. He was looking for Mark. That's when we closed ranks."

Satisfied with her disclosure, Clisten rose from the sofa causing all three to follow suit and stand. "It all fits."

"Then you know," she sighed deeply, not wanting to take the conversation any further.

"Yes. All of it." Clisten became silent. The message between them was clear. He would ask no more questions. The need was no longer there. He had the answers and more specifically, the motive for Amelia Grant's murder. That he wanted nothing more revealed sanctioned their precaution for hiding Mark.

Regardless of the outcome surrounding Amelia's death, Rebecca knew the detective would keep her secret safe. "Are you going to arrest me?"

"No. Although your actions were totally illegal, my investigation stops here. I think you and Gunther suffered enough. You can start using your real name again and live openly, after I close the case. I emphasize the word after. But these things take time." Then turning to Gunther directly, said, "You'll hear from me when it happens. I still have your phone number."

"What about Lily?" Twilla could not take her guardianship for granted. She had to know their intentions. "She's been with me and I'd like to keep her."

"You love that little rascal, don't you?" Rebecca caught Twilla's glowing nod. "I think Amelia would have liked that. She talked about your being a real friend to her," she added and grasping the impact of those words, noted the brightened look of a compliment well-received.

"Will someone else come?" Gunther returned to their original conversation. "What should we do?"

"Go through your regular routine. Do what you've been doing. Nothing out of the ordinary."

"Maybe I can slide my hand up her skirt."

Clisten began to choke with laughter. That action had been taken long before they had their first conversation. However, his comment prompted another thought related to the case. "I will need to send Amy's body somewhere at some point."

"I have your phone number too." Gunther reminded him. "I'll call after we discuss burial plans. I know she wanted to be cremated according to the will drafted by Thaddeus Stevens. Rebecca has it in her safety deposit box. It's crazy when you think about it. Amelia bequeathed everything to Rebecca should something happen, and Rebecca bestowed everything she has to me." His eyes were wet when he finished speaking.

"Thank you." Rebecca gave Clisten her hand. "We won't be seeing you again, will we?"

"No," he said quietly, a total understanding between them. "Give Rebecca the ring, Twilla."

Like a robot obeying a command, Twilla placed the gold ring in the woman's hand. "It's up to you now," she said as Rebecca and Gunther walked them to the door.

Clisten wanted to leave them on a high note. There was no sense in telling them Thaddeus J. Stevens was dead.

TWENTY-ONE

DINNER

"Someday you're going to tell me what the hell just happened," Twilla fumed as she entered the car. "I walk in there armed with papers, map and a ring, and I come out like an empty-handed mushroom eating cave shit."

Her furious tirade had Clisten chuckling for the next mile. Twilla's expressions of anger, struck with sprinkled obscenities, harmless ones at that, always brought touches of humor to his thankless job.

After a mile or two, Twilla's tone changed from anger to regret. "I shared everything with you and came to this hell hole of a place for one reason," she said, pointing to Mortimer's junk yard. "Instead of complying with Amy's last wish to find Mark, I'm listening to a conversation about her murder. There was nothing about finding Mark! Not one thing!" Then she turned directly to face him. "Why didn't you help me? Why was I told to give Rebecca Givens the ring?"

As Clisten listened to Twilla's harangue, he knew the venting was just a cover for her inward frustration. What she truly felt was monumental failure and disappointment at being unable to pursue Amy's last request.

What could Clisten tell her? What could he say? In the long run it was better this way. He had chosen the safer option…for all of them.

Feeling he could stand the diatribe no longer, Clisten parked the car in the middle of the rutted service road, grabbed Twilla and planted a long passionate kiss on her lips. "Now stop bitch-ing and think about where we're having dinner!" Then without so much as a glance, he started the car to continue the drive toward High Coventry.

Taken back by his sudden actions, the only response from his overwhelmed companion was a weak, "Ok."

It was not long after the two entered the hotel restaurant and were seated at a corner table, somewhat away from the clamor-ing dinner crowd, when the conversation began.

"I'm sorry," she apologized. "I totally lost it…but taking it out on you wasn't fair." Twilla stopped speaking when the waiter ap-proached their table. "I know what I want," she waved the menu away. "A filet, medium rare, a house salad and a glass of red wine."

"The same, but make the wine a good Cabernet Sauvignon," Clisten addressed the waiter then turned his attention back to Twilla. "Have you come to gripps with it? All of it, including the false identity of Amelia Grant?"

"I'm not surprised, considering the abuse. When she ran away, she had to assume a different name, but I'm not catching your drift. What do you mean?"

"By not finding Mark, you think you failed Amelia Grant and her dying request to find him. It was failure and disappointment that caused you to vent this afternoon. Of course, you're wrong."

"How can you say that?" She glared at him, her voice growing louder. "I didn't find Mark and now Rebecca has the ring!"

"That's exactly how Amelia planned it. She wanted Rebecca to have the ring all along."

"That makes no sense."

"Think about it logically. First, Amelia sets-up a code in your cookbook. Then she pastes a picture between two pages, knowing all the while her nosy colleague will check the tome for her mother's recipes. After being shot, the woman can't really say much, so she tells you to find Mark."

"Are you saying the whole code thing was to find Rebecca?"

"Exactly. Don't you get it?" he insisted with growing frustration. "It was imperative you find Rebecca. The ring symbolized confirmation that nothing had been uncovered or found. No records, no papers, nothing. As Amelia lay dying it was imperative Rebecca know their guarded secret was still secure. That Mark was safe."

"But if the ring confirmed Mark's safety," Twilla demanded, "why wouldn't she tell me about her son? He is her son, isn't he?" The detective's lack of understanding was beginning to irritate her. "She never mentioned him to me. Ever!" That Amelia put her in this situation frustrated her even more. They were more than colleagues: they were friends...just not close ones.

"Twilla." He ignored her questions deliberately. The detective felt some things were best left unsaid. "You still don't get it. Her son, Mark, is alive, but to us, he's in limbo. We have no real knowledge of him or his existence. That's the way it must be for his sake. His mother is dead. He's an orphan among people who love him, and they don't want him in the clutches of Amelia's miserable sister. Do you understand? Were you not listening to our conversation?"

"Of course, I was."

"Then you heard me tell Rebecca I would no longer be investigating her or going in that direction." Then questioning her facial expression, Clisten added, "You, of all people, must understand my reasons for determining that."

"What's that supposed to mean?"

"It means a full inquiry would include you, uncover Rebecca's hidden identity, the forging of Amelia's credentials, a secreted Mark and possibly get Gunther fired."

"So that's what you meant. Your investigation won't dig deeper than necessary."

"Twilla. There is no ring. Never was. No lengthy mention of Mark. There is nothing more to investigate, going forward. The man who murdered Amelia is in custody. We have the high-powered rifle he used and now we have the motive which is, 'The man hunted for the wife he continually abused and a possible son, we can't locate.' He planned to kill his wife and find the son. End of story."

Twilla nodded with understanding. "So, no ring, no side investigation of Mark. Problem solved. You're giving all three a chance to start over. In protecting them, you're protecting me too."

"I think Rebecca and Gunther suffered enough. They put their lives on hold, fearful Amelia's husband would find her, and then, through her, Mark. But you're a different story. Amelia's dying request turned your life upside down."

"Yes, but the ring also signified danger. Her last thoughts were on Mark and his safety when she gave me the ring."

"That was her thinking," he agreed.

"True, but I had no way of knowing who was involved in hiding Mark or anything about his father for that matter. I told you before. Amy never talked about family or friends. In fact, she never mentioned anything personal in the conversations we had. What would have happened if I found Rebecca on my own? What could I have told her?"

"That your colleague died in your arms and anything else you could remember. The ring would have told her Amelia divulged nothing: their secret, meaning Mark, was still safe. The ring was a code. Your transferring it told her that."

Twilla thought about Clisten's theory for a moment. "Then by telling Rebecca the man who murdered Amelia was in custody, you removed any fears of discovery." Although satisfied with his explanation, Twilla still had questions. "Why the ring? Why was it so significant?"

"It was personal, portable and something Rebecca could identify. While it was in Amelia's possession, Mark was safe. If a problem occurred, it could be passed along to keep his safety in check."

"But why, me?"

"Once Amelia realized her husband was watching her every move, she opted not to unmask Mrs. Benson as someone who helped her in the initial escape. That alone would have put the woman in danger. Although Henrietta knew the significance of the ring, Amy risked Mark's life on a trusted but nosy colleague to pass the wedding band and the code it carried."

"This was all for Mark's safety." Twilla thought she captured his full meaning.

"And Rebecca's," he clarified. "To determine whether the ring was still hidden, she would have had to come forward to claim the body as a member of the family. In doing so, her identity would have been revealed."

"Making her a possible target for Mark's father."

"Exactly. We know he searched the entire history of Amelia's family in his effort to find her. That's why he was so desperate to locate Rebecca Givens. Although a remote relative by her own choosing, the woman was next on his list. The man ran a complete check list of relatives and may have found Givens using the generational family name of Graham in the family tree."

"Now that he's arrested, giving her the ring ended an investigation that never began."

Now, she fully understood how morally ingrained the man was. Her mind went off somewhere as she smiled at the thought. She finally realized the full extent of Clisten's gesture and Rebecca's appreciative comment. This was a side of him she had never seen before…kind, generous and very giving.

"Now that we no longer must contend with them," he said, ending her quiet reverie, "I want to concentrate on you." He touched her wine glass with his. "Twilla, you look beautiful."

"You really are good at what you do," she teased. "So smooth at changing the subject."

While Twilla's playful attitude seemed light and spirited, it was really a cover for her innermost feelings. Did he think she looked beautiful because a well-coifed, tastefully dressed woman sat across from him, a complete departure of his past picture of her? Or was he laying the groundwork for a night together? Either way, it was something men always say to get what they want.

"I wasn't changing the subject. Sitting across from me is a very beautiful woman. I'm just surprised you're not in a relationship."

His comment caused Twilla to stop eating abruptly and fix her eyes directly on his in a long silent stare. There was no need for a response: an increasing chemistry between them spoke volumes.

He reached across the table and rubbed his thumb inside the palm of her hand, mesmerizing and stimulating her with a long steady stroke that conveyed its meaning. As his stroking pace steadily increased, he sensed the readiness of her body language and slowly slid his thumb upon hers.

"How's your steak?" he asked, clearing his throat.

"What steak?" Twilla spoke in a confused manner, her thoughts elsewhere. His foreplay had stirred an unrestrained fire deep within her, one only he could control.

"You ready?" he asked, as they arose from the table.

Although Clisten was not surprised by her simple nod, little did he know that circling Twilla's thoughts with anticipation was their spending the night together, his strong arms around her naked body, his lips slowly kissing the hollow of her throat. *Just like the dinner foreplay before both thumbs merged.*

⁓

After leaving the elevator, they walked down the long hall on the fifth floor, side by side, their hands dangling apart from each other. Seeing them together, one would think they were just friends, enjoying an evening together. When they reached Twilla's room, she took the entry card from her purse and turned to him, almost chewing her words as she opened the hotel door.

"Would you like to…?" Although obvious that extending an invitation of this sort seemed new to her, Clisten interrupted before she could finish the question.

"Twilla." he brought her to him, calling her name softly, as his lips met hers in an explosion of passion, their bodies linked as they moved toward the open entryway. "You make me crazy," he whispered, but soon realized his planned romantic evening was interrupted by the vibrating cell phone in the pocket of his trousers. *Answering it was unnecessary. Clisten already knew the identity of the caller. In his mind, however, the vibration kept repeating the same refrain: Damn Corky, Damn Corky, Damn Corky…*

"I have to go back," he mumbled, still holding her tight against him, the desire between them never ebbing. "There are times I hate this job."

"I understand," she sighed again. Although calm in manner, Twilla was seething inside as she moved away from him. The man had refused her offer. He had already notched her name on his belt of conquests, no need for a repeat.

Between her body language and the abruptness of moving away from him, Clisten knew something was wrong. Under normal circumstances Twilla would have asked his reason for going back at that moment.

"Do you really? I don't think so," he challenged with biting frustration.

"You want to bring the case to a quick resolution, now that you have a motive. That's what you said earlier." Her answer was short and to the point.

The remark made Clisten angry. Why could she not understand his dilemma? "Before that can happen, I have hours of work ahead of me, paperwork that needs to be done tonight." *This was not the time to explain his job.*

"Thank you for dinner." She turned away from him.

"You're not getting off that easy, Twilla!" He yelled angrily, spinning her around to face him. "I don't know what's going on in that crazy head of yours, but I don't go around kissing women as a matter of habit. And I sure as hell don't sleep with them either. Now, are we clear?"

"Very," she said, her own thoughts churning.

"Then you better think about it. Now, get inside so I know you're safe."

"Could you kiss me again?"

"You just want me to drive back in more pain."

"That your problem, I offered to remedy that situation." She pecked his cheek with a kiss, slapped his ass and slipped inside her room, closing the door in his face.

Clisten stood facing it with the same continuous thought that ran through his mind earlier. *This woman makes me crazy.*

Twilla stood on the opposite side with a different slant entirely. *Just what the hell was he talking about? Kissing me eliminates other women? And he's a fucking saint because I'm the only woman he's currently sleeping with? I don't think so.*

A short time later, Twilla removed her clothes and hung them carefully, still satisfied by Clisten's appreciation of her appearance. She looked in the mirror to check the style of her hair. It did seem to soften the shape of her face. She would keep it.

After getting into her pajamas, Twilla turned on the television and settled in bed to watch a movie. However, halfway through, her cell phone jarred her awake.

"Julie?" Twilla yawned, realizing she had drifted off to sleep. "Is something wrong?" Then clearing her head for a possible setback, asked again. "Is dad ok?"

"No. He's fine." Julie reassured her.

"Well that's good news." Although relieved by the report, Twilla knew something else was in the wind. It was probably about Russell.

"But I'm not," she wailed.

Here we go again, Twilla's thought. "What happened?"

"I'm in love, truly in love." Julie echoed her feelings.

Twilla sat on the bed, confused by her sister's statement. "Isn't being in love a good thing?"

"It's wonderful," Julie gushed before changing her tone, "and yet so bad."

"Then I don't understand the problem."

"What do I tell Russell?" she asked, surprising her sister.

"Doesn't he already know? You must have told him how you felt months ago." *Now Twilla was more confused than ever.*

"I did, but I don't," she moaned. "You have to help me."

"How the hell can I help you, when I don't understand what you're trying to tell me?"

"But you always understood my situations."

Although that reminder irritated her, Twilla's knew there was only one way to wade through Julie's layer of problems…and that was to start at the beginning…with Russell Weatherly.

"Where is Russell now?"

"He's in town. I'm sure of it. He left a message on my cell for dinner tomorrow night."

Sunday must be a slow night for him, Twilla thought to herself. Then as she wondered if Russell reserved Saturdays for his corral of other women, Twilla heard Julie clear her throat impatiently. "So, what's the problem? Have dinner with him."

"Brian wouldn't like it," her sister offered quickly.

"Is this the architect you met through Russell?" She remembered the mention of his name during their bedroom conversation.

"Yes." Her voice was shaky. "Brian's the one I care for. He's steady like a rock; always there for me and fun to be with."

"So, what's the problem? You're not in a relationship with Russell. There's no ring to contend with. He never proposed marriage. You were just dating."

"I had hope for more," she said, memories flooding her mind.

"Well that didn't happen. Your ring finger's bare and you shouldn't feel guilty about anything. There was no understanding." Twilla paused for a minute. There was no way to sugar coat her next question. "Tell me this. Are you and Brian in a relationship now? I think you know what I mean."

"I'm meeting his parents in two weeks. We've already talked about marriage." Then noticing a slight pause, Julie asked, "Are you still there?"

"I am so happy for you. At long last someone deserving of you," she said, her voice filled with expectation of a wedding. "But if you and Brian have been seeing each other, why wasn't Russell aware of it?"

"I left Russell three messages to call me. Everything went to voice mail. Brian left messages and sent him texts."

"Call Brian and tell him about Russell's plans for dinner tomorrow night. Suggest that you phone Russell to have him make reservations for three. He will get the picture very quickly. Some unexpected situation will pop-up and cause him to cancel."

"Should I call Brian now with your plan in mind?"

"That's your decision. Since both of you tried contacting him, Russell already knows something's up."

"Then why didn't he call Brian instead of me?"

"Who knows how men think?" Twilla answered. Although her sarcasm encompassed the entire male population, there was one whose behavior drove her crazy with the want of him.

However, Julie's case was different...from Twilla's point of view. She was not about to demean Russell as a coward and a player of women. Doing so, would only question the advice Twilla gave her sister in the bedroom of their family home, the night Julie spoke of her love for him. That night Twilla told her sister to be patient. What Twilla wanted was time to investigate the man's background and prove how shallow he was with women, all women. Julie would have been informed. She deserved better.

Although Twilla thought Russell was a complete rake after he tried seducing her at the family home and his subsequent visits to her condo, in retrospect, he was solely responsible for her night with Clisten.

Not true an inner voice challenged. Russell was merely a precursor of what she thought might happen. Without the chemistry between them, Twilla would never have yielded. She faced that fact a long time ago. Twilla wanted Clisten beside her that night, and he wanted her as much as she wanted him. But those thoughts were brought up short by Julie's next question.

"What if Brian wants to talk to Russell instead of me?" Julie asked with a great deal of uncertainty in her voice.

"Let him. Give him the phone message and go from there."

"You make everything sound so easy," she complained. "Wait until you meet someone and fall in love, Twill," she lamented, using her sister's pet name. "Then you'll know what it feels like to have your insides twisted in knots."

"Has my suggestion helped you at all?" Twilla changed the subject, ignoring her sister's warning.

"I'm going to call Brian right now. Thanks, Twill. Love you." She ended the call.

Twilla eyed her dead iPhone. *Lucky me. Julie makes 'being in love' sound like an intestinal problem. What I feel for Clisten is not some twisted obstruction. That's for damn sure.*

Later, as she crunched her bed pillow, their last conversation, particularly his parting words, kept running through her mind. It was the 'Are we clear?' that bothered her. Could it be true? Would this handsome man, one who could have his pick of any woman, really want her? Her mother always said she was plain. Did Clisten see her in a different way? When he said she looked beautiful, did he really mean it?

Maybe it wasn't a line. Maybe that's who Clisten really was: a man who comes on strong and arrogant, but is a straight shooter, expressing his thoughts. His parting words continued to linger in her mind as she tried raising objections to them.

It's always *'work first'* with him!

Face it, Twilla. Understand and accept it or get off the train. There won't be too many stops like him…..so drummed her thoughts.

What makes him think he's alone in the passion department? *Just being close to him makes me crazy too.*

Doesn't he understand where I'm coming from? What about my feelings? My needs?

Tears began falling from her luminous brown eyes, the heaving of her chest steadily increasing with each painful thought.

Why do I ache so much for him…?

Why am I not important enough…?

I need him to want me, love me…can't he see that?

Why does loving someone hurt so much?

Is this what Julie meant? Was she right?

After tossing and turning several times, Twilla finally fell asleep.

TWENTY-TWO

PAPERWORK

Shortly after entering the car, Clisten tapped a number on his cell phone. "I was indisposed when you called," he said turning a key in the ignition.

"I figured." Corky's voice blasted the airways. "I wanted to bring you up-to-speed. He lawyered-up after you left but was held over. The perp seems to know something about the way we work."

"Did you get anything?"

"Fingerprints identified him as Jonathan Grant from Cleveland. Records show a wife, Amelia, and a son named Mark. I thought you should know." He paused waiting for some response.

"Prints from the car?" Clisten asked, thinking it a natural assumption.

"On file as a stockbroker," Corky clarified, dropping the matter for something more important. "Did you get what you wanted?"

"The motive. It sets everything in motion for both cases." Clisten turned on the highway heading toward Stockton.

"So, what was it…money, revenge, infidelity? Don't make me go through the list," he threatened.

"Revenge was a big part of it. Once he found the woman, her life was essentially over. Although our boy killed her earlier than planned, that was his intention all along."

"Are you saying my partner's murder was connected to your female runaway?"

"Pretty much, but she took a new identity. The murdered woman had been constantly abused. I saw the x-rays."

"So, your Amy Gregson was really his wife, Amelia Grant."

"That's the way it looks," he sighed. "The whole thing's crazy."

"I don't follow."

"Think about it. He used a three-step plan to come here and kill her. Jonathan Grant became John Landis to escape being traced. As John Landis, he met and killed Tony Mistretta to finalize his plan."

Of course, the missing step was killing a suspicious Leggin ahead of his planned schedule, but this was not the time for a repeat. Corky never agreed with Clisten's theory about his partner's death.

"Yeah, but what kind of twisted mind kills for a spot in the police department?"

"A psychopath who found his hunted victim, then developed a long-range plan by murdering two policemen to position himself for a targeted kill." Clisten thought of Leggin again.

"I don't buy it. He could have made the shot, driven out-of-town and left us scratching our asses for clues."

"No." Clisten disagreed. "Two things were supposed to happen: your partner's body was to have sunk permanently; and as a detective, phony Tony planned to turn his wife's murder into a cold case before returning to his former life as a stockbroker. Who would have known he was an imposter, if you hadn't called?"

"That's true."

"And if Amy hadn't recognized him, the killing would have taken place later…as originally planned."

"You think he had a timetable." Although Corky's statement was logical, Clisten failed to mention the man's real plan, his true reason for coming to Stockton.

"Absolutely. He had to join in and be accepted by the force without arousing suspicion. With his likable personality, it wasn't hard. Who would suspect an incoming cop of a murderous plot?

Remember, Tony was a legal transfer." Clisten parsed his words. "This had been a long-range plan shortened by the recognition of his wife and then you."

"You already mentioned that," Corky conceded, causing Clisten to continue his narrative.

"After the killing, phony Tony would have continued his role of detective by erasing any possible clues. Later, when the case got cold, he would request a few weeks off with some excuse and just disappear."

"Obviously the plan didn't work."

"That's because I answered the phone when you called your partner. Although the murder had already taken place we could have wrapped it up sooner if Sergeant Qurlan wasn't so obliging."

"I wanted to arrest him for impersonating an officer, but you told me not to come."

"It was too late, by then," Clisten said, refreshing Corky's recollection. "When Tony called the station, Qurlan gave him a 'head's–up' about my *looking* for him. That's when Tony went missing. Now we know he was watching me, following Twilla Hale and searching for Rebecca Givens."

"What about the son? Where does he fit into all of this?"

"Our records show Amy Gregson living alone. So, he could be anywhere."

"Well, that's not really a part of our murder investigation." Corky ignored the comment, feeling triumphant. "We have means, opportunity and motive. It's a first-degree conviction anyway you cut it. He killed a cop and we have enough material evidence to put him away permanently."

"Anything good?"

"Witnesses and more fingerprints."

"Witnesses, maybe in the bar, but fingerprints? The man's too smart. He would have wiped Tony's apartment clean."

"That may be true, but he must have had a last-minute flush. There were prints on the handle. Can you believe?"

"No. That was sloppy."

"Our lab technicians are very thorough. They weren't going to let anything slip by when one of our own got killed." He gave a sigh of relief. "Now, it's up to the big guns for prosecution. Our work's done. Yours should be too, except for the paperwork."

"Don't remind me." Clisten groaned. "I know they'll adjudicate your case before moving to my jurisdiction. Yet, my gut still tells me Leggin was killed before Tony. I just can't prove it."

"We've gone through this before," Corky said, frustrated by the detective's repeated litany.

"But it makes sense in real terms if Jonathan Grant felt his role here as a detective was threatened or his identity revealed. Think about it. Can you imagine how much planning it took to go through with it?"

"Are you praising the SOB...after all he's done?"

Clisten sensed Corky's outrage with an anger of his own. "No. I am not!" He blurted loudly. "The man's a cold-blooded killer, but you can't underestimate him. He's smart and he's patient. He waited, watched and studied all three targets before activating his murderous plans. To accomplish this, it took an organized and disciplined mind, along with a pair of steel balls."

"You think he had help?"

"We'll never know. Anyone connected to him must be dead. He wouldn't make that kind of mistake."

"You're thinking blackmail."

"For the plan to succeed, anyone helping him search for his wife had to be eliminated. He could leave no witness alive. And murdering people came easy. It was part of his genetic makeup."

"I don't want to think about it anymore," Corky yawned. "Are you on the way home now...this late...after only two interviews?" Corky yawned again. "I don't think so."

"Think what you want. I stopped for dinner." The man's in-ference disappointed him. "What happened to the evidence in Tony's car?"

"Don't worry, it's been logged in. I took care of the paperwork, including the transfer. It was all done legally. I'll keep you in the loop. Don't fret."

"Fret?" Clisten mimicked him.

"Quit busting my chops!" Corky chortled, repeating one of Clisten's earlier refrains before hanging up.

Clisten thought about their conversation as he continued down the highway, the mileage signs signaling 21 more miles to his destination.

Although the motive was the same in both cases, there were things he could not discuss with Corky or anyone else until he determined the contents of his report, inclusions and exclusions. It had to be factual and accurate. Factual and accurate…his mind took over.

Clisten could not mention the real reason for Jonathan's rush to murder Amelia. Finding his son, before killing his wife, was the primary goal of the man's abominable plan. He needed her alive to accomplish this. Searching her apartment for clues was the first part of his plan. Then he continued following her from a sizeable distance thinking she would lead him to the son's location. Yet, to keep his disguise as a detective secure, he shied away from places she frequented to keep from being recognized.

It was then and only then, when the recognition took place, that Jonathan's plans had to change. Finding the son was second to his own survival. Amelia as Amy would have accused him openly, know-ing he would be jailed for fraud, despite the cost to her.

Yes. His report would only detail facts. That was his job. Since there was no room for speculation in a murder case, he could give no real intelligence on the son.

However, Clisten did have questions, ones he could not answer and would never be able to. Yet to protect those who suffered most, he had to remain silent. Still, those thoughts lingered.

Although she had a full description of Amelia's husband, Mrs. Benson never suspected Tony Mistretta as being Jonathan Grant. Why? The woman was mentally alert, although pretending to be a bit senile. Only one logical explanation existed. The man was a detective in the police department. She had seen him before, when Amelia's apartment had been ransacked. That had to be the simple explanation. She noticed the badge, not the man. But that was not the only thing that occurred to him.

During the interview with Rebecca Givens, Mark's location was never mentioned. But then again, Clisten never asked. He didn't have to. They had reached a silent understanding, one that was mutual. The assumption being, no one knew anything about the child or if he were still alive. He had never appeared with Amelia to anyone's knowledge: not when the woman moved into her apartment, nor when she asked Rebecca Givens for a job referral. Now that she was dead, the prospect of finding him died with her.

Then too, something like a ring never existed.

A wide grin crossed his face. *Clisten didn't need to ask where they had hidden Mark. He had determined the boy's location during the visit. Rebecca was well-aware of it, prompting an unspoken pledge between them. Clisten would never divulge their secret, even now, when Mark was safe.*

Clisten thought about the boy and wondered how he liked selling puppies.

Clisten was only a few miles from town when his thoughts turned to Twilla Hale. Could she not understand his reason for leaving her? Obviously not. The woman had no concept of his job as a detective or his priorities.

Had he not clarified his thoughts? Clisten thought so. He wanted to be with her, spend the night together, their bodies entwined. The desire was there. It had to be obvious from the foreplay at dinner: the signal of making love never left his thoughts. She understood. It was mutual. He wanted her; she wanted him; they hungered for each other.

All of that was changed by a phone call, one reminding him of the case, his primary reason for going to High Coventry.

Was she disappointed with the way he left her? No. Not disappointed. She felt rejected. That was a better word. He had made advances, bringing her to him and kissing her passionately with expectation, only to push her away when she yielded.

At that moment her desire clearly turned to anger, a resentment which Clisten refused to allow without an explanation or a demanding tone of his own. Her anger paled by his reproach for her misguided understanding of the situation. If nothing else, Clisten felt it necessary to clear the air. He was not some sweet-smiling lothario going through life kissing and seducing women. That he made abundantly clear, as was his interest in her. If she couldn't understand that, then she was dumber than the sandpaper in her lab.

Was she really that stupid to understand his situation? If so, he would never see her again. That kind of person would never understand anything short of a one-sided relationship, one demanding constant adoration.

Yet, Twilla was something unto herself...a different kind of dinosaur. When her ignited passion diminished...and after Clisten's litany on his behavior with women, she surprised him abruptly with a kiss on the cheek, a pat on the ass and goodnight asshole, although she s didn't call him that. She had reconciled to an evening without him…as in "ok, no big deal."

Had Clisten screwed up with her? In retrospect, he didn't think so. He was being honest. Although he hated leaving her, his work had to take precedence at the time. Twilla understood. He hoped she did. He wanted her to.

Clisten's thoughts continued as he pulled into the parking lot of the police station. On a factual basis he liked Twilla Hale. He wanted to know her better. She was an intelligent woman.

Oh, hell. Who am I kidding? The two of us fight like cats and dogs. She is one irritating bitch who drives me nuts!

He slammed the car door and entered the police station.

Except for Qurlan the station was deserted. "What are you doing here on a Saturday night?" Clisten asked, surprised by the man's presence. Aside from his duties, the officer was always busy on weekends with his wife and five children.

"Came back for this." He fingered his iPad, then added, "The kids want to use it and dad didn't remember bringing it to work this week. You know how that goes."

"Quiet night?" Clisten asked when the man finished explaining his presence.

"It is now. Pavarotti just left." Qurlan laughed, referring to a fellow officer who seemed to sing his way through life. The man would burst into song whether it be in the police car, the locker room, or anywhere an audience gathered. "I think we're all going bonkers. He left a pair of sneakers here." Then changing the subject, asked Clisten directly, "What's up with you? Saturday night, eight o'clock and no date?"

"Catching up on paperwork." Clisten gave a short reply as he strolled down the hallway. This was not the time for a lengthy conversation. "If Luciano comes back, tell him to keep it down."

"Tell him yourself. I'm leaving," Qurlan countered, as he watched Clisten enter his office. "You can lock up."

Within minutes, Clisten was studying an open file on Amy Gregson. He took a large yellow tablet from his desk drawer, wrote Amelia Grant aka Amy Gregson across the top sheet, and then turned on the computer to search for a report on the missing woman. He could not find one. Amelia Grant's absence was never recorded anywhere in the Cleveland area.

Clisten checked Motor Vehicles next. Within seconds, Amelia Grant's expired driver's license, a pictured one from many years earlier, appeared on the screen. After adding a printed copy to her file, he thought about the woman's abusive husband and began a search on him.

A pictured Jonathan Grant with a current driver's license from the state of Ohio flashed across the screen. Clisten immediately recognized him as the fake Tony Mistretta and added a printed copy to the file.

Clisten sat back in his desk chair, his thoughts on the battered woman and her son. How should he handle it? If Rebecca Givens' account of the local police were true, he would get nothing from them. An injury reported by the hospital would have been processed quietly by one of Jonathan's police friends as *'having been acted upon'* and filed. However, an extensive profile of Amelia Grant might give him the additional information he needed.

Within minutes, Amelia Grant's age, address, phone number and the absence of a criminal record appeared on the computer screen. Three other names emerged within the composite: Jonathan Grant, Mark Grant and Chloe Moss. A further digging gave the extent of these relationships: a husband, son, relative. Although the relationship of relative, not sister, gave him cause to wonder, he shrugged it off as an error and filed the information.

A further thought crossed his mind. Was this the file Corky spoke of, the one identifying the family? It had to be. The fingerprint file of a stockbroker would not give the kind of information needed. He must have cross-referenced both.

Clisten began to analyze one section of Amelia's profile with hypothetical thoughts. If Mark were under the age of two when she fled Cleveland, the child would be about nine now. The image of a boy with a howling dog caused him to smile. *That would be about right.*

Then he checked the Cleveland listing of a property on Aberdeen Road and browsed the computer for a deeper dig. According to the information gleaned, the area consisted of single family dwellings, one associated with planned neighborhoods. This brought on further questions. Did Jonathan Grant still own the property? Although the tax office could provide that information, it was of little use now that he was under arrest. Still certain questions remained. Was the property vacant? Was it used when Clisten couldn't find the imposter during his extensive search? A new hiding place would make sense since Clisten checked every hell-hole he knew of.

Clisten thought about the sadistic man. Would the neighbors remember anything about Amelia Grant's abusive marriage? Although questioning them directly could be a consideration, what would be the point? He had already seen the woman's X-rays of multiple fractures and no longer needed that information. The woman was dead, murdered by her husband and he had the evidence to prove it.

He studied the phone number for a moment and wondered whose name was on the billing, and if it was still in service. Taking the cell phone from his pocket, he tapped-in the number listed on the computer screen. After a few rings it went directly to voicemail for the caller's message.

How convenient. The man certainly knew how to take cover, particularly when his real identity was unknown.

Clisten returned to the computer screen profiling Amelia Grant.

Aside from her abusive husband, the two other names listed had to be considered. Clisten was well-aware of the situation concerning Mark Grant and his promise to shield the boy. Chloe Moss, however, was another matter entirely. *Handling the vinegar lady Rebecca Givens talked about could be difficult.* Did he dare visit her or would a phone call suffice? Either way could be very messy and extremely unsatisfying.

He eyed his watch. It wasn't quite nine o'clock. Perhaps it was too late for a lengthy conversation, but it was still early enough to arrange a meeting for a later date.

After checking the computer for her phone number, Clisten tapped-in the number on his office phone, just in case he needed a record of the call to Chloe Moss.

"Hello," a distinctively low voice answered.

"I would like to speak to Chloe Moss."

"What is the nature of your call?" The voice demanded.

"It's a personal matter. I'm Detective Clisten Barr from…"

Before he could complete his identification, the woman began an angry vent, interrupting him completely. "I already gave money to the police. Why are you…?"

Before she could finish the reprimand, Clisten reacted quickly with a few words of his own. "I'm not calling for a donation. It's about Amelia Grant, your sister."

"Ha. That's a laugh. She hasn't been my sister for years." Her voice hit a sour note.

"Nevertheless, I would like to make an appointment with you about her."

"I told you before. She's not my sister anymore. She just took-off and broke my father's heart. Husband's too. No goodbyes, no reason for leaving, nothing. So, I don't care anything about her. I have nothing to say and no need for a meeting."

"She's dead," he said flatly. "Amelia Grant is dead."

"Why are you telling me? Why should I care? I haven't seen that bitch in years." Clisten could hear the woman's heavy breathing. "I get it. You want me to bury her. That's why you called."

"No. I just wanted you to know."

"Where was she living?"

"Stockton, small town, eastern Pennsylvania"

"Alone?"

"Yes."

"Where's the son?"

"We have no record of him. She lived alone."

"That figures. Amelia only cared about herself. Family meant nothing to her. She had a good father, a wonderful husband and a beautiful little boy. Never appreciated what she had."

"I wanted to tell you in person."

"Not necessary," she paused again. "Why a detective? Was it an accident?"

"No. Amelia was shot. She was murdered."

"I'm not surprised," the woman blustered loudly. "We always knew she'd come to a bad end. We talked about it, Daddy and me, but never with her husband, Jonathan. He stopped coming around. It was just too painful; not knowing where she was or if she was still alive. That's too bad. She had it so good."

"I wanted to offer my condolences," he said with the right touch of politeness. "You needed to know."

"I know you're obligated to tell a family when something happens to one of its members. You have done your duty, officer…"

"Detective Barr," Clisten interjected.

"Right." Chloe Moss ended the conversation with droplets of vinegar.

When Clisten heard the abrupt click ending the call, he realized the depth of Amelia Grant's despair. Between her husband and the likes of Chloe Moss, the dead woman was living a miserable life surrounded by a wretched family.

Chloe Moss was not interested in what happened to her sister. That was obvious. Burial costs seemed to be her main concern as she questioned the purpose of his call. The inference was clear. She was not interested in paying for a burial. However, Clisten had that covered, if questioned by her or the legal authorities. The detective did make inquiries and found one candidate who would cover the cost.

Yet, how could he report contacting a sister whose unforgiving heart refused the burial of a sibling? He clearly understood Amelia's need for escape. It was a matter of survival.

Clisten sat back in his chair again trying to reorganize his thoughts. His paperwork on the murder of Amy Gregson, the alias used by Amelia Grant, had to be factual and accurate. He had to substantiate the facts of the case with material evidence that could lead to a conviction. The rifle immediately came to mind.

Clisten worked into the night detailing Jonathan Grant's murderous plan to kill his abused wife, while impersonating a transferring detective whom he murdered to assume the man's identity. Clisten verified the legality of Tony Mistretta's official move by including a copy of the transfer papers, the jurisdictions involved and his work with Detective Frank Corsi.

Three pictures topped the file. A caption under one was the name Amy Gregson; under the other, Amelia Grant. The third one simply named Jonathan Grant. But nowhere in the file was there an in-depth probe or picture of the son, Mark Grant. Nor was there a record of the boy being seen with his mother, who was now dead. A telephone interview with Miss Chloe Moss, the sister of the murdered woman indicated a deep estrangement, yielding no viable information on the family. Clisten made certain to record the date and time of his interview with Chloe Moss.

He sat back in his chair and looked at the fat file of paperwork that reinforced his arrest report. Essentially the case was over. So why didn't he feel some sense of satisfaction?

It wasn't the case that took over his thoughts. Compiling facts to make a case was nothing more than routine to him. He had done it many times before. What was so different about this one? Was it his involvement and her lack of support?

Oh, hell. It is what it is. She wouldn't understand.

Clisten signed the report, got up from his chair and went home.

TWENTY-THREE
CIGARETTE BUTT

Twilla awakened early Sunday morning, feeling depressed. Her weekend was not what she had planned. Clisten managed to screw it up again...all the way around. Granted, he did find Rebecca Givens, even clarified the mystery surrounding the woman...but the other, the rest of their time together was a complete disappointment.

What you really mean is the way the evening ended. You wanted to be with him, lay by his side and make love. She thought of his thumb messaging her palm, signaling his desire, stimulating within her his erogenous intentions.

She felt an ache beginning to heighten deep within her body as she imagined being swept in his arms, his lips on hers, their bodies blending so passionately. She could feel his chest hairs rubbing her breasts with each undulating motion, and in that instant of rhythmic progression felt the torrid heat of their togetherness throbbing deep within her loins for that moment of pure bliss.

That it didn't happen, made her feel unwanted and turned her frustration to anger. At first, she thought it contemptuous with the way he recoiled with rage, silencing her completely, her attention drawn to his words. His message could not have been more definitive.

The dinner foreplay was a precursor for his intentions that evening. And although a phone call ended those plans, he made it very clear that he was not the town player. His interest in her was real; his job, a priority.

While he didn't spell it out, his message resonated loudly within her clouded thoughts. If there was to be any kind of relationship, she had to understand the parameters: no kissy, kissy anything when duty called. Either shit or get off the pot, Twilla. The reasoning was not that hard to understand.

"No sense thinking about it," she said aloud, sliding out of bed before trotting to the bathroom. "A quick shower and I'm out of here." Yet the events of the previous day were still fresh in her mind.

Promises made: promises kept. The adage continued running through her thoughts like the ticking rhythm of a metronome.

She had to stop reflecting her pledge to Amy and concentrate on the present… like getting into my jeans and leaving High Coventry. After making a quick trip to the hotel coffee shop, she would be on her way home.

Of course, that wasn't quite true. Before heading to Stoneledge, Twilla had to stop by Mrs. Benson's apartment at Ravencrest for Lily. Fortunately, the two complexes stood within three or four miles of each other. So, time and distance presented no problem; however, Lily certainly would.

Her precious Peekapoo would probably give Twilla an Amish shunning for leaving her. She pictured those large black dots staring up at her with an aloof elegance that would scorn the nouveau riche. She was such a dammed elitist. Lily had not yet realized her role as a canine. She was the dog, and Twilla, her master. Had that thought never occurred to the little Prima Donna? Of course not. There were times when an uncompromising Lily would eye Twilla with disdain and walk away, flagging her tail with unwavering contempt.

As Twilla drove along the highway, her thoughts turned from Lily to Mrs. Benson. Should she mention meeting Rebecca Givens or being told that a man came to secrete Amy the day she was shot? Mentioning Amy's urgent phone call and Mr. Banks arrival could muddy the waters and raise questions. Then too, Rebecca might not want Mrs. Benson privy to their conversation or the information she imparted. But truth be told, the woman was really talking to Clisten, not her. Twilla just happened to be his robotic companion with an auditory capacity.

It would be far better if Twilla just stuck to the script. Mrs. Benson was caring for Lily while she was away for the weekend. It was much safer that way. Let Rebecca Givens be the one to divulge their meeting. The prerogative was hers. But if Twilla were a betting woman, she would say the lady from High Coventry would be tight-lipped about the whole encounter.

She thought about giving Rebecca the ring. Clisten's explanation could be right after all. Maybe in finding Rebecca, she had found Mark; perhaps not in the physical sense one would expect, but in a way, Amy had hoped. Passing the ring to Rebecca meant Twilla, *not his father,* had found Mark. The boy was still safe.

Passing the ring brought up another scenario that could be closer to the truth. The ring must have symbolized a coded message between the two women, one that revealed an outcome.

While Amy had the ring, her life, along with Mark's, functioned normally.

If the ring were found on her dead body, it signaled a dire warning that Jonathan was in the area and had been watching her, making contact impossible. The group had to take further precautions to protect Mark.

What if no ring were found on her body?

Although Mrs. Benson would search Amy's apartment for it, they would be crazy with worry over Mark's safety. So, where was it? There was no one *among them* who could ask that question without the risk of being questioned by the authorities or targeted by the abusive husband.

While uncertain of the facts, they would still point to Jonathan and his effort to find his son. Yet, he would have no knowledge of the ring's coded significance.

That the whole situation had now changed seemed to please her. Rebecca had the ring; Amy's husband had been arrested, and Mark was safe. Twilla felt good about it. She had kept her pledge to Amy.

As she continued along the highway, a question kept invading her thoughts. *"Why do you keep referring to her as Amy Gregson instead of Amelia Grant?"*

"That's how I knew her." Twilla insisted, before questioning an avenue she found puzzling: the start of the whole situation; *the why of it all.*

Why did Amy give Twilla the ring in the first place? She had so many people helping her. *It made no sense at all, and a scenario of fact and assumption began to play out in her mind.*

Fact: When Amy ran away from an abusive husband, she took Mark with her and assumed a new identity and safe location with a distant relative.

Assumption: Knowing Amy's husband would be searching for her, the two women had to plan everything down to the last detail.

Fact: Aside from coordinating the entire ongoing effort, Rebecca Givens was instrumental in getting Amy a teaching job and an apartment to make her life appear normal.

Assumption: Fitting into an academic setting was one way of seeming innocuous.

Fact: Three people involved with Amy's new identity conspired to protect her and Mark from the moment of their escape:

Rebecca Givens, Mrs. Benson, and Herman Banks. Aside from this triangle of main conspirators, Gunther Pratt and Tula Banks aided in the deception, although their roles were clearly defined.

Assumption: With her apartment near Amy's, Mrs. Benson could apprise the group of impending danger. Herman Banks would help Amy escape should a dangerous situation arise and Rebecca Givens, the driving force of the trio, would check on Amy's safety through linking with Herman Banks for Mrs. Benson's updates. Unfortunately, since Rebecca Givens was the only one who had seen a picture of Jonathan Grant, identifying him could have become problematic.

Fact: Clisten contacted Gunther Pratt because he worked in records at High Coventry where Rebecca Givens was an administrator before retiring.

Assumption: Somewhere during Clisten's investigation, the name Rebecca Givens popped-up, and when he contacted the school, the detective spoke with a Gunther Pratt who gave scant information.

After taking all these facts into consideration, Twilla was still clueless. Everyone had a role in protecting Amy. So why not give one of them the ring when her life was in danger? Mrs. Benson was the logical choice. The woman lived next door to Amy. She would have known if a threat were imminent. Amy would have told her. She was in the loop. It just seemed so illogical. Twilla was not sure she agreed with Clisten's narrative, although uncovering the role Mrs. Benson played could have proven dangerous. His reasoning made sense.

Twilla was close to Ravencrest when a possible scenario of Amy's last hours framed her thoughts.

Having been found by her abusive husband, Amy called Herman Banks for help, but needed a back-up plan in case something went wrong. Knowing she faced possible death, Amy could not risk having Mrs. Benson's role exposed. Mark had to be protected at any cost and her neighbor was the family link. So, Mrs. Benson could not be suspected of having a close relationship with Amy while her husband was still around looking for his son.

What would Amy do next? She was planning an early escape but needed to insure Mark's safety if it failed. The answer was obvious. At least, now it was.

Amy planned to meet Twilla that fatal morning, knowing all the while she would be leaving the campus forever, provided her arrangement with Herman Banks went accordingly. If not, her other plan would go into effect.

That meant Amy spent the previous night adding clues to Twilla's cookbook and a photograph of her with Rebecca Givens. The young woman knew Twilla would inspect the cookbook immediately, since it was a family history of food recipes passed down by generations. The tome was Twilla's prize possession.

So much for the cookbook, what about the ring? Amy must have hidden it somewhere in her clothing, just like Twilla did initially. But it must have been in her pocket the morning she was shot.

Still the scenario failed to explain the inventory file. Where did it fit into all of this?

"It didn't," Twilla said aloud, as she drove into the parking lot of Ravencrest. "They weren't related."

Twilla climbed the few steps fronting the apartment building and headed toward the elevator off the main foyer. She held a monied envelope in her hand for Mrs. Benson while thinking of the furry princess waiting to greet her.

"She had better be glad to see me. I am in no mood for one of her hissy fits," she grumbled, exiting the elevator. "Like I'm going to do something about it. I missed that little shit." Her words echoed as she walked down the hall.

The couple passing her shrugged in unison, stepped into the elevator and held combined thoughts. *There seemed to be an influx of flaky people in their building.*

"Did you miss me?" Twilla questioned Lily sitting beside her in the passenger seat of the car. "I missed you." As she spoke, Twilla sensed something was wrong. Lily seemed unusually quiet and listless. But as they came nearer Stoneledge, Lily stood up in the passenger seat and began to bark. "My baby's homesick," she cooed and after parking the car leashed Lily before entering her unit.

As they approached the front of the building, Lily tugged at the leash moving Twilla toward the bushes for its daily watering. "I'm sorry. I forgot our routine," she apologized, "but you better hurry, you're not the only one who has to pee."

Within minutes of being inside the condo, Twilla watched a barking Lily race to the bedroom yapping to be on the bed with her pillow.

"Why do I always come in second?" Twilla asked herself as she placed Lily on the bed and watched her scamper toward her pillow.

When she finally stretched out on the bed, Lily stopped barking and snuggled in her armpit. "So that's what you want, snuggling! Me too." She caressed her. As they lay quietly together, Twilla fell fast asleep with Lily in the recess area of her arm pit. Deodorized or not, it seemed to be Lily's favorite spot.

Somewhere around two o'clock that afternoon, Twilla awakened somewhat disconcerted.

"I feel stiff," she said aloud, getting out of bed slowly. "How about you?" She addressed Lily who stood on the bed watching her. "C'mon. We've things to do, like getting my luggage and your dog food."

Within minutes Lily was sitting on the couch watching Twilla drop a suitcase on the floor and take a bag of dog food to the kitchen before shrugging-off her coat.

As she filled Lily's bowl with water, Twilla said, "I don't know about you but I'm hungry." As soon as the words escaped her lips, Lily began to bark.

"Spaghetti sound good?" she asked to her continuous barking. "I'm glad because I don't have anything good in the refrigerator."

Within the hour, both Twilla and Lily were satisfied with a dinner of spaghetti, loads of dipping sauce for bread but no meat balls. It was obvious that neither minded as they dug in, and the few red splatters on Twilla's yellow polo shirt painted an unusual abstract...particularly for those who liked that kind of art.

Somewhat later, as she sat on the couch watching the news with Lily beside her, a warm feeling flooded over her. It was nice to get away, but there was nothing like coming home. "This is where we belong," she said stroking Lily, "a place that makes us happy and safe."

It was the last thought that jolted Twilla to the sudden reality of a previous ransacking. She was not safe, not by a long shot. Pete had warned her of another possible invasion. Had that happened while she was away? The unit looked intact, but Pete told her it would. Anyone prowling for the file would have to be sophisticated enough to know where to look and how to go about it without leaving a clue.

Cautioning Lily to stay on the couch, Twilla walked to her desk and, sliding the desk chair outward over the carpeting, opened the center drawer very slowly. A sense of relief engulfed her as she examined its contents. Nothing had been touched. She would remove the file from her safety deposit box tomorrow and give Pete a glowing report when they met in the park. Although colder weather had been predicted, snow was not in the forecast. However, she remembered how strong the winds were blowing off the lake and knew she would have to dress accordingly to keep warm. Still, Thanksgiving was not that far away and Twilla could not remember eating turkey without a backdrop of snow.

"They're not always right," she said aloud. "We'll have a short visit with Pete and Sam tomorrow. I'll give him the original file and the whole thing will end. No more worries."

As she attempted to replace the chair beneath the desk, her eyes fell on something that looked like a cigarette butt. However, a closer inspection unleashed a range of strong emotions when she recalled the incident in the backyard of her family home.

Russell Weatherly, that two-faced son of a bitch! Her thoughts raced wildly as she recalled the pocketed cigarette butt he crushed in the yard, the repeated attempts to entice her with his visits and the cruel false play for Julie that caused her sister months of pain and sleepless nights. And for what purpose? To get access to a file? Why? For whom? Dr. Shelden? What was the connection between her department head and Russell Weatherly?

"Thank God, Julie found Brian," she muttered.

Then her thoughts took a different turn when she remembered Julie's phone call the previous night, when Twilla was in High Coventry.

That clever son of a bitch is covering his ass! Russell called Julie yesterday for dinner tonight. He must have called her after rifling my condo on Saturday and used a Sunday dinner as an excuse for being in town. If he was out and about dining in New York, no one would suspect him of being in Stoneledge rifling her condo the day before. But he was. The evidence was there. The cigarette butt clearly belonged to Russell Weatherly. There was no one else to accuse.

Twilla stared at the cigarette butt lying on the floor and came to a quick decision. She walked to the kitchen counter, grabbed her cell phone and, turning the TV to mute, tapped Pete's number.

"We need to talk." She listened to his response before answering. "No. It can't wait until tomorrow. I have a problem." When Twilla explained finding Russell's cigarette butt under the desk, she was unhappy with his suggestion. "That's my only avenue? You're sure that's the way to go?" She nodded in agreement. "I'll see you tomorrow at two."

"This is not what I want." She told Lily who now stood on the couch, totally puzzled. Why was she being scolded? Why take that tone with her? She had done nothing wrong. It wasn't fair. She was a good girl.

As soon as Twilla sat on the couch, Lily crossed to her lap and began licking her face.

"You want attention." Twilla scratched her head. "I do too, but not the kind I'll be getting," she added, tapping a number on her cell phone.

"Detective Barr," a distinctive voice answered.

Twilla felt all crumbly inside, not knowing what to say, except, "You *make me crazy. I want to be in your arms.*" Instead, she cleared her throat.

"Hello." The voice repeated, sounding somewhat annoyed.

"Clisten. It's Twilla. I hate to bother you, but a retired detective told me you could gather some evidence for him since you have access to a lab."

"Slow down," he interrupted. "What kind of evidence and what are you talking about?" A second later she heard him ask, "Twilla, what are you into now?"

"Long story. Remember my telling you about my suspicions of Russell Weatherly?"

"The man with your sister." She heard him sigh in disgust.

"This has nothing to do with my sister!" Twilla snapped, annoyed with his disdain of anything personal. "Well, it does, but it doesn't. It involves a cigarette butt."

"You have a cigarette butt?"

"I didn't touch it."

"No. You smoked it." She heard him chuckle.

"Now, you're pissing me off." She tapped the end button, furious that he could make light of the situation. Russell Weatherly had been in her home, gone through her things for a file. It had to be the file. What else was in the unit to spark someone's interest in her possessions? Nothing. She had nothing of value except a patched heirloom vase.

As she continued to sit on the couch stroking Lily, another thought crossed her mind.

How did he know I'd be gone? Has he been following me? Was he responsible for ransacking my condo the first time? When he came by that evening Russell seemed genuinely surprised by the burglary. That was around the third week of October, if she recalled correctly, and her thoughts faded to that night. It was Russell's first visit after the backyard episode and the night he met Clisten. I had just returned home after dad's surgery and, never expecting to find my condo vandalized, had a neighbor call the police.

The only person who knew my schedule then was Dr. Shelden. That would make sense if she and Russell worked hand in hand. But that did not seem logical. According to Pete, the scam was small scale, a form of embezzlement by equipment rather than the normal stealing of funds. If it was so small scale, why would anyone need to steal the file back again? Was Shelden afraid of being sacked? Maybe she was afraid of being blackmailed.

Twilla continued questioning those thoughts when the doorbell rang, causing Lily to jump off the couch and race toward the door.

A very neat Clisten Barr stood in the doorway studying a very messy Twilla facing him. Behind him, almost hidden, was a short stocky man carrying a bag, the kind a doctor would carry.

"Perfect. Did the two of you have spaghetti again?" he asked, dropping his coat on a chair while Lily tried climbing his leg.

Twilla eyed her telltale shirt and smirked. "Why? Are you hungry or just interested in abstract art?"

"Funny girl." Clisten answered dryly, taking Lily in his arms. "Tell me where this evidence is and what else you've been hiding from me. By the way, this is Harry. He's going to gather the evidence for a home invasion, not me."

Twilla led them to her desk and pointed to the cigarette butt underneath. "It's a Parliament, the kind Russell Weatherly smokes. It must have fallen out of his pocket. That's where he keeps his cigarette butts when there's no ashtray available."

"When, exactly, did you find the cigarette butt?" Clisten asked, as he walked away from the desk area to give Harry working space.

"Within the hour. I didn't think about looking in my desk for clues when I got home. I took a nap. I was tired!" Emphasizing her weariness, Twilla's voice grew louder as she followed him to the kitchen. "My unit seemed to be the way I left it before going to High Coventry."

"Why would you be looking in your desk for clues?" The woman's statement boggled his mind and Clisten wondered what kind of mischief was following her now.

"To see if someone was looking for the file. I arranged the desk drawer like Pete told me to." As she spoke they could hear Harry humming as he took pictures, checked the desk for fingerprints and bagged the cigarette butt.

"What file and Pete who? What's his last name?"

"I don't know. He's a retired detective. I met him in Tavis Park when I walked Lily. He's trying to help me," she added as an after-thought. "He's very kind."

"Here, hold Lily." Clisten moved toward her. After the detective placed the dog in Twilla's arms, he spoke privately with Harry about a later meeting as they walked toward the door of the unit. However, once the man had gone, Clisten turned his attention back to the woman whose life was constantly in turmoil. "Ok. Talk to me. What is this about?"

"Dr. Shelden gave Amy a file by mistake."

"Wait," Clisten hastily interrupted. "Are you talking about Amy Gregson? Amy Gregson alias Amelia Grant?"

"Yes, why?" She found his question puzzling.

"Because nothing connected to this woman ever seems to go away."

"It wasn't her fault Shelden screwed up." Twilla defended her colleague. "If Shelden's hands are so clean, why is she searching so frantically for it and why my place?"

"Why didn't Amy return it?"

"She found something wrong, something illegal."

"Everybody wants to play detective! Like she didn't have enough on her plate."

"You can't fault her for wanting to do the right thing."

"Right! Her life is going up in flames and she's worried about a file? I don't think so."

Clisten knew his statement made her angry, but he didn't care. That a woman whose life was in danger cared about a file or its contents was totally illogical. He had to know what Twilla was talking about. All she gave him were bits and pieces of a screwed-up story. *Was that the way her quirky mind worked?*

"Well, you're wrong this time. I don't care what you say. You are wrong about Amy. She did find something illegal and Pete thinks so too."

"Twilla, stop!" His sharp voice silenced her. "You are making no sense. Not to me. I'll summarize your information snippets and you tell me if I'm on the right track. Are we clear?"

"Yes," Twilla answered, her manner subdued as she listened to him chronicle the events.

"By mistake, Dr. Shelden gives Amy a file that has some sort of disclosure. Before her death, Amy gives it to you. Worried about its contents, you discuss the file with a retired detective. Meanwhile, Dr. Shelden or someone else, like Russell, searches your apartment for it and inadvertently drops a cigarette butt. Upon finding it, you discuss the information with a retired detective named Pete who tells you to call me."

Clisten paused for a moment, then said, "Now, tell me if that narrative is correct."

"That's only part of it." Twilla agreed to disagree. "Although I found the cigarette butt, the same brand Russell smoked and crushed in the backyard of my home, there's more to this than meets the eye."

"Meaning?"

"The whole thing was a set-up. I told you weeks ago the SOB was after something…something I couldn't figure out…and it just wasn't a roll in the hay. Now we know he was playing me for the file, dropping by unannounced, pretending this unwavering attraction had to be satisfied." *Her narrative paused for a moment, reflecting a thought that took precedence.* "But long before that could happen, Russell had to stir my sister's emotions to full bloom by getting her to fall in love with him. That would provide a pathway to meeting the plain Jane sister, charm the bitch out of her drawers and have her give him the file willingly." She shook her head. "This is sick."

"Twilla," he cautioned, "you do not mention this to Julie."

"I'd like to know how the hell my sister was targeted to get to me."

"If you mentioned her work place in conversation, tracking Julie Hale's routine would have been easy."

"I'm sure I must have…somewhere along the line."

"What's in the file?" Clisten no longer cared about the cigarette butt or how Russell manipulated Twilla's sister. He needed more information. Full disclosure would determine the extent of a crime, if one had been committed. At this point he had no way of knowing, since there was so little information to go on. In any event, it did not look good for Russell Weatherly.

"Equipment theft…refrigerators, ranges, big ticket appliances."

"And the relationship between Russell and Shelden?"

"I don't know."

"How did he know your schedule?"

"He didn't. Shelden had my schedule when I left for dad's surgery, but she certainly didn't know about High Coventry."

"Something's not right with this scenario." He moved from the desk area to the front door and shrugged into his coat. "When are you seeing your retired detective again?"

"Tomorrow at two in Tavis Park. Why?"

"Then we better talk about this before the meeting."

"Now would be a good time."

"No. I'm meeting Harry. Expect me tonight around eight."

"Do you want dinner?"

"Are you on the pill?" He closed the door slowly.

TWENTY-FOUR

TOGETHER

Twilla sat on the couch deep in thought. As she petted Lily, she thought of the previous night when Clisten held her in his arms, kissing her in the hotel hallway. They had the perfect opportunity to be together. The night was totally theirs with a king size bed for added comfort. Although she had not asked for a bed that size, the hotel probably offered that type of room with the extra cost in mind. But it didn't matter. A phone call ended their encounter. *Duty calls.*

Yet, his statements made her feel he cared. Was he being honest?

Clisten had every opportunity to be with her again today. They could have spent the afternoon together...enjoyed each other thoroughly...right through the night.

But no. Not Clisten, the detective. He had to get that stupid cigarette butt checked-in with Harry...like a cigarette butt couldn't wait. It would turn to ashes, or even explode, at the stroke of midnight. *Once again, duty calls.*

"Well, they say, the third time's the charm." She directed the conversation to Lily. "It damned well better be or I'm going to put your leash on him and climb his leg." She tugged Lily's ears. "Yes, I am," she cooed and then stopped suddenly. "Just listen to me. I sound like some sex-starved nut looking for someone to seduce." Twilla shook her head and smirked. "I am hungry for him. So, what am I going to do about it?"

236

It wasn't long before Twilla began searching her closet for something nice to wear. Her pantsuits were too business-like; she needed something more casual. She thought about slack pants but decided against them. This was not going to be easy.

After searching her entire wardrobe, Twilla settled on a crisp pair of jeans and a long sleeve sweater that matched the dark coral sand of Bermuda. She categorized the outfit as semi-casual; the kind one wears for a friendly get together.

With the proper attire and a possible menu in mind, the evening would be complete. Since she always had red wine and some type of cheese in the refrigerator, Twilla would play the perfect hostess with a cheese plate offering. They would discuss Amy's file and Twilla's current involvement. However, tomorrow would be a different story. She would give the file to Pete and it would be out of her hands forever.

Twilla was sure Clisten would offer some suggestion for her retired detective. But that didn't really matter. Being together was more important. It was to her.

After a long shower and a final primping before the mirror, it was somewhere after seven when Twilla finished dressing for her appointment with Clisten. Lily had eaten her dinner along with a few other snacks while Twilla bounced around the kitchen, trying to make her cheese and crackers presentation look attractive.

Shortly before eight o'clock, when Twilla answered the doorbell, she stood in shock to see Russell Weatherly staring back at her. *Russell Weatherly, the man who used her sister and left a souvenir behind while searching her desk.* But grasping the dangerous reality of his being in her doorway, she quickly became composed.

"I'm sorry." Twilla apologized. "I thought it was Clisten. That's why I'm so surprised. Please come in."

"You look beautiful as ever," he said, his eyes capturing her entire appearance. "I was in the area and wondered how you were doing."

"I'm glad you stopped by. Sit down, please." She motioned to a nearby chair when the doorbell rang. "I have so much to tell you." She walked to the door with Lily following her.

"Hi, sweetheart." Twilla threw her arms around Clisten, kissing and whispering along the side of his face, "Same old, different chapter." She watched the detective remove his coat before leading him into the living room where a short exchange with Russell took place.

"What brings you our way?" Clisten asked sinking into a large upholstered chair. His casual air was the detective's way of drawing him out.

"I have a conference in Scranton this week and thought I'd stop by."

"I'm so glad you did," Twilla chimed in.

"This calls for a celebration." Clisten rose from his chair to face Twilla. "I have a bottle of wine in my car. It's a Thanksgiving gift from my car dealer."

"Don't bother." She waved him off. "I have red wine. It's one of my staples." She walked to the kitchen refrigerator and within minutes returned with a tray.

The two men watched Twilla set a bottle of Cabernet Sauvignon, and three wine glasses on the coffee table. A minute later she added a plate of cheese and crackers. Then Twilla removed a corkscrew from the pocket of her jeans and gave it to Clisten.

Once Clisten filled the glasses he proposed a toast. "To our families." He clinked their glasses before everyone took a sip.

"This is really good wine." Russell was the first to approve.

"It is," Clisten agreed.

"What are we drinking to? Whose families?" Twilla asked.

"The existing possibilities. We can't predict the future, but who knows? Maybe Russell and I might be related someday. You never know about relationships."

Although the comment could have been challenged, Russell remained silent. By itself, the comment was meaningless. No one really cared. It was just something to say. Being together now was more important than thinking about what was to happen in the future.

After another glass of wine, the finish of cheese and a huge lie about his continued relationship with Julie, Russell was on his way, without fear of discovery or suspicion.

As soon as Russell left the condo, Clisten cautioned Twilla not to remove his empty wine glass and requested a tea towel and large freezer bag. Twilla watched him carefully roll the glass in the tea towel before inserting it into the freezer bag and seal it closed. Almost automatically, Clisten placed the bag beneath his coat as a reminder.

"You did all this hanky-panky for his DNA?" Although obvious, she caught his facial expression of acknowledgement.

"It could not have worked out better. You gave me a cigarette butt this afternoon without a comparison."

"Now you have one." She cleared the coffee table. "Considering how friendly we were, he still thinks it's under the desk."

"I think you're right." He echoed her sentiments. "But you couldn't have planned it better," Clisten repeated his original statement. "I still can't believe it." He shook his head. "So smooth."

"Believe it," she sneered sarcastically. "It took everything I could muster to be nice to that SOB. He lied through his teeth."

Clisten knew she disliked the man but found the strength of her statement confusing. "I know he lied to Julie, but I gather something else is going on." He walked to the couch and sat down.

The moment Twilla sat beside him, her eyes filled with tears as she tried to explain. "I was so hurt when you left me last night. I wanted to be with you. I guess I'm not supposed to say that, but pretending I don't care about you is not who I am. There I go, double negatives!" She cracked a laugh and then emitted a large heaving gasp that caused Lily to come running.

"Feeling hurt and unwanted, you called Julie." His voice was almost inaudible.

"No. She called me after you left."

"About Russell leaving her?" Clisten had suspected that would happen long before this. The man was without scruples.

"No. Julie fell in love with Brian, an architect friend of Russell's, while pining away for him."

"How long have you known about Brian?"

"Since last night." She pulled a tissue from her pocket and blew her nose. "Russell called her last night, which, of course, was Saturday for a Sunday dinner. She hadn't seen him in weeks... pretending travel, I suppose. She didn't know how to handle it."

"So, she called you." Clisten found the protracted conversation taxing, while trying to ignore Lily, who was pawing his knees, begging for attention.

"Julie was confused. I told her to have Russell make a reservation for three. He'd get the picture really quick."

"Did she do it?" he asked, surrendering to Lily by placing her on his lap.

"I don't know what happened, but Russell was just here and it's Sunday according to my calendar. Although we haven't talked since last night, I'm really pissed at his continued pretense. Everything about him is a lie."

"He could have been in town when he made the call."

"How could you make a dinner reservation or plan one for Sunday and be here with us? I may not be as smart as you are putting facts together, but I'm not clueless either. This does not add up to me."

"His plans may have changed." Although Clisten did not like the man, he was willing to keep an open mind until facts proved otherwise.

"They damn well did. That wasn't his clone drinking my wine."

The remark made Clisten chuckle. "Enough of this. If your sister's happy, let's move on."

"You're thinking about Amy's file."

"No. Twilla. Its contents. I would take a different approach."

"I don't understand."

"Follow my logic, using one refrigerator. A new one can be shipped directly to a location with or without being a replacement. However, if a replacement's involved, the old one must be removed first. Where did it go, what location and who removed it? Did the person who removed the old one position the new one?"

"What are you saying?"

"If your retired detective can produce evidence of theft, he must identify the people involved and the location of the stolen equipment, new or old." His voice trailed off momentarily. "Maybe that's what Amy found."

"What do you mean?"

"Maybe after checking some numbers, she came across pieces of new equipment that should have been in her lab but were never delivered." Suddenly, Clisten stopped speaking. "Of course, all of this is speculation on my part."

"But I think that's exactly what happened. I tried checking numbers, but nothing matched. Your theory sounds like something she would do. Amy always knew if the least little thing was amiss. She was like a bloodhound. Call it instinct or street smarts. Since the file was a complete record of the equipment Dr. Shelden purchased for her department, Amy must have been concerned about theft. It goes back over twenty years, as I remember."

"Then it must be the original or the only one in existence, since your unit was searched for it. I wouldn't be surprised if an investigation is underway and your retired detective needs to produce it."

"You think so? Why wouldn't he tell me?" Clisten noticed her confused expression and felt a further explanation was necessary.

"He couldn't. Not until it was over. That's how cases work. Still, I wonder…"

"What?" Twilla interrupted his pause. "Don't look at me like I'm a deer caught in headlights. Tell me."

"I'd like to know who removed and replaced the equipment for Shelden. Someone did. What was in it for him?"

"Russell?"

"No. He was just an errand boy. I wouldn't be surprised if he's related to Shelden in some way."

"There couldn't be too many people involved if they took pieces over a twenty-year span," she agreed, "particularly if they took one every few years."

"You can't only talk numbers in this case. We're talking theft of college property. If a crime has been committed, suspects, cost and motive will all come into play. Your man might not know where the missing equipment went, but the file will be a record of its existence."

"I'm out of it tomorrow."

"I thought you were meeting him."

"I am. I'm giving him the original at two o'clock in Tavis Park where we always meet." Twilla felt it important that Clisten have all the information now. "I was very upset to find Shelden's file in my cookbook along with recipe clues for Ruth Graham. I had no idea what anything meant."

Clisten's mind raced as she spoke. He knew she had more information when he first interviewed her weeks earlier. Why didn't she speak up then? When he needed it. "When was this? When did you first learn of Ruth Graham?"

"When I went home for Dad's surgery...right after Amy was shot. I went to her apartment for Lily, remember? You were there. And so was my cookbook. So, I took it. You went through my shopping bag before I left. Then I stayed with my father longer than expected."

"Most of the stuff was for Lily as I recall," he said, returning to the original subject. "How did you know about Amy's code? What made you think of cookbook cyphers?"

"The food sections were all mixed-up and the recipes, altered. That was not the organized Amy I worked with. None of it made sense, so I started writing the altered words on a tablet and framing them into some pattern."

Clisten listened intently, impressed with her ability to recognize cyphering or its existence with little to substantiate the possibility. "So that's how you came-up with the clues to find Ruth Graham."

"That and Amy's last words. 'Find Mark.'"

"What about the file?"

"I was totally confused. Why did Amy keep it? That ran through my mind constantly. There had to be a reason. Shelden did say she gave it to Amy by mistake, but I didn't know anything about the file at the time. I hadn't seen it. Then when things started to happen, I turned to Pete for help. What made her think I had it?"

"You and Amy were friends."

"No. We were colleagues. Friends share private issues; Amy never disclosed anything. That's why the file surprised me. I had no idea what it meant. Say what you want. I was scared, and Pete helped me a lot…with this and caring for Lily. I gave him a copy, so he'd understand where I was coming from."

"What does he look like? I should have asked that question a lot earlier."

"He's older, gray hair, medium height, and very friendly. His grandson's dog plays with Lily in Tavis Park. They don't really play. She licks Sam's nose for the most part."

As soon as Twilla mentioned Sam, Lily began squirming in Clisten's arms. "She must really like him."

"Pete calls Sam, her boy toy." Her joke caused him to chuckle. "It is cute, isn't it? King Kong and Barbie."

Still chuckling at the thought, Clisten rose from the couch, set Lily on the floor and walked toward the chair that held his coat.

His action was more than a signal to Twilla. The night was at an end. She walked to the front door and flipped off the light switch. "Why are you leaving me again? I thought you cared."

In the darkened room Twilla felt Clisten strong arms pulling her to him, his lips hard on hers, his tongue eagerly penetrating her mouth. He slammed her body against the wall and slipped his hand up her shirt cupping her breasts, his emotions surging, his body begging for release. And without warning, Clisten lifted her high in the air, and, cradling her in his arms, carried her to the darkened bedroom, a yapping Lily racing behind, breaking the brisk silence.

"Twilla." His voice was hoarse with emotion as he brought her to him, their hunger for each other soaring. "I wanted you so much." He could feel his body dripping sweat as their undulating pace quickened. Placing his hands under her lower back he swayed her body in sync with his, her soft intermittent moans increasing, signaling what to come was near.

"Clisten!" She called his name, holding him tightly to her. She felt her body soaring upward…high among the cotton clouds… floating in a portrait sky…while redwoods below sang love songs to an instrumental wind, carrying their haunting melody…a symphony that ended much too soon.

After a few breathless moments, Twilla curled back into him and realized the unvarnished truth of their lovemaking. The thrill of the experience was due to her own true feelings for him and his masterful handling of her. She never wanted it to end.

"Clisten." Her soft voice caught his attention. "You turn me into putty when we make love. I have this out of body feeling and have no idea what's happening when it happens. I'm not making any sense."

"Lily quit barking. She stopped when I brought you to bed."

"I didn't know."

"I know you didn't."

"But that's not what I mean."

"I don't understand where you're coming from." Her statement made him curious. Their physical relationship seemed perfect. At least it was to him. He heard her sigh as she continued to cuddle in his arms.

"It's more than sex." She struggled with her words. "It's a sense of being. Who I am. When I'm in your arms, 'I'm home.' I feel loved and secure. It's where I belong. Where I want to be."

"Twilla." He slowly broke their embrace.

"We need to talk, don't we?" She stared up at him in the darkened room but couldn't see the expression on his face."

"What makes you say that?"

"Let's just call it intuition." *Had she scared him off with her implied declaration of unconditional love? It was in the air. She could almost feel it.*

"I care for you. You do know that, don't you?"

Here it comes. The big brush off. I'm too good. I deserve better. Yada, yada, yada. She felt tears beginning to form, her eyes becoming wet. "Yes. That's what you told me." She tried to sound calm.

"Am I too old for you, Twilla?"

"Are you serious?" She shot upright, bolted against the headboard and exploded with shock before catching herself. His question was not what she expected. "You take me to the friggin moon and you're worried about an age difference? What the hell is the matter with you? You sound like I'm screwing some calendar nut."

Clisten moved swiftly with her during the harangue, sharing the headboard.

"Well, this calendar nut is eight years your senior. You might want someone younger."

As expected. Twilla's quick reply never skipped a beat.

"I'll make a bargain with you. You keep me happy in bed and I won't worry about your age." Then Twilla became serious. "I'd rather be a person of interest to you, Detective Barr, *real interest*, not just one of the suspects you continually question, or in my case, take to bed."

Although she expected some response to her comment, he changed the subject completely.

"Aside from age, we have another obstacle to contend with. I must leave you when my job calls for it. Can you handle that? You couldn't last night."

"I was disappointed and angry. I wanted you with me."

Then wondering where the conversation was headed, Twilla took the lead and probed further, "Why are you asking? Are you thinking about a possible relationship?" The words no sooner escaped Twilla's lips when her mind began to race. If he cared for her, why not admit it? *No more of this dilly-dallying shit.*

"I told you before. I am not a player. Now answer my question."

"If I know, if you can assure me that it's just the two of us and there's no one else…"

Twilla couldn't finish the sentence. Clisten's lips were on hers once again, his tongue penetrating her mouth as he slid her down on the bed.

"You are all the woman I'll ever want," he whispered bringing her body to him.

Later that night, as Twilla lay fast asleep, Clisten shrugged into his coat and left the condo with Russell's wine glass in hand.

As he drove home, his thoughts fully on Twilla, Clisten began to chuckle. *When things went wrong in her lab, did Twilla resort to the vocabulary she spewed tonight? The woman was a pip. He'd never be able to restrain her.*

"What a dumbass." His thoughts took over. "You have handcuffs."

TWENTY-FIVE
THE ATTACK

Twilla awakened feeling fresh and rested Monday morning. Life had taken on a new meaning. She now knew the significance of reciprocal love. That Clisten cared for her was the only thing she could think about.

As she lay there, Twilla could still feel his soft hand inching down her body, his tongue slowly circling her mouth before licking the hollow of her throat. She felt an immediate hot surge flooding her thighs, pleading for release, aching for his body against hers again, fulfilling a desperate need.

As she turned on her side to think more about their night together, his earlier actions crossed her mind.

Clisten went for his coat before she turned off the lights. Would he have gone home had she left them on? Was he a kind of crazy triggered by a light switch? Now you're the one being crazy, she told herself.

"Hey Girl." Twilla addressed Lily who lay curled in her crate, totally unmoved by the greeting. "I know. You're pissed." Twilla ignored her surly mood. "Get over it, lady. I need attention too. So, go ahead and sulk. I'm taking a shower."

Within the hour, Twilla was dressed for class, had a breakfast of coffee and toast, and then promised Lily an afternoon visit with Sam. It was only then that the *Prima Donna* consented to the normality of barked communication and kibble consumption.

248

There were days when the slightest thing bothered the little shit, the Queen of the Realm, and this was one of them.

It would be a tough day and Twilla steeled herself for the hectic week ahead. She could feel the growing hoarseness in her voice already.

All classes were filled, every seat taken. And why not? Was it not predictable, the week of review? For this was the week students attended class with pages of questions before the scheduled mid-terms on two of her lecture courses, Family Economics and Home and Family Living.

As expected, the ones who cut class asked the most questions, some dating back to lectures given months earlier. However, groans from the conscientious students were loud and clear. They admonished the non-attendees for wasting precious class time on very elementary material. That was true. Not all who attended were happy. But then, Twilla was not there to be the happiness guru.

Since all students were nervous at mid-term, even the brightest, she tried helping them by revisiting the highlights of each course. Her lectures were very thorough. She reviewed subject areas in detail and offered possible exam questions. Those who attended and studied diligently would find the reviews most rewarding; those who did not had a problem.

Her throat felt dry from speaking too long and the image of a cold beer appeared in her thoughts when the last class ended. Although draining the contents of the little green Heineken bottle appealed to her, she knew that daydream would not materialize. Twilla had several errands to run before meeting Pete at two o'clock in Tavis Park.

❧

After leaving the Stockton campus, Twilla stopped at a su-permarket for needed groceries, retrieved and placed the file from the safety deposit box into the trunk of her car for the later meeting with Pete, and then headed toward the complex at Stoneledge. She would be glad to get home. Truth be told, she would be much happier once Pete had the file. Hopefully, it would happen that afternoon.

Somewhere along the way, when Twilla passed a billboard advertising Pistachio nuts, it triggered an immediate reaction. She parked on a side road and, after opening the trunk of her car, inspected the grocery bag for a container of walnuts. Yes, she had remembered to get both, the nuts and the apples. A Waldorf salad had been whetting her appetite for days, and within min-utes, Twilla was back on the road heading home.

Ignoring the envelope in the trunk, Twilla grabbed the bag of groceries and wondered if Pete would clarify something that bothered her. He said her unit could be searched again, but how did Dr. Shelden know she would be in High Coventry that week-end? That question needed to be addressed. Maybe Pete could find an answer to her satisfaction.

Nevertheless, it was going to be a great afternoon. She would finally rid herself of the file.

I'm going to get rid of the file, tra la, I'm going to get rid of the file.

The happy refrain kept circling her thoughts as she entered the complex. Upon opening the door of her unit, Twilla yelled, "Lily, I'm home." As she stepped inside, something came crashing down on her head as someone hurriedly pushed her aside. She could feel herself sinking, the bag of groceries sliding from her arms, down, down, then nothing.

❧

Hours later, when Twilla awakened, she lay prone on her bed, a curled Lily beside her and Clisten sitting in a nearby chair.

Totally confused, she managed to ask, "What happened? Why are you here?"

"Do you remember coming home after class?"

"Of course. I went to the supermarket before getting the file. Oh, God! Pete. What time is it?"

"It's almost four. Your two o'clock appointment is long gone. Do you remember being attacked?"

"The apples. I remember them rolling away."

"Someone hit you on the head and pushed you away for a quick exit."

"I don't understand." She tried to comprehend his meaning. "If Russell searched my place yesterday, why would he come back?"

"Maybe he came back for the cigarette butt and another search attempt. When you think about the logistics, it does make sense." Clisten rose from his chair, snapped on the night lamp and began to examine her head.

"Am I ok?" Twilla felt his fingers move along the upper side of her face.

"Yes, you are. As a favor to me, I had the medical examiner look at you rather than a rush to the hospital. I needed to keep this particular home invasion as quiet as possible, although a team did dust for prints."

"You're telling me Pete is getting close without telling me he is getting close." It took the detective a full second to digest the repeated meaning of her sentence.

"He called when you didn't show-up at the park."

"He called the police?" She sat-up abruptly against the head-board questioning his action. "How the hell am I going to explain this when they question me?"

"You're not listening, Twilla. He called your cell and then phoned me when you didn't answer. I am the police, remember?" She sighed with relief as he sat on the bed beside her. "Aside from the apples, can you remember anything about the intruder?"

"He was big in stature, someone a lot huskier than Russell. He seemed wide, had more bulk." She swung her arms from side to side. Then Twilla recalled the backyard incident. Russell had a toned muscular body as opposed to the bulky hulk banging her head and rushing by to escape. "I don't think it was Russell."

"What gives you that impression? Did you see him?"

"No." She closed her eyes, trying to recall the incident. "After being hit on the head, I remember being pushed aside and falling. It was more of a sinking feeling. That's when I must have dropped the groceries…the apples. Then everything went black. He was bigger than Russell. I could feel him, but I don't know how."

"Did he brush against you? Think back."

"Maybe. He had to raise his arms to hit me."

"What makes you so sure it was a man?"

"Women don't wear Old Spice."

"Do you happen to know anyone who uses it?"

"My dad. It's his aftershave. Did you want to consider him a suspect?"

Clisten ignored the question. "And you're sure it was Old Spice."

"Clisten. I don't go around sniffing men's faces. Well, that's not true. I liked your scent from the start. But I didn't need to get up close for a whiff. You splash it like I do with perfume. Although the scent was faint, I recognized it as my father's aftershave. Remember, the man was very close to me."

The remark caused him to chuckle. On Twilla's lab days, she needed more than perfume to cover the chemical odor that permeated her clothing. But commenting on that would only provoke her and he was not going there.

"The aftershave. That's good. Can you remember anything else?"

"The hit, the push and the smell. That's it."

"Where was Lily? Do you remember seeing her?"

"No. I called her name because she was not at the door to greet me. That's not like Lily." Twilla petted her. "Was she hiding again?" Without saying anything further, Twilla thought of the trauma Lily suffered when Amy's apartment had been vandalized. Now it was repeated by the invasion of hers. Lily had been there in both cases. It was so unfair.

"Under the bed." Clisten brought her thoughts to a halt. He mentioned the spot familiar to them. "This poor dog is becoming traumatized by intruders. It took her awhile to calm down. Lily was shaking when I found her. She ran to me immediately."

"I'm glad it was you and not some stranger taking care of her." Although Twilla was speaking about Lily, she soon realized Clisten's thoughts were elsewhere.

"Did they get the file, Twilla?" he asked, fearful of an answer that could stall the investigation. "Pete needs to know."

"Did you check the trunk? I was afraid to leave it on the car seat, so I tossed the envelope in there, thinking I'd get it before meeting Pete." His expression told her he had not considered that option. "My car keys are here somewhere. They were in my hand when I unlocked the door."

"I put them on your desk." Without saying anything further, he brushed her lips quickly and rushed out of the room.

Twilla watched him sprint like a pirate racing for treasure. "And there he goes!" She told Lily. "Nothing stimulates him more than working a case. Well, almost nothing."

Thinking of his actions the previous night made her giggle like a teenager recalling her first kiss. Clisten was stimulated all right, but then he wasn't alone in that department.

"What's going on?" Clisten raced back into the bedroom, after tossing the file on the coffee table. "Are you ok? Do you feel a little dizzy?" *His concern was real. She looked a little 'goofy' lying there, smiling for no reason.*

"You found it." She ignored the question. "Maybe I should call Pete."

"He already knows. I've been updating him all afternoon. Pete was, and still is, very worried. He feels responsible. I called him after checking the trunk. He's coming over."

"I'm glad. Now, you'll finally get to meet him. He's a great guy and very analytical like you. He's helped me so much." She moved to the side of the bed and tried to stand. "I don't want to be in bed when he comes. I'd like to sit in the living room."

Twilla took his arm and, within minutes, was sitting in an upholstered chair. But as soon as Clisten positioned Twilla, Lily began pawing his leg. "You want attention, too," he said, bringing her to him as he sat on the couch. It was not long before the doorbell rang.

"Twilla," Pete greeted the pale looking young woman. "Are you ok? I feel responsible for the attack. It should never have happened."

"Please don't feel that way." Twilla pleaded in earnest. "You warned me of the possibility."

"I warned you of a search, not an assault," he disagreed. "This is not the norm. Small scale theft never got this violent. He must have arrived just prior to your coming home and had to get out as quickly as possible, thereby hitting you on the head. Or, not finding the cigarette butt prompted him to do another search, which you interrupted."

"Well, he didn't get the file," she said pointing to the envelope sitting on the coffee table. "By the way, have you two formally met? I know Clisten called you."

The two men eyed each other and laughed.

"You tell her. I was in the dark on this one," Clisten answered.

"Clisten's my grandson. I think I may have mentioned walking his dog in Tavis Park when we first met."

Twilla stared at Pete in disbelief.

Inwardly, she was angry. Had she been played by these two men...Pete with Amy's file and Clisten with her colleague's murder? Were they comparing notes the entire time, while she sat fat, dumb and happy, thinking the file and murder investigations were being done separately by two total strangers? She felt betrayed.

"Did you tell him about Amy's file?" Her pointed question was filled with distrust.

"Clisten knew nothing about this case unless you told him." Pete answered her question in a straight forward manner. "We can't talk about his case work. So, I don't bother him with my business. In fact, I can remember only one time when my opinion was asked, and it was on a mugging."

"You walk his dog every day and don't tell him things? That's hard to believe."

"Believe what you want, I am telling you the truth," Pete insisted, his eyes fixed on her, his voice never wavering. Her faith in him was important. "Although retired and seemingly useless with so much time on my hands, I still had a lot to offer. So, when you shared Amy's file with me, it gave me a case to investigate, another chance to get the juices flowing again. I turned to my contacts for help, not my grandson."

Twilla grasped the heartfelt sincerity as she listened to his explanation. Although seemingly absurd, she did accept it.

In her mind, Pete could have been her father sitting in his chair watching football, idle with time, doing nothing meaningful day after day. That this man decided to do something more productive with his life instilled a belief in her of his truthfulness.

"I do believe you." She spoke with sincerity. "What about him?"

Before Pete could speak, Clisten answered her question. "I don't discuss my cases with anyone unless that person is directly involved. As for my grandfather, he leads a very productive private life. I am proud of him."

Of course, the exception was Leggin. Clisten still held the belief that his partner was murdered. No one, not even his grandfather, could convince him otherwise. Complain as he did, many times, the case still stood as a mugging death.

"I'm glad," Pete said, totally relieved. "I've always leveled with you."

Twilla pointed to the file on the coffee table. "Keep me posted."

"As soon as I get something, I'll call. Otherwise, we'll meet in Tavis Park." As he clutched the envelope in his hand, a thought crossed his mind. "Where are you staying tonight?"

"Here, why?"

"No. It might not be safe."

"What would be the purpose of someone coming back?"

"Maybe he didn't have enough time to retrieve the cigarette butt or you came home sooner than expected. So, I'm not comfortable with your staying here in any event."

"Twilla can stay with me. I have plenty of room."

"What?" Pete turned to his grandson, overcome with shock at the suggestion. He could not have planned it better. Maybe something would develop between the two people he cared about, but he had to stop thinking along those lines. The theft had to be his priority, not a growing relationship. "That's a great idea! If you stay at Clisten's, I'd like the key to your place."

"You think he's coming back?" *The thought of that happening could not possibly be real. Did the intruder believe the cigarette butt was still there?*

"It would have to be tonight if he does. He needs to find the cigarette butt and maybe do another file search. Staying with Clisten is perfect and I have an idea that's too good to pass-up."

"I smell trouble." Clisten reacted in a very negative manner.

"No. Not really. Twilla has to phone Shelden with an excuse for making the call, but she has to make it sound real."

The thought of talking to the woman who was responsible for her head injury infuriated her. "Phone her? I'd rather hit her with it!" Then calming down, she asked the retired detective, "What possible excuse could I use? It would have to be something believable."

"What if you misplaced your classroom keys and couldn't get into the lab tomorrow," Clisten interjected. "You had to call her now because you'll be getting home late from dinner in Easton with Julie and her boss. You want Shelden to unlock the door before she begins her daily schedule."

"That may work," Twilla agreed. "The department always keeps the lab locked. The projects could be stolen if we left it open. Maybe I should get the key from her tomorrow morning." She pondered the thought briefly before dismissing it. "When do I make the call?"

"You should do it now," Pete surprised her. "That would give me enough time to set a trap while she makes contact for another search. Think about what you're going to say before you call. Just make certain Shelden believes you."

They listened to Twilla's phone call and questioned her side of the conversation when it ended.

"I'm sure Shelden bought *'my seeing Julie.'* She asked if I was alright when I mentioned misplacing my keys. That's when you heard me tell her about slipping earlier when my grocery bag broke. I wanted to sluff-off the fall as nothing of consequence, no injury."

"I think she pulled it off." Pete studied his grandson for agreement then turned to Twilla. "We should leave now, but I still need a key."

"Check the rack in the kitchen, Clisten. There should be an extra one hanging on one of the hooks."

Clisten looked particularly somber when he returned. "No. Twilla. There is no key."

The room suddenly became silent; the same thought running through the minds of all three.

Addressing Pete, Twilla was the first to speak. "Russell. It had to be Russell's doing." Catching his agreement, she continued their thread of conversation regarding the key. "Take mine but make a copy until I get the lock changed. Drop it off at Clisten's in case I need to return for something."

"You sure?" he asked watching her slip the key from a circular ring.

"Just be careful," Twilla cautioned.

"I won't be alone." Pete reassured her. "If questioned about our presence, just remember, you gave me the key to take measurements tonight for a renovated kitchen design while you were out to dinner. Don't worry. I do have some experience in that area." Although Twilla's expression told him she understood his needed excuse, it was his experience in law enforcement that would be used tonight, if necessary.

"Are Jim and Larry coming with you?" A smirk crossed Clisten's face, causing Twilla to focus her attention on him and the people he mentioned. "Call, if you need me."

"That's the plan." Waving good-by to Twilla, Pete walked toward the door with Clisten following. Trailing behind him was his favorite fan, Lily.

‌⁓

"Who's Jim and Larry?" Twilla demanded as soon the door closed.

"Pete's contacts, his two poker buddies…The Three Stoolies."

"As opposed to the Three Stooges?" She caught the parallel.

"But they were all productive before retirement. They kid around calling themselves, Stoolies, or stool pigeons who know what to do with information, instead of just giving it to the police."

"Did he discuss Amy's file with them?"

"I have no idea. He's very private." Then changing the subject, Clisten asked, "How are you feeling now?"

Twilla knew the significance of his question even before answering. "Better, really. Do you think I should have stayed here?"

"That's no longer an option. It's not safe." Clisten's concern was real. The intruder had access to Twilla's unit. By having a key, the man could enter her condo at any time and hurt her. "Pack some clothes. You can stay with me until it's safe to return. I think teaching tomorrow is a good idea. We need to keep a low profile."

"What about Lily?"

"I'll get her stuff together, but you should think seriously about getting her fixed."

"You're talking about Sam."

"He may be big, but he's not dead."

"It's must be genetic." she said, taking his offered hands to help her stand. "I'm okay, really."

"After dinner, I think we should go to bed early. You need to rest."

"Where will I be sleeping?"

"Your choice. Alone in one of the four guest bedrooms or in a king-size bed with a detective who'll protect you." He kissed the tip of her nose.

"Am I being investigated?" She started to smile.

"Absolutely. The inspection starts when we get home."

"Then before that happens, I would like you to answer a question. Were you planning to leave me last night…before I turned off the light?"

"What was the last thing I asked before leaving you earlier?"

"About the pill?"

"You never answered so I needed protection. Are you?"

"Yes…after our first time together…," she stammered. "I didn't need to before."

Clisten's face took on a glow Twilla had never seen before. As he continued to embrace her, he brushed her lips saying, "Maybe we should forget dinner."

TWENTY-SIX

A TWISTY

It was early evening when Twilla followed Clisten's car to the outskirts of the town. She watched him enter a long treed driveway whose curve ended at a huge concrete square fronting a residence. He parked in front of a large stately home of weathered red brick and a white wrap-around porch. Not far from the house, but abutting the massive concrete section, two cylindrical trees framed a three-car garage. The picturesque scene, so treed and private, reminded her of a Thomas Kincaid Christmas card, but without the snow.

After parking behind his car, Twilla watched him leash Lily and walk her toward the bushes. The man was truly amazing! He knew 'the little lady' would leak with excitement the moment she saw Sam. Minutes later, Clisten gathered the Peekapoo in his arms and after unleashing her, headed toward the house.

As Twilla followed him up the front steps, he stopped abruptly and cautioned her. "Brace yourself. We're in for one helleva greeting."

As soon as the door opened Sam rushed to greet his master, his forepaws raised in excitement. However, when Sam saw Lily, his attention was drawn to 'the little lady' in his master's arms.

"Lie down, Sam." Clisten commanded as he set Lily on the floor.

As soon as Sam took a prone position, Lily crept between his front paws and lay flat facing him. She eyed Clisten with trepidation but received no frightening response.

261

"You better call Jay and get her fixed as soon as possible." He said in an aside.

"Can't I just give her one of my pills?" Twilla needled.

"Funny girl. Having the two of you pregnant would drive me crazy."

"I'm not pregnant."

"Not yet." Clisten dropped the subject and led her to a living room filled with sculptures and wall paintings. He motioned to a large couch and watched her sit down. "I know you feel okay, but I want you to sit here while I clear the trunk and get settled. Then we'll have dinner."

"Your home is beautiful."

"Thank you," he mused, growing wistful. "I love the house. It's our ancestral home. Been in the family for generations."

"And you're the last of the line."

"That's not my plan. Although I was young when my parents died, my grandfather raised me in this house. So, I plan to keep it in the family for generations to come."

"I'm so sorry Clis. You never talked about your parents to me."

"I was eight when my mother died. No accident or anything like that. She had cancer and suffered a lot in the end. I can still remember that. My mother had become so altered, so weak." He became quiet, as if remembering that moment in time, leaving Twilla hanging in midair while she waited in silence for more detail. "Dad went on the best he could without her, but I could tell how desolate he had become. How much he missed her. They had been inseparable…always together. They were so happy."

"It sounds like they had a great marriage. It gave you wonderful memories of their happy times together." She tried saying something to comfort him.

"They had the kind of marriage I want," he agreed, his sad expression changing. "Dad died a year later, in February, the same month as my mother. The doctor said it was a heart attack, but the child in me wants to believe he died because it was broken. Dad didn't want to go on anymore according to Pete. He continued to watch his son go through the motions of living until one day his body just surrendered to his wishes."

Surprised by the information and his sudden openness, Twilla did not push for anything further. Clisten was not one to offer background information or anything of a personal nature unless he felt it necessary to do so. Just saying he cared was hard enough, and he did it in anger of her stupidity at High Coventry. Although he wanted her physically, and maybe that alone wasn't enough for sustaining a relationship, it no longer mattered. She was in love with him.

"What about Pete? Is he living with you?"

"Aside from having use of the whole house, he has a separate wing of his own on the second floor, and since I don't pry, I don't know anything about his personal life unless he tells me. It works out well. He comes and goes as he pleases. He's very independent that way. I'll be back." He brought her up to present time.

After Clisten left the room, Twilla heard a loud command telling Lily to stay while he took Sam outside. Of course, this was new to the little elitist. Lily was accustomed to having things her way and did not like being told what to do. The stubborn Lilliputian stood confronting the immovable giant who wasn't giving an inch until Sam moved her bodily and forced her to lie down.

When Clisten and Sam returned, Lily had not moved from her prone position. She did not run to Sam and totally ignored Clisten. They left her sulking in the foyer and went on about their business of stowing everything before preparing dinner.

"I can see why you love the house," Twilla said, perched on one of the counter stools. "It's so beautiful. You must have spent a lot of money updating this kitchen. It has everything." As she spoke Twilla watched Clisten set Sam's kibble in one food dish and Lily's brand in another.

"I had help. Pete has a lot of friends."

Clisten ended their conversation momentarily when he went to the foyer to call Lily. Knowing she would resist, Clisten left her sulking and placed Sam's kibble dish on the kitchen floor. Listening to Sam chomp was more than Lily could bear. Within seconds, she stepped gingerly into the kitchen…to an ignoring Clisten who placed her food bowl on the floor without saying a word. She watched him sit beside Twilla on the kitchen stool before joining Sam for dinner.

"Ignore them," Clisten whispered. "It'll take time, but she'll learn to play by the rules."

"You really are tough."

"No. There are boundaries. Dogs must know what's expected of them. It's a means of communication."

"Really." *Good luck with that Twilla thought to herself. She couldn't wait until Lily peed on his shoes…*

"Absolutely," he said. "She has to be trained."

"Maybe, you're right." *She wanted to be around when it happened.*

Suddenly he was no longer engaged in conversation and she followed his quiet stare. The food bowls were empty, and they were resting in their normal prone position; Lily facing Sam, licking his nose.

"I'm glad you like the kitchen. It took a while to get it like this." Clisten turned to her.

"You mean with Pete and his Stoolies." The thought made her laugh. "He may have helped you with the kitchen, but his 'coming and going' could mean something else. Pete may have a friend."

"Think so?" *Somehow, he never thought of his grandfather that way…with his trousers down.*

"You know what they say about snow on the roof."

"You think someone's stoking the old boy's furnace."

"It sure isn't you fertilizing his crops."

"Where do you come up with this kind of stuff?" He surrendered to her repartee.

"C'mon," she teased. "He's happy, has a great personality and seems very well adjusted emotionally. The man's a hunk for his age. Women are not going to let that go to waste."

"You think my grandfather's sleeping around!" He couldn't believe what she was espousing.

"The man's not dead for Christ sake. I think he's just tastefully discreet."

"Wait until he hears this."

"What a blabbermouth. He doesn't question your sex life."

"Such as it is."

"You can always remedy that."

"Think so?" he smarted.

"Try me."

"I already did." *Now he had her.*

"You are such a smart ass!" Twilla watched him remove the plastic twist from a loaf of bread and set it aside. "Sandwiches?" she questioned.

"An assortment of lunchmeat and cheese with lettuce and tomatoes. I also have potato salad and fresh fruit. Pete went shopping for me while I stayed with you. Sorry about not having a cooked meal."

Clisten began placing dishes, silverware and platters of food on the counter before positioning himself on a stool near her.

"No. This looks wonderful! Why are you so good to me?"

"I honestly don't know." He turned facing her and grew serious. "You have managed to turn my quiet little world upside down. You literally make me crazy. You're so sassy and unpredictable. You have a mouth that won't quit, and profanity just seems to roll off your tongue; but, yet you are kind and very beautiful. And although it's only been a matter of weeks, I feel like I've known you forever." He stopped abruptly. "I'm not good at this kind of thing. I've never had a woman in my house before."

"Really?" Although she appeared calm, Twilla was in a state of shock. That this handsome man would bring her, and only her, into his home was beyond flattery. It was real. He did care for her.

"Twilla." He took her hand and grabbed something off the counter. "I know it's crazy, but I need to do this."

She watched him wrap a bread twisty around her ring finger.

"Grow old with me, Twilla. Marry me." As he spoke, his voice was low, somber and shaky. And although he was not comfortable expressing his emotions, the love he felt radiated between them, capturing that one solitary but precious moment.

Twilla's eyes never left his as he offered the terse marriage proposal. Deep within her, she knew growing old with this man was exactly what she wanted.

"I felt a chemistry between us the day we met. And to this day, I can't stop thinking about you and being in your arms." A tear slid down her cheek. "I never knew what loving someone really meant, until you left me in High Coventry with this ache in my heart. Although I know so little of your world, Clisten, I know mine would be empty without you."

Clisten lifted her from the counter stool and kissed the wetness from her eyes. "I love you, Twilla. I don't want to wait."

As he caressed her, Clisten heard her heave quietly. "Whatever you want. I love you."

"We'll drop Lily off at Jay's tomorrow. She must be fixed. He can take care of that while we shop for rings."

"I have classes from nine to twelve," she explained as they returned to their stools to resume eating. "You wanted me to follow my normal schedule."

"Then meet me at the vet's when you're done."

He watched Twilla outstretch her arm, look down at the white twisty on her ring finger and display it proudly. "I love it."

"Good. I have the matching band in the breadbox."

For once in her life, Twilla couldn't come up with some snappy remark. She was too busy laughing…they both were.

At bedtime, Lily refused to sleep in her crate. Her obstinate display of bad behavior annoyed Twilla to no end. Clisten had placed her crate in one corner of the bedroom and Sam's large bed in the other, thinking it a great arrangement. Now, Twilla stood scolding Lily for this unexpected outburst and had no idea what to do next. Clisten was right. She had to be trained. When Clisten entered the bedroom, Lily sped through the doorway and raced downstairs to be with Sam.

"She was never like this," Twilla complained bitterly.

"Think about it. If you can sleep with your boyfriend, why can't she?"

Twilla watched him take an old quilt from the closet shelf and place it next to Sam's padded but very large bed. When called, Sam immediately rushed up the stairs to the bedroom with Lily trailing behind him. But her secondary position made no difference once she entered the room. Lily whizzed by the sheepdog and made a dash for his large bed, leaving him to sleep on the folded quilt for the night.

"I can see where this marriage is headed."

"Come to bed and I'll give you better directions," Twilla said turning off the bed lamp.

"You must be with Triple A." He felt the soft skin of her naked body against his.

"I am. Our service provides the right directions with no detours."

"No detours." He silenced her with a kiss.

❧

What happened in Clisten's big bed was of no consequence. Lily had Sam. She liked having his shaggy hair overlap hers. It was nice to cuddle with him on the quilt.

It was a smart lady who chose to cuddle with a warm body than sleep in a large padded bed alone.

TWENTY-SEVEN

THREE STOOLIES

On the same evening that Twilla was safely tucked at Clisten's home, three men sat inside her darkened condo at Stoneledge waiting to catch an intruder. They came separately and at different intervals, thinking it would attract less attention than a group arriving at the same time.

Pete Barr was the first to enter. Aside from a tablet and tape measure, *his needed excuse for being there*, he came completely equipped with a flashlight, handcuffs, rope and a baseball bat. Aside from bottled water, he also carried a fully charged cell phone and a hand gun strapped to his leg. Although he could hold his own in a fight, the man felt it safer to carry his *'back-up equipment,'* legality aside.

One of his first actions was to unscrew the light bulb from the lamp connected to the wall switch adjacent the door. If the intruder tried flipping it, nothing would happen. He would stand in the darkened living room and express sudden shock when the light from a different lamp illuminated the room. At that point, the group would hold him until Clisten arrived. That was the plan. Whether it would work was an entirely different matter. It all depended on the intruder showing up. And Pete based the odds of this happening on a hunch, not a scientific probability.

Pete took his place on the couch and waited.

Jim Petro was the second to arrive. He was a big man whose broad body had not weakened with age. Temperamental as hell, he was not one to mess with. Commenting on his baldness or any of his body tattoos equated pain. Of course, no one knew his world encompassed very mean people during his younger days. At that time, he was known as a young boxer who had fast moves and was swift on his feet. The man moved away from Philadelphia years earlier and kept a low profile until he met Pete, his best friend, who was now flashing him toward a chair with his little flashlight.

Larry Johns, a retired chef, arrived last with a bag of sandwiches, snacks and bottled water. He was a pudgy little man whose bright disposition matched his sunny colored hair. Always looking at the bright side of things, the fun-loving cook could turn a nightmare of leftovers into a gourmet delight and on many occasions did exactly that. Hs bubbly disposition was a real contrast to Jim Petro, who tolerated him for Pete's sake.

Someone looking at these three men, all of whom were somewhere in their sixties and seventies, would wonder how they got together in the first place, and how they were able to tolerate each other once they met.

The glue of the mix was Pete, the man who listened more than he spoke. He got along with everybody, never getting excited, always there for someone with a problem. And although this was part of his genetic make-up, Pete always had something going on, something to keep busy, something to enjoy. They would go fishing, shoot pool or watch the ponies, but never were they involved in a stakeout. This may have been routine for Pete Barr, but not for Jim Petro or Larry Johns.

According to them, this was entirely different from anything either one of them had ever experienced.

When it came right down to it, what did they know about stakeouts? Nothing. In the movies, the good guys sat in a car and waited for something to happen. But they weren't going to be in a car. In fact, Pete only gave them two things: an address and a reason for meeting there.

Going to an address was a simple matter. The reason for going was not. The short of it, according to Pete, had to do with protecting a young lady, a teacher at the college, the one he met in the park who knew nothing about dogs. Apparently, someone at the school thought she had something incriminating and attacked her that very afternoon in her home.

Since she interrupted the intruder during his search, Pete thought the stakeout was a good idea. And for some reason, he insisted they do it that night.

And so, the three sat in the darkened condo, Pete and Larry on the couch and Jim sitting in an upholstered chair…waiting.

"I brought sandwiches because there wouldn't be any smell. I really wanted to bring a pizza." Larry broke the silence.

"No. That was a good thought." Pete thanked him appreciatively.

He was glad Larry hadn't thought of whipping up a batch of lasagna. The man seemed to link everything to food. In fishing season, they always enjoyed a repast of sandwiches during their quiet time. Of course, anything caught automatically signaled a glorious fish fry ala Larry.

"So, what are we doing here? What's the plan?" Jim Petro spoke first. "You mentioned a possible break-in."

"Someone thinks she's hiding something, like a paper or a file. Isn't that what you said?" Larry interrupted, directing his statement to Pete.

"I did. Someone was searching the place when she came home earlier than expected, but I think the man was looking for a cigarette butt, hoping it had been overlooked." He went on to explain its importance relative to a file search when the cigarette butt inadvertently fell on the floor under the desk.

"So, he's coming for a butt, not a file." Jim wanted assurance he understood their function.

"The butt, I think primarily. Remember he's slipping in here thinking it's safe, but I don't think he'll hang around long. It's sneak in for a quick search then out. I don't think he even knows about the dog. Lily has a history of hiding when she's scared. So, she didn't bark when he broke-in today. Still, we can't be certain of anything," he paused. "It could all come together or tonight could be a bust."

"But you think he'll come. That's why we're here, isn't it?" Now Larry wanted reassurance.

"Tonight's a golden opportunity. The intruder knows she won't be home until late. Since Twilla didn't report today's incident to the local authorities, he may think she wanted it to remain private. She has something to hide. Her concern was theft, not an overlooked cigarette butt." Pete gave a deep sigh. "This unit was vandalized several months ago, and it was reported then."

"That I understand," Jim assured him. "But what's our course of action? What's the plan when someone comes in, if it does happen?"

"Jim and I should stand behind the door," Larry offered.

Although his expression was not noticeable in the darkened room, Jim wondered what the hell he and this pudgy little runt were going to accomplish behind the door. 'Was he going to yell, 'Boo' or 'Welcome to our Neighborhood?' The man should stick to cooking. It was safer.

"What did you have in mind?" Pete asked.

"I don't know. Maybe we could close the door when he enters and jump him. Then you could turn on the lamp." After a slight pause, Larry said, "That won't work."

"Why not?" Pete demanded.

"We don't know how he's getting in. Does he have a key?"

"No. He's going to ring the doorbell and shout, 'Lucy, I'm home!'" Jim answered sarcastically.

The remark caught everyone off guard and they began to snicker at the stupidity of it. However, when they heard the click of the lock, Jim sprang instantly behind the door, a pudgy Larry trailing him, while Pete crawled behind the couch. It was at best an unplanned jumble of three men scrambling in different directions.

A burly man entered the condo immediately and closing the door quickly behind him, flipped on his flashlight. At that instant Jim and Larry tackled the man bringing him face down on the carpeted floor while Pete flipped on the light switch from the nearby lamp.

The intruder lay prone of the floor unable to move with Jim's hulk restraining him.

"Identify yourself," Pete demanded handcuffing him. Getting no response, he turned the man's head and after taking a picture of his face, sent it to Clisten. Then tapping a cell phone number, Pete said, "Give the picture a look and come over. But leave Sam home." *He knew his grandson would understand the message: Twilla was to stay put.*

Upon terminating the short conversation, Pete said, "He's coming, but without that damn dog."

"You can let go now!" Jim turned his head to face Larry who had inadvertently grabbed his friend's leg during the shuffle and was still holding on to it.

"I didn't know." He flinched his hands, shaking them. "I'm sorry. I was holding tight, or thought I was, because he had muscles and could get away. But it was you. You have the big muscles. You are a very strong man."

If something could ever have been said to reach someone's heart, it had just been done. In apologizing to Jim for his stupidity, Larry inadvertently touched a nerve complimenting him on his muscular build and fitness. That statement took their friendship to a new level and Jim began to view the pudgy little cook as a man of talent.

Pete brought a kitchen chair to the living room and had Jim manipulate the handcuffed man from a prone to a sitting position while being tied.

"I'm not going to waste my time asking questions, since you obviously won't talk. Nor am I going to search you. I'll leave that for the police."

After Pete's statement, the three men sat facing the intruder and waited…it was, after all, a stakeout.

When Pete phoned, Clisten gently nudged Twilla awake from an early night of rest. "Sorry honey," he flipped on the lamp. "You have to see this."

With the sudden illumination and Clisten's conversational voice, the dogs raced to his bedside barking for attention.

"What?" Twilla sat up against the headboard scrunching her eyes open. When Clisten flashed the picture Pete had sent him, Twilla's response was one of shock.

"I don't believe it!"

"Do you know him?"

"Of course, he's helped me so many times. Delsin Peck. He's head of operations at the college. This must be a mistake."

"No. Twilla. They caught him inside your condo. He used the key. I guess he came to retrieve the cigarette butt."

"Where are you going?" She watched him get dressed.

"I have to arrest him."

"Then I'm coming too." She started to climb out of bed.

"No. Pete was definite about that. You are not to be involved in any of this. Remember, you know absolutely nothing, if asked. You were with Julie. This is how it's going to be with you as my wife. You will be privy to things you cannot discuss."

"I understand," she said, climbing back into bed. "Am I still meeting you after class?"

"If I'm not home before you leave this morning, I'll call you." He brushed her lips before racing down the stairs and out of the house."

"And there he goes!" Twilla yelled aloud, sounding like an announcer at a race track. Feeling somewhat cold, she hopped out of bed suddenly to grab a nightgown from her suitcase. Within minutes, Twilla switched off the lamp and lay quietly in bed, her thoughts racing.

Was this the way her life would change with him as her husband? She had to understand and accept his work ethic. He could be called at any time, night or day.

Yes. Accept it. He told you this at High Coventry or at least tried to, but you wouldn't listen. You were too busy feeling sorry for yourself because he wouldn't stay with you. It wasn't wouldn't, as much as couldn't.

Twilla snuggled under the covers and got comfortable. Facts were facts. She loved the man. If Clisten had to work all hours, so be it. He would always come back to her with open arms. Isn't that what he told her? The man was no player. He wanted her but on his terms.

"Really, Twilla. You are an asshole. The man is talking about your understanding his job, not his love for you. Can you imagine a life with this man? How great the two of you are together? Don't create problems where they don't exist." Within minutes, Twilla fell asleep.

∽

When Clisten arrived at Twilla's condo it was only a matter of minutes before he sprang into action.

"What is your name," he asked the intruder.

When the man refused to answer his question, Clisten's quick response surprised the man. "Well, we'll know soon enough. You are under arrest for breaking and entering." Then he immediately turned away from the man and ordered a police squad to the Stoneledge address.

"How do you want to work this?" Clisten addressed his grand-father. "I need your statements."

"Does he mean now?" Larry asked.

"We witnessed the break-in." Jim explained. "That's why they want us to make a statement."

"What are you thinking?" Pete saw the troubled look on Larry's face.

"Nothing's going to be open for a burger."

"There's always the diner." Pete said, referring to the greasy spoon at the edge of town.

"That works for me," he brightened, not seeing the eye signals between Pete and Jim. "What do you think?" He turned to the friendly giant whose leg he previously held.

"I think we should keep our Nexium handy."

TWENTY-EIGHT
RING PLANS

It was early Tuesday morning when the alarm rang. Clisten turned it off quickly before the dogs started barking and awakened Twilla. A quick glance at the clock told him it was 6:30 and time to get up. But he waited five more minutes then rolled over to shake her gently.

"Wake up, Twilla." He brushed the side of her face with his lips. "We have to talk."

"What time is it?" Her one eye opened as she lay on her side facing him. "It's still dark outside, isn't it? Catching his response, she said, "I don't want to get up. My class starts at nine."

"That's why you have to get cracking now." Clisten pulled the bed covers down. "Take your shower and get dressed," he insisted. "We have serious business to discuss."

"Why didn't you wake me when you got in?" Her question was hardly audible with Sam and Lily clamoring for attention.

He watched Twilla climb out of bed and wished he had a camera as she faced him. She stood before him, her pink-flowered flannel nightgown hanging lopsided; Lily pulling at the longer portion and barking intermittently, while Sam stood yapping at everybody.

"You were fast asleep, and I didn't want to bother you."

"Oh."

"Oh…That's all?" Clisten echoed. *He expected some response expressing his 'being considerate.'*

"I'll take a shower and get dressed." She started for the bathroom, then turned around and walked toward him. "Would you mind terribly if I kissed you? My breath must smell like the inside of a toilet." She threw her arms around him and pressed her lips on his.

"Miss Hale you have a charming way of putting things."

"Thank you. I was Amy Vanderbilt's best student."

"And she is?"

"The etiquette lady of what to do when, where, why and how."

"Take your shower." He dismissed her. "I'll feed the dogs. What do you want for breakfast?"

"Coffee and toast."

"That's it?" He watched her walk into the bathroom and close the door. His question remained unanswered.

"Good morning." Clisten looked at her appreciatively when she stepped into the kitchen. She looked so beautiful, he wanted to undress her immediately and take her to bed. Instead, he placed a cup of coffee on the counter and watched her sit down while he popped bread slices into the toaster.

"Good morning, again," she answered knowingly, flattered by his approving look.

The man had no idea that she dressed for the occasion. In fact, she had taken extra time fixing her hair and applying makeup. And the tailored two-piece suit was the perfect attire for a day of shopping. Still, looking at rings and having one on her finger were two different things, and she wondered if the serious talk he mentioned would be the catalyst screwing everything up. Well, it mattered and then it didn't…in the long run. She still had the promise of a ring and slipped the twisty into her suit pocket.

"We need to talk," he said, placing two slices of toast and a butter dish in front of her. He reached inside the silverware drawer for a butter knife and set it on the counter.

"It has to do with last night, doesn't it?"

"Yes. It does." Clisten stood across the counter, watching her butter toast, his voice filled with caution as he began to speak. "Twilla, you must act like you know nothing about Delsin Peck's activity last night. He was not identified until questioned at the station. Remember, you came home late after having dinner with Julie. Pete wants you out of the investigation."

"I thought I was. People were supposed to think Amy released the file to someone with influence." Her expression told him she was puzzled.

"That will happen, but I'm talking about last night. When you go to class, someone might question Delsin Peck's absence. You do not respond by offering information. Do you understand? You are not to say anything. For all intents and purposes, you know absolutely nothing."

"You're talking about Dr. Shelden. You feel she may question me when she unlocks the lab, thinking I know something about it."

"Why would she ask that?"

"Because she knew Delsin Peck was going to search my unit and I wasn't there when he was arrested. She must know that by now."

"If pressed, you can tell her dinner with Julie was great, and although it was good being with her, you missed a bit of activity. On the elevator this morning a neighbor told you about a possible burglary last night but never clarified it when he got off."

Twilla studied the detective and became more dismissive by the minute. "You don't think she'd buy that kind of drivel, do you?"

"Assuming she has the information already, I think it would seem logical to her. Remember, after the officers took him, we left immediately for the station to give statements and there was no one in the hall. After processing, I came home, but I think Pete and company went to the diner at the edge of town." Then Clisten's thoughts turned to another area. "It's funny, thinking about it now."

"Funny, how? Humor funny or strange?" Twilla wasn't following him. *What was his analytical mind telling him now?*

"After Peck lawyered up, the whole arrest procedure seemed to change. I think the attorney notified someone with clout at the college. Remember you weren't notified of the break-in either."

"So, where does that leave me?" She waited for a response that seemed slow in coming.

"Just stick to the story. Remember, you have no knowledge of the anything. You were not home when the disruption occurred, and that part of the story is true."

"If really pressed, I can say that I found it strange to be happening again in our building." Twilla added to his narrative. "Shelden knew I reported the break-in when I returned after dad's surgery."

"That's very good, Miss Hale."

"Thank you, Detective Barr. We at Hale communications try very hard to get our stories straight."

"So, you are no longer with the triple A?"

"No. As a matter of fact, I am moving into the jewelry business as a specialized buyer of diamonds. I start at noon today."

Clisten began to laugh. The woman's nimble mind was always racing, and he found her word play on jobs very clever and funny. "We are meeting at Jay's," he confirmed the appointment. "I'll pick-up Lily and drop her off. He is keeping her overnight. That's a definite decision and cannot be negotiated."

"Really? Why?" *This was another thing she could not understand.*

"The answer is right over there." He pointed to Sam and Lily resting quietly on the floor, facing each other. "It's better that way. She may be very uncomfortable, and Jay can look after her. You can take Lily back to Stoneledge tomorrow. I'll help you."

"Then what's the immediate plan? Are we still shopping for rings when we meet?"

"Yes," he said, "but with a caveat. You can't wear your engagement ring openly until the Shelden case is closed, probably a week or ten days. I want no connection or an appearance of one. It's safer that way."

"Then tomorrow, I go back to Stoneledge." Without meaning to, Twilla sounded depressed.

Clisten reached for two keys that sat idly on the far end of the counter. "One is the key you gave Pete. It's to your place. The other opens my front door. I want you to have it. Although I love you, Twilla, we cannot live together until we're married. We have reputations to maintain and I don't want yours tarnished. Call me old fashioned."

"When did you want to get married?" She clutched the keys, almost afraid of his answer.

"As soon as possible. We should apply for the marriage license next week to avoid any kind of waiting period." Although his answer caught her by surprise, he was relieved by her response.

"Since you'll be meeting my parents over Thanksgiving, what about a quiet wedding then? We could do it without a big production."

"Are you're sure you don't want a reception with all the bells and whistles?" Clisten wanted her to be happy. His future bride could have any type of wedding she wanted. The decision was hers. He didn't want her looking back some day with regret. This was the day of a girl's dreams, *so he was told by friends*, and he would agree to a big affair if that was her desire.

"Yes. I'm sure." She stared at his handsome face. "People will think I'm pregnant and had to get married, but I don't care. I don't want to wait. What about you? What do you want?"

"Four kids would make me happy," he said unexpectedly, waiting for some snappy comeback.

"I guess we'll be ordering in…a lot." Twilla mused, watching Clisten move toward her as she stood up.

"Twilla." He drew her to him, kissing her. "We're going to be so good together."

The attraction was there, strong, unmeasured and surging, but he checked his emotions to a priority that was more serious in nature, one that needed attention and could affect the woman he loved directly.

"I'll see you at noon," she said composing herself as she slipped the keys into her purse and shrugged into her coat.

"Remember what I said about Shelden and Delsin Peck. You know nothing." He opened the front door for her.

"I'll give you an update at noon," she said, stepping into the new fallen snow.

Clisten watched her car disappear, and then raced upstairs to get ready for work. The morning would go quickly. He had an appointment with his grandfather who had some news of his own. He also had a 'little lady' who needed fixing.

It might have not been high on Twilla's priorities, but it sure as hell was high on his. After all, what did she know about dogs? Better still, what did she know about Sam? It was better he kept his buddy's social life secret. Sam had more of a history with females than Clisten ever did. Someone looking at him would think all he ever did was sleep. That was true, but Sam picked seasons when he wasn't sleeping alone.

Shortly before her class started, Twilla found Dr. Shelden near her lab, greeting students passing by and chatting briefly with the nutrition teacher who took over Amy's schedule. She found it curious that the department head would engage in conversation with Dr. Grace so willingly. There was no love lost between them, particularly when Dr. Shelden was named department head over her. Those in the know felt Grace was more qualified, published more educational material and had a softer approach with people than Shelden, who in affirming her title distinction, drew a separate definitive line from the colleagues in her department. Nevertheless, the woman did a good job and maintained a very positive relationship with the top administrative brass.

"Hello," Dr. Shelden greeted Twilla by dropping the lab key in her hand. "When you're done, lock-up the lab before returning the key." Then changing the subject completely, she said, "I'm checking to see who will be here during Thanksgiving vacation."

"Are you having them over for Thanksgiving dinner, the ones staying?" Twilla knew the woman's statement was just an excuse to question her.

"I was thinking more of a get together lunch at one of our local restaurants."

"That's a nice thought." Twilla said nothing further.

"You will be going home to your family, I suppose," she said trying to draw Twilla into a conversation.

"Family traditions are hard to break."

"Good," Shelden said, coming to the real reason for the conversation. "We will be doing a maintenance cleaning over the holidays, and if there is something you want Delsin to do, I can add it to the list."

"He could sharpen the carving tools. They're beginning to get dull."

"I haven't seen him today, have you?" She watched her closely.

"He might have been around, I don't know. He's a very busy man." Twilla replied in a normal fashion, knowing she was still being scrutinized. "I'll return the lab key after class, Dr. Shelden. I really appreciate your doing this for me."

"I hope you find your keys."

"I'm going to check the vet's office right after class." Twilla could feel the woman's eyes following her as she walked into her lab.

Did she pull it off or was Shelden still suspicious of her? She wasn't sure.

When Twilla met Clisten, she related the conversation and questioned the validity of her comments.

"Whether or not she believes you doesn't matter now. You gave her no reason to think you knew anything about Delsin Peck's arrest. She may still think you know something but can't prove it. They never found the file in your possession and the cigarette butt was something you could have overlooked. But Delsin was arrested on suspicion of theft. Although he was unresponsive, we kept asking him about your valuables."

"Not the cigarette butt? That means I'm out of it."

"Exactly," he said at the entrance of the jewelry store. "Jay is taking care of Lily and I'm going to take care of you." He noticed a strange expression crossing Twilla's face. "What is it?"

"He knew I would be out of town Saturday night. I just remembered."

"Who?"

"Delsin Peck. I ran into him Friday while shopping. He told me they were cleaning the floors on Saturday, so I wouldn't go to my lab for anything. I told him not to worry. I was going out of town for the weekend. That's how he knew my unit could be searched. The only thing he didn't know was where I was headed. I didn't mention High Coventry." Twilla paused for a moment, becoming even more silent.

"What are you thinking?"

"I completely forgot about a memo in the inventory file. It said, 'See DR.' Shelden must have been referring to Delsin and Russell."

"Then it all fits," Clisten said and began to explain the sequence of events. "He told Shelden about your overnight and she called Russell to search your unit for the missing file. When he accidently dropped the cigarette butt, Shelden sent Delsin to retrieve it."

"You're a regular Sherlock Holmes, young man."

"The name's Barr, Clisten Barr, agent double 01."

"You must be very busy."

"Yes, I am. Right now, I plan to finger someone."

His unexpected comment caused them to burst with laughter as they entered the jewelry shop.

Later that night in bed, long after Twilla broke the news of her engagement to her parents and sister, she raised her left hand in the air and flashed her engagement ring. "I'm going to miss my twisty," she said, cuddled in Clisten's arms.

"That shouldn't be a problem." Clisten kissed her forehead.

"Oh, really, Detective Barr," she answered smugly, "and how to you propose to fix that?"

"No problem. Left foot, 4th toe."

The bed started shaking, their laughter bouncing off the walls while Sam stood on all fours, barking.

It was a helleva night for a couple celebrating their engagement.

Hundreds of miles away, a conversation was taking place in the living room of the Hale home.

"It's too wonderful. I couldn't believe it at first."

"I never had any doubt," Matthew addressed the issue. "I always knew there would be someone who would fully appreciate her."

"She has so much to offer," Agatha rattled on. "I could hear the excitement in her voice."

"That's true," he said, surprised by her statement.

"She's invited him for Thanksgiving dinner. I want to make it perfect. We'll have a 20-pound turkey with all the trimmings."

"I'm more concerned about the wedding."

"What do you mean?" Agatha demanded. "Do you know something I don't?"

"An engagement usually precedes a wedding to my way of thinking. I don't think a big affair is in their plans."

"Why you would say that? I think you are totally wrong. When that happens, she would want something extraordinarily beautiful."

"I don't think you really know our Twilla."

"Twilla? Who mentioned her? I'm talking about Julie."

Tired of her incessant favoritism, Mathew became extremely angry and began shouting at his wife in no uncertain terms. "We are talking about meeting Twilla's fiancé at Thanksgiving. At that time, they may tell us their plans for a wedding. We will have a wonderful dinner and enjoy their company. That's the plan."

"And Julie?"

"Oh," he said, in consideration. "She'll bring her current boyfriend here at Thanksgiving, but we'll have no idea who her flavor of the month will be in December."

"How can you be so cruel?"

"It comes with years of living with you. It's always been Julie in your book of favorites."

"And yours was Twilla. It's always been Twilla."

"You know that's not true." Mathew took on a hard expression. "Had I left this child alone, she would have been scarred from neglect, the complete indifference of a loving mother."

"What exactly are you telling me?" She shrieked back at him. "That I'm so wretched I would hurt my own daughter? I suppose you think Millie Haskell would have been a better mother."

"That avenue's getting stale. You need new material to fall back on," he said dryly. "But I will tell you this. I expect to have a wonderful Thanksgiving with my future son-in-law, one without incident or currying favor to this architect Julie's bringing home. If not, I will make it very plain to both men that their future mother-in-law is a consummate bitch of the highest level, and one who has emasculated me for years."

"You wouldn't do that. That's not who you are."

"Try me. Years of living with you could alter any man's mentality."

"You're goading me, Matthew. You're angling for something. A divorce, so you can be with your precious Millie."

"Are you really that stupid?" Matthew oozed sarcasm. "I'm not going anywhere. If we did divorce, I would be attracted to someone much younger than you or Millie. Isn't that what your romance magazines tell you? Your interest in that kind of reality only exacerbates your total lack of common sense."

"I am not listening to this anymore."

"As long as the engaged couple find us happy for them, I don't give a good shit what you listen to."

"Now I know where Twilla gets her profane streak!" she screamed, walking toward the hall.

As he watched her leave the room, several thoughts entered his mind.

After so many years of marriage, did men his age come to terms with being ignored and left to paddle through life with cold, uncaring wives who favored their friends and activities more than spending a solitary hour with them? It seemed their immediate concerns were being heir to the estate and beneficiary to their insurance.

Was he being bitter with Agatha for constantly favoring Julie or was he angry because she no longer favored him? No. They had been drifting apart for years, with nothing more to bond them than the daily routine of living together.

There was no longer a touch or caress. Physical love was a thing of the past. The only evidence of togetherness was sleeping in the same bed. Even that was less than exciting. Agatha spent half the night traipsing to the bathroom and the other bounding into bed with a heavy thud, jarring him awake from a night's rest.

He thought about other women he knew. Millie Haskell was not even a consideration. He thought about the woman across the street, the new neighbor, an attractive widow. Now she was more of a consideration, if that was his bent.

If Matthew got down to basics, would he ever leave Agatha? Deep in his heart, he didn't know the answer. His mind, however, did.

TWENTY-NINE

WEDNESDAY

The next morning, *the day Twilla was to return to Stoneledge*, came too soon. Clisten slid his lips along the side of her face, kissing her awake, while bringing her close to him. They lay in bed quietly, neither acknowledging the other's thoughts, each regretting the parting that would soon take place.

"It's time," he said quietly, slipping into his sweat pants.

A quiet air prevailed as they duplicated the previous morning's schedule, and although they went through the motions, both found the idea of waking alone again distasteful.

When Twilla stepped into the kitchen and greeted him, Clisten smiled approvingly and placed a cup of coffee and plate with two slices of toast on the counter as he watched her sit on one of the kitchen stools. He stood across the counter, his eyes fixed on her.

"You look beautiful."

Had she become increasingly concerned about her appearance or did he not realize how lovely she really was beneath her lab coat so reminiscent of chemicals? Or were those thoughts connected with his love for her, causing him to see her in a different light?

"So, do you." She slid off the stool to kiss the man who seemed to have an endless supply of lounge Jockeys in his wardrobe. "It has to be this way, doesn't it?" She looked up at the man she loved and, slipping off her engagement ring, placed it on the counter.

Twilla watched him take the ring and disappear to the living room where he placed it with the wedding bands. "I hate doing this," he said returning to the kitchen. "The ring may be a symbol of eternal love, but what good is it, if something happens to you?"

"You still think I could be in danger, don't you?"

"I'm not willing to chance it. Flashing that rock this morning guarantees an afternoon visit."

"Shelden's going to find out sooner or later."

"But the case will be closed by then. We should concentrate on the present right now: moving you back to Stoneledge and getting Lily settled. It will work out, I promise." He gave her a light kiss. "Lily should be healed in two weeks, Pete's case will be over and hopefully, we will be married."

"I'm going to hold you to that."

He watched Twilla slip into her coat and kiss him before exiting the front door.

"Wait!" Clisten shouted from the doorway. "Jay's at 4 o'clock."

The detective watched her car disappear and wondered if she got his shouted message. The word…message…reminded him of an earlier text from Pete and he immediately tapped the man's contact number.

What was on Twilla's mind, as she drove away, was an ivory-colored ankle-length dress she had seen in a store window. She only hoped it looked as good on her as it did the mannequin.

When Pete entered the house, Sam ran to him for a quick head pat and followed him into the living room where Clisten sat waiting for his arrival.

"What was so important that we had to meet at the house privately?"

"I'm in a bind." Pete said, sinking into a nearby chair.

"Since our meeting?"

"It's not what I hoped. No notoriety, everything sanitized."

"You went up the ladder?"

"Just the lower contact rungs. They did my bidding with the upper echelon to call a special meeting of the Board. The charges and documentation cover all three: Felicia Shelden, Delsin Peck and Russell Weatherly."

"And the outcome?"

"Quiet and none of my business. At least that's today's menu. I'll tell you this though. When Thanksgiving vacation ends, a new department head will be in. I've seen it before."

"So where does that leave us?"

"Us?" He gave Clisten a quizzical look. "There is no us. I'm the one who called the police and although you just happened to show up, I'm still on record."

"You're talking about Delsin Peck, breaking and entering."

"No. I'm talking case dismissed. The college wanted it swept clean with no trace evidence."

"I don't think they can do that."

"Really? The man was in a drunken stupor and entered the wrong address while we were there, supposedly taking measurements. I don't know the full extent of his fairy tale, but it must be a beaut. Someone's pulling strings. You and I both know that."

"A drunken stupor!" Clisten shouted, ridiculing the excuse used. "That's baloney! The man had the key for an intended break-in."

"They didn't find one."

"What are you saying?" Now, Clisten was angry.

"There was no key. Although we heard him use it last night, the men at the station didn't find one on his key ring or in his clothing. Twilla's door was magically unlocked and being drunk, he mistakenly entered the wrong unit." Suddenly, Pete's mind took a different turn. "Since we didn't find the key, Twilla has to change the lock for her own safety. She can't afford losing the spare or have it floating about somewhere."

"I'll remind her when she goes back to Stoneledge," Clisten said returning to their original conversation. "So where does that leave us?" He repeated himself once again.

"Us? I keep telling you there is no us. It's me, period and we're leaving it that way. End of story."

"That's not possible. It can't be, and you know it. Cases aren't handled that way, no matter how small."

"Forget procedure! Peck lawyered-up immediately and I think the attorney called someone influential. The college wants no publicity of wrong doing. They wanted the break-in dropped like it never happened, and I agreed on Miss Hale's behalf, saying the instructor would never think of pressing charges under those circumstances. She realizes things happen when one drinks too much and does not want to pursue the matter."

Listening to the man's narrative, Clisten could not understand why his grandfather surrendered to the attorney's tale of a drunken Delsin Peck, particularly, if he were acting on Twilla's behalf. However, the reasoning became very clear when Pete clarified his position.

"I had to agree for her, if Twilla wants to continue teaching at Stockton or some other college later in life. I've seen their handiwork. Their tentacles are far reaching; they could ruin a budding career in nothing flat."

"And you're here because of the case results or for Twilla's benefit?"

"Neither. I want you to be prepared. Don't question anything you hear at the station. There are two separate issues at work and I don't want you to get involved. From what I understand, the college will handle the theft by Shelden, Peck and Weatherly as an internal affair and they are pressuring law enforcement to dismiss the case against Delsin Peck as a drunken disorderly issue since no one's pressing charges. This clears the way for the college to act without any side disputes muddying the waters."

"And you're pissed."

"That doesn't begin to cover it. The appliances are sitting in Shelden's house big as you please when they are supposed to be in a college classroom. A year-old refrigerator and stove. The file numbers match. Delsin's did too but his appliances were older. I took pictures of the appliances, numbers and kitchen setting."

"You didn't…"

"Right after I got the file from Twilla. I needed more evidence and Shelden was on campus at the time. Then later, when you held Delsin for questioning, I couldn't miss that opportunity for adding on."

"I can't believe you did this."

"How could they could be so dumb? Putting those appliances in their own homes! The greedy twosome must have felt safe after a twenty-year heist."

"You're damn lucky you didn't get caught."

"Give me some credit," Pete groused. "I know more about breaking and entering than you ever will, and I wouldn't get caught either. Besides, I had help," he added, his memory taking over.

Although they had planned on eating at the diner after Delsin's arrest, Pete realized then and there, that a golden opportunity lay open before them. The timing for a quick look at his place was much too perfect to pass up. When they found the evidence necessary to incriminate the divorced man, it pleased them even more. In fact, the burgers that night were the best they had ever eaten. All three were probably salivating over the job they had just pulled off.

"I don't want to know," Clisten said, his gruff response intending to end that aspect of their conversation; however, he could visualize the three stoolies at work…Jim moving the refrigerator, Pete, standing behind with camera, matching model numbers and Larry, facing the appliance, checking its contents.

"All I'm saying is I worked my ass off, and for what?"

"The possibility of a different outcome." Clisten nailed his grandfather's frustration. "But you already knew they'd be covering their asses. They almost had to in this case with a twenty-year theft and no accountability. Not knowing where their funds are being spent would make any college look bad. Even so, you knew what could possibly happen; what always happens when something incriminating is being swept under the rug."

"Of course, I do!" His loud response was filled with anger. Over the years of his career, he had been fully conditioned to concealing scandal, whether it be protecting the college, the politicians, or the wealthy, it was all corrupt. And Pete's hopes for a different outcome failed once again. "They will ride into the sunset fully pensioned while a fistful of evidence gets buried." He added, his anger still at fever pitch.

"What are you going to do?"

"Nothing. It's over. The Board wasn't happy with this, but they couldn't allow the theft to continue, so I am not the apple of anyone's eye for bringing it to their attention."

"They can't hold you responsible."

"No. They know I'll say nothing about the situation. Our relationships have been long standing. Some, I knew as a detective," he mused. "I also helped many of them keep a clean name, but that's not the issue."

"I do get it." Clisten's emphasis was overly strong. "Other than Delsin's almost arrest, I know nothing of Shelden's theft."

"How the hell am I going to explain this to Twilla? She trusted me." The man was obviously disappointed by the turn of events.

"I'll tell her before the wedding."

It took his grandfather a few seconds to digest his grandson's statement, which, of course, was the announcement of his coming marriage.

"You and Twilla?" For the first time in a long time, Peter Barr was confused. "I'll be damned." Then becoming somewhat composed, he asked, "When?"

"Over Thanksgiving. Got the rings yesterday."

"I'll be damned."

"Isn't there something else you could say?"

As if a bolt of lightning suddenly struck the older man, he yelled, "Call her. Do it now. Tell her to take off the engagement ring. She could still be in danger until this thing's settled."

"Stop shouting!" Clisten took the ring case from a nearby drawer to calm him. "See. She's not wearing it. We already discussed Shelden's seeing the ring and my involvement with Delsin's arrest."

"Thank God for that." Then studying the ring, Pete said, "It's beautiful. Must have cost a fortune with that size carat."

"You're fishing."

"And I'm good at it."

"Not today."

"You got a lot to learn. Henry's a friend of mine."

"Henry?"

"Boxwich. The name of the jewelry store on the box."

"You wouldn't go that far."

"Sure, I would. I could cook up a story so believable he'd tell me anything for another sale."

"Don't bother. It was almost two thousand."

"I'm proud of you. She deserves it."

"You really like her, don't you?"

"I'd been thinking of ways to get you two together, but when Twilla mentioned your name as the detective handling her colleague's murder, I knew it was hands off. I couldn't interfere with your case."

"You are one sneaky Pete!" Clisten laughed at the pun. "We'll spend Thanksgiving with her family and get married that weekend, if all goes according to plan. Then dinner is with you on Sunday."

"You want me to watch Sam?"

"If you would."

"What about Lily?"

"She comes with us. We had her fixed yesterday."

"Sorry, Sam." Pete spoke to the dog curled at his feet. "You're stuck with me."

"Are you staying here at the house?"

"Just for the time being."

"Time being for what? An invitation to Thanksgiving dinner?"

"Maybe." Pete arose from the chair and bristled. "You ask too many questions."

"It's my job. I'm a detective."

"Well, go interrogate someone else."

"Tell me her name and I will."

"I'm leaving." Pete raced toward the door. "Remember what I told you about Shelden and company."

Clisten watched his grandfather leave the house in a rush and smiled to himself. This was something he had never noticed before. *Was Twilla right? Did his grandfather have a girlfriend or did he have several? Who would have thought? Not him.*

As soon as Clisten entered his office at the police station, there was a memo from the District Attorney's office acknowledging the receipt of Amy Gregson's file. Receiving any kind of message from that department was unusual, if not unheard of. It essentially told him he was out of the loop and to move on.

Suspicious of the memo, Clisten tapped-in Corky's number.

"I was waiting to hear from you," Corky's raspy voice blasted.

"The DA's office has my file…I got a memo …"

Before Clisten could finish the sentence Corky interrupted, "That makes two of us."

"I don't get it."

"Welcome to the world of politics."

"Meaning?" Clisten was confused.

"Your guy must be running for something. Mine wants to be Attorney General."

"No. He still wants to be the DA."

"There's your answer. Both cases are a lock. They'll look good to the public and that's all that matters."

"We're completely out of it."

"We already were when the arrest was made and processed."

"What about Leggin?"

"It's time to move on for your own good. Don't let this eat at you and ruin your life."

"Do you feel that way about Tony…the moving on part?"

"I thank God we met. He was a great partner and a real friend. We had a lot of good years serving together, a lot of laughs and memories. I'll always remember him for that. You should do the same."

"Maybe, I will," Clisten said, thinking of his future, his life with Twilla. Leggin would have liked that.

"When you're out this way, stop and we'll have a beer."

"You have a deal, but I have a question I've been meaning to ask," Clisten said, abruptly halting an end to their conversation. "Why Corky, instead of Frank? It's not even your real name."

"I don't know but it kinda made sense. When I was growing up, the Italian families in the neighborhood made wine, barrels of it. You could smell the fermentation from house to house, including ours. Since my last name's Corsi, the kids at school started calling me Corky and it just stuck. I guess it was all related to the wine and corks back then. My name goes straight with arrests and investigations, business cards too, but I'm known as Corky around the precincts. Good thing. No one would know me by my real name."

"And Lupo?"

"That's two questions."

"Who else am I going to ask? Him?" Clisten persisted. "I can still feel the compression after his handshake, and I don't want to get on his bad side, thinking I'm getting too personal." Although Clisten grew more and more serious with his comments, he could hear Corky exploding with laughter.

"Wait til *Giovanni* John Lupone hears this one." His laughter became a chuckle.

"I just wanted to know the names of the players. Isn't that what we do?"

"It is. I'm pulling your chain. Lupo was impressed with the way you gave us phony Tony. You know, sending him to the parking lot so we could grab him. He likes the way you think." His raspy voice took over. "It was nice working with you, Barr. The beer offer still stands."

"Thanks, Corky." Although Clisten ended the call, the real issues troubling him were still on his mind.

Court cases taking on a political bent always saddened him. It was nothing new. It happened all the time.

He thought about the college and its strong influence on local jurisdiction. That a college could quell an investigation, suppress the evidence and release a pensioned criminal troubled him even more.

Was this the state of our nation? No, he determined. It was the core element of ambition that drove these people. They took the underlying work of others as their own accomplishments, while those *in the know* looked the other way, feeling helpless to say anything, fearing job loss. Clisten did not like the world of politics, although he clearly understood it.

Then following his normal routine, Clisten walked down the hall to Sargent Qurlan's desk. "Anything new on that arrest last night?"

"I think the case was dismissed on all charges."

"No kidding."

"I believe so."

"Wasn't much of a case anyhow," Clisten said, walking slowly back to his office. There was no point in letting Qurlan know his true feelings about the college or the world of politics. If anything, his admiration for his grandfather increased a hundredfold, if that word even existed. The man had smarts.

At four that afternoon at Jay's office, Twilla and a spayed Lily met with Clisten who was helping them move back to Stoneledge. Of course, Twilla had been back to her unit sometime earlier with a large box containing a very special dress.

"Did Shelden come by again?" Clisten asked when they met.

"No, why?"

"Just checking," he said, his thoughts turning elsewhere. "I have Lily's things in the trunk. You take her, and I'll meet you at Stoneledge."

"What about Delsin Peck? What happened to him?"

"We'll talk about it when we get to your place."

"Saying that makes me curious."

"It shouldn't. There's nothing to tell." Clisten blew it off as unimportant and felt satisfied that she accepted his statement. However, he anticipated an entirely different reaction when Twilla heard the whole story, but Clisten also knew that Jay's office was not the place for that kind of conversation.

Somewhat later, Twilla's reaction was right on target. "Drunk and disorderly? How could they dismiss the case when Delsin Peck had a key to my place?" She screamed, becoming more steamed by the minute.

"You weren't home. No harm done."

Disliking his answer, Twilla pushed further. "What about Pete and his friends?"

"They were there taking kitchen measurements. So, their actions were accounted for and not suspicious. But speaking of keys, Pete wants you to call a locksmith. They never found the spare. It was not in his possession when they searched him, and it made his drunken break-in much more plausible. So, we are clueless on that score. If it wasn't on him, where is it? What happened to the key?" After his last question, when Clisten gave a more detailed account of the case, her reaction was not unexpected.

Learning she was not pressing charges against Delsin Peck angered her. Then to discover Pete acted on her behalf, when the college attorney demanded the case be dismissed, infuriated her even more. In her mind, it wasn't fair. She could speak for herself. Although she could understand his acting for her benefit, it made her feel powerless. "I guess my rights don't really count either."

"Do you want them to be accountable?"

"Of course, I do."

"Then think about it from another point of view. The break-in was just so much fluff that clouded a real crime involving money or in this case, kitchen equipment. The Board doesn't care about a file search. It's a non-starter, meaningless. The big picture took center stage: the actual theft. Something is being done about it now; steps are being taken without the addition of a break-in. You should be grateful to Pete. He's taking good care of you from every angle possible."

"You mean by not involving me with Delsin Peck's break-in?"

"Consider it a cipher when a college career is at stake, here or down the road. That's what Pete did for you. He has seen it before and doesn't want it to happen to you. My grandfather cares for you, Twilla."

"I feel stupid," she said, her eyes fixed on him. "I didn't know the sphere of influence extended that far. What do I say?"

"Nothing. Not one word. You have done a great job on your own," Clisten responded, growing serious. "Amelia would have been so proud of you."

"You have a habit of making me feel so good."

"That young lady is my plan." He gathered her in his arms and carried her to the bedroom. Although Lily trailed him, she never barked. Maybe she was hoping to see Sam later.

As they lay curled in each other's arms, Clisten was the first to address the situation.

"We have to come to terms, Twilla. We leave next week for Mount Penn."

"I've given some thought to the wedding."

"And?"

"I'd like to get married in the chapel of our church, have dinner at some nice local restaurant and then come home."

"Are you sure you don't want a big wedding?" he asked again. "I want you to be happy. We can wait a month or two if that's what you want." He needed the strong assurance now, not a later disappointment.

"Are you backing out on me?" She peered into his dark brown eyes for some hidden meaning.

"Twilla, if it were up to me, I'd get the license Friday and have some Judge marry us. I know quite a few who would accommodate me."

"Saturday," she said, "the Saturday after Thanksgiving."

"I'll take care of the license and rings; you make all the other arrangements." He pulled up the bed covers and cuddled her to him. The plan was beginning to take shape.

After listening to the separation of duties, Twilla enjoyed the thought of making all the other arrangements. Her family knew everyone involved personally: the minister, florist and baker. It was only a matter of contacting them. Then, she would make reservations at her favorite restaurant for the wedding dinner.

Everything would fall into place…after she called the locksmith.

THIRTY

THE WEDDING

They drove home in silence Saturday evening, each reliving the past four days in disbelief. Who would have thought the dream of a lifetime would turn into an absolute nightmare? Were all of them to blame or could the catastrophe be shifted to one or two people?

It had been spelled out…every detail of the whole damn plan! Who would have thought an event so carefully organized would turn into a blueprint for disaster?

It had started out so peacefully when they arrived in Mount Penn that crisp Wednesday evening before Thanksgiving. Although Agatha and Matthew Hale were happy to meet their future son-in-law, Twilla's mother had reservations. Since she was meeting him just days before the wedding, the woman didn't have enough time for a full cross examination of his credentials. Matthew, on the other hand, was very pleased with Twilla's choice and the men got on famously from the start.

The one area they both agreed on was the exquisite ring on Twilla's finger. However, Agatha did quietly wonder if the man planned on living in her daughter's condo after blowing his wad on the engagement ring.

303

As Agatha led Clisten to the guest room, she apologized for the loud squeaky floors that kept everyone awake at night. Being the detective, he was, Clisten understood clearly that the distance between Twilla's room and his was being monitored by the old gumshoe herself. He had not expected that kind of Victorian reception.

As he started to unpack, Clisten heard the woman comment on a possible age difference, and expecting some agreement, was surprised when the woman was immediately silenced by her husband who wanted to avoid any possible conflict with his future son-in-law. However, the drama was to continue at the dinner table.

Although Twilla had detailed their wedding plans a week earlier during a phone conversation, she felt it necessary to review the timeline once again over dinner. Then after a short discussion, the four of them knew exactly what was to occur Saturday, the day of the wedding. According to plan, Twilla had handled every detail of the nuptial arrangements: the minister, flowers, restaurant and cake. Clisten oversaw the license and rings.

The review proved satisfactory and the evening passed quickly and quietly, although Agatha did ask a few pointed questions of her own, which, of course, had nothing to do with the wedding plans. But to her satisfaction, she learned that her future son-in-law did, in fact, have a house of his own, quite a large one, and Twilla's intentions were to rent her unit at Stoneledge for supplemental income.

However, after that lengthy inquisition no effort was made to give gumshoes a trial run at bedtime.

On Thanksgiving morning, somewhere around ten o'clock, Julie breezed into the Hale household on the arms of a young man and flashed a huge diamond ring of her own.

"Isn't it the most gorgeous ring you've ever seen?" Julie shouted, flashing the brilliant stone as her mother greeted her in the front hall. "This is my Brian, Brian Mills." She spun the architect around to meet her father who stood slightly behind his wife and marveled at the showy display by his daughter. "Where's Twilla and her detective?" Catching her mother's nod, she rushed into the kitchen to find them peeling potatoes.

"Hey! Twill! We're engaged! We wanted to surprise everybody." She flashed her ring, making Twilla wonder if she was supposed to kiss the damn thing and kneel for the pompous occasion or bring hers forth to compare.

Instead, the ring remained in her pocket while she admired Julie's. After introducing Clisten, Twilla went back to peeling potatoes when Brian sauntered into the kitchen. After an introduction, the two couples joined together in cooking the Thanksgiving dinner. Glasses of wine and conversation flowed freely, as it does with all opinionated cooks, and when all was said and done, it turned out to be a great meal.

Matthew was very pleased, but Agatha felt supplanted by strangers. The kitchen had always been her domain, hers and hers alone. But she had very little to say at dinner because Matthew took the conversation to new heights when he toasted Twilla and Clisten about their engagement and the happiness he felt regarding it. Then Matthew toasted the couple again on their up and coming nuptials. In giving Clisten his approval to marry the daughter he cherished, he commented on her intelligence and wit, knowing in his heart the love they felt for each other would be everlasting.

Although her father's toast brought tears to her eyes, Twilla could feel the silence surrounding the dinner table. However, seconds later, Clisten stood-up with a toast of his own...to his bride to be. Brian rose to the occasion with a few words for the couple and to his own future bride.

Although nothing was said about Brian's sleeping arrangements, the den featured a blow-up bed for his convenience. Agatha never mentioned squeaks, noises, or bumps in the night to Julie's young man. She didn't have to. Brian would have to traverse the same second floor hall used by Clisten. But truth be told, Agatha had heard those squeaks to Julie's room many times before. But as with all mind purges she just continued the pretense of house decorum.

As they settled-in for the night at the Hale household, particularly after a lengthy Thanksgiving dinner, an incident occurred that jaded the happiness of a future bride.

A bristling visit by Julie made Twilla cry herself to sleep.

At eight o'clock Friday morning, after Clisten fed Lily, he wandered around the house looking for Twilla when he ran into Matthew Hale.

"It's not like her," he insisted. "Rules or no rules, something's wrong." Clisten raced up the steps, and by-passing Agatha, marched into Twilla's room. He found her lying on her side, fully awake.

"Hey!" He went to her bedside and brought her to him. "Want to talk about it?"

"Do you think I'm selfish? Julie thinks I am." She swallowed hard, tears filling her eyes. "If I'm not pregnant, I shouldn't be getting married and bringing shame to my family. She wants me to wait and have a double wedding in June."

"Twilla, that's not going to happen. Get dressed. We're going out for breakfast."

Clisten bounded down the stairs two at a time and ran into Matthew Hale who was sitting in the living room.

"Is there anything you would like to ask me concerning your daughter or our plans for tomorrow?"

"No. I think your plans were very clear." He shook his head and, fixing his eyes on his future son-in-law's steely expression, sensed the man's anger. "What's wrong? Did Agatha say something?"

"Julie." That Clisten's voice was filled with rage was exceedingly obvious. "You settle this, or I will."

"She made a judgment."

"A very bad one, and then implanted a wish of her own."

"Don't let this cloud your love for each other. It's not worth it."

"My sentiments exactly." He turned to greet Twilla who had just entered the room. "Tell your father where you're taking me to breakfast."

"Pancake House."

"Good Choice," he said watching them leave.

Within minutes, Matthew Hale entered Julie's bedroom to have a very frank discussion with her, one that had been a long time coming. After he had finished, Matthew moved on to enlighten and silence his wife. It was time to clear the air and 'put things right.'

As the day dragged by, the estrangement between the two sisters continued and the only safe conversation was commenting on some television program. Even the Thanksgiving leftovers were tasteless for a family torn apart by hurtful rhetoric.

The end of the day found Julie crying for forgiveness in her sister's arms.

On Saturday morning, Twilla showered and dressed very carefully for her big day. As she looked in the mirror, her reflection showed an attractive woman, slim in build, wearing an ankle-length dress with a V neckline and three-quarter sleeves. Stylish pumps with French heels matched her ivory-colored silk dress, while around her neck lay a solitary string of pearls. She was the picture of a bride filled with happiness on her special day. Within the hour she would be married to the man she adored.

As Twilla glided into the living room, she met Clisten who stood waiting for her. He looked magnificent in his dark suit, his masculinity oozing every thread. She wanted to rip-off his clothes and say, 'the hell with everything, let's go to bed.' Instead, she greeted him with a kiss.

"You look so beautiful, Twilla."

"I'm so happy, Clis…," she started, but her conversation was interrupted by a father filled with worry as he entered the room.

"I think we should call the florist. The flowers should have been here by now."

Twilla immediately tapped a contact number only to hear a recording. "They must be out on deliveries. No one's at the store."

"We have exactly thirty minutes before the ceremony, what should we do?"

Although her father asked the question, the family had gathered together as a group by that time and offered a multitude of suggestions.

"Ok!" Clisten quieted them suddenly. "We're to be married at ten with or without flowers. So, Matthew and Agatha must come with us to give the bride away. Brian and Julie can buy a bouquet at the supermarket and meet us at the church."

"I ordered pink tea roses," Twilla cited her flower selection, then added, "with boutonnieres for the men and orchids for mom and Julie."

"We'll have to forget that and concentrate on your bouquet," Clisten instructed, knowing Twilla fully understood the situation.

They were interested in tying the knot with or without needless frills.

And according to plan, one car headed to church; the other, the supermarket.

As they filed into the little chapel, a small room off the main church area, Twilla wondered why Pastor Mike wasn't there to greet them. They sat in a pew near the small altar and waited.

Shortly before ten, Brian and Julie arrived holding a cone of red carnations.

"It's the best we could do," Brian explained. "We got a dozen. They're wired together and covered with tissue paper to make a bouquet, well, sort of."

"We would have bought pink roses," Julie interjected, "but they only had five. We didn't have time to go anywhere else."

If the explanation of their wonderful effort was intended to appease Twilla, it didn't work. It made her wonder if this was a precursor of things to come.

"Where's Pastor Mike? He's late," Julie asked, looking at her watch.

"We know, dear." Agatha said firmly, wanting to silence her daughter. Julie's 'sisterly conversation' had created a chasm that could never heal inwardly. It was then, at that hurtful time for Twilla, that Agatha had to face the reality of Julie's vanity, her sole interest in herself.

Maybe Matthew had been right all those years, trying to open her eyes to the one who put family above all else. Maybe the ugly duckling had turned into a swan without her notice. Or perhaps she was a swan all along and Agatha was too blind to look. However, her thoughts were suddenly interrupted.

An elderly woman, wearing an apron over a cotton house-dress entered the chapel and approached Clisten. "Are you the Hale party?"

"We are." Twilla spoke up.

"I'm Pastor Mike's housekeeper. He suggested you go to Starbucks for coffee. It's just down the street. He's going to be an hour late."

"Why didn't he call us?" Twilla asked the woman who scrunched the apron to wipe her hands.

"I don't know. The police called me with the message. Some sort of bad accident. Must have wanted last rites, I guess."

They watched her leave the chapel and wondered about having coffee at Starbucks. Fortunately, the delay would not interfere with their dinner plans at Listone, the French restaurant Twilla especially liked.

It was after the ceremony when they arrived at the Hale house that things moved quickly. Since their departure after dinner had already been planned, Twilla and Clisten left the family to prepare lunch while they went in different directions to pack, gather Lily's things and change into something appropriate for dinner yet comfortable enough for lunch and the trip home.

Within the hour, Twilla and Clisten joined the family so noisily engaged in conversation as they sat around a table loaded with an assortment of food.

"Well, Mrs. Barr, how does it feel to be married?" Clisten spoke first, flashing a wide smile in appreciation of his beautiful wife.

"Pretty good. I'm glad Pastor Mike finally showed up. It's too bad he didn't make it to Starbucks earlier. I don't think they've ever had a wedding there." She began to laugh.

"Are you finished packing?" Catching her nod, Clisten then asked, "Where's your suitcase?"

"Front hall, along with Lily's crate and things. We'll get her after dinner and be on our way."

"To Gray's Inn," Julie quipped, referring to a hotel some twenty-miles away and known for their hospitality with newlyweds.

As Julie spoke, Clisten watched the straight line forming along Twilla's mouth and knew a challenge was imminent.

"I am not spending my wedding night in some strange hotel," Twilla snapped back, the edge in her voice, obvious. "Clisten will carry me over the threshold of his beautiful home where I will cherish him for the rest of my life."

Although her words were few, they had a sobering yet felt effect on the family: the newly joined couple, so fueled with love for each other, had definite ideas of their own.

"I'll drink to that." Matthew Hale raised his water glass and paused. The rest of the family soon got his intended message and joined him. *If things were to go smoothly for the rest of the wedding, Julie had to hold her tongue.*

They were shown to a private table for six upon entering Listone's Restaurant at five o'clock that evening. It was set farther away from other patrons and the clatter of kitchen dishes, and in fact, was a lovely setting for a special celebration.

What made it even more special was the beautiful floral centerpiece sitting front and center of the newly married couple. Twilla elbowed Clisten but said nothing. What was there to say? Was it planned or coincidence that the centerpiece held tiny pink tea roses? Apparently, none of this dawned on the rest of the party; not the parents sitting directly across from them or to

Julie and Brian sitting at each end of the table. No one seemed to notice.

Not wanting to draw attention to it, the wedding couple passed it off to enjoy a wonderful dinner from an extensive menu. To that end, the entire meal with a featured wine was an unforgettable repast. In fact, everything that followed was also unforgettable.

At the very end of the dinner when the table was cleared of all used dishes, the waiters lined up around the family and the maître d' approached the table carrying a large cake while the waiters sang 'Happy Birthday to Twilla Ann Clisten.'

Twilla looked at her father who suddenly joined the chorus in song and began to laugh hysterically when two other waiters placed boutonnieres and orchids on the table.

While that was occurring, the maître d' placed the knife and birthday cake in front of Twilla's mother, who quickly pushed it toward Twilla sitting across the table from her, only to upset it on the floral centerpiece.

"Oh, Mon Dieu! mon Dieu!" the Maitre d' started yelling, causing Clisten to spring immediately into action.

Like a runner in a relay, he sprinted to Agatha's place at the table, righted the toppled cake and, lifting it over the centerpiece to his own place setting, waved to a waiter nearby for the misplaced cake knife before retaking his seat. Another quick-thinking waiter placed dessert plates on the table.

"Coffee," Clisten said as he studied the broken cake, trying to determine the best approach for knifing the damn thing. Without question, the pieces would be unidentified hunks rather than slices.

Nevertheless, no one questioned Clisten's servings. In fact, the family enjoyed dessert and sipped coffee while making very polite conversation without drawing attention to the chunks being devoured or reproaching anyone.

Of course, the restaurant had no idea they had substituted a birthday for a wedding dinner. To them, it was all about that elderly lady who was fearful of cutting her cake! If only they had been forewarned.

Twilla, on the other hand, had defined the occasion at the time of reservation and was now too upset to say anything. At the end of the day, what was there to say? She wanted to cry…tell the world how unhappy she was…how her beautifully planned wedding was a complete disaster through no fault of her own. With a challenge at every turn, her wedding plans ended now… like this…without any help. Clisten and Twilla were participants in name only to the day's debacle.

If God was sending her a message, why couldn't it have been forwarded earlier? She had nothing against elopement.

Within the hour, two family members were in 'snicker mode' as they recounted the day's events from the living room of the Hale home. However, still hurting from the day's fiasco, Twilla and Clisten found their comments insensitive and especially cruel as they listened to them mock their special occasion.

You could not have planned it better." Brian laughed as he spoke. The remark caused a further giggle from Julie.

"I'll remember that in June." Twilla responded, her voice filled with disgust. She was far from amused. Her beautiful wedding plans had been destroyed through no fault of her own. It was so unfair.

"I did not mean it that way." Brian went on to apologize. "Really, I didn't. You have a reputation for being a very smart and organized young lady. I could see Julie's reaction if today's disaster happened to her. Let's face it. She gets scattered when things go wrong, so distraught at times and really needs help. You're the exact opposite, totally frustrated but composed. If something like this can happen to you, heaven help us."

"Thanks a lot," Julie sneered sarcastically. "This is the one who has a blueprint for everything."

"Apology accepted," Twilla interrupted, sensing the man's sincerity.

She had enough excitement for one day, and not wanting to witness an argument that seemed to be brewing, signaled Clisten for a hasty departure.

After gathering Lily and a private word with her parents, Twilla took Clisten's arm as they headed to their car.

"So, is your next job going to be something of a party planner?" Clisten teased, breaking the silence on their way home, a very broad smile crossing his face. What had just happened could never have been planned.

"Only if I can recommend you as the head pastry chef."

"Twilla." He grew serious.

"What?" She fell into his trap.

"Can we sing Happy Birthday to us on our anniversary?"

"Absolutely. We'll sing it together. Maybe I should invite my father. Did you see him join in song?"

"This is going to be one helleva marriage." His chuckle said it all.

"I know." She placed her hand on his thigh and slid it inward."

"Stop that, young lady or we'll end up at that inn Julie mentioned."

"Gray's Inn." Twilla removed her hand. "No. I want to spend our wedding night at home."

"I like how you think."

"And I like the way you cuddle."

"I will promise you a lifetime filled with embraces."

"I needed to hear that. I love you so much, Clis." Her voice filled with emotion. "At the end of the day, when all is said and done, we are man and wife. That's all that matters."

Their conversation continued until Clisten carried her over the threshold of their home. As he held her in his arms and brushed her lips, he said, "Twilla Barr, I will love you forever."

As she lay in his arms, a tear slid slowly down her cheek, a one drop chorus that echoed, '*I'm home.*"

Adding her name on the deed to the family home was scheduled for a meeting with his lawyer that coming Monday morning, an unknown present for his new bride and the family he wanted.

THIRTY-ONE

SUNDAY BRUNCH

On the morning following their return to Stockton and according to plan, Pete, Clisten and Twilla drove to a nearby restaurant known for their Sunday brunch. This was more to their liking rather than a late dinner. The early reservation was really Pete's idea. Without going into detail, he had plans for later that day, arrangements he had scheduled weeks earlier and couldn't cancel. The comment caused the newly married duo to smile inwardly, their thoughts racing.

As fate or mere coincidence would have it, Dr. Grace passed by their table and stopped to acknowledge Twilla.

Twilla rose from her seat, and after addressing her colleague, introduced her husband and his grandfather who had followed her lead by standing to greet the woman.

"I am so happy for you," she said with a great deal of sincerity. "I take it you married over the holidays."

"I did not want a lengthy engagement," Clisten intervened. "Nor was I interested in waiting for a wedding to take place. Life is much too short when you plan to build a life together."

"My grandson is a very wise man," Pete interjected.

"Yes. He is. I lost my husband years ago, so I know exactly where he's coming from." Then turning to Twilla, added, "You can change your status sometime this week. Dr. Shelden retired suddenly, and I am her replacement."

"Congratulations! I am so happy for you. This is a great day for both of us." With a glee in her voice so undeniable, Twilla watched her walk away and turned to face Pete who was watching the slender woman amble slowly down the aisle between tables.

"Pete." Twilla tried bringing him up to present time.

"Do you happen to know if she likes live theater?"

"I could ask." Twilla's responded quickly. "Maybe tomorrow after class."

"Stop!" Clisten halted the two conspirators, knowing his grandfather's intentions.

"What's wrong with that?" Pete snapped abruptly. "There goes a beautiful woman who should have all the attention she deserves."

"I totally agree." Clisten's answer surprised him. "But you can ask the woman about live theater when you see her on your own. Have Twilla get her schedule so you can bump into her accidently and go from there."

"Now you know why he's such a good detective."

"He does think of everything," Twilla admitted, thinking back to Rebecca Givens, Guenther Pratt and Mark. Although her husband was a good detective, he was also a kind, considerate man.

"Before you ask," he said, changing the subject. "There's a rumor going around campus that Dr. Shelden had to leave unexpectedly for Utah. And just as sudden, Delsin Peck moved to New Jersey. Of course, we know the real story behind that fairy tale!" he fumed. "That they were fired with their pension intact pisses me off, but I can't say anything. As for Weatherly, I think he was fired from his job at Simex and moved out of New York."

"I'm not surprised," Twilla reminded them. "I distrusted him from the first time we met. His actions are obvious now. He used Julie, playing her emotionally as a pathway to me, hoping his charm would work. This was all done to recover a file, a stupid file! Can you imagine the planning involved to meet her initially?"

"It had to be organized to be effective," Pete agreed. "The file was too damaging and had to be recovered. When Shelden gave it to Amy by mistake, she had to get it back. The consequences were too great. After Amy was killed Shelden thought you had the file, so she sent 'charm boy' out with a plan that obviously backfired. You were too quick. You saw him as a rogue two-timing your sister, and not as someone involved in a theft scheme. That came later."

"I know Russell dropped the cigarette butt in my unit, but that doesn't explain Delsin Peck's role there. I thought appliance theft was his primary function."

"I think Russell must have been unavailable when he discovered the missing cigarette butt...maybe a conference or something. Shelden had no choice. She had to send Delsin to retrieve it both times."

"Then who took my spare key?"

Before Pete could give an opinion, Clisten answered her question. "Russell took it from the hook in your kitchen when he broke-in for the file search. He was to make a duplicate according to plan, giving them total access if needed. Delsin was to return the key while you were at class. Of course, everything went to hell after Russell dropped the cigarette butt and you came home earlier than expected that Monday afternoon."

"That's why Delsin came back the same night, knowing you were out to dinner with your sister. Thanks to your convincing Shelden." Pete added, clarifying the whole situation."

"Wait a minute. Let's go back. If Russell searched my unit Saturday, he must have called Julie from here for the Sunday dinner in New York, knowing all the while it wouldn't happen. Julie and Brian had been calling and texting him, so he knew something was going on between them." She paused, somewhat confused. "I don't understand. Why would he spend Sunday night drinking my wine?"

"He wanted to see if you were suspicious about his search. Russell hadn't discovered the missing cigarette butt until later. In fact, he wasn't sure where he dropped it," Clisten added. "That's the only scenario that makes sense."

"And they had to check my place to be sure."

"I guess we're not supposed to know all this," Clisten hinted.

"That's true, but I know you won't repeat it." Pete cleared his throat to broach another subject and took a long hard breath before speaking. "Listen, I'm going to be looking at apartments next week. I just wanted you to know my intentions."

"What are you talking about?" Twilla demanded loudly. His news was something she had not expected, a total surprise and not a pleasant one. "Absolutely not!"

"You think the newlyweds need privacy. Is that it?" Clisten chimed in.

"What the hell is the matter with you two?"

"I've become dependent on you." Twilla's voice cracked as she spoke.

"You can't be serious."

"No. I really love you. Please don't leave us." Twilla's eyes began to glisten. It was obvious her affection for the man was deeply felt.

"I think your moving no longer applies." Clisten told his grandfather.

"But only with my same routine," Pete insisted.

"What routine? There never was one!" Clisten exploded. "Just because we're married, nothing's changed: You still have full run of the house, your bedroom suite and Sam. We've never had a schedule. You always come and go as you please. And your private life is none of our business."

Although Clisten was the one who spoke, he and Twilla understood the man wanted the freedom to go places or be with

someone of his choosing for any number of calendar days without their concern or inquiry.

"Okay, if that's what you really want, but you're supposed to
be newlyweds." He shook his head. "I guess I don't understand
you two." Then Pete sheepishly asked, "Who's for dessert? They
have some fine-looking cakes."

For the life of him, the man could not understand why Clisten
and Twilla sat glued to their chairs in fits of laughter.

Although Sunday was an eye-opener for Twilla and Clisten,
Agatha Hale had one of her own as she sat beside her husband on
the couch. Except for the dog, Luke, they were completely alone.

Julie and Brian had left them shortly after dinner leaving the
clean-up chores to Agatha. That, alone, was something else to
reflect on. Although a simple comparison, it was there. Twilla
would have cleaned-up everything before leaving. That was the
way of her younger but independent daughter. How could she
have been so mistaken, so blinded by outward beauty when
Twilla had so much within?

It reflected wasted years…a confession of sorts.

Agatha had someone dear and loving at her side and it was
high time she did something about it. And that something had
to be now.

"Matthew, we need to talk. I owe you an apology for the past
twenty some years."

This was the last thing Matthew Hale ever expected to hear
from his wife. He turned abruptly and focused on the woman
who seemed to have developed a softer voice.

"I'm wrong. I have been for years about our daughters, the
neighbors and just about everything. I want us to be together
again as we once were."

Although taken by her words and heartfelt sincerity, he wondered if she were sick or just mesmerized by the overwhelming love between Twilla and Clisten.

"Can we start over, Matthew? I don't want to live like this anymore. Please give me a chance."

"What exactly did you have in mind?"

"I was thinking Gray's Inn."

"That's a good idea for next weekend, but I have a better one that can't wait." He took her hand and led her quietly upstairs.

Several weeks later, Twilla received a refund check from the florist charged with her wedding flowers. It made her wonder if they realized their mistake, or upon discovery, the restaurant complained to them and the bakery about their errors and how it reflected a giant embarrassment for them.

Since the family had used the florist for many years, Twilla felt justified in calling her father for a further explanation. After all, the owner knew Matthew from high school.

"I got a refund check from Dovesky," she said getting straight to the point.

"Stanley apologized big time. They were out of town for the holidays and had their nephew fill the orders on hand. He read *banquet* instead of *bouquet*, but that's only the half of it. Your *bouquet* became the *table centerpiece* and the young man thought the boutonnieres and corsages were part of the celebration *banquet* honoring someone special. Having mistakenly tossed your phone number and address, he called around to see where your event was being held and the rest was history. If Stan had filled the order, your flowers would have been delivered to the house that morning."

"I thought you'd check to see what happened," Twilla sighed, never acknowledging the fact that she and Clisten had noticed the floral bouquet centerpiece when they were seated at Listone's. "I was too stressed-out to care at that point. I watched all of my wedding plans go up-in-smoke, from the ceremony to dinner."

"Granted." Her father agreed. "What happened was no small screw-up. It could be one of those 'Believe it or not, by Ripley.'"

"Got nothing from our bakery lady," Twilla continued their thread of conversation.

"Aside from an apology, Grace Furlong was really embarrassed. This was the first time something like that ever happened."

"I don't understand."

"There was a mix-up with the extra holiday help. When you ordered the cake by phone, *BD*, meaning *birthday*, was written on the order sheet for Twilla Ann Clisten, *instead of Twilla and Clisten on a wedding cake*. So that night at Listone's, the maître de thought we were celebrating a milestone event for an older lady with the table decoration, corsages and boutonnieres. That's why the waiter placed the cake in front of Agatha."

"It also explains the Twilla Ann Clisten on the cake. But by that time, I was so depressed, I wanted to cry. Thank God for Clisten," she sighed thinking how fast he reacted in removing the mashed cake from the table centerpiece. "Grace can't be too happy with the outcome."

"Neither was Listone's when I spoke with them."

"And?"

"They credited my card for the dinner and you'll get a refund from the bakery."

"I love you, dad," she said in appreciation of the father she adored.

"The same here, my Twilla."

She heard him end the call and wished she could hug him just one more time. She would do just that in three weeks. Christmas was a time for family, a time of loving.

Later that night when they were in bed, Twilla turned to Clisten and, after repeating the conversation she had with her father, had a declaration of her own.

"I love you so much, Clis. I can't imagine my life without you." She paused momentarily and, reflecting her earlier years, began a confession of sorts.

"Although I was never popular and considered more of a geek in school, I still dreamt of being loved, just like the other pretty girls in my class. I never pictured your face, but I knew you'd come into my life some day and be my reason for living. I know it sounds corny, but I believed it with all my heart."

"Loving your soul mate works both ways." He faced her in the darkened room. "I'll always be here for you, Twilla. Remember that. In thick and thin. No matter how crazy life gets."

"You mean like our wedding?"

"Just think of the story we can tell our kids. If nothing else, it was memorable."

The thought made him chuckle. He could still picture Twilla's zombie-like state. With every chaotic turn, her depression deepened. He could not remember a time when Twilla looked so lost or defeated. Unfortunately, it had to be on her wedding day.

However, this was not the case now as she brought him up to present time. "If we have a daughter, her wedding won't duplicate ours. I will personally re-check the flower and cake orders until they are sick of hearing from me." Her voice held a definite edge.

"And I'll sit with groom, just to make sure he has the rings." *After all, there was a limit to the groom's obligations.*

They started to giggle at their combined thoughts when Clisten quelled her laughter with a whisper. "Come to me." He bought her to him and, holding her close, brushed her lips with a whisper, "I love you, Twilla. I always will. I think we were meant to be together."

"Wherever it's written, I will always love you, Clis. That test of time is on our side."

Lying in the arms of the man she adored, Twilla knew in her heart…she was truly home.

Wherever life's journey took them, they would face it together and their love would be stronger for it.

Suddenly, time seemed to stop. Two people pledging their love and devotion were locked in an embrace, a symbol of what was to come in a lifetime together.

Who would have thought that a colleague's murder and a wedding with unmistakable disasters could bring this couple closer than ever…this paradigm of unconditioned love.

Forget Twilla's careful wedding plans. What happened was a crazy but precious memory. It was theirs alone, one they would share together, through a lifetime of much laughter and a few tears.

When Twilla and Clisten renovated the unit at Stoneledge for a rental property, they noticed a key standing on edge against the baseboard, formerly hidden by a couch. They stood staring at the key, wondering how it got there the night Delsin broke in.

"What do you think?"

"It must have flown out of his hands, obviously. How it got there? I don't know. It doesn't really matter now, Twilla. It's over."

Watching him grab the key and toss it in a trash bag made her realize the entire episode involving Russell Weatherly, Delsin Peck and Felicia Shelden had finally come to an end.

On the second weekend in January, Clisten surprised his wife with tickets to a Broadway play in New York City. The next day they enjoyed lunching with an elderly lady named Bessie Long, who had much to say about Twilla's husband being a man of his word. Twilla always knew it, of course, but it was nice to have someone else acknowledge his integrity. Clisten Barr, whose core principles never faded, was the man she would always love and cherish.

###

OTHER NOVELS BY THE AUTHOR

Pursuit of the Frog Prince

Continued Pursuit

A Game of Wits

24918070R00185

Made in the USA
Columbia, SC
01 September 2018